Charles George Harper

The Brighton Road

Old Times and new on a Classic Highway

Charles George Harper

The Brighton Road
Old Times and new on a Classic Highway

ISBN/EAN: 9783744729932

Printed in Europe, USA, Canada, Australia, Japan

Cover: Foto ©Andreas Hilbeck / pixelio.de

More available books at **www.hansebooks.com**

GEORGE IV.

THE BRIGHTON ROAD

OLD TIMES AND NEW ON A CLASSIC HIGHWAY

BY

CHARLES G. HARPER

AUTHOR OF "ENGLISH PEN ARTISTS OF TO-DAY"

WITH NINETY ILLUSTRATIONS BY THE AUTHOR
And from Old-time Pictures and Engravings

London
CHATTO & WINDUS, PICCADILLY
1892

PREFACE.

Do you remember that old and curiously shrewd passage in one of the Quarterly Reviews—I think it was the "Edinburgh"—"There are two questions to be asked respecting every new publication: Is it worth buying? Is it worth borrowing?" Perhaps you do not call it to mind. It occurs to me, however, as I write the last lines of this book, and commands attention.

To him who creates, an impartial and impersonal view of that creation he would fain judge impartially is impossible, so that the only criterion of worth to be gained is the reception accorded by Press and Public. That lies yet in the future, but if you who read these pages take an equal pleasure with the writer in writing them, then those questions quoted above are likely to be answered in the affirmative.

The subject seems, on the face of it, to claim an interest both in its aspects of yesterday and of to-day. The days of the Regency are done: the Corinthianism of that time has utterly vanished. Tom and Jerry we know because they are enshrined in the pages of Pierce Egan's writings, but their ways are not the ways of this more subdued generation. What was brilliant in that period shines now with the added lustre of romance; what was sordid has mostly escaped record. An historic glamour pertains to their days, and to the road that was then fashionable and travelled above all others. There is, too, a modern and more living interest in this road, now that the pastimes of pedestrianism and cycling have peopled the ways anew: now that coaching, too, is revived on this, as on other highways.

It is not for the sake of its destination alone, or, indeed, to any great extent, that this road may claim attention: it has interest on its course quite apart from that which lies at either end, and I would not have you think that, if opportunity offers, I would not turn aside from it into the bye-ways and lanes of Surrey and Sussex. Pictures and interesting notes of the quiet corners and villages lying off the road, but within hail of it, you shall find who seek in these pages: notes, too, of the lingering superstitions and quaint customs still left to the peasantry of the Weald and the South Downs.

As for literary and artistic gossip upon writers

and artists who have lived, or travelled, or sketched, or written upon this road, that forms a very large portion of this book. Occasion, too, has offered of conscientiously cleansing the mud-spattered character of a very Great Personage indeed, whom every, or almost every, writer upon history (we will not say Historian) has contrived to vilify; possibly, like Goldsmith's mad dog, "to gain some private ends."

However that may be, it cannot be gainsaid that the pendulum of History has been swung too violently when George IV. has been under discussion. It is time (and we are upon the threshold of that period when that King's day shall belong solely to history) that we should have a normal notation. Thackeray is probably the greatest sinner among those who have recklessly vilipended the Fourth George. He set out upon a crusade against that august if (excepting the last of that name) unpicturesque quartette, and the result, the "Four Georges," shall afford you both interest and excellent literature; but neither those Lectures nor that book are History: they are, indeed, merely the record of a bias.

To speak thus of Thackeray is, I know, to do the accursed thing, and, I doubt not, the hero-worshippers will fall, shrieking, upon me; but I will maintain that that great writer was indeed something of the moral snob. There! I have said it.

Coaching has been very fully treated in these pages, and in them will be found many reproductions of old coaching prints relating to this road. One only do I know of that makes no appearance here.

To the courtesy of Mr. Stewart Freeman, Mr. Bishop, and Mr. J. B. Muir I owe the inclusion of several of these interesting coaching pictures, and to Mrs. Mayall and Mr. Macdonald I am indebted for the portraits of the late Mr. Mayall and the late James Selby. For permission to reprint such portions of this book as originally appeared in the "Pall Mall Budget," "Cycling," "Bicycling News," and "Northern Wheeler," acknowledgments are due the proprietors of those journals.

CHARLES G. HARPER.

LONDON, *October* 1892.

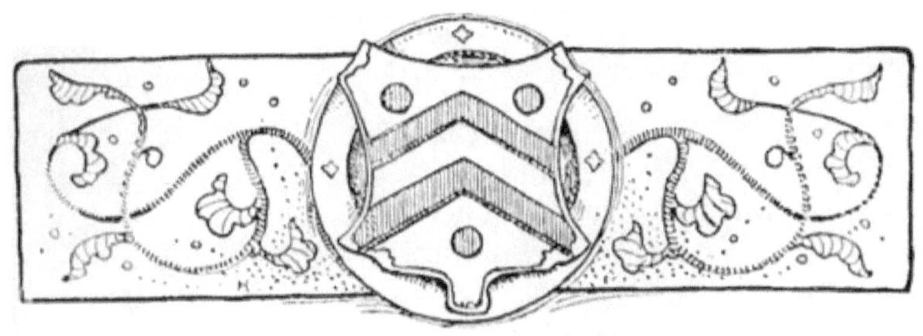

CONTENTS.

FIRST DAY.

SECOND DAY.

THIRD DAY.

FOURTH DAY.

LIST OF ILLUSTRATIONS.

SEPARATE PLATES.

ILLUSTRATIONS IN TEXT.

PAGE

Initials, Decorative Devices, and Tailpieces.

THE BRIGHTON ROAD.

FIRST DAY.

THE winter was over and past, and yet, by reason of its long-continued and almost unprecedented severity, there was in us little of that buoyancy which spring generally gives. London fogs, too, had done their worst, and, together with a subtle and insidious scourge which had been prevalent throughout the land during the winter months, had taken away much of the delight of living. Therefore it was with eagerness that this tramp to Brighton, once suggested, was undertaken in the sweet spring-time.

Many and various are the ways in which they travel who go down to the sea at London-super-Mare. *Imprimis*, there be they who journey by rail, a goodly crowd; cyclists of all kinds (and their kinds are many) fall into the highway below

Croydon—the wheelman's "unspeakable Croydon;" coaches, in these days of revival, take the road gaily; pedestrians of the amateur kind there are a few, and tramps pure and simple (if such an expression may pass respecting these tribes of uncleanly and guileful wanderers) infest this classic way. And we walked, too, in an age of wheels, and were without doubt objects of pity to the cyclists who "scorched" the fifty-two miles of road between London and the sea in a fraction over three hours and three-quarters. Well, the advantage lay entirely in their minds, for we were content to pass, if needs or inclinations were, the whole of our few days' holiday upon the road, so only some fresh air might be encountered on the way, careless if Brighton were reached only in time to return.

Now, there are many roads by which those who will may reach this smaller London of the southern coast. The most direct is that which goes by way of Streatham, Croydon, Redhill, Horley, Crawley, Cuckfield, and Clayton, and this, the Record Route, the Classic Road, is that we took. Others of foremost importance there are two, in addition to those variations of the first route, which, avoiding Croydon, go through Sutton and Reigate, and lower down at Hand Cross branch out by way of Hickstead and Albourne, rejoining the foremost road by the *Plough* at Pyecombe. These are (1) that by way of Ewell, Dorking, Horsham, and Mockbridge; and (2) that other, of greatest length, through Croydon, Godstone Green, East Grinstead, Maresfield, Uckfield, and Lewes, which last is the oldest of these

THE "COMET," 1876, STARTING FROM THE WHITE HORSE CELLARS.
(*From Photo.*)

quoted routes, and is over fifty-eight miles in length. This is, without doubt, the most picturesque route of any, contrived as it is out of country lanes, aimless and wandering, that, existing before any one wished to get to Brighthelmstone, reached that place almost fortuitously and with many doublings—a route little travelled in these days. Even though one goes a-pleasuring along the roads, in these hurrying times the shortest route is certain of selection.

To the purist in these matters, one should "take off" from the White Horse Cellars in Piccadilly, even though the original cellars are gone the way of all old houses in London, and though the coaches in these days of their exotic revival have, many of them, changed their venue to the more convenient centre of Northumberland Avenue. But to make a detour for the purpose of passing that historic starting-point were surely sentiment gone mad; so we held on from our start in the Bayswater Road, through the Parks to that point whence the Brighton Road is measured—that is to say, the Surrey side of Westminster Bridge. But, not to suffer the memory of "the Cellars" to be dismissed so summarily, I have turned to Hazlitt for his description of the starting of the mail-coaches from this historic spot in Piccadilly.

That the old White Horse Cellars were situated on the south side of Piccadilly is a fact known to but few modern Londoners. The majority think upon the old "Hatchett's," pulled down in 1884, as the only possible cellars; but they, and the coach-office, were in Regency times situated two doors from what is now the Bath Hotel (itself memorable as the death-place of Gustave Doré), at the corner of Arlington Street.[1]

Well, Hazlitt thought the morning scene in the Piccadilly of his time a very fine sight indeed. "The finest sight in the metropolis," he says, "is the setting off of the mail-coaches from Piccadilly. The horses paw the ground and are impatient to be gone, as if conscious of the precious burden they convey. There is a peculiar secrecy and dispatch, significant and full of meaning, in all the proceedings concerning them. Even the outside passengers have an erect and supercilious air, as if proof against the accidents of the journey; in fact, it seems indifferent whether they are to encounter the summer's heat or the winter's cold, since they are borne through the air on a winged chariot."

But I like better a passage referring to Piccadilly which I found the other day in a work published in Corinthian days, and steeped to the full in the spirit of that remarkable time. The book I refer to is a pseudonymous work entitled "Real Life in London," purporting to be by "Bob Tally-ho," and recounting the adventures of himself and "Tom Dashall" in town. It is a work suggested by the great success which attended Pierce Egan's "Life in London," wherein may be read the strange and fearful doings of "Corinthian Tom" and his two companions, "Jerry Hawthorn" and

[1] The original White Horse Cellars were in existence in 1720, and were so named by Williams, the landlord, as a compliment to the House of Hanover, the newly established Royal House of Great Britain.

"Bob Logic," the Oxonian. Apart from its illustrations, the merit of "Real Life" is fully equal to its forerunner, and, indeed, is likely to prove of greater real historic interest, inasmuch as it deals, under a very thin veil, with real persons and personages, whose identity he who cares to may discover with little trouble.

In the passage just mentioned, Tom Dashall and his friend are setting out to a prize-fight to be held on Copthorne Common, a contest between Jack Randall, the Nonpareil, and Martin, a baker by trade, and for that reason endeared to "the Fancy" by the nickname of "Master of the Rolls." Naturally, on that important occasion, the roads were thronged; "the lads of the Fancy were on the *qui vive*," and "Piccadilly was all in motion—coaches, carts, gigs, tilburies, whiskies, buggies, dogcarts, sociables, dennets, curricles, and sulkies were passing in rapid succession, intermingled with tax-carts and waggons decorated with laurel, conveying company of the most varied description. Here was to be seen the dashing *Corinthian* tickling up his *tits*, and his *bang-up set-out* of *blood and bone*, giving the go-by to a *heavy drag* laden with eight brawny, bull-faced blades, smoking their way down behind a skeleton of a horse, to whom, in all probability, a good feed of corn would have been a luxury: *pattering* among themselves, occasionally *chaffing* the more elevated drivers by whom they were surrounded, and pushing forward their nags with all the ardour of a British merchant intent upon disposing of a valuable cargo of foreign goods on 'Change. There was a waggon full of *all sorts* upon the *lark*, succeeded by a *donkey-cart* with four insides; but *Neddy*, not liking his burthen, stopped short in the way of a Dandy, whose horse's head, coming plump up to the back of the crazy vehicle at the moment of its stoppage, threw the rider into the arms of a dustman, who, hugging his *customer* with the determined grasp of a bear, swore, d—n his eyes, he had saved his life, and he expected he would stand something handsome for the Gemmen all round, for if he had not pitched into their cart, he would certainly have broke his neck; which being complied with, though reluctantly, he regained his saddle, and proceeded a little more cautiously along the remainder of the road, while groups of pedestrians of all ranks and appearances lined each side."

On their way they pass Hyde Park Corner, where they encounter one of a notorious trio of brothers, friends of the Prince Regent and companions of his in every sort of excess—the Barrymores, to wit, named severally Hellgate, Newgate, and Cripplegate, the last of this unholy trinity so called because of his chronic limping: the two others' titles, taken with the characters of their bearers, are self-explanatory.

Dashall points his Lordship out to his companion, who is new to London life, and requires such explanations.

"The driver of that tilbury," says he, "is the celebrated Lord Cripplegate,[1] with his usual equipage; his blue cloak with a scarlet lining hanging loosely over the vehicle gives an air of importance

[1] Henry Barry, Earl of Barrymore, in the peerage of Ireland.

to his appearance, and he is always attended by that boy, who has been denominated his Cupid: he is a nobleman by birth, a gentleman by courtesy (oh. witty Dashall!), and a gamester by profession. He exhausted a large estate upon *odd and even, seven's the main*, &c., till. having lost sight of the *main chance*, he found it necessary to curtail his establishment and enliven his prospects by exchanging a first floor for a second, without an opportunity of ascertaining whether or not these alterations were best suited to his high notions or exalted taste: from which. in a short time, he was induced, either by inclination or necessity, to take a small lodging in an obscure street, and to sport a gig and one horse, instead of a curricle and pair, though in former times he used to drive four-in-hand, and was acknowledged to be an excellent whip. He still. however, possessed money enough to collect together a large quantity of halfpence, which in his hours of relaxation he managed to turn to good account by the following stratagem:—He distributed his halfpence on the floor of his little parlour in straight lines, and ascertained how many it would require to cover it. Having thus prepared himself, he invited some wealthy spendthrifts (with whom he still had the power of associating) to sup with him, and he welcomed them to his habitation with much cordiality. The glass circulated freely, and each recounted his gaming or amorous adventures till a late hour, when, the effects of the bottle becoming visible, he proposed, as a momentary suggestion, to name how many halfpence, laid side by side, would carpet the floor, and offered to lay a large wager that he would guess the nearest.

"'Done! done!' was echoed round the room. Every one made a deposit of £100, and every one made a guess, equally certain of success; and his Lordship declaring he had a large stock of halfpence by him, though perhaps not enough, the experiment was to be tried immediately. 'Twas an excellent hit!

"The room was cleared; to it they went; the halfpence were arranged rank and file in military order, when it appeared that his Lordship had certainly guessed (as well he might) nearest to the number. The consequence was an immediate alteration of his Lordship's residence and appearance: he got one step in the world by it. He gave up his second-hand gig for one warranted new; and a change in his vehicle may pretty generally be considered as the barometer of his pocket."

And so, with these piquant biographical remarks, they betook them along the road in the early morning, passing on their way many curious itinerants, whose trades have changed and decayed, and are now become nothing but a dim and misty memory; such as, for instance, the sellers of warm salop, the forerunners of the early coffee-stalls of our own day.

The early postman, too, would be starting his rounds: a radiant vision he, of scarlet coat with bright blue facings, drab breeches and gaiters, and a wonderful hat, low-crowned and black, and girded round with a deep gold band, carrying in one hand a lock valise, and in the other a brass bell, which he would ring to herald his coming. *Our* postmen are as nothing to this brilliant being in appearance; to compare the two orders were as the comparison of the peacock with the raven. I cannot here present him in his colours; but in this sketch from a contemporary print you have something of his cut.

LONDON POSTMAN OF THE REGENCY.

'Twas half-past six o'clock as we entered Hyde Park by the Marble Arch, and the daylight was but little advanced. We had each of us a knapsack, carried on the back, containing necessary articles for a few days' sojourn, and these were our only burdens, save that at starting we were only too conscious of those knapsacks. The entirely British sense of shame in presenting any but the most orthodox of appearances was, indeed, chiefly responsible for our early start, as we had hoped at this unusual hour to meet few people; but at the outset we ran the gauntlet of criticism at the hands of the workmen partaking of an early breakfast at an open-air coffee-stall. There is something particularly annoying in being criticised by the British workman, inasmuch as it is difficult, if not impossible, to come down to his level, and to fire into him the only replies which he would feel acutely; which, by the way, explains also the unanswerable nature of arguments emanating from 'busmen and the like.

Big Ben struck the hour of seven as we left the Parks behind and walked down the grey length of Great George Street on to Westminster Bridge. Here all was mist. Westminster towers and spires loomed ponderously overhead, poised apparently on nothing more substantial than eddying vapours, and the river below was invisible. A ghostly shape, indeed, spanned the void to the eastward, which we took to be Charing Cross Bridge, and the huge pile of Whitehall Court lent romance to the scene, with its picturesque sky-line; and again, a something far away and to the right hand glittered faintly high in air, doubtless the gilded cross of St. Paul's touched by the mist-swaddled sun. Earth, we thought then, had little fairer to show than this same view from Westminster Bridge.

The Brighton Road, measured from the Surrey side, just here, takes its course along the Westminster Bridge Road, turning at Newington Causeway to the right, and then follows the Kennington Road to its junction with the Park Road and the weary length of Brixton.

Though 'twas yet early, the insistant tinkle, tinkle of tramway horses' bells filled the air, and the shops of the cheap tailors and bootmakers and furnishers, with which the Bridge Road is filled, were already opening; so we made haste to leave its sordid neighbourhood behind, and pursued the broad pavements of Kennington with all speed, stopping only

KENNINGTON GATE, 1830: DERBY DAY.
(*From an Engraving after J. Pollard.*)

to note the fortuitously happy composition which the spires of Christ Church make viewed from adown the road. 'Tis another matter at Kennington, whose Church of St. Mark, standing where the Brixton Road begins, is a fearsome specimen of pagan architecture done in plebeian brick and stucco, the tower, cupola-crowned, bearing aloft funeral urns and sacrificial tripods in plenty, equalling in hideousness only its near neighbour of Brixton.

Here, as you go toward this pagan temple, stood, in times not so far removed but that some yet living can remember it, Kennington Gate, an important turnpike at any time, and one of very great traffic on Derby Day, when, I fear, the pikeman was freely bilked of his due at the hands of sportsmen, noble and ignoble. There is a view of this gate on such a day drawn by James Pollard, and published in 1838, which gives a very good idea of the amount of traffic and, by the way, the curious costumes of the period. You shall also find in the "Comic Almanack" for 1837 an illustration by George Cruickshank, of this same place, one would say, although it is not mentioned by name, in which is an immense jostling crowd anxious to pass through, while the pikeman, having apparently been "cheeked" by the occupants of a passing vehicle, is vulgarly engaged, I grieve to state, in "taking a sight" at them. That is to say, he has, according to the poet, "Put his thumb unto his nose and spread his fingers out."

And here begins the Brixton Road.

The Brixton Road is given over in great part

to schools, and the district is inhabited largely of City men, wealthy tradesfolk, retired and active, and so is become, as it were, a veritable Philistine stronghold, where the money-market article in the morning papers seems the sweetest and most enthralling literature ever writ, and where the clangour of the conventicle bell ceaseth not out of the land, but jars for ever upon the exasperated ear. Memories of the Regency are impossible in the Brixton Road; Corinthian days, even though they be chronicled by Pierce Egan, are powerless of recall. Conceive me, if you can, at the same time the Barrymores and the Bon Marché. You cannot! Let us away!

It came on to rain when we reached the church on Brixton Hill; so, while sheltering by its dreadful Doric, we had the opportunity of, willy-nilly, studying the tombstone inscriptions to dead and gone Brixton Philistines, who apparently possessed all the virtues of their several classes, and certainly, when they were gathered to their fathers, were buried with tons of stone a-top, designed in horrid taste, eloquent alike of vulgarity and long purses.

One bleating epitaph in especial forced itself upon our gaze. It was in this wise, not to give it here in its fulness of gush :—

"Oh, Miles! the modest, learned, and sincere
Will sigh for thee, whose ashes slumber here;
The youthful bard will pluck a floweret pale
From this sad turf whene'er he reads the tale."

Right glad were we when the showers ceased and we could leave this Golgotha behind to follow the way, which now gained something of rurality, in so

Kennington Road

far at least as lay in the substitution of wide lawns and detached villas for the frowsy gardens and fore-courts and continuous houses of the Brixton Road.

And now, as there is little or nothing worthy mention until we reach Streatham, let us beguile the uninteresting way with some historical gossip upon this road to Brighton.

If these pages had been devised solely for showing a picture of the road during the Regency and the reign that succeeded it, there would be not the slightest difficulty in creating a lengthy and light-some narrative of its many and distinguished travellers. Some of these may in succeeding pages be dismissed with little ceremony; but there is one great personage connected with the Brighton Road, without whom it would never have attained its once great vogue, who will be mentioned frequently in this book. The mention of George, Prince of Wales, Prince Regent, and fourth King of that name, could no more be omitted from a gossip of its travellers than could the Prince of Denmark go unrepresented in the play of "Hamlet." Indeed, without him, it is fairly arguable, having all due regard to the tricks of that jade, Fashion, that there would be no Brighton Road to-day, and but a ghost of Brighton herself.[1] So I have, bearing these things in mind, caused a portrait of Prince Florizel to appear on the frontis-piece of this book, and a brave appearance he makes there too.

[1] Brighton, familiarly *Doctor* Brighton, must really be masculine; but figure to yourself the egregious phrase "Brighton himself." It [illegible] impossible of use; so this, it would seem, must be a female d[illegible];

Thackeray would have, indeed *has*, told us that the curly hair waving so picturesquely on those princely temples was a wig, and I will not say he was in error; but it was an unkind thing to proclaim, especially after the P.R.A., the courtly Lawrence, had achieved so excellent a piece of flattery in paint as this is; and when the well-paid poet had so perjured himself as to write such lines as these, it was too bad to batter so splendid an idol as that here presented:—

"Seek you the Brave, the Generous, and the Free,
The Pride, the Hope of Britons?—This is He!
From Albion's Kings he boasts his splendid Fame,
The Patriot King, shall grace his future name:
E'en now the cause of Europe he sustains,
And from the groaning World removes the Tyrant's chains."

Alas! he has been handed down as doing nothing, or being none, of these things.

The character of George IV. has been the theme of writers upon history and sociology, of essayists, diarists, and gossip-mongers without number, and most of them have shown him in very lurid colours indeed. But Horace Walpole, perhaps, after all, the clearest-headed of this company, shows us in his "Last Journals" that from his boyhood the Prince was governed in the stupidest way—in a manner, indeed, but too well fitted to spoil a spirit so high and so impetuous, and impulses so generous as then were his.

It seems, unfortunately, only too clear that George III., himself of a narrow and obstinate mind, given to pettinesses, public and private, was jealous of his son's superior parts, and endeavoured to hide them beneath the bushel of seclusion and inadequate training. It was impossible for such a father to appreciate either the qualities or the defects of such a son. "The uncommunicative selfishness and pride of George III. confined him to domestic virtues," says Walpole, and he adds, "Nothing could equal the King's attention to seclude his son and protract his nonage. It went so absurdly far that he was made to wear a shirt with a frilled collar like that of babies. He one day took hold of his collar and said to a domestic, 'See how I am treated!'"[1]

The Duke of Montagu, too, was charged with the education of the Prince, and "he was utterly incapable of giving him any kind of instruction. . . . The Prince was so good-natured, but so uninformed, that he often said, 'I wish anybody would tell me what I ought to do; nobody gives me any instruction for my conduct.'" The absolute poverty of the instruction afforded him, the false and narrow ways of the royal household, and the evil example and low companionship of his uncle, the Duke of Cumberland, did much to spoil this Prince.

To quote Walpole again: "It made men smile to find that in the palace of piety and pride his Royal Highness had learnt nothing but the dialect of footmen and grooms. . . . He drunk hard, swore, and passed every night in[2] . . . ; such were the fruits of his being locked up in the palace of piety."

[1] "The Last Journals of Horace Walpole," edited by Dr. John Doran, 2 vols., 1889.

[2] *Hiatus* in the Journals, arranged by the editor for the benefit of the Young Person!

He proved, too, as might have been foreseen, an intractable and undutiful son; he was the faithless husband of a flippant and vulgar wife; and, in the circumstances, least excusable, an indifferent father to his only daughter. These things cannot be explained away, even did one wish to do so; but the responsibility for this evil warping of what was originally a generous and kindly nature is fixed by incontrovertible facts upon those whose charge it was.

He it was who peopled these roads with a numerous and brilliant concourse of whirling travellers, where before had been only some infrequent plodder amidst the depths of Sussex sloughs. To his royal presence, radiant by the Old Steyne, hasted all manner of people: prince and prizefighter, statesmen, noblemen; beauties, noble and ignoble, jostled one another on these ways in chaises, stage-coaches, mail-coaches, phaetons, gigs, whiskies, and divers other vehicles of yet more singular nomenclature, and severally cursed and shrieked when, as was not an uncommon occurrence, they were stuck fast in ruts or overturned altogether.

Travelling even this short distance of fifty-two miles was a serious business when the fare to or from London to Brighton varied from sixteen to twenty-five shillings for every passenger, and when the journey rarely took less than twelve hours to perform, and not infrequently longer than that.

Before 1796, when the stage-coaches were first put on these more direct roads, the only method of public conveyance was by the heavy, lumbering so-called "fly-waggons," drawn by eight horses, and

STAGE WAGGON, 18[illegible]

taking circuitous routes by way of Steyning and Horsham or Lewes, and carrying goods in addition to passengers; or, to put it in a stricter sense, passengers in addition to the usual load of goods.

These cumbrous conveyances supplanted a yet more primitive means of transit. Pack-horses had previously been used on what were then the extremely narrow lanes which wound by intricate ways to the coast: the infrequent lady-travellers rode then upon pillions, a method of progression which, however picturesque it may seem to us who have the advantage of Time's enchanting perspective, must have produced in but few miles an utter weariness and an intolerable aching in the jolted fair.

There were, it is true, stage-coaches of an earlier establishment in these counties of Surrey and Sussex, but they ran to towns which had been in existence for centuries while yet Brighthelmstone was the "miserable fishing-village" of early chroniclers, and then only to those which were within a reasonable distance from the metropolis; a distance, that is to say, which a moderately good pedestrian of our times would find no difficulty in covering in a long day's walk. Thus we are told that the earliest public conveyance from London towards the Sussex coast ran only to Tunbridge, whence journeys were performed on horseback. This coach is that referred to in the diary of Samuel Jeake, junior, of Rye, who writes in 1682: "May 22nd, Monday, I rode with my wife and mother-in-law to London for diversion; came thither 23, Tuesday: had hot and dry weather. June 23, Friday, we returned from London in ye stage-coach to Tonbridge, and 24, Saturday, came to Rye at night." In a later passage this gentleman of the peculiar views in the matter of diversions thanks God for his having escaped the dangers of the execrable roads they travelled.

Erredge, the Brighton historian, gives an interesting, if somewhat ungrammatical, note respecting stage-coaches :—

"In 1801 two pair-horse coaches ran between London and Brighton on alternate days, one up, the other down, and they were driven by Messrs. Crossweller and Hine. The progress of these coaches was amusing. The one from London left the Blossoms Inn, Lawrence Lane, at 7 A.M., the passengers breaking their fast at the Cock, Sutton, at 9. The next stoppage for the purpose of refreshment was at the *Tangier*, Banstead Downs—a rural little spot, famous for its elderberry wine, which used to be brought from the cottage 'roking hot,' and on a cold wintry morning few refused to partake of it. George IV. invariably stopped here and took a glass from the hand of Miss Jeal as he sat in his carriage. The important business of luncheon took place at Reigate, where sufficient time was allowed the passengers to view the Barons' Cave, where, it is said, the barons assembled the night previous to their meeting King John at Runnymeade. The grand halt for dinner was made at Staplefield Common, celebrated for its famous black cherry-trees, under the branches of which, when the fruit was ripe, the coaches were allowed to draw up and the passengers to partake of its tempting produce. The

ME AND MY WIFE AND DAUGHTER.
(From a Caricature by Henry Bunbury.)

hostess of the hostelry here was famed for her rabbit-puddings, which, hot, were always waiting the arrival of the coach, and to which the travellers never failed to do such ample justice, that ordinarily they found it quite impossible to leave at the hour appointed; so grogs, pipes, and ale were ordered in, and, to use the language of the fraternity, 'not a wheel wagged' for two hours. Handcross was the next resting-place, celebrated for its 'neat' liquors, the landlord of the inn standing, bottle in hand, at the door. He and several other bonifaces at Friar's Oak, &c., had the reputation of being on pretty good terms with the smugglers who carried on their operations with such audacity along the Sussex coast.

"After walking up Clayton Hill, a cup of tea was sometimes found to be necessary at Patcham, after which Brighton was safely reached at 7 P.M. It must be understood that it was the custom for the passengers to walk up all the hills, and even sometimes in heavy weather to give a push behind to assist the jaded horses.

"About 1809 a great revolution took place in coach-travelling. Some gentlemen—at the head of whom was the late Mr. William Bradford, or, as he was then styled, 'Miller' Bradford—twelve in number, formed a capital by shares of £100 each, and established two four-horse coaches. The cattle were cast horses of the Inniskilling Dragoons, then stationed at Brighton.

"In 1805 another vehicle of the same class, the 'Bellerophon,' a huge concern, built with two compartments, one carrying six, the other four inside.

and with several out, was driven by Mr. Hine. This coach received its name from the ship in which Bonaparte, after his defeat at Waterloo, was conveyed to exile at St. Helena. The 'Bellerophon' was soon found to be too heavy for the improving speed, and was abandoned for lighter vehicles, until travelling attained its perfection on the Brighton Road, the time taken in the transit having diminished from twelve hours to five, and on one occasion the 'Quicksilver,' with a King's Speech of William IV., made a journey down in three hours and forty minutes. From the year 1822, at different periods of the year, no less than sixty coaches were on the road, thirty each way."

What a grand and glorious procession that must have been, and especially when the light four-inside fast coaches came into use in 1823. The imagination pictures them careering along at all hours, the coachmen all with red, weather-beaten faces, wearing uncanny, low-crowned beaver hats and portentous overcoats with those amazing seven capes; the passengers, who have started some of them maybe at 7 A.M., sleepy, and (in winter) horribly cold, and the elder ones in terror at the astonishing pace, to which they could not by any possibility become accustomed. Such old fogeys mostly patronised the "Life Preserver," which started every morning at 8.45 from the Cross Keys, Cheapside. The rushing "Vivid" would have been altogether too great a terror to them.

Many and distinguished were the amateur whips of this road, which, though it can boast no such

THE BEAUFORT COACH STARTING, FROM THE BULL AND MOUTH OFFICE, PICCADILLY CIRCUS, 182[illegible]

(From an Aquatint after W. J. Shayer.)

artists of the ribbons as were Jack Moody and Charles Ward, can at least claim a social refinement wanting elsewhere. It is curious to see how coaching has always been, even in its serious days, before steam was thought of, the chosen amusement of wealthy and aristocratic whips. Of those who affected the Brighton Road may be mentioned the Marquis of Worcester, who drove the "Beaufort," Sir St. Vincent Cotton of the "Age," and the Hon. Fred. Jerningham, who drove the day-mail. The "Age," too, had been driven by Mr. Stevenson, a gentleman and a graduate of Cambridge, whose "passion for the *bench*," as "Nimrod" says, superseded all other worldly ambitions. He became a coachman by profession, and a good professional he made; but he had not forgotten his education and early training, and he was, as a whip, singularly refined and courteous. He caused, at a certain change of horses on the road, a silver sandwich-box to be handed round to the passengers by his servant, with an offer of a glass of sherry, should any desire one. Another gentleman, "connected with the first families in Wales," whose father long represented his native county in Parliament, horsed and drove one side of this ground with Mr. Stevenson.

Coaching authorities give the palm for artistry to whips of other roads: they considered the excellence of this as fatal to the production of those qualities that went to make an historic name. This road had become, as even "Viator" acknowledges, "perhaps the most nearly perfect, and certainly the most fashionable of all;" and private vehicles, light and airy of build, were driven along its excellent surface, that would not have been trusted on the very much less admirable roads of other parts of the kingdom. Indeed, in these latter years of the coaching age were to be seen on these vastly improved roads many and curious vehicles. Phaetons, barouches, sociables, curricles, gigs, and whiskies, driven by their owners, were used as private conveyances, and jostled the numerous stage- and mail-coaches plying for hire. Young sprigs derived a fearful joy from driving the smart but essentially dangerous contrivance known then as "the high-perch phaeton." It was generally two-horsed, and was, as its name foreshadows, of a giddy and amazing altitude. When you learn that it was of a thin and spidery build, and that these amateurs of the ribbons prided themselves on their high-spirited cattle, you are not surprised at hearing of constant and dangerous spills.

But here we are at Streatham, the sometime village of a certain literary repute, and an uncertain and long-dead fame as a Spa; for here did folks come, in the early years of the eighteenth century to drink the waters issuing from what the quaint Aubrey calls the "sower and weeping ground" by the Common.

It is only when this Streatham is reached, built on the downward slope of its long hill, that one realises fully the fact of being on that famous road to Brighton which was at once so notorious and so brilliant in the days of the Prince Regent and the Augustan age of coaching. Streatham, indeed, still retains something of its character of roadside village,

a village dating from the formation of the Roman Stane Street, and to which it owes both name and existence. True, it owns nothing of even a reputable age, and the glory of that brief-lived Spa has departed. Even Thrale Park has gone the way of all suburban estates in these days of the speculative builder, the house having been pulled down in 1863, and its lands laid out in building plots. Lysons, writing of its demesne in 1792, says that "Adjoining the houfe is an inclofure of about 100 acres, furrounded with a fhrubbery and gravel-walk of nearly two miles in circumference." Trim villas now occupy the spot, and the memory of the house itself is fading. Here is a view of it, taken just before operations were commenced for pulling down. Such a view was, singularly enough, difficult to obtain; there is not even a representation of the place in the local history. Save for its size, the house makes no brave show, it being merely one of many hundreds of mansions built in the seventeenth century, of a debased Classic type. One regrets the house because of its literary associations, and the estate for twofold reasons.

Even now, as these lines are being written, another, and the largest, of Streatham estates is being given over to the builder. Seventy acres or thereby of delightful gardens at Leigham Court are given over to destruction, and Streatham is welded by one more link to London.

But yet and yet, though now merely on the inner suburban circle of London, the air of the village clings about Streatham, seemingly inalienable, and the hillside, roadside common, wonderfully preserved through the mystic agency of the Statute of Merton: so long as they do not rail it round parkwise, the "villagers" shall still be something more than are ordinary suburban dwellers under the mighty shadow of London: they shall still continue with that fine sense of space and elbow-room with which it endows them.

Then they have their traditions, with which not many villages are so well endowed. First there is Dr. Johnson, a figure which will always be remembered, thanks to his biographer, and shall ever live in their memory, as coming down from London to Thrale's house, a grumbling, unwieldy figure, with the manners of a bear and a heart as tender as a child's beating beneath that unpromising exterior. Wig, too, awry and singed in front, from his short-sighted porings over the midnight oil, his was no pacifying presence when he happened upon that literary-artistic tea-table at Thrale Place. He met over those teacups a brilliant company, Reynolds and Garrick, and the lively Fanny Burney among other lesser lights, and partook there of innumerable cups of tea, dispensed at that hospitable board by Mrs. Thrale. That historic teapot is still extant, and has a capacity of three quarts; specially chosen, doubtless, in view of the Doctor's visits. Ye gods! what floods of congo were consumed within that house in Thrale Park!

Johnson once, we are told, went a-hunting at Streatham, and acquitted himself well upon that notable occasion. Would that we had been there to see!

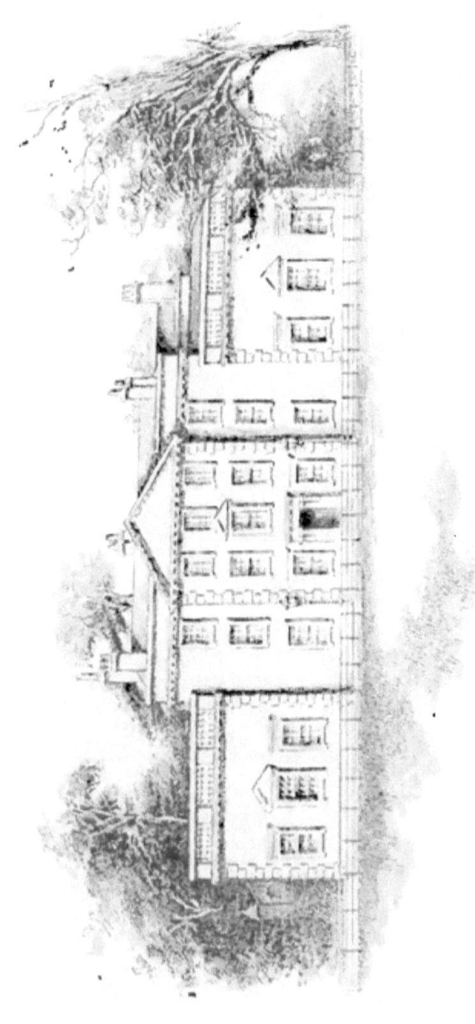

But all things have their end, and the day was to come when Johnson should bid his last farewell to Streatham. This he did in this wise, to quote from his diary :—"Sunday, went to church at Streatham. *Templo valedixi cum osculo.*" And so, kissing the old porch of St. Leonard's, the lexicographer departed with heavy heart.

This Church of St. Leonards still contains the Latin epitaph which the Doctor wrote to commemorate the easy virtues of his friend Henry Thrale, but alterations and restorations have changed almost all else. It is curious to note the learned Doctor's indignation when asked to write an English epitaph for setting up in Westminster Abbey. The great authority on the English language, the compiler of that monumental dictionary, exclaimed that he would not desecrate its walls with an inscription in his own tongue. Thus the pedant!

There is one Latin epitaph at Streatham that reads curiously. It is on a tablet by Richard Westmacott to Frederick Howard, who *in pugna Waterlooensi occiso.* The battle of Waterloo looks strange in that garb.

But Latin is frequent and free here. The mural tablets that jostle one another down the aisles are abounding in that tongue, and the little brass to an ecclesiastic, now nailed upon the woodwork toward the west end of the north aisle, is not free from it. So the shade of the Doctor, if ever it revisits the scenes of his life, might well be satisfied with the quantity of Latin to be read here, although it is not inconceivable he would cavil at the quality of it.

The swelling graveyard of this parish church, hard by the clear ringing anvil of the blacksmith's forge, holds the remains of many victims of the footpads and cut-throats who infested these outskirts of London in the "good old times." The Common and Thornton Heath were the lurking-places of so many desperate characters that it was extremely unsafe to venture abroad o' nights unless escorted and heavily armed. Even in daytime the wayfarer, if well advised, carried his pistols handy.

Meanwhile, on a neighbouring gallows there swung in chains, creaking in the wind, the corpse of an occasional highway murderer or robber as a warning to his surviving fellows. There is a curious old book in the British Museum with an interminable title, called "Britannia Depicta, or Ogilby Improv'd," published in 1731, which shows engraved plates of roads from London, and gives on the way from town to Croydon two such gallows, one where the road branches to Tooting, and another at, approximately, Thornton Heath for the use of Croydon. These, it would seem, were permanent structures, and Croydon's was extra large—a significant commentary either upon the size of that town or its proportion of evil-doers.

Down through Lower Streatham, passing on the way a cyclist's rest and a tiny stream, a branch of the Wandle, we came to Norbury, where a pleasant park skirts the way, and a railway bridge at Norbury Station spans the road, where once, in "the good old times," the footpad plied his dreadful trade. "Then," to quote Mr. Ruskin, "the Crystal Palace

STREAM AT NORBURY.

came, for ever spoiling the view through all its compass."[1]

It haunts you, indeed, all the way down Streatham Hill and through Norbury, sparkling away to the left in the sunshine with all the radiance of that "polished handle of the big front door" which Gilbert sings—and with as vulgar a lustre. And yet there were who likened this coruscating abomination to much that is beautiful in nature. But that was in '51, when the Great Orgie was held.

To Norbury succeeds Thornton Heath, now a continuation of Croydon, eminently respectable and dull. Here an ancient roadside horse-pond, a survival from those times when Thornton Heath was a name of some considerable dread to travellers, has been fenced round and furnished with a Jubilee fountain, which (of course) runs dry, as an Irishman might say. That fact suggests what might prove an interesting inquiry into the causes of so-called ornamental fountains so rarely fulfilling those functions which alone excuse their existence.

Presently we looked our last at the Great Conservatory and came at length into Croydon, as into another metropolis in the full tide of business. It was now past nine o'clock, and belated business men were hurrying to catch their trains to London city. Cyclists, too, there were in numbers, cursing by all their gods, consigning tramways and their promoters to regions where the earning of dividends is unknown, and where the fires burn unfailingly, because they could not steer clear of the rails that run through

[1] "Præterita," p. 70.

Croydon's busy streets. Croydon is not beloved of the cyclist. What of antiquity and picturesqueness this place possessed has well-nigh all gone in the incursion of villadom and the building of shops whose huge plate-glass fronts would not discredit Bond Street itself, and Archiepiscopal Croydon stands revealed only in the Palace remains, the Whitgift schools, the parish church, and the charming Hospital of the Holy Trinity. But this last makes amends for much else. A solitude amidst the throng, it stands in North End, by the High Street, remarkable in the simplicity of its screening walls of dark red brick, elbowed on one side by a draper's shop in all its impertinence of flashing plate-glass. Once within the outer portal of the Hospital, ornamented overhead with the arms of the See of Canterbury and eloquent with its motto, "*Qui dat pauperi non indigebit*," we were in another world. The building is, as old Aubrey quaintly puts it, "a handsome edifice, erected in the manner of a College, by the Right Reverend Father in God, John Whitgift, late Archbishop of Canterbury." The dainty quadrangle, set about with grass lawns and bright flowers, is formed on three sides by tiny houses of two floors, where dwell the poor brothers and sisters of this old foundation, twenty brothers and sixteen sisters, who, beside lodging, receive each £40 and £30 yearly respectively. The fourth side, and the farthest from the street, is occupied by the Hall, the Warden's rooms, and the Chapel, all in very much the same condition as they were in at their building. That old oak table in the Hall is dated

1614, and much of the stained glass is of sixteenth-century date.

But it is in the Warden's rooms above that the eye is feasted with old wood-work, ancient panelling, black with lapse of time, quaint muniment chests, curious records, and the like.

These were the rooms specially reserved for his personal use during his lifetime by the pious Archbishop Whitgift.

Here is a case exhibiting the original titles to the lands on which the Hospital is built, and with which it is endowed; formidable sheets of parchment, bearing many seals, and, what does duty for one, a gold angel of Edward VI.

These are ideal rooms, rooms which delight one with their unspoiled sixteenth-century air. The sun streams through the western windows over their deep embrasures, lighting up finely the darksome wood-work into patches of brilliance; and as we leave, we envy the Warden his lodging, so perfect a survival of more spacious days. Indeed, we scrupled not to tell him so, at which he is well pleased, for he has a loving interest in the old place and his old people. Then he shows us the Chapel, quite a little building, and a dusky.

Here is not pomp of carving nor vanity of blazoning, for the good Archbishop, mindful of economy, would none of these. The seats and benches are contemporary with the building and are rough-hewn. On the western wall hangs the founder's portrait, black-framed and mellow, rescued from the boys of the Whitgift schools ere quite destroyed, and on the other walls are the portrait of a lady, supposed to be the Archbishop's niece, and a ghastly representation of Death as a skeleton digging a grave. But all

these things are seen but dimly, for the light is very feeble.

At length we leave this harbour of refuge, and are out upon the roaring street once more. The Warden, who is kindness itself, accompanies us, and points out some timbered houses of a prodigious age in a disreputable quarter of the town, and occupied as fourpenny lodgings by tramps. Among other things here, he shows us the inn which John Ruskin's grandmother kept. You shall find particulars of it set forth fully in "Præterita," thuswise:[1]—

". . . Of my father's ancestors I know nothing, nor of my mother's more than that my maternal grandmother was the landlady of the 'Old King's Head' in Market Street, Croydon; and I wish she were alive again, and I could paint her Simone Memmi's 'King's Head' for a sign." And Mr. Ruskin adds farther on:[2] "Meantime my aunt had remained in Croydon and married a baker. . . . My aunt lived in the little house still standing—or which was so four months ago,[3]—the fashionablest in Market Street, having actually two windows over the shop, in the second story" (*sic*).

This is a quarter of Croydon that will soon be entirely of the past. As it is the oldest, so also it is the most disreputable part of the town; more squalid than the London slums, dirtier than a Glasgow rookery, more offensive to the sense of smell than Drury Lane o' summer evenings, and at the same time more picturesque than Venice. Here the true-born British tramp lolls, free as air and ineffably foul, in the dark and cavernous doorways of these crazy old buildings, and when the sunlight comes down and lights upon the cobble-stones and makes

[1] "Præterita," p. 9. [2] "Præterita," pp. 12, 18.
[3] The Preface to "Præterita" is dated 10th May 1885.

great patches of glory here, and mysterious black shadows there, and tender half-lights otherwhere, I declare he and the place both wear an extremely paintable look. But then that tramp has such a vocabulary, and the scent of the place smites you so forcibly in the face, that you flee.

This is Middle Street, at whose end stands the "Old King's Head," fronting on to the open space of Market Street, where a street-market of the type familiar to most Londoners is held. Opposite stands the building of the old jail, now disused from its old-time purpose and converted into business premises. In its basement are still to be seen the prisoners' cells, empty of prisoners, filled with store of corn and flour, and seeds, and closed still with their original doors, whereon you may read, carved in the wood, how so-and-so had free lodging within for six months, and others for other periods.

At one end, with an iron-barred window looking out upon the street, is the debtors' cell. That time is within the memory of living townsmen when debtors were imprisoned here, and when a written notice was exhibited at that window imploring passers-by to "Remember the poor debtors." They do not need cells for debtors now at Croydon; but in the other departments the business has so greatly increased that the establishment has been "removed to larger and more commodious premises."

An you are interested in the Croydon of the past, you may learn many facts of an amazing antiquity, even that this town, which we look upon as ancient enough, is, properly speaking, New Croydon; for this mediæval town had a hoary predecessor, which was situated otherwhere, a mile or so to the east, where is no trace nor relic to be found at this day, but which antiquarians have proved among themselves to have existed in Roman civilisation under the name of Noviomagus.

But coming down to Elizabethan times, we shall find the Croydon of that glorious reign to have been a veritable Black Country by reason of the great charcoal-burning industry carried on then, and even until the end of the eighteenth century.

These counties of Surrey and Sussex were at one time little else than huge forests, in which the oak predominated, and charcoal was manufactured here for the use of London in days when coal was practically unknown. Indeed, it was not until coal became generally used that Croydon lost its evil reputation, and that the iron-smelting industries of these southern counties became extinct. What the town was like in the sixteenth and seventeenth centuries we may gather in some sort from these curious excerpts from contemporary plays and poems. Thus Patrick Hannay writes in one of his songs, published during the reign of Charles the Second :—

"In midst of these stands Croydon clothed in blacke,
In a low bottom sinke of all these hills ;
And is receipt of all the durtie wracke,
Which from their tops still in abundance trills.
The unpav'd lanes with muddie mire it fills :
If one shower falls, or if that blessing stay,
You well may sent, but never see your way.

"And those who there inhabit, suting well
With such a place, doe either *Nigro's* seeme,
Or harbingers for *Pluto*, Prince of Hell,
Or his fire-beaters one might rightly deeme;
Their sight would make a soule of hell to dreame;
Besmeared with sut, and breathing pitchie smoake,
Which (save themselves) a living wight would choke.

"These, with the demi-gods still disagreeing
(As vice with virtue ever is at jarre),
With all who in the pleasant woods have being,
Doe undertake an everlasting warre,
Cuts downe their groves, and often doe them skarre;
And in a close-pent fire their arbours burne,
Whileas the *Muses* can doe nought but mourne.

. . . . .

"To all proud dames I wish no greater hell,
Whoe doe disdaine of chastly profered love,
Then to that place confin'd there ever dwel;
That place their pride's dear price might justly prove:
For if (which God forbid) my dear should move
Me not come nie her—for to passe my troth—
Place her but there, and I shall keep mine oath."

That is a sufficiently vivid picture of an ancient Black Country, and this, from an Elizabethan play, is not less convincing:—

"Marry," quoth he that looked like Lucifer, "though I am black, I am not the Devill, but indeed a collyer from Croydon."

The town is not grimy nor black-canopied now, although grown to a monstrous size, and with a population of some ninety thousand souls, a vast increase upon the meagre six thousand of 1801.

A place well beloved of City men, its distance of a short ten miles from town has resulted in this huge growth, absorbent of much fair country and responsible for the remarkable number of railway stations, from West to East Croydon, from South Croydon to Addiscombe, that are dotted about.

'Twas long past one o'clock ere we left the town, and almost two before its southern outskirts had been passed. Not far from the roadside in this direction is another place where Croydon's gallows trees held aloft in other times their dreadful fruit.

In olden days were but few townships but had their wild commons or dreary heaths whereon local malefactors expiated their crimes and swung, rattling in the breeze, a terror to timid folk who chanced their way of eventide, in receipt of stray whiffs of well-hanged murderer or common thief. Those were truly robust times. The law in these days, we are told, executes assassins not in revenge, but by way of warning, as a deterrent, in fact; but where is your warning in this era of private executions and speedy interments in quicklime-bestrewn graves? Our forefathers had a better way. *Their* criminals hung rotting *in terrorem* in chains on gibbets in public places, disappearing only to give place to fresh subjects, and their brethren yet in life were thus constantly reminded of what end awaited their evil courses. Nay, remoter ancestors were yet more grim; one political offender, or murderer, or highwayman, one horse-thief or sheep-stealer, would then serve half a county, with one piece in this village, another fragment in that, a leg or so otherwhere, and so on, as often as not seethed in pitch for their better preservation, and stuck on poles for the edification of the lieges. There is a certain delightfully horrid picturesqueness in all this. You might then go abroad o' nights and get a fine romantic thrill of horror by encountering unawares one of these ghastly objects; now you may find nothing savouring more of romance than skeleton jerry-built houses, but of these more than a sufficiency.

It is not until the twelfth milestone is passed that one emerges from pavement upon really open country, passing to it through South Croydon and Purley, whose mean roadside houses affront the fair face of Nature.

It was here, at Purley House, to the left of the road, that John Horne Tooke, that contentious partisan and stolid begetter of seditious tracts, lived—when, indeed, he was not detained within the four walls of some prison for political offences. He was the author of that deep philological treatise, "EΠΕΑ ΠΤΕΡΟΕΝΤΑ, or the Diversions of Purley," which some rash scribe, blissfully unconscious of fallacy, recently called "that amusing book." He ought to know and be compelled to read it, and then be called upon to give his views upon its amusing qualities.

Tooke had intended to be buried in the grounds of his residence, Purley House, but when he died in 1812 at Wimbledon, his mortal coil was laid to rest at Ealing; and so it chanced that the vault he had constructed in his garden remained, after all, untenanted, with the unfinished epitaph:—

John Horne Tooke,
Late Proprietor and now Occupier
of this spot,
was born in June 1736,
Died in
Aged years,
Contented and Grateful.

Purley House is still standing, though considerably altered, and presents few features reminiscent of the eighteenth-century politician, and fewer still of the Puritan Bradshaw, the regicide, who once resided here. It stands in the midst of tall elms, and looks as far removed from political dissensions as may well be imagined, with its trim lawns and trellised walls, o'ergrown in summer by a tangle of greenery.

It is a welcome contrast to the mean ravellings of Croydon town along the high-road. But though they do much to spoil the country-side here, this is not to say that folk have not their appreciations in these parts; for just here, where the old road branches to the left, a sign-post states, in bold letters, "To Riddlesdown, the prettiest spot in Surrey," a surprise in sign-posts, which generally confine themselves to bald, dry statements of facts, leaving controversial matter to rival guide-books.

But then, 'tis possible some advertising scheme accounts for this enthusiasm.

So we mused as we ascended the long hill of Smitham Bottom; but of a truth the Brighton Road is singular in sign-posts, as in other respects, not the least remarkable feature along its course being the extraordinary number of asylums, public institutions, and schools seen on either hand. The Warehousemen and Clerks' Schools are on the crest of Russell Hill, as you leave Croydon; the Reedham Asylum for fatherless children is away to the left: at Cane Hill the huge building of the Surrey County Lunatic Asylum looks down upon the road from its lofty perch; and away through Redhill down to Brighton occur the Earlswood Asylum, and many

COULSDON: A ROADSIDE STATION.

more, and, as you at length reach your destination, the Brighton Workhouse frowns a-down the road.

The little hamlet of Smitham Bottom, in the pass of that name, in the North Downs, is, in all but the fairest weather, a very forlorn concourse of about a dozen houses, occupying a little elevated plateau amid the hills. The London, Brighton, and South Coast Railway follows beside the road, and has a new station for Coulsdon a little way beyond, where the road begins to descend again in the direction of Merstham.

The fretful rookeries of Coulsdon woods were already echoing with their early evening clamour as we drew near, the circling homeward flight of their inhabitants livening the pale sky where the windy elms revealed their lofty nests, seen clearly through the thin foliage of spring. There was in all the air a freshness, a stimulus, a certain life-giving quality which this season alone, of all the four, possesses, and everything spoke eloquently of the coming glory of summer.

A-down the road, where some few sorry outlying houses of Chipstead village and a mean settlement known as Hooley line the way, the railway plunges into a deep cutting of some 120 feet in depth, driven through the chalk. Running irregularly beside it is the smaller, shallower cutting of the abandoned iron tramway from Merstham to Wandsworth, made in 1805 and still traceable, though disused these fifty years and more. Alders and hazels grow on its sides, and its bridges are ivy-grown; primroses and violets, too, grow there, wondrously profuse.

And here, by your leave, we will turn aside up a lane to the right hand, toward the village of Chipstead, where lies Sir Edward Banks in the little churchyard. He began life in the humblest manner, and worked as a labourer, a "navvy," upon this same obsolete tramway, afterwards rising to be an employer of labour and a contractor to the Government. You shall see all these things recorded of him upon

CHIPSTEAD CHURCH.

a memorial tablet in the church of Chipstead, a tablet which lets nothing of his worth escape you, so prolix is it.[1]

It was while delving amid the chalk of this tramway cutting that Edward Banks first became acquainted with this village, and so charmed with it was he that he expressed a desire, when his time should come, to be laid to rest in its quiet graveyard. Fifty years later, when he died, after a singularly successful career, his wish was carried out, and here, in this quiet spot overlooking the highway, you may see his handsome tomb, begirt with iron railings, and overshadowed with ancient trees.

The little church of Chipstead is of Norman origin, and still shows some interesting features of that period, with some interesting Early English additions that have presented architectural puzzles even

[1] "Sir Edward Banks, Knight, of Sheerness, Isle of Sheppey, and Adelphi Terrace, Strand, Middlesex, whose remains are deposited in the family vault in this churchyard. Blessed by Divine Providence with an honest heart, a clear head, and an extraordinary degree of perseverance, he rose superior to all difficulties, and was the founder of his own fortune; and although of self-cultivated talent, he in early life became contractor for public works, and was actively and successfully engaged during forty years in the execution of some of the most useful, extensive, and splendid works of his time; amongst which may be mentioned the Waterloo, Southwark, London, and Staines Bridges over the Thames, the Naval Works at Sheerness Dockyard, and the new channels for the rivers Ouse, Nene, and Witham in Norfolk and Lincolnshire. He was eminently distinguished for the simplicity of his manners and the benevolence of his heart; respected for his inflexible integrity and his pure and unaffected piety: in all the relations of his life he was candid, diligent, and humane; just in purpose, firm in execution; his liberality and indulgence to his numerous coadjutors were alone equalled by his generosity and charity displayed in the disposal of his honourably-acquired wealth. He departed this life at Tilgate, Sussex . . . on the 5th day of July 1835, in the sixty-sixth year of his age."

to the minds of experts. Many years ago, the late Mr. G. E. Street, the architect of the present Royal Courts of Justice in London, read a paper upon this building, advancing the theory that the curious pedimental windows of the chancel and the transept door were not the Saxon work they appeared to be, but were the creation of an architect of the Early English period, who had a fancy for reviving Saxon features, and who was the builder and designer of a series of Surrey churches, among which is included that of Merstham.

Within the belfry here is a ring of five bells, some of them of a respectable age, and three with the inscription, with variations—

"OUR HOPE IS IN THE LORD, 1595."

From here a bye-lane leads steeply once more into the high-road, which winds along the valley, sloping always toward the Weald. Down the long descent into Merstham village tall and close battalions of fir-trees lend a sombre colouring to the foreground, while "southward o'er Surrey's pleasant hills" the evening sunlight streams in parting radiance. On the left hand as we descend are the eerie-looking blow-holes of the Merstham tunnel, which here succeeds the cutting. Great heaps of chalk, by this time partly overgrown with grass, also mark its course, and in the distance, crowned as many of them are with telegraph poles, they look by twilight curiously and awfully like so many Calvarys.

Merstham is as pretty a village as Surrey affords, and typically English. Railways have not abated, nor these turbid times altered in any great measure, its fine air of aristocratic and old-time rusticity. At one end of its one clearly-defined street, set at an angle to the high-road, are the great ornamental gates of Merstham Park, setting their stamp of landed aristocracy upon the place. To their right is a tiny gate leading to the public right-of-way through the park, which presently crosses over the pond where rise fitfully the springs of Merstham Brook, a congener of the Kentish "Nailbournes," and one of the many sources of the River Mole. Beyond, above the tall trees, is seen the shingled spire of the church, an Early English building dedicated to St. Catherine, not yet destroyed, despite restorations and the scraping which its original lancet windows have undergone in misguided efforts to endue them with an air of modernity.

The church is built of that "firestone" found so freely in the neighbourhood, a famed specialty which entered largely into the building and ornamentation of Henry the Seventh's Chapel at Westminster. Those wondrously intricate and involved carvings and traceries, whose decadent Gothic delicacy is the despair of present-day architects and stone-carvers, were possible only in this stone, which, when quarried, is of exceeding softness, but afterwards, on exposure to the air, assumes a hardness equalling that of any ordinary building-stone, and has, in addition, the merit of resisting fire, whence its name. Merstham church is even at this day of considerable interest. It contains brasses to the Newdegate, Best, and Elmebrygge families, one of which records in black letter:—

> "Hic iacet Johēs Elmebrygge, armiger, qui obiit viij° die Februarij A° Dñi Mᵒcccclxxij, et Isabella uxor eius quae fuit filia Richī Jamys quondā Maioris et Aldermañ London: quae obiit vij° die Septembris A° Dñi Mᵒcccclxxij° et Annae uxor ei: quae fuit filia Johēs Prophete Gentilman quae obiit . . . A° Dñi Mᵒcccc . . . . quorū animabus ppicietur Deus."

The date of the second wife's death has never been inserted, showing that the brass was engraved and set during her lifetime, as in so many other examples of monumental brasses throughout the country. The figure of John Elmebrygge is wanting, it having been at some time torn from its matrix, but above his figure's indent remains a label inscribed *Sancta Trinitas*, and from the mouths of the remaining figures issue labels inscribed *Unus Deus—Miserere Nobis*. Beneath is a group of seven daughters; the group of four sons is long since lost.

A transitional Norman font of grey Sussex marble remains at the western end of the church, and on an altar-tomb in the southern chapel are the poor remains of an ancient stone figure of the fifteenth century, presumably the effigy of a merchant civilian, as he is represented wearing the *gypcière*. It is hacked out of almost all significance at the hands of some iconoclasts; their chisel-marks are even now distinct, and bear witness against the Puritan rage

COFFEE ROOM

which defaced and buried it face downwards, the reverse side of the stone forming part of the chapel pavement until 1861, when it was discovered during the restoration of the church.

Before that restoration this interior disclosed a Georgian orgie of high pews, among which the "squire's parlour" was pre-eminent, with its fire-place and well-carpeted floor, its chairs and tables: a snuggery wherein that great man snored unobserved or partook critically of his snuff during the parson's discreet discourse. But now the parlour is gone, and the squire must slumber with the other sinners.

These things we noted during the walk we took while high tea was being prepared at the "Feathers." Now, there is hardly any other satisfaction so hearty as that experienced when, toward the close of a day's walk, the traveller sits him down to that cheering meal tea. For one thing, the repast seems well and truly earned; a pleasing langour steals upon mind and body as the hour of six approaches, and thought turns involuntarily to rest and refreshment. I have observed this even in City offices, where clerks yawn wearily at this hour. We had sped the day with exploration, quip, and jest, and were not aweary indeed, but here was a village where everything conspired to give content, and foolish, nay, criminal were he who should hie him forth with never a halt, be it never so short.

The world is viewed charitably over the teacup, even the rabidest of American art critics could hardly fail to be somewhat mollified under such circumstances as these, though, certainly, his is an extreme case. They have not evil tongues who can ply their evening knives and forks to such good purpose as the sharp-set pedestrian, to whom, an he be happily placed in his hostelry, everything is rosy-hued and the world young again.

At length, that important office of tea despatched, 'twas time to depart, but (we argued) what need was there to urge our course farther this eve? Why tempt Fortune by pursuing the road to Redhill, than whence we could not hope farther to reach this night? Knew we not already by common report what manner of town that town might be—a creation of the present age, called into being by the railway; a modern model town, rhythmic, local boarded to the extreme; an orgie in the newest and most vivid of red brick—an impossible town, indeed, from the point of view of him who seeketh after the fortuitously picturesque.

So we stayed the night at Merstham, and an aimless walk, begun in the gathering twilight, was a fitting close to an irresponsible day.

Such experiences as these evening walks are of the sweetest; conversation which in daylight would perhaps become absolute chatter seems in the vagueness of evening around you of the most luminous quality (it appears so, harking back to it). Perhaps though, if it were reported verbatim, 'twould be of the sorriest. It seems, indeed, almost desecration to attempt to analyse those optimist utterances, for optimist under such circumstances they always are; at such times to be a weeping philosopher were surely impossible. Analysis here would be a dese-

BYE-ROAD, MER[illegible]

cration worse than that of which we were guilty, that of burdening the scented air of the spring evening with tobacco, though that was bad enough.

But as darkness came on apace, it was the crowning touch of witchery to note the ruddy glow of one's neighbour's tobacco as, side by side, we paced the bye-lanes. The bat had now left his church-tower and the owl his clinging ivy, and they flitted overhead or haunted the trees with gruesome cries; the crake, too, commenced his harsh creaking, while blundering moths flew full tilt into the wayfarer's face, and from ditches and long grasses came the chirping of the grasshopper.

Now came from the ale-house open door a bar of light across the path. From within one heard the rustic discourse in accents of beer on matters political, following that unwritten law by whose decree he who knows little says much. You shall hear the yokel at these times denounce the Government with all his florid vocabulary of invective. 'Tis no matter, his wife shall presently haul him home, and his voice will be heard no more this night; for your disputatious rustic is in so far like "Gelert the faithful hound," that though a lion abroad, he is "a lamb at home." Thus Hodge.

Cottage windows, through diamond panes, lent their glimmer to intensify the gathered night as we made to return. Coming at length into the high-road to seek the village for the night, we encountered quite an array of cyclists speeding with flying wheels towards Brighton at what pace they might. One moment a blaze of lamps rounding the corner, the next a blank darkness and a confused babel of ringing bells and hooting pneumatic alarms (*cyclorns* they call them) as they swept past us down the road upon something in their way. They would reach the coast to-night, no doubt, while we—we chuckled as having the better way.

And so (as Pepys might have said) to our inn and to bed well pleased.

SECOND DAY.

I LOOK back upon this as a day of great good-humour, a day when the sun shone gaily and all nature seemed to smile in response; a day, too, when all went well with us, from that excellently appreciated breakfast at Merstham to the equally enjoyable evening repast at Crawley; an ideal spring day, when all we met or passed were pleasant and happy seeming, except indeed an ungodly tramp, who swore roundly at us for that we would give him nothing—a morally ill-conditioned fellow, but physically well-cared for: of such are all his tribe. And yet this lazy, hulking, well-fed rascal was not without a touch of the picturesque—ragged picturesqueness of a theatrical exaggeration. It was a marvel to see how his tattered duds held together as he walked, so looped and windowed were they with raggedness. It seemed indeed almost as if he had made to himself a covering of dried leaves pinned together, so many were his fragments and without so much as a suspicion of cut or fit. Buttons had fled him long since: string and wire romantically replaced them where fastenings became imperative; and where his many windows afforded glimpses of his skin, inconceivable griminess was disclosed, so that one instinctively stood to windward of him. Yet all this must have been but an elaborately contrived get-up to induce pity in all who should behold him; for it was plain to see that this was a lusty, able-bodied, well-fed vagabond, with round face and well-covered ribs, one of the sort that will not work while they can so readily beg a living.

You shall happen upon many of his order along these pleasant roads in spring, summer, and autumn; whole families of them, father, mother, and children. Not hard-working hop-pickers these, not gipsies even, but whining, hypocritical wanderers, incorrigibly nomadic, with the morals of a mudlark and language equalling only the awful profanity of an Australian sheep-shearer from the "back blocks."

Such a family was that we passed later in the day by Earlswood Common. They were cooking their mid-day meal near to the roadside by the aid of a fire of dried twigs. The man, head of the family, I suppose, was stretched full length upon his stomach, chewing the blades of grass he had plucked, while the woman tended the fire and the children gathered yet more twigs. As we approached, this bullet-headed, evil-looking creature raised himself slightly, irresistibly recalling the action of some reptile, and called to us, with dull wit, "Hi! Guv'nor, wait for us; we're going your way." The children, too, came pell-mell after us, crying, "Gie me a penny, sir, gie me a 'a'p'nny," and would not be denied; so, because of their importunity, we pitched them some coppers and were left in peace.

But, ere these folks were encountered, we had left the lime-burners and apple-orchards of Merstham

behind, and had walked that featureless two miles or so into Redhill, whose uninteresting streets we paced hot-foot, eager to have done with its suggestions of town, its pavings, asphalte or stone-flagged, and its unpicturesque but withal unkempt High Street or London Road, by whatsoever name they call that part of the town that borders the Brighton Road.

But atop of that steep ascent lying before all who fare southward, you have a not unpleasing view over the town. True, there is nothing more romantic down there in that welter of junctions, reformatories, and asylums than the huge building of St. Anne's Society; but distance lends a something that (though enchantment here were an impossible word) extenuates the view, backed as it is by the swelling bosom of the North Downs, parti-coloured in fields of different growths.

And so, with but little delay, we turned an unreluctant heel upon this place, which commands no interest, saving only that little which may lie in the fact that here is found fuller's earth, a distinction shared only by one other neighbourhood in this land.

The road, here narrowed for some distance and enclosed on either side by high brick walls, leads presently upon Redhill and Earlswood Commons, where movement is unrestrained and free as air, and the vision is bounded only by Leith Hill in one direction, and the blue haze of distance in another. Earlswood Common is a welcome change after Redhill. It gives sensations of elbow-room, of freedom and vastness, which are not justified by a reference to its acreage, and this by reason of its broken, irregular surface, grey-green, picturesquely uncared-for, and still with a certain wildness; the little pools which fill many of its hollows reflecting, as so many mirrors, both sunshine and passing clouds.

This had surely been in other times the ideal spot for an encounter with a knight of the road. What pity it is that these days of the cyclist were not synchronised with those of the highwayman! Imagine with what delightful "creeps" the nocturnal wheelman would have wheeled himself out of an incipient Redhill on to the lonely Common, larger, wilder, and lonelier than now, and all haggard under the occasional rays of a fitful moonlight. With what suspense and misgiving he would have heard the tinkle of a horse's gallop on the frosty road somewhere in his rear! *How* he would have pedalled as the horseman drew nearer and yet more near, and with what a sinking of his heart into his shoes he would have regarded such an apparition as that you shall see depicted on the opposite page, crape-masked and armed with horse-pistol of generous calibre! Then, being compelled by the moral suasion of that "barker" to dismount, one can very vividly imagine the Cut-throat Dick or Sixteen-string Jack of this involuntary encounter demanding the unhappy wheelman's valuables, and cursing him for that he wore, instead of a gold chronometer jewelled in Lord knows how many holes, only the humble inexpensive Waterbury.

And then, the better to escape pursuit, the knight of industry, being keen-witted, would doubtless de-

mand his pedals of that cyclist, who, reduced thus to walking both himself and his machine, would return a sadder and a poorer, if not a wiser wight to that place whence he came.

One can imagine how splendid an opportunity would thus be afforded the Munchausens of the pastime (of cycling, not of highway robbery) of exercising their powers, now so poorly used in competitive lying on feats of pace. They might begin in the old familiar style of the Christmas numbers we know so well, and work up the interest by picturesque exaggerations of their prowess, and——But who am I that I should presume to coach the mendacious wheelman in his very own subject?

But now-a-days the wheelman has nothing to fear, unless it be the puncturing of a tyre, or the happening upon the fortuitons brick upon the highway. He may wheel along this or any other public road, and none shall say him nay. This stretch across Earlswood Common is very much after his heart; it has those "switchback" properties that are dear to the heart of the tourist on wheels, inasmuch as he is called upon for little or no exertion. And so, this being thus, he would, in dashing past that old inn which lies at the Common's farthest southern limit, have missed that talk which ourselves had with as aged a specimen of the Sussex peasant as it had ever been our fortune to light upon out o' doors.

He was drinking from a tankard of the pea-soup which they call ale in these parts, sitting the while upon a bench whose like is usually found outside old country inns. Ruddy of face, with clean-shaven lips and chin, his grizzled beard kept rigidly upon his wrinkled dewlap, his hands gnarled and twisted with toil and rheumatism, he sat there in smock-frock and gaiters, as typical a countryman as ever on London stage brought the scent of the hay across the footlights. That smock of his, the "round frock" of Sussex parlance, was worked about the yoke of it, fore and aft, with many and curious devices, whose patterns, though he, and she who worked them, knew it not, derived from centuries of tradition and precept, had been handed down from Saxon times, ay, and before them, to the present day, when, their significance lost, they excite merely a mild wonder at their oddity and complication.

He was, it seemed, a "hedger and ditcher," and his leathern gauntlets and billhook lay beside him on the ale-house bench.

"I've worked at this sort o' thing," said he, in conversation with us, "for the last twenty year. Hard work? yes, onaccountable hard, and small pay for't too. Two and twopence a day I gets, an' works from seven o' marnings to half-past five in the afternoon for that. You'll be gettin' more than two and twopence a day when you're at work, I reckon."

One of us modestly admitted the truth of that surmise, but submitted that living and housing in London being far and away more costly than country life, town and country earnings, comparatively and without personal experience, were not so widely different as might be imagined. London, too, we urged, both of us, was not the ideal residence; the country was preferable. The old man agreed in this last proposition, for he had been to the metropolis, and "a dirty place it was, sure-ly;" also he had been atop of the Monument, to the Tower, and to Tussaud's, to which places we, being merely Londoners from our

FLOODS ON THE BRIGHTON ROAD AT SALFORD MILL.

birth up, had never been. Thus the country cousin in our gates is more learned in the stock sights of town than townsfolk themselves.

From here the road slopes gently to the Weald, past Petridge Wood and Salford, where a tributary of the Mole crosses it beneath a little bridge, and, constrained to service, turns the water-wheel of a new and an extremely ugly mill. It is nearly always a puny rivulet; but let there be a continuous month or three weeks of rain, or a sudden melting of winter snows, and the Mole shall show you how powerful for evil it may become.

To take the latest instance, the floods of October 1891. There had been weeks of more or less heavy rains following upon one of the wettest summers experienced of late years, and the earth had arrived at that soaked condition under which it had lost for the time its absorbent power. Rain continued falling, and the Mole, which runs in countless little arteries throughout the level lands, rose in power and flooded the country-side, isolating farm-houses and flooding high-roads and bye-lanes alike. Here, at Salford, and again at Horley, the highway became a rushing torrent, along whose nut-brown October flood tumbled the remaining apples from drowned orchards, with trees and bushes and hurdles. The postman on his rounds had to wade it, as had all those whose business called them this way on foot. The meadows, too, to the south of Horley and at Gatwick were flooded, and the water, stretching for great distances, flooded Horley churchyard itself.

WADING.

This God's acre boasts two fine yews, notable even in a county whose soil seems particularly

The Chequers
Horley.

favourable to the growth of this tree. The church itself, with its shingled spire and white walls, composes finely with the noble trees surrounding, but has not much to show beyond a mail-clad effigy of the fourteenth century and two brasses of but mild attractions to the archaeologist.

Of greatest interest is the churchwardens' account book, dating from the sixteenth century, but not to be seen of the curious here. After many wanderings in the land, it was at length purchased at a second-hand bookseller's and presented to the British Museum, in which mausoleum of literature, in the department of manuscripts, it is now to be found. It contains a curious item, which shows that even in the rigid times that produced the great Puritan upheaval congregations were not unapt for irreverence. Thus in 1632 "John Austy is chosen by the consent of ye minister & parishioners to see y^t^ ye younge men & boyes behaue themselves decently in ye church in time of diuine service and sermon, & he is to haue for his paines ij^s.^"

The village of Horley has only one building of any picturesqueness, and that is one so well known to all them that travel this road that this drawing of it must come even as the picture of an old familiar friend. The "Chequers" is an inn that commands attention as much by its position as by its appearance, standing as it does at the centre of Horley, where several roads meet. A long rambling building, its several parts added as expediency dictated, it is of uncertain date, and of a certain uncalculated irregularity that is only the outcome of needs supplied as they arose, an irregularity that charms by its artless air where a premeditated quaintness would fail to please.

The Brighton Parcel Mail, which goes now-a-days by road, changes here every night. The down van, running from the London Bridge office, and leaving there at 9.45 P.M., meets the up mail from Brighton at 12.55; vans are exchanged, the Brighton van and London driver go back to London, the London van and Brighton driver back again to the Brighton office, which is reached at 4.45 A.M. To view this strange practical revival of old-time mail-carrying is to almost fancy one's self back in the early years of this dying century. The lateness of the hour, the changing of the horses, the appearance of the great vans, each with its three powerful lamps in front and its two red lights behind; all these things are impressive indeed. And not less remarkable facts are the regularity with which the service is maintained and the swiftness which characterises the transport of the heavy loads which compose the parcel mail for Brighton or London; for this is not by any means a performance to be set on all fours with the doings of the light passenger drags that in the summer cover these fifty-two miles in a matter of six hours. To exceed their time by only an hour is an achievement of note when the construction and weight of the vans and their heavy loads are taken into consideration.

There has very recently been opened just below Horley, at Gatwick Park, a new racecourse to keep alive the name and fame of this classic road as a

THE BRIGHTON PARCEL MAIL.

sporting highway. Of such import is it that a new station (Gatwick) has been built on the Brighton Railway to serve the needs of the sporting community. Here foregather sportsmen of every description; bookmakers and an eager crowd throng the roads when important events are run.

This, the more important of all the roads to Brighton, has unfortunately too distinct an air of the modern suburb to altogether please men who find aught of pleasure in history and old associations. Villadom has pitched its tents at too frequent intervals along the highway for any great survival of romance. Streatham, Croydon, Redhill, and Horley beckon each to each, and shall embrace ere long, to the approximate extinction of rurality along this entire stretch of country down to the sea-shore. Every village that stands directly in the path has its belt of bungalows, its arteries of asphalte.

But turn for any distance right or left, and the fair country-side, innocent of building estates, smiles fresh and free, and hardly in Cornwall itself shall you find such solitudes as may successfully be sought in these two home counties.

Horley is a typical example of modern growth. It will doubtless be, ere many years have passed, a town, with town-hall and other signs of size, so energetic is the builder in these gates. Yet to turn aside to the neighbouring villages of Charlwood and Newdigate is to experience a plunge from the restless hurry of to-day into the restfulness of bygone centuries, when Brighthelmstone was a fishing village unknown beyond its neighbours, and when, the watering-place being as yet undreamt of, there were no highways worthy the name leading toward the coast. In what, for some inscrutable reason, are called the *Statutes at Large* may be seen titles of Acts of Parliament authorising the making of roads in these parts. Among the earliest of them is that of 1770, entitled "An Act for repairing and widening the road leading from Brighthelmstone to the County Oak on Lovell Heath, in the county of Sussex." "Lovell Heath" we recognise in these days as the modern hamlet of Lowfield Heath. The Heath, in a strict sense, is to seek; it has been

improved away utterly and without remorse. The road here, and indeed all that portion lying between Horley and the approach to Crawley, is level and particularly smooth; it is a little paradise for cyclists, who frequent this highway in great numbers on Saturdays and Sundays of the spring and summer months; but, all the same, it is extremely uninteresting.

Turn we then to the remoteness of Charlwood and Ifield.

Few indeed are they who find themselves in these lovely spots. Hundreds, nay, thousands, are continually passing within almost hail of their slumberous sites, and have been passing for hundreds of years, yet they and their inhabitants doze on, and ever and again some cyclist or pedestrian blunders upon them by a fortunate accident; as, one may say, some unconscious Livingstone or Speke discovering an unknown Happy Valley, and disturbing with a little ripple of change their uneventful calm.

We broke in upon their unknown beauties in this wise. We knew well the uninteresting flatness of three miles or so between Povey Cross and Crawley, and proposed to take that bye-road that leads by devious turns along the valley of the Mole, and promises on the map a pleasing journey. And that promise is not, like too many on the sinful Ordnance, unsatisfied; for the way is a way of delightful greenery, and Charlwood, when reached, a revelation.

A happier picture than that of Charlwood Church, seen from the village street through a framing of two severely-cropped elms forming an archway across the road, can rarely be seen in these home counties. The church is an ancient building of the eleventh century, with later insertions of windows when the Norman gloom of its interior assorted less admirably with a more enlightened time. In plan cruciform, with central tower and double nave, it is of an unusual type of village church, and presents many

features of interest to the archaeologist, whose attention will immediately be arrested by the fragments of an immense and hideous fresco seen on the south wall. A late brass, now mural, in the chancel, dated 1553, is for Nicholas Sander and Alys his wife. These Sanders, or, as they spelled their name variously, Saunder, held for many years the manor of Charlwood, and at one time that also of Purley. Sir Thomas Saunder, who was Remembrancer of the Exchequer in Queen Elizabeth's time, bequeathed his estates to his son Edmund, who sold the reversion of Purley in 1580. The church is built of Charlwood stone, a stone quarried from the earliest times in this parish, but now rarely used. It is of two varieties, one of a yellowish-grey colour, the other, fossiliferous in character, of a light bluish

tint, and capable of taking a high polish, like that of Purbeck marble, which it greatly resembles.

One of the loveliest spots in Surrey is the tiny village of Newdigate, on a secluded winding road that leads from here past a picturesque and diminutive inn called the "Surrey Oaks," fronted with aged trees. It is probably the loneliest place of any in the county, and is worth visiting, if only for a peep into the curious timber belfry of its little church, which contains a hoary chest, contrived out of a solid block of oak, and fastened with three ancient padlocks.

But probably very few will go so far abroad: hie we then along the road to Ifield. Tramping along the road here, one presently becomes aware of a row of large flat blocks of stone, continued from the village paving along the grassy margins of the ditches, and forming a kind of primitive pavement in themselves. They were placed here long ago, in the days when the Wealden clay asserted itself much more emphatically than it does now, and were supposed to form a means of pedestrian progression wanting in the miry tracks which then gained for Sussex and Surrey a most unenviable notoriety.

Beside those travellers' tales of miry ways, there is preserved for our information the old county metrical saying—

> "Essex full of good housewyfes,
> Middlesex full of stryves,
> Kentshire hood as fire,
> Sowsecks full of dirt and mire."

And here we came across the border-line into this last county.

Now we came within sight of Ifield Church spire, after passing through the park, in whose woody drives the oak and holly most do grow. It has been remarked of this part of the Weald, that its soil is particularly favourable to the growth of the oak. Cobbett indeed says, "It is a county where, strictly speaking, only three things will grow well—grass, wheat, and oak trees."

It had really long been a belief that Sussex alone could furnish forth sufficient oak to build all the royal navies of Europe, and this, notwithstanding

A Corner in Newtimber Church

the ravages among the forests of forges and furnaces.

In the church at Hield, whose somewhat unprepossessing exterior gives no hint of its inward beauty, is an oaken screen which should prove of great attraction to those who take an interest in old landmarks, for it is made from the wood of an old oak tree cut down in the "forties," which had stood for centuries on the Brighton Road at Lowfield Heath, where the boundary lines of Surrey and Sussex meet. The tree was known far and wide as "County Oak." For the rest, the church is interesting enough by reason of its architecture to warrant some lingering here, but it is, beside this legitimate attraction, also very much of a museum of sepulchral curiosities. A brass for two brothers, with a curious metrical inscription, lurks in the gloom of the south aisle on the wall, and sundry grim and ghastly relics in the shape of engraved coffin-plates, grubbed up by ghoulish antiquarians from the vaults below, form a perpetual *memento mori* from darksome masonry. On either side the nave, by the chancel, beneath the graceful arches of the nave arcade, are the recumbent effigies of Sir John de Ifield and his lady. The knight died in 1317. He is represented as an armed Crusader, cross-legged, a position, to quote "Thomas Ingoldsby," "so prized by Templars in ancient and tailors in modern days." But so dark is the church that details can only with difficulty be examined, and to emerge from the murk of this interior is to blink again in the light of day, however dull that day may be.

From Ifield Church, a long and exceeding straight road leads in one mile to Ifield Hammer Pond. Here is one of the many sources of the little river

Mole, whose trickling tributaries spread over all the neighbouring valley. The old corn-mill standing beside the hatch bears on its brick substructure the date 1683, but the white-painted, boarded mill itself is evidently of much later date. But before a mill

IFIELD MILL POND.

stood here at all this was the site of one of the most important ironworks in Sussex, when Sussex iron paid for the smelting. It will come as a surprise to many who know but little of the county history to learn that this was for a considerable period a veritable Black Country—but so it was.

Ironstone had been known to exist here even in the days of the Roman occupation, when Anderida, as this great district, extending from the sea to London, was called, was one vast forest. Heaps of slag and cinders have been found in which have been discovered Roman coins and implements of contemporary date, proving that iron was smelted here to some extent even then. But it was not until the latter part of the Tudor period that the industry attained its greatest height. Then, according to Camden, "the Weald of Sussex was full of iron-mines, and the beating of hammers upon the iron filled the neighbourhood round about with continual noise." The ironstone was smelted with charcoal made from the forest trees that then covered the land, and it was not until the first year or two of the present century that the industry finally died out. The last remaining ironworks in Sussex were situated at Ashburnham and ceased working about 1820, owing to the inability of ironmasters to compete with the coal-smelted ore of South Wales.

By that time the great forest of Anderida had almost entirely disappeared, which is not at all a wonderful thing to consider when we learn that one ironworks alone consumed 200,000 cords of wood annually. Even in Drayton's time the woods were already very greatly despoiled, and in his "Poly-olbion" he thus bewails their fate in that peculiar convention of Nymphs and Dryads which obtained so greatly in his day, and whose vogue he did so much to work to death :—

> "These forests, as I say, the daughters of the Weald
> (That in their heavy breasts had long their griefs concealed),
> Foreseeing their decay each hour so fast come on,
> Under the axe's stroke, fetched many a grievous groan,
> When as the anvil's weight, and hammer's dreadful sound,
> Even rent the hollow woods and shook the queachy ground;
> So that the trembling Nymphs, oppress'd through ghastly fear,
> Ran madding to the Downs with loose dishevell'd hair.
> The Sylvans that about the neighbouring woods did dwell,
> Both in the turfy frith and in the mossy fell,
> Forsook their gloomy bowers, and wandered far abroad.
> Expelled their quiet seats, and place of their abode,
> When labouring carts they saw to hold their daily trade,
> Where they in summer wont to sport them in the shade.
> Could we, say they, suppose that any would us cherish,
> Which suffer (every day) the holiest things to perish?
> Or to our daily want to minister supply?
> These Iron Times breed none that mind posterity.
> 'Tis but in vain to tell what we before have been,
> Or changes of the world that we in time have seen;
> When, not devising how to spend our wealth with waste,
> We to the savage swine let fall our larding mast,
> But now, alas! ourselves we have not to sustain,
> Nor can our tops suffice to shield our roots from rain:
> Jove's Oak, the warlike Ash, veyned Elm, the softer Beech,
> Short Hazel, Maple plan, light Ash, the bending Wych,
> Tough Holly, and smooth Birch, must altogether burn.
> What should the Builder serve, supplies the forger's turn,
> When under public good, base private gain takes hold,
> And we poor woeful woods to ruin lastly sold."

Fuller, writing in 1662, says that it is to be wished that "a way may be found out to char the sea-coal in such a manner as to render it useful for the making of iron."

Iron smelting and working had been considered the chief industries of the county, and many families became enriched in their pursuit: among them may be mentioned the Burrells of Cuckfield. Relics of these days may be seen even now, scattered over the country-side, in some of the many curious old farm-houses that remain: relics in the shape of cast-iron chimney-back and andirons, many of them very effectively designed. They are now greatly sought after.

The motive power used in the ironworks and at the furnaces was water, the difficulties caused by there being no river of sufficient volume being overcome by the embanking of small streams to form ponds, from which a stream was allowed to escape by hatches over the water-wheels, whose motion gave life to the somewhat primitive machinery of that day.

There are very many of these ponds remaining even now in Sussex and Surrey: they were called Hammer Ponds, and still frequently retain that name in common speech.

Ifield ironworks became extinct at an early date; but from a very arbitrary cause. During the fierce conflicts of the Civil War, the property of Royalists was destroyed by the Puritan soldiery wherever possible; and after the taking of Arundel Castle in 1643, a detachment of troops under Sir William Waller wantonly wrecked the works then situated here, since when they do not appear to have been at any time revived.

It is a pretty spot to-day, and extremely quiet; the

splash, splash of the moss-covered water-wheel slowly revolving, and the flutterings and chirpings of birds alone breaking the silence. The pond itself, rush be-grown, mirrors the tall and close trees, whose reflections are only now and again disturbed by the circling ripples of some leaping fish; and these distractions are all you shall find, saving only the

A QUIET CORNER AT CRAWLEY.

whisperings, like some silken rustle, of the wayward breeze in feathered rushes.

By way of Gossop's Green we reached Crawley, after these pleasant lingerings in unfrequented ways, coming upon the village through a quiet lane, which had the tiled roofs of cottages and the grey tower of Crawley Church, crowned with flaming vane, at its farther end. And here we were, twenty-nine miles only from London, and yet soothed with peaceful rurality.

The somewhat steep ascent by the highway from London to Crawley village, and the extreme length of its long street, together with the quaint cottages and their homely front gardens, give the place so pleasing an air of rusticity, that, inconstant traveller! you vote it the compeer of Merstham in its old world charm. The large and long patches of grass that take up so considerable a selvedge of Crawley Street, seem to speak with eloquence of those dead days of coaching necessity, when even this generous width of roadway cannot have been an inch too wide for the traffic that crowded the village when Crawley was a stage at which every coach stopped, when the air resounded with the guards' winding of their horns, or the playing of the occasional key-bugle to the airs of "Sally in our Alley" or "Love's Young Dream." Then the "George," an inn where cyclists now do mostly congregate, was the scene of a continual bustling, with the shouting of the ostlers, the chink and clashing of harness, and all the tumults of travelling, when travelling was no light affair of an hour and a fraction, railway time.

Now there is little in this place to stir the pulses or make the heart leap. Occasionally there is some great cycle "scorch" in progress, when the whirling enthusiasts speed through the village on winged wheels beneath the sign of the "George," which spans the street, swinging in the breeze; a sign on which the saintly knight wages eternal warfare with a blurred and very invertebrate dragon. Sometimes a driving match brings down sportsmen *and* bookmakers, and every now and again some one has a record to cut, be it in cycling, coaching, walking, or in wheelbarrow trundling; and then the roads are peopled again.

Even so it was when Selby drove his famous drive to Brighton and back, on 13th July 1888, in seven hours and fifty minutes, a drive which awakened the utmost enthusiasm at that time, and which has not been bettered in coaching exploits of our day, nor is ever likely to be, now that the dragsman's pursuit is that of pleasure. During the season of 1888, the time-bill of Selby's coach, the "Old Times," showed a drive of variously five and a half and six hours, good pace for every-day work. The "Comet," too, of the same season, starting from Northumberland Avenue, made a journey of six hours ten minutes, and varied the route in going round by Albourne.

For a description of a drive from Brighton on the "Old Times," I think I cannot do better than give you this account from a sporting paper of 1888. Acknowledgments are due "J. S. P.," whose initials appeared beneath the article :—

"Hand-in-hand with Selby in this enterprise will be found Messrs. Becket, M'Adam, and Walter Dickson, whose names alone will be sufficient to load the old 'shay' with popularity, each one of them having the enviable reputation of being capital fellows and good coachmen. Some difference of opinion naturally exists as to the respective merits of summer and winter coaching. Although personally a chilly mortal, I must confess to a greater degree of partiality to the latter portion of the year. To begin with, the spring is usually so thundering cold, and the March winds so bitterly piercing, that it takes you all your time to keep upsides with them; then later on, you get any quantity of dust, which is not altogether desirable, and, in addition, the fatigue to cattle must be greater in a sweltering sun than when rattling along with the roads hard, and crisp, clear, frosty air to breathe. At any rate, I never enjoyed a drive more than that from Brighton to London recently. The King's Road was alive with carriages, equestrians, and people, who all seemed to be of opinion that it was a big lark to be alive, and the crowds which congregated at the 'Old Ship' as the hour of departure drew near plainly indicated the pleasurable interest taken in the 'Old Times' and its supporters. On pulling up at the door, the first to welcome me was the genial Mr. Beckett, who I was delighted to find ready and willing to take charge of my precious carcass on this particular day, and as on more than one occasion during the years I have known him I have had cause to congratulate myself on the ready resource, strong arm, and excellent judgment of this gentleman-whip under somewhat trying

circumstances, I considered myself particularly fortunate in this instance.

"Punctually to the tick of the clock we are off with a spanking team of skewbalds and chestnuts, driven chess-board fashion, which, for the benefit of the uninitiated, I may explain is composed of a skewbald and a chestnut as near and off wheelers, and a chestnut and a skewbald near and off leaders. As they jump into their collars and settle down to work with the merry notes rattling out of one of Boosey's horns, admirably played by Walter Godden, who, take him all round, is as good a guard as ever tackled a yard of tin, I felt an exhilaration to which I had been a stranger some time, and wondered that ever a day passed without this coach being besieged by passengers. On this particular morning we had a capital load, and as we shake down into our places, and get on terms with each other, the same conclusion is arrived at by the rest of the passengers, if their faces are any index to their feelings.

"Through pretty Preston and Patcham village we rattle at a good eleven miles an hour on to 'Friar's Oak,' where our first change is waiting. This team is composed of two browns, a bay, and a grey. Mr. Beckett again mounts the box, and it is pretty evident that both horses and man understand this job as well as the manner in which it should be done. Now it isn't every one that *can* drive a galloping stage, but the way in which this one is accomplished is a rare treat. As we dash along through St. John's Common, up and down the sharp hills between there and Ansty, and so on past Major Sergison's picturesque seat (which, by the way, is presumed to be the scene of Ainsworth's 'Rookwood,' to the old 'Talbot' at Cuckfield, the conclusion one naturally comes to is that we have a nailing good coachman and a first-class coach, for although the six miles and a half is done in a trifle under twenty-five minutes, there is not the slightest 'wobbling' to be detected. Our next team consists of three blacks and a bay, all strong useful sorts, and they need be, for it is a stiffish stage from Cuckfield to Pease Pottage, although a sweetly pretty and thickly wooded country, the autumn tints lending an additional charm to the beautiful scenery. At Pease Pottage we have a sharp team in, to run us over some of the best trotting ground in England, and the way they do it is a credit to them. Nearing Crawley, a wag inquires whether we are aware that this is the longest village in the world, and on admitting our ignorance of this geographical fact, he points out the 'Sun' at one end and the 'Moon' at the other. Soon the 'Chequers' at Horley looms in sight, and it is with no small amount of satisfaction that we bustle up the few steps into the luncheon-room and find an excellent spread provided by jolly host Brown, who I firmly believe would rather provide for the passengers gratuitously than not have the coach at his place. The crisp autumn morning has put us all on good terms with the provender, and the 'tooth powder,' as Jim facetiously calls it, completely puts a stopper on conversation for the time. The thirty minutes' grace for this all-important operation being up, Godden reminds us, with a very pretty call I heard years ago from Blackburn, who at that time was with Captain Blythe, that our seats must be taken, and with a spanking team of sporting greys, we trot along at a merry pace past Earlswood Asylum, and on through Redhill to Merstham. Formerly this stage was extended to Smitham Bottom, a distance of eleven miles (like the Irishman's, too long and narrow), but the present proprietors have very wisely cut this into two, making the second stage from Merstham to Purley Bottom. From Merstham we have a mixed team, but all good ones, and they must be good on this road, for the fifty-two miles and a half from the 'Cellars' to the 'Old Ship' is covered in six hours, including half an hour for lunch and seven changes. Arrived at Purley Bottom, we have a clever team, composed of a roan near wheel, grey off wheel, and a couple of chestnut leaders, quick as light and clever as cats. In Mr. Beckett's hands the way they rattle through Croydon, with its beastly tram-rails, narrow streets, and crowded traffic is a caution, and so on to Streatham, where our last change is effected.

"The shades of night are now falling fast, and the five powerful lamps which this coach carries gives it a very imposing appearance, and serves to show us the pick of the basket in the London team.

This is made up of three browns and a bay, all very fast, with ripping action and in the pink of condition. We hop on quickly with these past Clapham Common, over Chelsea Bridge, and, all too soon, Grosvenor Place and Piccadilly are reached, the whole journey having been completed in masterly style, and the advertised time to half a minute. Better coach, better cattle, better waggoners, and better road cannot be found, and if the winter season of the 'Old Times' in 1887-88 is not a success, it ought to be. If my good wishes will keep these plucky and high-spirited sportsmen in their venture, they are heartily welcome to them, and as one of my fellow-passengers hit it off poetically in the form of a toast :—

Here's the 'Old Times,' it's one of the best,
Which no coaching man will deny,
Fifty miles down the road with a jolly good load,
Between London and Brighton each day.
Beckett, M'Adam, and Dickey, the driver, are there,
Of old Jim's presence every one is aware,
They are all nailing good sorts,
And go in for all sports,
So we'll all go a coaching to-day."

Of very great interest, also, is this table of time occupied in the "Record drive," with remarks. The times were taken throughout by chronograph, and may be relied upon as thoroughly accurate :—

COACHING FEAT—LONDON TO BRIGHTON AND BACK, 14th July 1888.

Place.	Time of Arrival.	Time of Departure.	Remarks.
London . . .	...	10.0	
Streatham .	10.28	10.29	Changed in 47 secs., Mr. Blyth, Mr. M'Adam, and Mr. Beckett personally assisting.
Croydon .			Passed through; passed West Croydon Church at 10.45.
Purley Bottom	10.57	10.58¾	Changed in 1 min. 5 secs.
Merstham .	11.27	11.29	Plate greased; relay; accomplished in 2 mins.
Horley . . .	11.51½	11.52½	Changed horses in 55 secs.; 28 miles accomplished in 1 hour 51½ mins.; lunch.
Crawley. . .	12.11		Ran through; short stoppage, as the level-crossing railway gates were closed.
Pease Pottage .	12.23¾	12.25	Changed in 1 min. 2 secs.; passed Tom Sayers' late residence; thirty-third milestone passed 12.31¼.
Hand Cross .	12.33½		Ran through.
Cuckfield .	12.53½	12.54¾	Changed in 1 min. 8 secs.
Friar's Oak. .	1.17		Changed in 1 min.
Patcham . .	1.40	1.41	Changed in 47 secs.
Ship Inn, Brighton. . . .	1.56		Turned round: Mr. Blyth ran in for wires; telegram from Duke of Beaufort; work.

Place.	Time of Arrival.	Time of Departure.	Remarks.
The Kennels .	2.17½	2.20	Company got down for first time.
Friar's Oak . .	2.35	2.36	Changed horses; greased plate.
Cuckfield . .	2.54	2.55	
Hand Cross	3.21½		Passed M'Calmont's coach 3.27½.
Pease Pottage .	3.29	3.30	Changed in about 1 min.
Crawley . .			Passed through; out of Sussex into Surrey at 3.34; dust.
Horley .	3.57½	3.58½	56 secs. in changing.
Redhill .	4.12		Turned Corner galloping.
Merstham .	4.24	4.25	Greased plate again: Godden presented with a bouquet.
Purley Bottom	4.51	4.52	Change, 50 secs.
Croydon			Right through; carts made way; Mr. Blyth thanked local police:—"Thank you very much, officer."
Streatham . .	5.20	5.21	Change, 55 secs.; company joyful; remarks—"50 to 1 on us:" 'busmen, "Bravo, you'll do it."
Piccadilly .	5.50		Cheers.

The *Times* report of the record drive is as follows:—"The 'Old Times' coach was driven from the 'White Horse Cellars' to Brighton and back for a wager of £1000 to £500, that the matter could not be accomplished in eight hours. The proprietors of the coach accepted the bet, in the interests of Mr. James Selby, at the recent meeting at Ascot, with the resolve that, if they won, the £1000 should be presented to that well-known driver. The proprietors of the coach accompanied the team, with only a few friends. Mr. James Selby, the whip, has driven the 'Old Times' for many years, and is well known on the Brighton Road; for the past twenty years having taught more men to drive in England than any man in the kingdom. Mr. Percy Edwards, watchmaker, of Piccadilly, started the team, and the times were taken throughout by Benson's chronograph. The start was effected from Hatchett's Hotel punctually at 10 A.M. The police did all they could to keep the road clear; and, soon after the start, twelve miles an hour was kept up. Streatham ('Horse and Groom') was reached at 10.28, and the horses changed in forty-seven seconds, some of the gentlemen getting off and assisting in performing the feat. A bicycle rider named O'Neill joined the coach hereabouts, and followed it as far as Merstham. Everywhere the coach was enthusiastically received and cheered. West Croydon was passed at 10.45. In passing Croydon a uniform pace of thirteen miles an hour was maintained. At the 'Windsor Castle,' at Purley Bottom, another change of teams took place, which occupied one minute five seconds. The roads after leaving Redhill at times became heavy; but nevertheless a good pace was maintained throughout, increased at times, between Earlswood and Horley, to twenty miles an hour.

"Horley was reached at 11.51½, and Crawley at 12.11. Here the only hitch took place, through the level-crossing gates being closed; but the coach was allowed to go on after a delay of only about two minutes. The coach arrived at the 'Old Ship' at 1 hour, 56 minutes, 10 seconds, having accomplished the journey just under four hours. The stay at Brighton was only momentary; the halt at the 'Old Ship' was only long enough to satisfy the party that it was still there. The horses were merely turned round and a few telegrams handed up. One to Captain Blyth from the Duke of Beaufort read:—'Thank you much; sorry could not go; fine fresh day. Hope six o'clock will find you at the Cellars. Sharp work.—BEAUFORT.'

"The whip proceeded to work, and drove off amid the cheers of a large crowd at Brighton. The party came back by the same route. Every one made way, and at numerous places *en route* bouquets were thrown on the coach. Stoppages were made at the Kennels, Friar's Oak, Cuckfield, Pease Pottage, Horley, Merstham, Purley Bottom, and Streatham, to change teams, and ultimately Selby brought his party safe to town in splendid style, arriving at Piccadilly at 5.50, or ten minutes under the stipulated time to win the bet. Many members of the Coaching Club and naval and military officers were present, and greatly cheered Selby on his success."

A great drive this, and a great driver; one who worthily resuscitated the good old traditions of the road. One who has had the good fortune to go down to Brighton on the "Old Times" coach, with Selby on the box and Godden as guard, will not readily forget so enjoyable a drive, for good stories and good company were assured.

But Selby did not live long to enjoy the world-wide repute his great performance gained him. He died when only forty-four years of age, at the end of the same year that saw this splendid feat of the accomplished dragsman. This sympathetic notice, written at the time by one who knew him well, I take from the *Sporting Life* of Monday, December 17, 1888:—

"THE LATE MR. JAMES SELBY.

'His form was of the manliest beauty,'
'His virtues were so rare.'

"Coaching men of every degree will hardly realise the sad fact that Jim, 'Dear Old Jim,' has departed from our midst, never more to hear the cheery note of the horn, the musical rattle of the bars he loved so well, or to unfurl that double thong which in his hands was used with such unerring judgment and discrimination. Never more for us to see that square-built manly form and sunny face; sure index of the true warm heart that was always open to the sorrows of others. Ah me! that such a man has departed at the comparatively early age of forty-four will be regretted alike by peer and peasant. Articled as a youth to an auctioneer, he soon grew tired of the monotony of the desk, and when asked his reason for throwing up the appointment, replied that it was all very well as far as it went, but they hadn't any horses in the business. He remained with his father, who then kept the 'Railway Hotel' at Colney Hatch, together with a considerable livery stable business, afterwards removing to a similar business at Potter's Bar, where he confined his attention to perfecting by practice those matchless hands which have subdued some of the hottest equine tempers that have ever carried leather. He had a peculiar mastery over horses, achieved by an iron nerve and complete command of his own temper. I have seldom in the course of a long number of years seen him really angry with or punish them. A whisper—as he quaintly termed it—was sufficient, but if the necessity did arise for a salutary lesson, it was administered "hot with." His first appearance as a professional whip was on the Tunbridge Wells road, in 1870, with the Earl of Bective and Colonel Clitherow as proprietors, and afterwards on the same road with Colonel Hawthorn, who, he used to say, had the best cattle that ever drew a road coach. When this ceased running, he accepted an engagement with Mr. Charles Hoare and Lord Arthur Somerset, the joint proprietors of the 'Rapid' West Wickham and London coach. Many a happy

JAMES SELBY.

(From a Photo by Mr. H. W. Macdonald, Eton.)

afternoon and evening did the writer spend with him in those days, driving to West Wickham with the coach and back to Mr. Charles Hoare's mansion at Beckenham, where the old buggy was waiting to bring us back to town, drawn by a roan mare that no one could do with but Jim. On November 4, 1879, he made his first journey as proprietor of the 'Old Times' to St. Alban's, with the late Major Harry Dixon and a few other friends as subscribers. In 1881 saw a fresh departure, Virginia Water being the destination in summer and Windsor the winter route. It was their proud boast that the coach had never been off the road a single day (Sundays excepted), and as an instance of his dogged determination that it should run as advertised, it may be mentioned that the terrible snowstorm of January 18, 1881, did not prevent him from doing the journey, accompanied only by the Major. The exposure of that fearful day, however, told its tale. Poor Harry Dixon was never quite the same man afterwards, and I fear that in Jim's case the seeds were sown which eventually undermined his iron constitution.

"For a little over a year now the 'Old Times' has been running to Brighton, and it was in this connection that his sensational performance on the 13th of July last of driving the whole distance from London to Brighton and back (108 miles) in the unprecedented time of seven hours fifty minutes came about.

"To many this may not appear such a gigantic undertaking as it really is, but to experienced coaching men the performance of the task, and the qualities of strength and endurance necessary to bring it to a successful issue, were appreciated at their true value.

"He was indeed a man whose like we do not often see. Loved and respected by high and low, rich and poor, for his honest, sunny nature, his loss will be felt by all. To the writer personally he was a warm-hearted friend for many years—in fair weather or foul, ever the same kindly welcome, the same cheery smile and shake of the hand, now, alas! cold in death. May his memory be kept green in the hearts of those who knew him intimately!"

Coaching and coachmen have always inspired the poetic Muse equally with hunting and other manly sports; so I need make no apology for inserting this metrical lament for his colleague by the "Old Times" guard:—

In Memoriam

OF

THE LATE JAMES SELBY,

BY HIS GUARD.

Air—"Good Old Jeff."

"They say it's just ten years ago since Selby's coach first ran,
With good old Major Dixon on, a thorough coaching man,
The coach has never missed a day, no matter hail or snow,
Jim Selby's motto always was, 'The "Old Times" still must go.'

CHORUS.

"We'll ne'er see more that dear old face, those eyes in death are dim;
He's done his stage, and done it well, our friend and favourite, Jim.

"In January eighty-one the snow lay far and wide,
Still Selby struggled bravely on, the Major by his side;
The best of friends they were in life, now both are gone to rest;
It seems that those who leave us now are those we love the best.

"The last ride that our old friend had was on the Brighton Road,
Whilst he with favourite anecdote amused his sporting load;
But now he's left us all to mourn for him, so kind and true,
Respected both by rich and poor, in fact, by all he knew.

"Ne'er shall I ride another stage with him I loved so well,
Or tootle on his favourite horn the tunes to me he'd tell;
For now he's gone to realms above, all pleasure here is marred:
A good old master and a friend was he to me, his Guard."

WALTER GODDEN.

It was not to be supposed that the ubiquitous and emulative cyclist would be content to leave the coaching record alone. Cycling has indeed ever been industriously pursued on this road; for it was in ancient days (in cycling chronology), before cycles had earned their present name, and when they were known as velocipedes—in 1869, in fact—that the first cyclist, or, as he then was termed, velocipedist, essayed to ride from London to Brighton. That he accomplished his task reflects credit upon his name and powers of endurance; for all who have experimentally ridden the "boneshaker" of that time know that the physical qualities required for such a feat on such a machine are of no mean order. The pioneer's credit (on the Brighton Road) belongs to the late Mr. John Mayall, junior, who died during the summer of 1891. He started with two companions from Trafalgar Square on Wednesday, 17th February 1869. The party of three kept together until Redhill was reached, when Mayall took the lead, and eventually reached Brighton alone. The time occupied was about twelve hours.

THE LATE JOHN MAYALL, JUN.

(From photo taken in 1886, lent by Mrs. Mayall.)

As cycling became more popular, and as cycles progressed in speed and lightness, rides to Brighton became more and more frequent. Such, and even very much longer journeys, in one day were soon so common as to be accounted of no importance whatever. Then came the era of records, which is still with us. Early record rides on this road are of little account, both by reason of bad timing and of the different starting-places chosen. But after Selby's coach drive records became many and scientific, the recognised points being Hatchett's Hotel (old White Horse Cellars) and the "Old Ship," Brighton.

Many unsuccessful attempts were made to break the coach record. The first successful attempt was that of 10th August 1889, when four cyclists—E. J. Willis, G. L. Morris, C. W. Schafer, and S. Walker—did the 108 miles out and home in 7 hours 36 minutes and $19\frac{2}{5}$ seconds, dividing the journey between them, and using the same machine. M. A. Holbein and P. C. Wilson made (singly) unsuccessful attempts somewhat later. The next team of four—J. F. Shute, T. W. Girling, R. Wilson, and A. E. Griffin—on 30th March 1890, reduced the previous team's record by 4 minutes $19\frac{2}{5}$ seconds, and their time was beaten on the 13th April by E. and W. Scantlebury, W. W. Arnott, and J. Blair, who left the record at 7 hours 25 minutes 15 seconds. Then Wilson tried again single-handed, without success. It was left to F. W. Shorland, a very young rider, to be the first of a series of single-handed breakers of the coaching time. He accomplished the feat in June 1890 upon a pneumatic-tyred "Facile" safety, and reduced the time to 7 hours 19 minutes, being himself beaten on July 23rd by S. F. Edge, riding a cushion-tyred safety. Edge put the time at 7 hours 2 minutes 50 seconds, and, in addition, first beat Selby's outward journey, the times being—coach, 3 hours 36 minutes; cycle, 3 hours 18 minutes 25 seconds. Then came yet another stalwart, C. A. Smith, who, on September 3rd of the same year, beat Edge by 10 minutes 40 seconds. Even a tricyclist—E. P. Moorhouse—essayed the feat on the 30th September, but failed, his time being 8 hours 9 minutes 24 seconds.

On June 1 of this present year S. F. Edge again held the record, beating Smith's time by 63 seconds.

THIRD DAY.

THE morning was not of the most promising description, saving only in the promises of evil weather that met our glances at an early hour; but the spring showers that fell so briskly during breakfast-time fell at last through a glorious burst of sunshine that seemed to dry up the weeping heavens as by magic power.

Down the street the air was full of the scent of those old-fashioned flowers that gladden the heart by their artless beauty, their rich odours, and their gladsome profusion at the year's awakening. If Patrick Hannay, that sweet seventeenth-century singer, melodious but little known, had writ these lines *à propos* of Crawley on such an occasion as this, he could hardly have better fitted the time and scene to his tuneful rhyme :—

> "The blooming borders fresh and faire,
> Were clad with cloathes of colours rare,
> Which fairest *Flora* fram'd :
> The Hyacinth, the selfe-lov'd lad,
> *Adonis*, *Amaranthus* sad,
> Their pleasing places claim'd.
> The Primrose pride of pleasing Prime,
> With roses of each hew :
> The Cowslip, Pinke, and Savory Thyme,
> And Gilly-flower there grew.
>
> The Marygold
> Which to behold
> Her lover loaths the night,
> Locking her leaves
> She inward grieves,
> When Sol is out of sight."

And

> "Upon the boughs and tops of trees,
> Blythe birds did sit as thicke as Bees
> On blooming Beanes doe bait :
> And every Bird some loving note
> Did warble thorow the swelling throat
> To wooe the wanton mate.
> There might be heard the throbbing Thrush,
> The Bull-finch blyth her by ;
> The Blacke-bird in another bush,
> With thousands more her nie.
>
> The ditties all,
> To great and small,
> Sweet *Philomel* did set,
> In all the grounds
> Of Musicke sounds,
> Those darlings did direct."

We have it on the authority of writers who fared this way in early coaching days that Crawley was a "poor place."

As many of the houses now standing in the village are of Georgian times, and are, some of them, not inconsiderable buildings, we may assume that the village owed much to its receipt of highway custom. There are yet remaining a few cottages of ancient build in its one long street, and its grey, embattled church-tower lends an assured

OLD COTTAGE, CRAWLEY.

antiquity to the view; but there is, in especial, one picturesque cottage of sixteenth-century date that is worthy notice. Its timbered frame stands as securely, though not so erect, as ever, and is eloquent of that spacious age when the Virgin Queen ruled the land. Here, indeed, Victoria and Elizabeth foregather, for against that sunny wall the postal authorities have placed a flaming letter-box, whose cypher of V.R. gives in this conjunction an ample field for reflection in the philosophical mind. They are, too, conservative folks at Crawley. When that ancient elm of theirs that stands directly below this old cottage had become decayed with lapse of years and failure of sap, they did not, even though its vast trunk obtrudes upon the roadway, cut it down and scatter its remains abroad. Instead, they fenced it around with as decorative a rustic railing as might well be contrived out of cut boughs, all innocent of the carpenter, and still retaining their bark, and they planted the enclosure with flowers and tender saplings, so that this venerable ruin is become a very attractive ruin indeed.

REGENCY BUCKS.

There is but one literary celebrity whose name goes down to posterity associated with this village. At Vine Cottage, near the railway station, resided Mark Lemon, editor of *Punch*, who died on the 20th May 1870. The only other inhabitant of Crawley whose deeds informed the world at large of his name and existence was a character very much more in harmony with the traditions of this classic road, this Appian Way of Corinthianism. I name Tom Cribb. But though I lighted upon the statement of his residence here at one time, yet, after hunting up details of his life and the battles he fought, after pursuing him through the classic pages of "Boxiana" and the voluminous records of "Pugilistica," after consulting, too, that sprightly work "The Fancy," after all this I find no further mention of the fact. It was fitting, though, that the pugilist should have his home so near Crawley Downs, the scene of so many of the Homeric combats witnessed by thousands upon thousands of excited spectators, from the Czar of Russia and the great Prince Regent downwards to the lowest blackguards of the metropolis. An inspiring sight those Downs must have presented from time to time, when great multitudes, princes, patricians, pimps, and plebeians of every description hung with beating hearts and bated breath upon the performances of two men in a roped enclosure battering one another for so much a side. But, at any rate, the spectators generally saw what they went to see; the combatants earned their pay, and those who paid the piper were not baulked of the tune. Now-a-days the pugilist does most of his fighting in the papers; the pen is mightier than the fist.

These things considered, it cannot be matter for surprise that the Brighton Road, on its several routes, witnessed brilliant and dashing turn-outs, both in public coaches and private equipages, during that time when the last of the Georges flourished so flamboyantly as Prince, Prince Regent, and King. How other could it have been with the Court at one end of it and the metropolis at the other, and between both the rendezvous of all such as delighted in the "noble art"?

Many were the merry "mills" which "came off" at Crawley Downs, Copthorne Common, Blindley Heath, and other parts of these two counties, frequently attended by the Prince and his merry men, conspicuous among whom at different times were Fox, Lord Barrymore, Lord Yarmouth ("Red Herrings"), and Major George Hanger. As for the tappings of claret, the punchings of conks and bread-baskets, and the tremendous sloggings that went on in this neighbourhood in those virile times, are they not set forth with much circumstantial detail in the pages of "Fistiana" and "Boxiana"? There shall you read how the Prince Regent, together with an immense concourse of Bucks, witnessed with enthusiasm such merry sets-to as this between Randall and Martin on Crawley Downs. "Boxiana" gives a full account of it, and is even moved to verse, in this wise, with great display of title:—

THE FIGHT AT CRAWLEY

BETWEEN

THE NONPAREIL

AND

THE OUT-AND-OUTER.

"Come, won't you list unto my lay
About the fight at Crawley, O!" . .

with the refrain—

"With his tilaloo trillaloo,
Whack, fal lal de dal di de do!"

For the number of rounds and such-like technical details I refer the curious to the classic pages of

CRAWLEY, LOOKING NORTH.

"Boxiana" itself; but this description, curiously italicised, of the crowd that went to see is worthy the extensive quotation I append:—

"GRAND PUGILISTIC COMBAT,

Between Randall and Martin, at Crawley Down, thirty miles from London, on Tuesday, May 4, 1819.

"The *Fancy* were all upon the alert soon after breakfast-time, on the Monday, to ascertain the seat of action, and as soon as the important *whisper* had gone forth, that Crawley Down was likely to be the place, the *toddlers* were off in a *twinkling*. The gigs were soon brushed up, the *prads* harnessed, and the 'boys' who intended to enjoy themselves on the road were in motion. Heavy *drags* and waggons were also to be witnessed *creeping* along full of people and plenty of *grub*. Between the hours of two and three o'clock in the afternoon upwards of one hundred gigs were counted passing through Croydon. The Bonifaces *chuckled* again with delight, and *screwing* was the order of the day. Long before eight o'clock in the evening every bed belonging to the inns and public-houses in Godstone, East Grinstead, Reigate, Bletchingley, &c., &c., were *doubly* and some *trebly* occupied. The country folks also came in for a *snack* of the thing, and the *simple* JOHNNY RAWS, who felt no hesitation in *sitting up all night*, if they could turn their beds to account, with much *modesty* only asked one pound and fifteen shillings each for an hour or two's sleep. The private houses were thus filled. Five and seven shillings were also charged for the stand of a horse in any wretched hut. But those *customers* who were *fly* to all the tricks and fancies of life, and who would not be *nailed* at any price, preferred going to *roost* in a barn; while others, possessing rather more *gaiety*, and who set sleep at defiance, blowed *a cloud* over some *heavy wet*, devouring the *rich* points of a *flash chaunt*, and thought no more of *time* hanging heavily than they did of the *Classics*, *chaunting*, and *swiping* till many of the young *sprigs* dropped off their *perches;* while the *Ould Ones* felt the influence of the *Dustman*, and were glad to *drop* their *nobs* to obtain *forty winks*. Those persons whose *blunt* enabled them to procure beds could not obtain any sleep, for carriages of every description were passing through the above towns all night. Things passed on in this manner till daylight began to *peep*. Then the *swells* in their barouches and four; and the swift-trotting fanciers, all hurried from the Metropolis; and the road exhibited the bustle of the *primest* day of Epsom Races. The *Brilliants* also left Brighton, Worthing, &c., about the same period, and thus were the roads thronged in every direction. 'The pitiless pelting shower' commenced furiously at six o'clock on the Tuesday morning, but it *damped* nothing but the *dust*. The *Fancy* are too *game* to prevent anything like weather interrupting their sports. The *ogles* of the turnpike men let not half a *chance* slip through their fingers, and those persons, either from carelessness or accident, who had not preserved their tickets, were *physicked* by paying twice at the same gate. The weather at length cleared up, and by twelve o'clock the amphitheatre on Crawley Down had a noble effect, and thousands of persons were assembled at the above spot. It is supposed, if the carriages had all been placed in one line, they would have reached from London to Crawley. The amateurs were of the highest distinction, and several noblemen and foreigners of rank were upon the ground."

Martin, familiarly known as the "Master of the Rolls," one of the heroes whom all these sporting blades went out to see contend for victory in the ring, died so recently as 1871. He had long retired from the P.R., and had, upon quitting it, followed the usual practice of retired pugilists, that is to say, he became a publican. He was landlord successively of the "Crown" at Croydon, and the "Horns" tavern, Kennington.

As for details of this fight or that upon the same spot, from which Hickman "The Gas-Light Man," came off victor, I am not going to set them forth in these pages. How the combatants "fibbed" and "countered," and did other things whose nomenclature is equally abstruse to the average reader, you may, who care to, read in the pages of the enthusiastic authorities upon the subject, who spare you nothing of all the blows given and received.

But while on the subject of pugilism, it remains to remark upon the connection of it and its exponents with Brighton and the Brighton Road. That Bayard of the Noble Art, the "Commander-in-Chief" of the prize-ring, Gentleman Jackson, commenced his fistic career upon it in 1788, when on June 9 he beat Fewterel at Smitham Bottom. Major Hanger rewarded the victor with a bank-note from the enthusiastic Prince of Wales.

Tom Sayers, with whom died the reputation of prize-fighting, was born at Brighton, the son of a

PAST AND PRESENT—TWO GENERATIONS OF ENGLISHMEN.

man descended from a thoroughly Sussexian stock. He was not, as so often erroneously stated, an Irishman. Indeed, the name of Sayers is one well known throughout Sussex, and is particularly frequent at Hurstpierpoint, Hand Cross, and Burgess Hill. Sayers Common, indeed, is the name of a hamlet in the parish of Hurstpierpoint, situated on the road to Brighton by way of Albourne and Hickstead.

The future champion of England was born at Brighton in 1828, and worked as a bricklayer on the Preston viaduct of the Brighton and Lewes Railway at its building. His first encounter was near Patcham, at Dale Vale. He died in 1865.

This was fine company, you will say, for the Heir-Apparent to keep here at Crawley Downs; but see how picturesque the Regent rendered these "times," he and the crowds that followed in his wake. What diversions went forward on the roads, such roads as they were! One chronicler of a fight here says, in all good faith, that on the morning following the battle, the remains of several carriages, phaetons, and other vehicles were found bestrewing the narrow ways in which they had collided in the darkness.

The House of Hanover has not been at any time largely endowed with picturesqueness, saving only the gruesome picture afforded by that horrid legend which accounts for its name of Guelph; but the Regent had as much of that quality, and more, than almost any other of his family: more, certainly, than any member of it that ever reigned in this land. The reign of George III. was the culmination of dulness and *bourgeois* respectability at Court, from whose weary routine the Prince's surroundings were entirely different. Himself and his *entourage* were dissolute indeed, roystering in lawlesswise, drinking, cursing, dicing in excess, visiting prize-fights on these Downs of Crawley, and hail fellow, well met, with the blackguards there gathered together. But whatever his surroundings, they were never dull, for which saving grace much may be excused the memory of this peculiar Prince.

Thackeray, in his "Four Georges," has little that is pleasant to say of any one of them; but he is astonishingly severe upon this last, both as Prince and King. For a thorough-going condemnation, commend me to that book. To the faults of George IV. the author is very wide-awake, nor will he allow him any virtues whatsoever. So bitter is he, he will not even allow him to be a man, as witness this passage:—"To make a portrait of him at first sight seemed a matter of small difficulty. There is his coat, his star, his wig, his countenance simpering under it: with a slate and a piece of chalk, I could at this very desk perform a recognisable likeness of him. And yet, after reading of him in scores of volumes, hunting him through old magazines and newspapers, having him here at a ball, there at a public dinner, there at races, and so forth, you find you have nothing, nothing but a coat and a wig, and a mask smiling below it; nothing but a great simulacrum."

Poor fat Adonis!

And yet Thackeray is obliged reluctantly to acknowledge the grace and charm of the detracted George and some of the kind acts he performed, although at these last he sneers consumedly, because, forsooth, those thus benefited were quite humble persons. It was not without reason that Thackeray wrote so much concerning snobs: in those unworthy sneers speaks one of that race.

Here is a curious little item of praise which the author of the "Four Georges" is constrained to allow the Regent:—"Where my Prince did actually distinguish himself was in driving. He drove once in four hours and a half from Brighton to Carlton House—fifty-six miles."[1]

So the altogether British love of sport compelled even Thackeray, who set out upon his "Four Georges" with (so to speak) a mouth filled with all manner of cursings and revilings, to concede a point in favour of this "simulacrum."

Unhappy shade of him that wore the crown! I trust (if this-worldly matters come within the ken of the other world), you have had no opportunities of foregathering with your scurril essayist. I think it unlikely, though, that your circles *la bas* are very similar.

But Thackeray to the contrary notwithstanding, I admire, in some sort, a man who goes whole-souled to the devil, as we are told went George IV.,[2] not, let me hasten to say, by reason of his choice of destination, but in a frank appreciation of a remark-

[1] A slight error on the part of Thackeray. The Prince did the journey twice, in the same space of time. He *rode* on the one occasion to Carlton House, and *drove* on the other to the Pavilion.

[2] "George the First was reckoned vile:
Viler George the Second:
Has any mortal ever heard
Any good of George the Third:
And when from earth the Fourth descended,
Heavens be praised! the Georges ended!"
—*Leigh Hunt.*

able single-heartedness of purpose. Such courses are evil—granted; but they are eminently picturesque.

This being thus, the creator of "Becky Sharp" should have gratefully recognised a character ready to the novelist's hand, and should have adapted this lurid career to the purposes of his art.

But then Thackeray was ever oppressively moral. His preachments, even in "Vanity Fair," are the inevitable spots on the sun of his genius.

Crawley Down is in these days a quiet hamlet, entirely dissociated from pugilism. It lies some miles to the east of the village whose name it bears, in the direction of Worth.

But Crawley itself was recently the scene of a sporting event that occasioned a very great deal of interest. The Shrewsbury-Lonsdale driving match, driven on that exceedingly flat stretch of road between Reigate and Crawley on 11th March 1891, was one of the most important matches of late years. It was a match agreed upon between the Earl of Lonsdale and the Earl of Shrewsbury and Talbot, with the object of settling the respective merits of trotting and galloping, and it arose out of a discussion amongst a shooting party assembled at Ingestre in the previous autumn. A wager of the nominal value of £100 was laid between the two competitors about the covering of the course in one hour, and each one was to drive his own team. The course was fixed at twenty miles, divided equally between the four recognised methods of driving—four-in-hand, pair, single, and postillion—and, after many different roads had been under discussion, the referee.

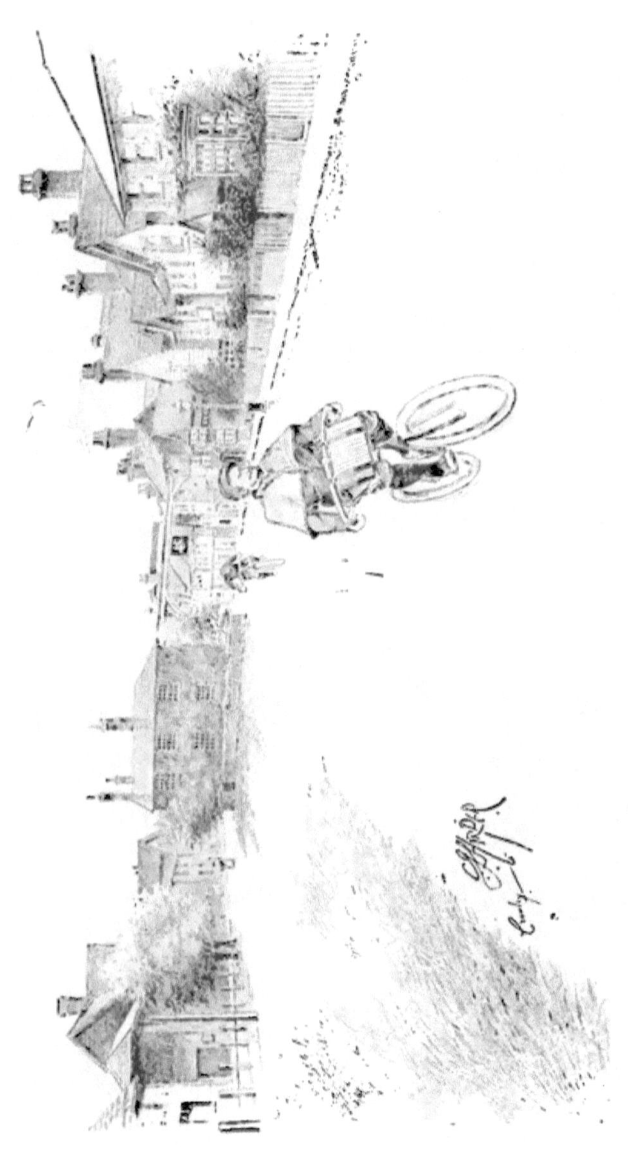

Mr. Arthur Coventry, decided for this, than which, probably, no better course could have been selected. The weather, which had suddenly become very wintry, greatly interfered with arrangements for the match, and a lengthy despatch of verbal messages, telegrams, and letters, duly published in sporting and other papers, caused misunderstanding and some recrimination between the two competitors, until the Earl of Shrewsbury declared off the match and paid his £100 forfeit. Lord Lonsdale, in the interests of sport, and in order to satisfy the public, who had taken a very lively interest in the match, about which a very large amount of money had been wagered, decided to drive over the course alone, and justified his belief in trotting by the results achieved.

The following account of the drive is taken from the *Sportsman*:—

"The Earl of Lonsdale was a disappointed man when he learned that the Earl of Shrewsbury and Talbot had paid forfeit. For fully eight weeks the head of the House of Lowther had been making extraordinary preparations for the driving match between himself and the chairman of the S. and T. Cab Company. His experience in matters pugilistic led him to go into regular training, and out at five o'clock was his chief order of the day for some time. Lord Lonsdale 'trained,' if the word may be permitted, at Barley Thorpe, his place in Rutlandshire, near Oakham, and in reply to the inquiry of an ardent supporter, expressed himself 'as fit as a buck rat.' Certainly he looked in excellent trim when at an early hour he made his appearance at breakfast at the 'White Hart' at Reigate. It was expected, when the Newmarket Heath officials refused permission for the race to be decided on their grounds, that a road in Leicestershire would have been selected. Lord Lonsdale had two in his mind, but on Mr. Arthur Coventry, the referee, fixing on the Reigate road, it became necessary for the owner of Barley Thorpe to at once move his horses and carriages to the scene of action. This he did by means of a special train. Altogether fifteen horses, as many men, and thirteen carriages were transported to Reigate at enormous expense, the cost of maintaining them whilst there being at least £150 a day. Lord Shrewsbury's stud was located at Caterham close by, at Mr. Woodland's place, and he did not need any special trains.

"Such was the state of affairs on the Monday morning on which the match was fixed to take place. The Earl of Lonsdale thought his horses should have time to settle themselves after their special train experiences, and obtained a postponement until the Tuesday. When that morning arrived, Lord Shrewsbury's cattle were snowed up in their boxes, and everything looked against the proposed contest. In the meantime the most elaborate preparations had been made. Special newspaper correspondents journeyed down on Sunday night to Reigate, within three miles of where the race was to take place, and a number of members of the Pelican Club also took up their temporary abode in the little Surrey town, prominent among them being Mr. Arthur E. Wells, Captain H. L. Beckett, Captain Broadwood, Major Candy (father of the Duchess of Newcastle), and many others. Flags manufactured of Lord Lonsdale's colours, yellow and blue, had been prepared, and men were sent to the front to fix them up in their allotted places. Mr. Arthur Coventry could not have selected a better road than the one ultimately settled upon. A five-miles stretch was agreed to, this being on the Reigate road, from Kennersley Manor, Mr. Brocklehurst's place, three miles from the White Hart, to within a furlong of the Sun Inn at Crawley, and about half a mile from the centre of the latter named village. It is curious here to notice that Mr. W. Wragge, who, with Mr. Coulard, of Coulard and Selby, had been making the arrangements for the match, chained the whole five miles on the Tuesday morning at six o'clock, and found that the milestones were wrong in several instances. As may be expected, great care was taken that the road should be exactly measured. Just now we said that a better course could not have been selected. This is borne out by the fact that for years past important trotting, walking, and running matches have been decided on the same road. At Crawley we met an ancient resident who remembered a great time-test affair, in which a horse called the Ranger, belonging to Mr. Bob Percival, was backed for large sums to cover three miles in nine minutes. This feat he would readily have accomplished but for the fact that Mr. Percival was anxious not to expose his animal's form too much, and on cutting it fine, he lost by three seconds, the race being timed by Mr. 'Ned' Smith, of the now defunct *Bell's Life*. This same ancient resident had seen over twenty prize-fights in the same district, which sport he placed on the same level as trotting, holding the votaries of both pastimes to be on the same level of morality.

"Uncertainty and postponement are twin enemies to sport. They combined to work destruction to the Shrewsbury-Lonsdale driving match, but happily were not altogether successful. Lord Shrewsbury having forfeited, he disappears from the affair. No sooner did Lord Lonsdale learn the position of affairs on Tuesday night, than he determined, at all hazards, to give the public a show for their money. Indeed, after the trouble and expense he had gone to, it would have been a lame ending to leave Reigate without mounting a vehicle. It must be remembered that Lord Lonsdale had had special harness made for every one of his nine horses, this being light yet strong, whilst not a single one of his carriages escaped the most scrupulous examination, time after time. Accordingly the word went forth that he would ride over the course just to prove what he really could do. An urgent telegram from Mr. Arthur E. Wells, who knows the value of publicity, caused a *Sportsman* reporter to breakfast early, in fact at half-past six, and to make his appearance in frozen condition at London Bridge Railway Station just before eight o'clock. Everything, in the immortal words of Mr. Mantalini, had a 'dem'd moist unpleasant' look. The streets were cold and penetrating, the water dripped wearily from the eaves, whilst the pavement was in such a state that one step forward meant two backward. Two Pelicans were flapping their wings at the station, and presently were joined by Mr. H. L. Beckett in attire which may be dismissed in a word as 'coachy.' Search the whole world over, and nothing will be found to approach in originality of design and picturesqueness of appearance the clothing, from boot to brimmer, worn by the coaching man of to-day. We all booked to Reigate, and, after sundry shuntings, arrived there about half-past nine. The 'White Hart' was within easy distance, and the coffee-room at once became a subject of interest. To one whose breakfast had consisted of a hurried gaze at a coffee-stall, the ham and eggs at the famous old hostelry were welcome indeed. Here must be mentioned a characteristic incident. No sooner did our reporter, for the first time in his life, set foot in Reigate, than he recalled the fact that Mr. Walter W. Read was born there. Not to know 'W. W.' is to argue oneself unknown, but an unexpected surprise was in store. Speak of angels and their wings flutter. Who should stroll up to the station as we emerged but the identical Mr. W. W. himself, quite oblivious of the coaching match. Breakfast over, talk turned on the drive to be undertaken by Lord Lonsdale.

"It was not until twelve o'clock that the party made a move from the 'White Hart' to the scene of action. Brakes, waggonettes, and carriages were brought round to the entrance, and mounted amidst the open-mouthed wonder of the inhabitants. Mr. Wells, whose first, second, third, and every thought is for creature comforts, caused a nice fat hamper to be hoisted into his conveyance, which conveyed the *Sportsman* representative 'to the front.' A pleasant drive it was in all respects. The snow-laden foliage glistened in the pale sun's rays, making matters overhead of the most delightful description. The long string of vehicles was followed and surrounded by a crowd of persons interested in the affair, and slowly made its way along the Reigate road for about three miles. At length we came to Kennersley Manor, Mr. Brocklehurst's place, almost opposite the gates of which, on either side of the road, were posted two of the well-known blue and yellow flags. This, then, was the starting-place. For nearly a mile in front stretched an undulating road, perfectly clear in the middle from a vestige of snow. We had previously learned that Lord Lonsdale had borrowed the snow-plough from the Reigate local authorities, and sent it over the course. The result exceeded the most sanguine expectations. As much of the road as was required was perfectly clear, and the going, whilst a trifle heavy, was much better than might have been expected. Most of the visitors alighted near the start, but others preferred to go farther on before pulling up. The different vehicles were drawn into neighbouring fields and side roads, so as not to interfere in the slightest manner with the trial which was to take place.

"The Earl of Lonsdale, with whom was Mr. Paget, drove up at 12.35 in a pair-horse brougham, but it was not until twenty-five minutes later that he sped away on his adventurous journey. It will be remembered that four modes of driving were to be employed—single-horse, pair-horse, team, and postillion fashion. Accordingly the pair-horse and the postillion buggy were sent to the Crawley end, five miles away, the char-à-banc with the four-in-hand being drawn up in close contiguity to the starting-place. His Lordship, who was dressed in a brown covert coat, with leather breeches and brown Wellingtons to match, took his seat in the single-horse buggy shortly before one, when everything was in readiness. The horse was the well-known thoroughbred War Paint, aged, by Uncas out of Toilette. He was claimed for Lord Lonsdale from Mr. C. Lane at the Dunstall Park Meeting. It is stated that War Paint has only twice been in harness. The buggy—of American make—was lent to his Lordship by Mr. R. K. Fox of New York. Its construction was light yet strong, and a small clock was placed in front to enable the driver to see how he was getting along. It may be mentioned that it was synchronised with three other clocks placed on the other vehicles, from which fact will be gathered the care with which each minute detail was attended to. Further, each vehicle contained a large pair of blue spectacles, and these, as it turned out, were of especial value in view of the muddy condition of the roads.

"Lord Lonsdale trotted up to the flags, shouted to the timekeeper, 'Are you ready?' shook the reins, and away bounded old War Paint at full gallop. Save for a big crowd, which drew back, the road was quite clear, and in a second or two the buggy, which his Lordship was keeping straight as an arrow, went flying over the hill. It should have been mentioned that a couple of *avant couriers* had been despatched to clear the way; and this they did with such success, that no obstruction was met with until nearly reaching Crawley. Then a brewer's dray, to which were attached a couple of horses, tandem, obstructed the road. Lord Lonsdale shouted, and the driver did his best to clear out of the way, but the leader becoming restive, it caused the racer to lose fully twenty seconds. This will account for the comparatively slow time accomplished by the single horse, the time on reaching the flags at Crawley being 13 minutes 39⅗ seconds. In trials his Lordship had done the five miles in 11 seconds over 13 minutes.

The pair-horse was in waiting, and with extraordinary celerity the driver jumped from one to the other, the change only taking three seconds. In less time than it takes to write it, the return journey was commenced. This buggy was also from New York, having been bought. The horses attached were two American trotters, Blue and Yellow, a pair of French trotters originally intended not being used. Just at the start of the second journey, a couple of policemen made a faint protest, but did not actively interfere, and the road was again found beautifully clear. Excellent progress was made this time, and a great cheer went up as the vehicle was descried in the distance from the starting-post. At breakneck pace up galloped the Americans, steaming hot, making, with Lord Lonsdale, all mud-bespattered and blue spectacled, driving, a remarkable sight. Quickly leaping out, he ran a few yards and mounted the box of the char-à-banc, in waiting handy. The second journey had been accomplished in 12 minutes 51$\frac{3}{5}$ seconds, giving 26 minutes 33$\frac{2}{5}$ seconds for the ten miles; and now everything pointed to a record of under one hour for the complete twenty miles. The change to the coach, one by Holland & Holland, freighted with two grooms, occupied 36$\frac{2}{5}$ seconds, rather longer than at the other end; and here occurred the most picturesque scene of all.

"When Lord Lonsdale mounted the coach, it was a few yards behind the starting-post, and whilst his Lordship adjusted his position, the groom drove the coach. A yard before reaching the proper place, the chief of the Lowthers 'caught up,' and standing on the box, he sent the team away in grand style. As he swept by the crowd on the rise a hundred yards away, a chorus of admiration was raised, many old coaching hands expressing their surprise at the manner in which his Lordship handled the reins. He had a splendid team, supplied him by Mr. W. Wragge of Whitechapel. The leaders were thoroughbred geldings, Silk (near) and Everton King; the wheelers being Conservative and Whitechapel. Again the road was all clear, and this journey Crawley was reached in 15 minutes $9\frac{2}{5}$ seconds, the slowest of the four, as was to be expected. Last of all was the change to the postillion fashion. The change took $40\frac{2}{5}$ seconds, the reason being that Lord Lonsdale had to strip off his covert coat, jacket, and hat before mounting. In the vehicle attached, made by Benny of New York, sat a groom, whose face, by the way, was in a dreadful condition of muddiness by the finish of the gallop. On Draper, a chestnut gelding, Lord Lonsdale rode, the other being Violetta, a bay mare. Little need be said about the fourth and last ride. At full tilt it was carried on throughout, and when the flags were reached, the five miles had been covered in 13 minutes $55\frac{4}{5}$ seconds. The time for the full distance, including changes, was 56 minutes $55\frac{1}{5}$ seconds."

Thus ended the long-talked-of Shrewsbury-Lonsdale driving match; but the matter cropped up again on 21st March at the Horsham Police Court, to which tribunal the Earl of Lonsdale was summoned "for driving furiously, to the danger of the public." The summons was eventually dismissed, after the chairman of the magisterial bench had expressed an opinion to the effect that the public highway is not a fit place for use as a racecourse; but not before the constable-witnesses had played the parts of buffoons in the comedy. As thus:—

Mr. Wightman Wood (appearing for Lord Lonsdale) to constable giving evidence—

"You have said the horse was going as fast as he could. Are you a judge of horses?"

Witness.—"No, sir."

"Have you ever seen a horse go as fast as it could?"

"I don't know."

"You don't know how fast a horse can go?"

"No."

"You stopped in the middle of the road. Why was that: to be run over?"

"No, I took care to get out of the way—(Laughter)—our endeavour to stop Lord Lonsdale was confined to throwing up our arms. We took care to get out of the way before he reached the point where we were standing. We were not going to stand there to be run over." (Laughter.)

"A groom followed his Lordship, I believe?"

"Yes."

"And another came in front, a sort of pilot-engine?" (Laughter.)

"Yes."

The Brighton Road has ever been a course upon which the enthusiastic exponents of different methods of progression have eagerly exhibited their prowess. But to-day, although the road affords as good going as, or better than, ever, it is not so suitable as it was for these displays of speed. Traffic has grown with the growth of villages and townships along these fifty-two miles, and sport and public convenience are, on the highway, antipathetic. Yet every kind of sport has its will of the road. Pedestrians, with others, find the London to Brighton records alluring, and walking matches are by no means infrequent here. The best performance in this division of athletics on this road remains to the credit of the late J. A. M'Intosh of the London Athletic Club, who, on April 10, 1886, walked down in 9 hours 25 minutes 8 seconds, beating the record of 9 hours 48 minutes established by C. L. O'Malley in 1884, on the occasion of a match with B. Nickels, who conceded 30 minutes start, a handicap which, the result proved, should have been reversed.

Callow finished second to M'Intosh on the record walk, his time being 10 hours 14 minutes 6 seconds.

On 20th March 1891, E. Cuthbertson walked from London to Brighton in 10 hours 6 minutes 18 seconds, winning two wagers, that (1) he could not beat J. Chinnery's performance of 11 hours 15 minutes; and (2) that he could not do the distance between Hatchett's Hotel and the "Old Ship" inside twelve hours. At the same time H. K. Paxton walked from "Hatchett's" to the "Greyhound," Croydon, in 1 hour 43 minutes 37 seconds.

The Prince of Wales on July 25, 1784, on the occasion of his second visit to Brighthelmstone, mounted his horse there and rode to and from London on that day. He went by way of Cuckfield, and was ten hours on the road, four and a half hours going, five and a half hours returning. On the 21st of August in the same year he drove from Carlton House to the "Pavilion" in four hours and a half. The turn-out was a phaeton drawn by three horses harnessed tandem-fashion.

These feats were surpassed by "Mr." Webster, of the 10th Light Dragoons, in May 1809. He accepted and won a wager of 300 to 200 guineas with Sir B. Graham about the performance in three and a half hours of the journey from Brighton to Westminster Bridge, mounted upon one of the blood horses that usually ran in his phaeton. He accomplished the ride in three hours twenty minutes, knocking the Prince's record into the proverbial cocked hat. The rider stopped a while at Reigate to take a glass or two of wine, and compelled his horse to swallow the remainder of the bottle.

This spirited affair was preceded in April 1793 by a curious match which seems to deserve mention. A clergyman at Brighton betted an officer of the Artillery quartered there 100 guineas that he would ride his own horse to London sooner than the officer could go in a chaise and pair, the officer's horses to be changed *en route* as often as he might think proper. The Artilleryman accordingly despatched a servant to provide relays, and at twelve o'clock on an unfavourable night the parties set out to decide the bet, which was won by the clergyman with difficulty. He arrived in town at 5 A.M., only a few minutes before the chaise, which it had been thought was sure of winning. The driver of the last stage, however, nearly became stuck in a ditch, which mishap caused considerable delay. The

Cuckfield driver ran his stage to Crawley, nine miles, within the half hour.

In later years, on 1st January 1888, a trotting match against time was made from London to Brighton, when the horse "Ginger" won; time, 4 hours 16 minutes 30 seconds. Another horse, "The Bird," trotted from Kennington Cross to Brighton in 4 hours 30 minutes.[1]

And so an end to these sporting reflections at Crawley, the half-way house, as it were, of a sporting road.

Rowlandson has preserved for us in one of his drawings a view of Crawley as he saw it in 1789. It was published with a few others just a hundred years ago in that intolerable work of Henry Wigstead's, "An Excursion to Brighthelmstone in 1789," a work of the dreadfullest ditchwater dulness, saved only from oblivion by the artist's illustrations. That *they* should have lived, you who see this reproduction of Crawley will not wonder.

Passing southward along the rising street, you leave on the left hand the grey church-tower, and presently pass over the abomination of a railway crossing on the road-level that renders the road always unsightly and often dangerous. Of the church, one who lives not at Crawley, and waits not upon its opening for services, can say little, for its doors are at other times rigidly locked. All that can be done is to poach upon the preserves of one's Murray, and cite him to the effect that upon one

[1] It seems well to place these records in tabulated form (p. 119) for readier reference:—

GEORGE

SOME BRIGHTON ROAD RECORDS.

Date.		Time. h.	m.	s.
1784, July 25.	Prince of Wales rode horse back from "Pavilion" to Carlton House. . . .	10	0	0
	Going, ...	4	30	0
	Returning, ...	5	30	0
,, Aug. 21.	Prince of Wales drove phaeton, three horses tandem-wise, Carlton House to "Pavilion,"	4	30	0
1809, May.	"Mr." Webster, of 10th Light Dragoons, rode horseback, Brighton to Westminster Bridge, ...	3	20	0
1834, Feb. 4.	"Criterion" Coach, London to Brighton, .	3	40	0
1869, ,, 17.	John Mayall, jun., rode on velocipede from Trafalgar Square to Brighton, (about) .	12	0	0
1884.	C. L. O'Malley walked from Westminster Clock Tower to Aquarium, Brighton, .	9	48	0
1886, April 10.	J. A. M'Intosh walked from Westminster Clock Tower to Aquarium, Brighton, .	9	25	8
1888, Jan. 1.	Horse "Ginger" trotted to Brighton, . .	4	16	30
,, July 13.	James Selby drove "Old Times" Coach from "Hatchett's," Piccadilly, to "Old Ship," Brighton, and back.	7	50	0
	Going, ...	3	56	0
	Returning, ...	3	54	0
,, Aug. 10.	Team of four cyclists, E. J. Willis, G. L. Morris, S. C. Schafer, and S. Walker, dividing the distance between them, cycled from "Hatchett's," Piccadilly, to "Old Ship," Brighton, and back, . .	7	36	$19\frac{2}{5}$
1890, Mar. 30.	Another team, J. F. Shute, T. W. Girling, R. Wilson, and A. E. Griffin, reduced first team's time by 4 min. $19\frac{2}{5}$ secs. .	7	32	0
,, April 13.	Another team, E. and W. Scantlebury, W. W. Arnott, and J. Blair, reduced the time to	7	25	15
,, June.	F. W. Shorland cycled from "Hatchett's" to "Old Ship" and back, ...	7	19	0
,, July 23.	S. F. Edge cycled from "Hatchett's" to "Old Ship" and back.	7	2	50
Sept. 3.	C. A. Smith cycled from "Hatchett's" to "Old Ship" and back, ...	6	52	10
,, ,, 30.	E. P. Moorhouse cycled (tricycle) from "Hatchett's" to "Old Ship" and back,	8	9	24
1891, Mar. 20.	E. Cuthbertson walked from "Hatchett's" to "Old Ship,"	10	6	18
1892, June 1.	S. F. Edge cycled from "Hatchett's" to "Old Ship" and back. . .	6	31	7

Note.—The fastest L. B. & S. C. R. train, the 5.0 P.M. Pullman Express from London Bridge, reaches Brighton at 6.5 P.M. . . . . 1 5 0 of the tie beams of its curious open-timbered roof is carved the inscription in old English characters :—

> "Man yn wele bewar, for warldly good makyth man blynde
> Bewar befor, whate comyth behynde."

Also the church contains two brasses, and its architecture is Decorated and Perpendicular. This last you can gather from a glance at the exterior; for the rest, original impressions are for the passing stranger impossible.

Now come we in less than an hour to Hog's Hill, where the modern coach-guard regales his passengers with apocryphal tales as to the derivation of that name, and from Hog's Hill it is but a matter of another mile and a quarter or thereby to Pease Pottage Gate, whose etymology is equally uncertain.

Rash folk there be to whom this striking, if homely, name offers all the charms of a conundrum, and they will give you essays many and varied as to its derivation. I do not propose, however, to venture a theory of my own. Let it suffice to quote others to the effect that in the old route-marching times the Tommy Atkins of the day was halted here and regaled upon "pease-pottage," a name for pease-pudding, I take it, as nearly poetic as that eminently prosaic compost admits.

Or, again, the gossips say that prisoners on their way for trial at the Assizes, holden at Horsham and East Grinstead alternately, were conveyed in wagons between the two places, and were rested here and given each a bowl of pease-pottage. It may

be shrewdly suspected that these explanations are the wildest guesses at the solution of a tempting puzzle; but who will have the courage to adventure a theory as to the name of the neighbouring hamlet of Warninglid?

Right away from here to Hand Cross the road is bordered and shaded by the most delightful of forest greenery, and indeed the highway seems not so much a public as a private road through some lordly park. The hedges are frequently of laurel and other evergreen shrubs. The white track of roadway, too, is bordered by a dainty edging of grass neatly kept.

Half a mile after passing the thirty-second milestone, on the left-hand side of the road, is a rather singular sight—a beech and an oak growing out of one trunk. Shortly after passing this you come to a settlement of a few houses set down beside the road in a clearing of the forest, Tilgate Forest Row, so called. St. Leonard's and Tilgate forests, or their remains, line the way for some miles until you come, past the spectre-haunted laurel hedges near Hand Cross Park, to Hand Cross itself.

The Hand Cross ghost is, by all accounts, an extremely eccentric but harmless spook, with peculiar notions in the matter of clothes, and given, in days when the turnpike gate stood here, to Egyptian-Hall-like tricks with bolts and bars, whereby pikemen were not only scared, but were the losers of sundry tolls. But still, a harmless wraith, and (evidently) the wayfarers' friend.

Hand Cross is a settlement of forty, perhaps

fifty houses, situated on the borders of this delightful land of forests, where several roads meet. Its name clearly derives from this convenient position, and antiquarians have a theory that a combination of wayside-cross and direction-post anciently found here, and indeed throughout the country, during pre-Reformation times, originated the name. These posts were furnished with a pointing hand at the end of the directing arm; hence their generic names, "finger-post," "hand-post," and here, in combination with the votive cross or shrine, "hand-cross."

From this friendly arm, erected for guidance and devotion on the, at that time, lonely roads, springs this offshoot of Slaugham village. We may see, in imagination, how the hamlet grew from a mere halting-place on the old "fly-wagon" route through Sussex, before the Brighthelmstone stage-coach was; before, indeed, the new-grown popularity of that fishing-village had caused a direct road to be constructed to it from London. We may conceive its progress through the early days of the coaching era to the present time, increasing always in importance, until, when steam came to depose road-travel utterly for a time, the place was of greater consideration than its parent village, dozing away on a road that leads to nowhere in particular.

It is its being on the main road, and on the junction of several routes, that has made Hand Cross what it is to-day; though that condition, speaking with the voice of the tourist, may not

THE
RED
LION

be altogether pleasing to the eye; for, after all, it is a *parvenu* of a place, and lacks the Domesday descent of, for instance, Cuckfield. Now, the *parvenu*, the man of his hands, may be a very estimable fellow, but his raw prosperity grates upon the nerves. So it is with Hand Cross, for its prosperity, which has not waned with the coaching era, has incited to the building of many houses, cottages of that cheap and yellow brick we know so well and loathe so much. Also, though there is no church, there are two chapels; one of retiring position, the other conventicle of aggressive and red, red brick. One could find it in one's heart to forgive the yellow brick; but this red, never. In this lurid building is a harmonium. On Sundays, the wail of that instrument and the hooting and ting, tinging of cyclorns and cycling gongs, as cyclists foregather by the "Red Lion," are the most striking features of the place.

The "Red Lion" though, (alas! that I should say it!) is of greater interest than all other buildings at Hand Cross. It stood here in receipt of coaching custom through all those roystering days, as it stands now, prosperous at the hands of another age of wheels. What does my Shergold say of it, but that its landlords in olden times knew more of smuggling than what came by hearsay.

And at Hand Cross the ways divide. The cyclist who knows his Brighton Road, and who, I am afraid, cares more for smoothness and easy gradients than for scenery or associations, goes more frequently by the Hickstead and Albourne route than by the left-hand road, which includes such hills as the one that leads down to Staplefield Common immediately after leaving Hand Cross, and that famous hill at Clayton, of which more later.

But there is no reason why we should follow in the track of the wheelman, who is ever easefully inclined; there are cogent considerations, indeed, which urge to the other course, for by following the course of that pneumatic pilgrim, Cuckfield, that delightful old town, would be missed, to speak of that place alone. So let us away down Hand Cross Hill, past that gnarled and eccentric-looking fir-tree that overhangs the road in so astonishing a manner, as striking a landmark as ever earned a glance by day or caused a delightful sensation of "creeps" o' nights. There is an unexplainably bodeful effect to be experienced in passing under this fantastic growth. When the sun has set, its remarkable form looms overhead like some gigantic outstretched hand, ready and willing to crush, as the veriest blackbeetle, the puny wayfarer.

Going down the hillside, there opens as fine a view over the Weald as you could wish, bounded by the blue barrier of the South Downs, with an enchanting middle-distance of copses, cottages, and winding roads, and, nearer, the sparkle of Slaugham mill-pond; while in the foreground is Staplefield Place, with lodge-gate beside the road, and white-capped Equatorial amid the trees. Now you come upon Staplefield Common, bisected by the highway, with its group of recent cottages and modern church. There

is an Elizabethan-like spaciousness about the place for all the modernity of its few buildings: it is the elbow-room remaining that gives the effect. Staplefield is, unlike St. John's Common, what its name implies. Here you do not expect an open space, and find instead a jostling town, as will hap further on the way, hard by Burgess Hill.

Staplefield stands, with Hand Cross, in the parish of Slaugham. If, being a stranger, you inquire the way to that village, pronouncing its name as spelled, it is probable you will not be understood of the natives. "Slaffam," on the other hand, wins instant recognition, and the direction will be along the right-hand pathway. Half a mile along a leafy lane leads to the Hickstead route to Brighton, crossing the bye-road at right angles, and just beyond, to the left hand, in a watery meadow, stand the ruins of Slaugham Place, the deserted home of the Coverts, a vanished family, once among the most powerful, as they were of the noblest, in the county.

The Coverts were of Norman descent. They, to use a well-worn phrase, "came over with the Conqueror;" but it is not until toward the close of the fifteenth century that they are found settled at Slaugham. They were preceded as lords of this manor by the Poynings of Poynings, and by the Berkeleys and Stanleys. Sir Walter Covert, to whose ancestors the manor fell by marriage, was the builder of the Slaugham Place whose ruins still remain to show the almost palatial character of his conception. They cover within their enclosing walls of red brick, which rise from the yet partly filled moat, over three acres of what is now orchard and meadow-land. In spring the apple trees bloom pink and white amid the grey and lichen-stained ashlar of the ruined walls and arches of Palladian architecture; the lush grass grows tall around the cold hearths of the roofless rooms. The noble gateway leads now, not from courtyard to hall, but doorless, with its massive stones wrenched apart by clinging ivy, stands merely as some sort of key to the enigma of ground plan presented by walls ruinated in greater part to the level of the watery turf.

The singular facts of high wall and moat surrounding a mansion of Jacobean build seem to point to an earlier building, contrived with these defences when men thought first of security and afterwards of comfort. Some few mullioned windows of much earlier date than the greater part of the mansion remain to confirm the thought.

That a building of the magnificence attested by these crumbling walls should have been allowed to fall into decay so shortly after its completion is a singular fact. Though the male line of the Coverts failed, and their estates passed by the marriage of their womankind into other hands, yet their alienation would not necessarily imply the destruction of their roof-tree. The explanation is to be sought in the situation and qualities of the ground upon which Slaugham Place stood, a marshy tract of land, which no builder of to-day would think of selecting as a site for so important a dwelling, home as it is of swamps and damps, and, quashy as it is even

now, it must have been in the past the breeding-ground of agues and chills innumerable. Indeed, from near by three rivers, the Arun, the Adur, and the Sussex Ouse, take their rise. Slaugham, in fact, derives its name from the mires and bogs and "sloughs" of its river-bearing lands.

A true exemplar this of that Sussex of which in 1690 a barrister on circuit, whose profession led him by evil chance into this county, writes to his wife:—"The Sussex ways are bad and ruinous beyond imagination. I vow 'tis melancholy consideration that mankind will inhabit such a heap of dirt for a poor livelihood. The county is in a sink of about fourteen miles broad, which receives all the water that falls from the long ranges of hills on both sides of it, and not being furnished with convenient draining, is kept moist and soft by the water till the middle of a dry summer, which is only able to make it tolerable to ride for a short time."

Such soft and shaky earth as this could not bear the weight of so ponderous a structure as was Slaugham Place: the swamps pulled its masonry apart and rotted its fittings. Despairing of victory over the reeking moisture, its owners left it for healthier sites. Then the rapacity of all those neighbouring folk who had need of building material completed the havoc wrought by natural forces, and finally Slaugham Place became what it is to-day. Its clock-tower was pulled down and removed to Cuckfield Park, where it now spans the entrance drive of that romantic spot; its handsomely carved Jacobean stairway is to-day the pride and glory of the "Star" Hotel at Lewes.

The Coverts are gone; their heraldic shields, in company of an architectural frieze of greyhounds' and leopards' heads and skulls of oxen wreathed in drapery, still decorate what remains of the north front of their mansion, and their achievements are repeated upon their tombs within the little church of Slaugham on the hillside. You may, if heraldically versed, learn from their quarterings into what families they married; but the deeds which they wrought, and their virtues and their vices, are, for the most part, clean forgotten, even as their name is gone out of the land who once, as tradition has it, travelled southward from London to the sea on their own manors.

The squat, shingled spirelet of Slaugham Church and its Decorated architecture mark the spot where many of this knightly race lie buried. In the Covert Chapel is the handsome brass of John Covert, who died in 1503; and in the north wall of the chancel is the canopied altar-tomb of Richard Covert, the much-married, who died in 1547, and is represented, in company of three of his four wives, by little brass effigies, together with a curious brass representing the Saviour rising from the tomb, guarded by armed knights of weirdly-humorous aspect, the more diverting because executed all innocent of joke or irreverence. Here is a rubbing, nothing exaggerated, of one of these guardian knights, to bear me up.

Another Richard, but twice married, who died in

1579, is commemorated in a large and elaborate monument in the Covert Chapel, whereon are sculptured, in an attitude of prayer, Richard himself, his two wives, six sons, and eight daughters.

FROM A BRASS AT SLAUGHAM.

Last of the Coverts whose name is perpetuated here is Jane, who deceased in 1586.

Beside these things, Slaugham claims some interest as containing the mansion of Ashfold, where once resided Mrs. Matcham, a sister of Lord Nelson's. Indeed, it was while staying here that the Admiral received the summons which sped him on his last and most glorious and fatal voyage. Slaugham, too, with St. Leonard's Forest, contributes a title to the peerage, Lord St. Leonards' creation being of "Slaugham, in the county of Sussex."

And now to return to Staplefield, and thence to make along the three miles of highway, past Slough Green and Whiteman's Green to Cuckfield. Passing the new and magnificent mansion of Holmstead on the right hand, the road rises sharply commanding views over the Ouse Valley toward Balcombe and Ardingly, where the Ouse Railway

I

viaduct stalks with gaunt brick arches across the meadows. As you look, a puff of steam and smoke from a passing train trails across it, and you think, sadly, it may be, upon the utilitarian spirit which thus disfigures the country-side with this array of arches. Now, if you were assured of this being a Roman aqueduct, to which, indeed, it bears a striking resemblance, the case would be different; a halo of romance would surround the structure. It is purely a matter of sentiment how you look upon these things; the mind, not the eye, settles such questions of taste.

And so we tramped along, passing Slough Green, with its quaint and recently added-to old house of Slough Place, and we presently came to Whiteman's Green, as picturesque as its name.

Before going on into Cuckfield, we sat down a while beside the road, for 'twas hot, and we were in lazy mood.

From our resting-place we could command a view down the road to where stood a roadside inn, and we were dreamily regarding this prospect, one of interest on a hot day, when suddenly, as if shot out, a figure emerged from that hostelry, and fell grovelling in the dust, amid imprecations and a general commotion, whose sounds reached us distinctly. This was interesting, but it was enough to watch from afar. But presently he who had been so shamefully entreated arose, and painfully made his intricate way uphill; and as he drew near, it was evident that he was very drunken.

He proved to be a pedlar, one who sells laces

A CORNER OF STAPLEFIELD COMMON.

and buttons and needles, pins and tapes, and such small wares; and his stock-in-trade was in a case slung upon his back.

Figure to yourself a man below the middle height, yet thin and wiry, habited (it were impossible to say dressed) in clothes which years ago had been black, but which were now rusty with age and ragged with hard usage; a man whose age it were impossible to guess with near approach to accuracy, but who might be anything from thirty-five to near upon fifty years of age. From under an absolutely shapeless hat, his face, red and streaky, could be seen, here and there scratched by his fall. Though it was now spring, he wore a once white muffler tied in a wisp about his neck, its long ends hanging down in front of him. Great rents showed in his trousers at either knee, and from them the torn cloth hung down, as it were, on hinges, and flapped and waved as he moved. His boots were large and bulbous, and one of them was tied around the toe of it with a cloth. For support he leaned upon a ragged stick, so that he was, indeed, rags in all his equipment. Had this fellow been an Italian and in Venice, he would have been accounted almost invaluable as a model for (say) a picturesque beggar; but this was England, and the pedlar spoke our own tongue, so his appearance was merely sordid, with no qualification.

AND THUS WE PARTED.

When at length he came up, the pack was unstrapped and opened, disclosing his small stock.

"Anything in my line, gentlemen?"

We bought some laces, and one of us produced a sketch-book, and began some rough pencillings.

"Well," said the subject of those jottings, noticing this, "I ain't never before bin a artis' moddle; I ain't pritty enough, I reckon."

He drew himself up into a ridiculously formal attitude, and failed absurdly in the attempt to look sober, so that we laughed loud and long.

"I don't see nothin' to laugh at," said he of the tatters. "I've got to tramp into Reigit, an' I ain't took enough to get me a bed to-night."

It was extremely unlikely that this unsteady fellow would think of walking that eighteen miles, and as to his takings, that story of his was probably as apocryphal as is the first edition of an evening newspaper; but before we turned away, we put some silver into his hand. Presently, turning round to look after the pedlar, we saw him still regarding the Queen's shilling in his outstretched palm, and thus we parted.

And so into Cuckfield, that pleasant old town, which, standing on no railway, having no manufactures, and being on the slightly hillier road of the two short routes to Brighton, is consequently but scantily favoured of your "scorching" cyclist, and nods drowsily in summer sunshine and winter snows, all round the calendar. It pleased the engineers of the Brighton Railway to bring their line no nearer Cuckfield than Hayward's Heath, some two miles distant, where they built a station of that name, giving thereby satisfaction, if not to the commercial population of this Sleepy Hollow, at least to the private inhabitants, and to the perhaps selfish tourist, who would rather happen upon such quiet backwaters of life as this than upon the bustling prosperity of a town so situated as to snatch every commercial advantage a sordid and grasping age may offer. For I don't think the Cuckfield shopkeepers grow rich upon Cuckfield trade. What of business was left to the town when the coaches ceased running, fifty years ago, has been taken away by the already greater town of Hayward's Heath, that has sprung up fungus-like round the rail. And Hayward's Heath is in Cuckfield parish! Ah! ingrate parasite, that kills the friendly growth to which it owes existence. County business has left Cuckfield for the more convenient settlement on the railway. Everything else follows, and, to the tourist's delight, if to the freeholder's disgust, Cuckfield is left to its traditions and natural beauties.

At how many places have you seen an inn so redolent of old coaching days as is the "Talbot" here, whose embayed frontage of such height and length looks down upon the High Street with solid primness of Georgian red brick, earnest of the solid comfort obtainable within? What ranges of stables here and at the "King's Head!"

Cuckfield, for all the day being not yet advanced beyond tea-time, was insistent in its claims to be regarded as the end of that day's journey; so we to our inn for toilette and tea, and afterwards an exploration of the town before the twilight quenched the dull red tone of its red-bricked High Street in an impartial mantle of tender grey.

FOURTH DAY.

We remained at Cuckfield the greater part of this morning. To see Cuckfield thoroughly, and to gain an adequate impression of it, demands some morning hours spent in its streets; some leisured inspection of its large and handsome church, which runs the gamut of Pointed architecture and is filled with memorials of the Burrells and the Sergisons of Cuckfield Park; and lastly, requires a tour of that romantic home of deer and tradition, acknowledged by Harrison Ainsworth to be the original of "Rookwood." Cuckfield Place stands amid the groves and avenues of this charming domain, its grey Elizabethan front and greyer roof visible at some points from the road, that descends abruptly on leaving the town as you go southward, lined on either side with cottages and fir trees, whose branches and dark evergreen foliage frame the vista as artistically as ever foreground was contrived by artist. Lower down this road the entrance-lodge leads to the Chase, a long avenue of ancient lime trees, in whose midst stands that clock-tower from Slaugham Place of which I have already spoken. The Park is 242 acres in extent, and, wooded as it is, and traversed throughout its picturesquely broken surface by a deep-burrowing stream, is surpassed by few estates in natural beauty; and over Cuckfield Park and Place is cast a spell of romantic interest by the

CUCKFIELD PLACE.

incidents of "Rookwood," that grim and gory tale by which Ainsworth made his literary repute, such as it is. "Rookwood," commenced in 1831, was not finished till 1834. Its author died at Reigate, 3rd January 1882. It is thus, in his preface, he acknowledges his model:—

"The supernatural occurrence forming the groundwork of one of the ballads which I have made the harbinger of doom to the house of Rookwood, is ascribed by popular superstition to a family resident in Sussex, upon whose estate the fatal tree (a gigantic lime, with mighty arms and huge girth of trunk, as described in the song) is still carefully preserved. Cuckfield Place, to which this singular piece of timber is attached, is, I may state for the benefit of the curious, the real Rookwood Hall; for I have not drawn upon imagination, but upon memory in describing the seat and domains of that fated family. The general features of the venerable structure, several of its chambers, the old garden, and, in particular, the noble park, with its spreading prospects, its picturesque views of the hall, 'like bits of Mrs. Radcliffe' (as the poet Shelley once observed of the same scene), its deep glades, through which the deer come lightly tripping down, its uplands, slopes, brooks, brakes, coverts, and groves are carefully delineated."

"Like Mrs. Radcliffe!" This romance is indeed written in that peculiar convention which obtained with her, with Horace Walpole, with Maturin, and Lewis—"Monk" Lewis; a convention of Gothic gloom and superstition, delighting in gore and apparitions, which was responsible for the "Mysteries of Udolpho," "The Italian," "The Monk," and other highly seasoned reading of the early years of this century. All this sort of thing was then extremely popular, but who reads those blood-boltered romances now! Ainsworth deliberately modelled his manner upon Mrs. Radcliffe, changing the scenes of his desperate deeds from her favourite Italy to our own land. Ainsworth, I suppose, is still read, chiefly by an admiring *clientèle* of schoolboys, who

HARRISON AINSWORTH (*from the Fraser Portrait*).

devour incident, however improbable; and Ainsworth is both full of action and wild improbability. In "Rookwood," too, his workmanship is of the poorest; you are allowed full view of the frame upon which the canvas is stretched—a canvas painted upon with bright, nay, lurid colours and the heaviest of hands. The songs and ballads, too, scattered up and down those pages are the merest shoddy, and his jokes the most hob-nailed of witticisms. You deplore his verses, his puns; your gravity is endangered by what he intends to be horrible, but is, after all, only repulsively ridiculous. These pages from the close of "Rookwood" exhibit this trait. Alan Rookwood visits the family vault:—

"He then walked beneath the shadow of one of the yews, chanting an odd stanza or so of one of his wild staves, wrapped the while, it would seem, in affectionate contemplation of the subject-matter of his song:—

THE CHURCHYARD YEW.

"———Metuendaque succo
Taxus."

A noxious tree is the churchyard yew,
As if from the dead its sap it drew:
Dark are its branches, and dismal to see,
Like plumes at Death's latest solemnity.
Spectral and jagged, and black as the wings
Which some spirit of ill o'er a sepulchre flings:
Oh! a terrible tree is the churchyard yew:
Like it is nothing so grimly to view.

Yet this baleful tree hath a core so sound,
Can nought so tough in the grove be found:
From it were fashioned brave English bows,
The boast of our isle, and the dread of its foes,
For our sturdy sires cut their stoutest staves
From the branch that hung o'er their fathers' graves:
And though it be dreary and dismal to view,
Staunch at the heart is the churchyard yew.

"His ditty concluded, Alan entered the churchyard, taking care to leave the door slightly ajar, in order to facilitate his grandson's entrance. For an instant he lingered in the chancel. The yellow moonlight fell upon the monuments of his race; and, directed by the instinct of hate, Alan's eye rested upon the gilded entablature of his perfidious brother Reginald, and muttering curses, 'not loud, but deep,' he passed on. Having lighted his lantern in no tranquil mood, he descended into the vault, observing a similar caution with respect to the portal of the cemetery, which he left partially unclosed, with the key in the lock. Here he resolved to abide Luke's coming. The reader knows what probability there was of his expectations being realised.

"For a while he paced the tomb, wrapped in gloomy meditation, and pondering, it might be, upon the result of Luke's expedition, and the fulfilment of his own dark schemes, scowling from time to time beneath his bent eyebrows, counting the grim array of coffins, and noticing, with something like satisfaction, that the shell which contained the remains of his daughter had been restored to its former position. He then bethought him of Father Checkley's midnight intrusion upon his conference with Luke, and their apprehension of a supernatural visitation, and his curiosity was stimulated to ascertain by what means the priest had gained admission to the spot unperceived and unheard. He resolved to sound the floor, and see whether any secret entrance existed; and hollowly and dully did the hard flagging return the stroke of his heel as he pursued his scrutiny. At length the metallic ringing of an iron plate, immediately behind the marble effigy of Sir Ranulph, resolved the point. There it was that the priest had found access to the vault; but Alan's disappointment was excessive when he discovered that this plate was fastened on the underside, and all communication thence with the churchyard, or to wherever else it might conduct him, cut off; but the present was not the season for further investigation, and tolerably pleased with the discovery he had already made, he returned to his silent march around the sepulchre.

"At length a sound, like the sudden shutting of the church door, broke upon the profound stillness of the holy edifice. In the hush that succeeded, a footstep was distinctly heard threading the aisle.

"'He comes—he comes!' exclaimed Alan, joyfully; adding, an instant after, in an altered voice, 'but he comes alone.'

"The footstep drew near to the mouth of the vault—it was upon the stairs. Alan stepped forward to greet, as he supposed, his grandson, but started back in astonishment and dismay as he encountered in his stead Lady Rookwood. Alan retreated, while the lady advanced, swinging the iron door after her, which closed with a tremendous clang. Approaching the statue of the first Sir Ranulph, she passed, and Alan then remarked the singular and terrible expression of her eyes, which appeared to be fixed upon the statue, or upon some invisible object near it. There was something in her whole attitude and manner calculated to impress the deepest terror on the beholder, and Alan gazed upon her with an awe which momentarily increased. Lady Rookwood's bearing was as proud and erect as we have formerly described it to have been, her brow was as haughtily bent, her chiselled lip as disdainfully curled; but the staring, changeless eye, and the deep-heaved sob which occasionally escaped her, betrayed how much she was under the influence of mortal terror. Alan watched her in amazement. He knew not how the scene was likely to terminate, nor what could have induced her to visit this ghostly spot at such an hour and alone; but he resolved to abide the issue in silence—profound as her own. After a time, however, his impatience got the better of his fears and scruples, and he spoke.

"'What doth Lady Rookwood in the abode of the dead?' asked he at length.

"She started at the sound of his voice, but still kept her eye fixed upon the vacancy.

"'Hast thou not beckoned me hither, and am I not come?' returned she, in a hollow tone. 'And now thou askest wherefore I am here. I am here because, as in thy life I feared thee not, neither in death do I fear thee. I am here because——'

"'What seest thou?' interrupted Alan, with ill-suppressed terror.

"'What see I—ha—ha!' shouted Lady Rookwood, amidst discordant laughter; 'that which might appal a heart less stout than mine—a figure anguish-writhen, with veins that glow as with a subtle and consuming flame. A substance, yet a shadow, in thy living likeness. Ha—frown if thou wilt; I can return thy glances.'

"'Where dost thou see this vision?' demanded Alan.

"'Where?' echoed Lady Rookwood, becoming for the first time sensible of the presence of a stranger. 'Ha—who are you that question me?—what are you?—speak!'

"'No matter who or what I am,' returned Alan; 'I ask you what you behold?'

"'Can you see nothing?'

"'Nothing,' replied Alan.

"'You knew Sir Piers Rookwood?'

"'Is it he?' asked Alan, drawing near her.

"'It is,' replied Lady Rookwood; 'I have followed him hither, and I will follow him whithersoever he leads me, were it to——'

"'What doth he now?' asked Alan; 'do you see him still?'

"'The figure points to that sarcophagus,' returned Lady Rookwood—'can you raise up the lid?'

"'No,' replied Alan; 'my strength will not avail to lift it.'

"'Yet let the trial be made,' said Lady Rookwood; 'the figure points there still—my own arm shall aid you.'

"Alan watched her in dumb wonder. She advanced towards the marble monument, and beckoned him to follow. He reluctantly complied. Without any expectation of being able to move the ponderous lid of the sarcophagus, at Lady Rookwood's renewed request he applied himself to the task. What was his surprise, when, beneath their united efforts, he found the ponderous slab slowly revolve upon its vast hinges, and, with little further difficulty, it was completely elevated, though it still required the exertion of all Alan's strength to prop it open and prevent its falling back.

"'What does it contain?' asked Lady Rookwood.

"'A warrior's ashes,' returned Alan.

"'There is a rusty dagger upon a fold of faded linen,' cried Lady Rookwood, holding down the light.

"'It is the weapon with which the first dame of house of Rookwood was stabbed,' said Alan, with a grim smile:—

'Which whoso findeth in the tomb
Shall clutch until the hour of doom;
And when 'tis grasped by hand of clay,
The curse of blood shall pass away.'

So saith the rhyme. Have you seen enough?'

"'No,' said Lady Rookwood, precipitating herself into the marble coffin. 'That weapon shall be mine.'

"'Come forth—come forth,' cried Alan. 'My arm trembles—I cannot support the lid.'

"'I will have it, though I grasp it to eternity,' shrieked Lady Rookwood, vainly endeavouring to wrest away the dagger, which was fastened, together with the linen upon which it lay, by some adhesive substance to the bottom of the shell.

"At this moment Alan Rookwood happened to

cast his eye upward, and he then beheld what filled him with new terror. The axe of the sable statue was poised above its head, as in the act to strike him. Some secret machinery, it was evident, existed between the sarcophagus lid and this mysterious image. But in the first impulse of his alarm Alan abandoned his hold of the slab, and it sunk slowly downwards. He uttered a loud cry as it moved. Lady Rookwood heard this cry. She raised herself at the same moment—the dagger was in her hand—she pressed it against the lid, but its downward force was too great to be withstood. The light was within the sarcophagus, and Alan could discern her features. The expression was terrible. She uttered one shriek, and the lid closed for ever.

"Alan was in total darkness. The light had been enclosed with Lady Rookwood. There was something so horrible in her probable fate that even *he* shuddered as he thought upon it. Exerting all his remaining strength, he essayed to raise the lid, but now it was more firmly closed than ever. It defied all his power. Once, for an instant, he fancied that it yielded to his straining sinews, but it was only his hand that slided upon the surface of the marble. It was fixed—immovable. The sides and lid rang with the strokes which the unfortunate lady bestowed upon them with the dagger's point; but these sounds were not long heard. Presently all was still; the marble ceased to vibrate with her blows. Alan struck the lid with his knuckles, but no response was returned. All was silent.

"He now turned his attention to his own situation, which had become sufficiently alarming. An hour must have elapsed, yet Luke had not arrived. The door of the vault was closed—the key was in the lock, and on the outside. He was himself a prisoner within the tomb. What if Luke should *not* return? What if he were slain, as it might chance, in the enterprise? That thought flashed across his brain like an electric shock. None knew of his retreat but his grandson. He might perish of famine within this desolate vault.

"He checked this notion as soon as it was formed—it was too dreadful to be indulged in. A thousand circumstances might conspire to detain Luke. He was sure to come. Yet the solitude, the darkness was awful, almost intolerable. The dying and the dead were around him. He dared not stir.

"Another hour—an age it seemed to him—had passed. Still Luke came not. Horrible forebodings crossed him; but he would not surrender himself to them. He rose, and crawled in the direction, as he supposed, of the door—fearful even of the stealthy sound of his own footsteps. He reached it, and his heart once more throbbed with hope. He bent his ear to the key; he drew in his breath; he listened for some sound, but nothing was to be heard. A groan would have been almost music in his ears.

"Another hour was gone! He was now a prey to the most frightful apprehensions, agitated in turns by the wildest emotions of rage and terror. He at one moment imagined that Luke had abandoned him, and heaped curses upon his head; at the next, convinced that he had fallen, he bewailed with equal bitterness his grandson's fate and his own. He paced the tomb like one distracted; he stamped upon the iron plate; he smote with his hands upon the door; he shouted, and the vault hollowly echoed his lamentations. But Time's sand ran on, and Luke arrived not.

"Alan now abandoned himself wholly to despair. He could no longer anticipate his grandson's coming —no longer hope for deliverance. His fate was sealed. Death awaited him. He must anticipate his slow but inevitable stroke, enduring all the grinding horrors of starvation. The contemplation of such an end was madness, but he was forced to contemplate it now; and so appalling did it appear to his imagination, that he half resolved to dash out his brains against the walls of the sepulchre, and put an end at once to his tortures; and nothing, except a doubt whether he might not, by imperfectly accomplishing his purpose, increase his own suffering, prevented him from putting this dreadful idea into execution. His dagger was gone, and he had no other weapon. Terrors of a new kind now assailed him. The dead, he fancied, were bursting from their coffins, and he peopled the darkness with grisly phantoms. They were round about him on each side, whirling and rustling, gibbering, groaning, shrieking, laughing, and lamenting. He was stunned, stifled. The air seemed to grow suffocating, pestilential; the wild laughter was redoubled; the horrible troop assailed him; they dragged him along the tomb, and amid their howls he fell, and became insensible.

"When he returned to himself, it was some time before he could collect his scattered faculties; and when the agonising consciousness of his terrible situation forced itself upon his mind, he had nigh relapsed into oblivion. He arose. He rushed towards the door: he knocked against it with his knuckles till the blood streamed from them; he scratched against it with his nails till they were torn off by the roots. With insane fury he hurled himself against the iron frame: it was in vain. Again he had recourse to the trap-door. He searched for it; he found it. He laid himself upon the ground. There was no interval of space in which he could insert a finger's point. He beat it with his clenched hand; he tore it with his teeth; he jumped upon it; he smote it with his heel. The iron returned a sullen sound.

"He again essayed the lid of the sarcophagus. Despair nerved his strength. He raised the slab a few inches. He shouted, screamed, but no answer was returned; and again the lid fell.

"'She is dead!' cried Alan. 'Why have I not shared her fate? But mine is to come. And such a death!—oh, oh!' And, frenzied at the thought, he again hurried to the door, and renewed his fruitless attempts to escape, till nature gave way, and he sank upon the floor, groaning and exhausted.

"Physical suffering now began to take the place of his mental tortures. Parched and consumed with a fierce internal fever, he was tormented by unappeasable thirst—of all human ills the most unendurable. His tongue was dry and dusty, his throat inflamed; his lips had lost all moisture. He licked the humid floor; he sought to imbibe the nitrous drops from the walls; but, instead of allaying his thirst, they increased it. He would have given the world, had he possessed it, for a draught of cold spring-water. Oh, to have died with his lips upon some bubbling fountain's marge! But to perish thus!

"Nor were the pangs of hunger wanting. He had to endure all the horrors of famine as well as the agonies of quenchless thirst.

"In this dreadful state three days and nights passed over Alan's fated head. Nor night nor day had he. Time, with him, was only measured by its duration, and that seemed interminable. Each hour added to his suffering, and brought with it no relief. During this period of prolonged misery reason often tottered on her throne. Sometimes he was under the influence of the wildest passions. He dragged coffins from their recesses, hurled them upon the ground, striving to break them open and drag forth their loathsome contents. Upon other occasions he would weep bitterly and wildly; and once—once only—did he attempt to pray; but he started from his knees with an echo of infernal laughter, as he deemed, ringing in his ears. Then, again, would he call down imprecations upon himself and his whole line, trampling upon the pile of coffins he had reared; and, lastly, more subdued, would creep to the boards that contained the body of his child, kissing them with a frantic outbreak of affection.

"At length he became sensible of his approaching dissolution. To him the thought of death might well be terrible; but he quailed not before it, or rather seemed, in his latest moments, to resume all his wonted firmness of character. Gathering together his remaining strength, he dragged himself towards the niche wherein his brother, Sir Reginald Rookwood, was deposited, and, placing his hand upon the coffin, solemnly exclaimed, 'My curse—my dying curse—be upon thee evermore!'

"Falling with his face upon the coffin, Alan instantly expired. In this attitude his remains were discovered."

How to repress a smile at the picture conjured up of Lady Rookwood "precipitating herself into the marble coffin!" How not to refrain from laughing at the fantastic description of Alan "piling up coffins in the vault and jumping upon them?"

This is the veriest burlesque of horror.

Cuckfield Park is picturesque and romantic indeed, but it, as might any place, refuses to lend itself to such preposterous romanticism as this. And, because of that tale's appalling vulgarity, we may be thankful that only in its preface does "Rookwood" reveal Cuckfield. The descriptions in those pages of Place and Park would fit a hundred other manors and mansions of this land; and it is well that this should be thus, for to thoroughly identify the place with the novel, would be for ever to taint so fair a retreat.

But the town has a legitimate air of romance, arising from memories of old times, which are not so old but that to go back two generations would land us in their midst.

There is a fine air of the Regency still lingering about Cuckfield and the Brighton Road for they who list to hear of those wild days and the brilliant end of the Coaching Age. I always think upon "Ruddigore" and the Brighton Road together; of frogged frock-coats, blucher-boots, curly wigs, and all the fopperies of Corinthian days; of Prince George and his crew of roysterers, who, like "old Q.," "swore like ten thousand troopers;" and I must confess I like to read of these times, and to dwell upon this old town and these storied ways.

Rowlandson realises the picturesqueness of the Cuckfield of his time for us very finely in that book of his and Wigstead's making. "At Cuckfield," says our Wigstead, "a fair is held in September, resorted to by a great number of pretty rustic females, and by a multitude of happy swains." This view, by Rowlandson, gives an impression of that fair, in which you notice one of those "happy swains" being choused out of his liberty by an artful, ostentatiously friendly recruiting sergeant. Poor recruity! To-morrow the sergeant will not be so robustiously good-humoured with you; his demonstrativeness will shape itself in other moulds.

Down the street, meanwhile, goes a carriage, well horsed, with postboys ready for the ill-conditioned roads that awaited travellers just beyond the town. These roads, to dignify those early tracks by that name, were comparatively little travelled ere the Prince had popularised Brighton, for they had a most unenviable name for miriness, as indeed had all the ways of Kent, Surrey, and Sussex. Horace Walpole, indeed, travelling in Sussex in 1749, visiting Arundel and Cowdray, acquired a too intimate acquaintance with their phenomenal depth of mud and ruts, inasmuch as he—that finicking little gentleman—was compelled to alight precipitantly from his overturned chaise, and to foot it like any common fellow. One quite pities his daintiness in this narration of his sorrows, so picturesquely are they set forth by that accomplished letter-writer from the safe seclusion of Strawberry Hill. He writes to George Montagu, and dates this account the 26th August 1749:[1]—

"Mr. Chute and I are returned from our expedition miraculously well, considering all our distresses. If you love good roads, conveniences, good inns, plenty of postillions and horses, be so kind as never to go into Sussex. We thought ourselves in the northest part of England; the whole county has a Saxon air, and the inhabitants are savage, as if King George the Second was the first monarch of the East Angles. Coaches grow there no more than balm and spices: we were forced to drop our post-chaise, that resembled

[1] "Letters of Horace Walpole." Ed. Peter Cunningham, 1857, vol. ii. pp. 180 181.

nothing so much as harlequin's calash, which was occasionally a chaise or a baker's cart. We journeyed over alpine mountains"—(Horace, you will observe, was, equally with the evening journalist of these happy times, not unaccustomed to exaggerate)—"drenched in clouds, and thought of harlequin again, when he was driving the chariot of the sun through the morning clouds, and was so glad to hear the *aqua vita* man crying a dram. . . . . I have set up my staff, and finished my pilgrimages for this year. Sussex is a great damper of curiosity."

Thus he prattles on, delightfully describing the peculiarities of the several places he visited with this Mr. Chute, "whom," says he, "I have created *Strawberry King-at-Arms.*" One wonders what that "mute, inglorious" Chute thought of it all; whether he was as disgusted with Sussex sloughs and moist unpleasant "mountains" as his garrulous companion.

Then the pedantic Doctor John Burton, who journeyed into Sussex in 1751, had no less unfortunate acquaintance with these miry ways than our dilettante of Strawberry Hill. To any, and these are as the sands of the sea-shore for multitude, who have small Latin and less Greek, this traveller's tale must ever remain a sealed book; for he records in those languages, scornfully entreating those who have not their acquaintance, his views upon ways and means, and men and manners in Sussex. As thus, for example —

"I fell immediately upon all that was most bad,

upon a land desolate and muddy, whether inhabited by men or beasts a stranger could not easily distinguish, and upon roads which were, to explain concisely what is most abominable, Sussexian. No one would imagine them to be intended for the people and the public, but rather the bye-ways of individuals, or, more truly, the tracks of cattle-drivers; for everywhere the usual footmarks of oxen appeared, and we too, who were on horseback, going along zigzag, almost like oxen at plough, advanced as if we were turning back, while we followed out all the twists of the roads. . . . My friend, I will set before you a kind of problem in the manner of Aristotle:—Why comes it that the oxen, the swine, the women, and all other animals (!) are so long-legged in Sussex? Can it be from the difficulty of pulling the feet out of so much mud by the strength of the ankle, so that the muscles become stretched as it were, and the bones lengthened?" This is always the burden of his doleful tale. Presently he arrives at the conclusion that the peasantry "do not concern themselves with literature or philosophy, for they consider the pursuit of such things to be only idling," which is not so very remarkable a trait after all in the character of an agricultural people.

Our author eventually, notwithstanding the terrible roads, arrived at Brighthelmstone, by way of Lewes, "just as day was fading." It was, so he says, "a village on the sea-coast, lying in a valley gradually sloping, and yet deep." . . . "It is not, indeed, contemptible as to size, for it is thronged with people, though the inhabitants are mostly very needy and wretched in their mode of living, occupied in the employment of fishing, robust in their bodies, laborious, and skilled in all nautical crafts, and, as it is said, terrible cheats of the custom-house officers." As who, indeed, is not, allowing the opportunity? This was before the advent of the coaching era, when the old Sussex carriers were performing their laborious journeys. First, the long, broad-wheeled waggons, plying painfully between the more important towns, were introduced, and to them the title of "stage" was first applied. Their rate of progression was snail-like. Persons were in the habit of travelling in company with these conveyances, forming a kind of caravan for mutual protection; safety lay in numbers.

In 1746 there was being continued by the widow of the Lewes carrier a weekly service between Lewes and Southwark: Brighthelmstone was not yet of sufficient importance to warrant an extension of the itinerary to the coast. Neither, at this time, was the conveyance other than a waggon.

Ten years later, in 1756, the *Sussex Weekly Advertiser* of May 12th contained the following advertisement:—

"NOTICE IS HEREBY GIVEN, that the LEWES ONE DAY STAGE COACH or CHAISE sets out from the Talbot Inn, in the Borough, on Saturday next, the 19th instant.

"When likewise the Brighthelmstone Stage begins.

Performed (*if God permit*) by

JAMES BATCHELOR.

There is no means of ascertaining how many hours were occupied on the road between Southwark and Lewes, but it apparently took two days to reach Brighthelmstone, for in May 1757 James Batchelor advertised his "two days' stage-coach."

In the course of time there rose up a rival to this coaching pioneer, a certain "J. Tubb," who, in partnership with "S. Brawne," started in May 1762 a

"LEWES and BRIGHTHELMSTON new FLYING MACHINE (by Uckfield), hung on steel springs, very neat and commodious, to carry FOUR PASSENGERS, sets out from the Golden Cross Inn, Charing Cross, on Monday, the 7th of June, at six o'clock in the morning, and will continue MONDAY'S, WEDNESDAY'S, and FRIDAY'S to the White Hart, at Lewes, and the Castle, at Brighthelmston, where regular Books are kept for entering passenger's and parcels; will return to London TUESDAY'S, THURSDAY'S, and SATURDAY'S. Each Inside Passenger to Lewes, Thirteen Shillings; to Brighthelmston, Sixteen; to be allowed Fourteen Pound Weight for Luggage, all above to pay One Penny per Pound; half the fare to be paid at Booking, the other at entering the machine. Children in Lap and Outside Passengers to pay half price.

Performed by { J. TUBB.
S. BRAWNE."

Batchelor, however, determined to be as good a man as his opponent, if not even a better, for he started in the succeeding week, at identical fares, "a new large FLYING CHARIOT, with a Box and four horses (by Chailey) to carry two Passengers only, except three should desire to go together." The better to crush the presumptuous Tubb, he later

TALBOT INN, BOROUGH, ABOUT 1815.

(From an old Drawing.)

on reduced his fares. Then ensued a diverting, if by no means edifying, war of advertisements; for Tubb, unwilling to be outdone, inserted the following in the *Lewes Journal*, November 1762:—

"THIS IS TO INFORM THE PUBLIC that, on Monday, the 1st of November instant, the LEWES and BRIGHTHELMSTON FLYING MACHINE began going in *one day*, and continues twice a week during the Winter Season to Lewes only; sets out from the White Hart, at Lewes, MONDAYS and THURSDAYS at Six o'clock in the Morning, and returns from the Golden Cross, at Charing Cross, TUESDAYS and SATURDAYS, at the same hour.

Performed by J. TUBB.

"N.B.—Gentlemen, Ladies, and others, are desired to look narrowly into the Meanness and Design of the other Flying Machine to Lewes and Brighthelmston, in lowering his prices, whether 'tis thro' conscience or an endeavour to suppress me. If the former is the case, think how you have been used for a great number of years, when he engrossed the whole to himself, and kept you two days upon the road, going fifty miles. If the latter, and he should be lucky enough to succeed in it, judge whether he wont return to his old prices, when you cannot help yourselves, and use you as formerly. As I have, then, been the remover of this obstacle, which you have all granted by your great encouragement to me hitherto, I, therefore, hope for the continuance of your favours, which will entirely frustrate the deep-laid schemes of my great opponent, and lay a lasting obligation on,—Your very humble Servant,

J. TUBB."

To this replies Batchelor, with an idea of vested interests pertaining to himself:—

"WHEREAS, Mr. TUBB, by an Advertisement in this paper of Monday last, has thought fit to cast some invidious

Reflections upon me, in respect of the lowering my Prices and being two days upon the Road, with other low insinuations, I beg leave to submit the following matters to the calm Consideration of the Gentlemen, Ladies, and other Passengers, of what Degree soever, who have been pleased to favour me, viz. :—

"That our Family first set up the Stage Coach from London to Lewes, and have continued it for a long Series of Years, from Father to Son and other Branches of the same Race, and that even before the Turnpikes on the Lewes Road were erected they drove their Stage, in the Summer Season, in one day, and have continued to do ever since, and now in the Winter Season twice in the week.[1] And it is likewise to be considered that many aged and infirm Persons, who did not chuse to rise early in the Morning, were very desirous to be two Days on the Road for their own Ease and Conveniency, therefore there was no obstacle to be removed. And as to lowering my prices, let every one judge whether, when an old Servant of the Country perceives an Endeavour to suppress and supplant him in his Business, he is not well justified in taking all measures in his Power for his own Security, and even to oppose an unfair Adversary as far as he can. 'Tis, therefore, hoped that the descendants of your very ancient Servants will still meet with your farther Encouragement, and leave the Schemes of our little Opponent to their proper Deserts.—I am, Your old and present most obedient Servant. J. BATCHELOR.

December 13, 1762."

The rivals both kept to the road until Batchelor died in 1766, when his business was sold to Tubb, who took into partnership a Mr. Davis. Together they started, in 1767, the "Lewes and Brighthelm-

[1] "Who deniges of it, Betsy."

stone Flys," each carrying four passengers, one to London and one to Brighton every day.

Tubb and Davis had in 1770 one "machine" and one waggon on this road, fare by "machine" 14s. The machine ran daily to and from London, starting at five o'clock in the morning. The waggon was three days on the road. Another machine was also running, but with the coming of winter these machines performed only three double journeys each.

In 1777 another stage-waggon was started by "Lashmar & Co." It loitered between the "King's Head," Southwark, and the "King's Head," Brighton, starting from London every Tuesday at the unearthly hour of 3 A.M., and reaching its destination on Thursday afternoons.

On May 31, 1784, Tubb and Davis put a "light post-coach" on the road, running to Brighton one day, returning to London the next, in addition to their already running "machine" and "post-coach." This new conveyance presumably made good time, four "insides" only being carried.

Four years later, when Brighton's sun of splendour had begun to rise, there were on the road between London and the sea three "machines," three light post-coaches, two coaches, and two stage-waggons. Tubb now disappears, and his firm becomes Davis & Co. Other proprietors were Ibberson & Co., Bradford & Co., and Mr. Wesson.

About 1796 coach offices were opened in Brighton for the sole despatch of coaching business, the time having passed for the old custom of starting from inns. Now, too, were different tales to tell of these roads, after the Pavilion had been set in course of building. Royalty and the Court could not endure to travel upon such evil tracks as had hitherto been the lot of travellers to Brighthelmstone. Presently, instead of a dearth of roads and a plethora of ruts, there became a choice of good highways and a plenty of travellers upon them.

TOWN AND COUNTRY, 1784.

Numerous coaches ran to meet the demands of the travelling public, and these continually increased in number and improved in speed. About this time first appear the names of Henwood, Crossweller, Cuddington, Pockney, & Harding, whose office was at 44 East Street; and another firm, Boulton, Tilt, Hicks, Baulcomb & Co., at 1 North Street. Now, in addition to the old service, ran a "night post-coach" on alternate nights, starting at 10 P.M. in the season. One then went to or from London generally in about eleven hours,[1] if all went well. If you could only afford a ride in the stage-waggon, why then you were carried the

[1] Coaches were timed at "about" nine hours, an unpleasant equivoce.

distance by the accelerated (!) waggons of this time in two days and one night.

In 1802 a company, the Royal Brighton Four Horse Coach Company, was started, and, as competitors with the older firms, seems to have aroused much jealousy and slander, if we may believe the following contemporary advertisement:—

"THE ROYAL BRIGHTON Four Horse Coach Company beg leave to return their sincere thanks to their Friends and the Public in general for the very liberal support they have experienced since the starting of their Coaches, and assure them it will always be their greatest study to have their Coaches safe, with good Horses and sober careful Coachmen.

"They likewise wish to rectify a report in circulation of their Coach having been overturned on Monday last, by which a gentleman's leg was broken, &c., no such thing having ever happened to either of their Coaches. The Fact is it was one of the BLUE COACHES instead of the Royal New Coach.

"*** As several mistakes have happened, of their friends being BOOKED at other Coach offices, they are requested to book themselves at the ROYAL NEW COACH OFFICE, CATHERINE'S HEAD, 47 East Street."

In an advertisement offering for sale a portion of the coaching business at No. 1 North Street, it was stated that the annual returns of this firm were more than £12,000 per annum, yielding from Christmas 1794 to Christmas 1808 seven and a half per cent. on the capital invested, besides purchasing the interest of four of the partners in the concern. In this last year two new businesses were started, those of Waldegrave & Co., and Pattenden & Co. Fares now ruled high—23s. inside; 13s. outside.

In 1809 Crossweller & Co. commenced to run their "morning and night" coaches, and "Miller" Bradford formed his company, of which mention has been made in earlier pages.[1] In the following year the "Royal Night Mail Coaches" were started by arrangement with the Postmaster-General. The speed, although greatly improved, was not yet so very great, eight hours being occupied on the way, although these coaches went by what was then the new cut *viâ* Croydon. It was in this year, on June 25, that an accident befell Waldegrave's "Accommodation" coach on its up journey. Near Brixton Causeway its hind wheels collapsed, owing to the heavy weight of the loaded vehicle. By one of those strange chances when truth appears stranger than fiction, there chanced to be a farmer's waggon passing the coach at the instant of its overturning. Into it were shot the "outsides," fortunate in this comparatively easy fall. Still, shocks and bruises were not few, and one gentleman had his thigh broken.

By June 1811 traffic had so grown that there were then no fewer than twenty-eight coaches running between Brighton and London. On February 5th in the following year occurred the only great road robbery known on this road. This was the theft from the "Blue" coach of a package of bank-notes representing a sum of between three and four thousand pounds sterling. Crosswellers were proprietors of

[1] Page 19.

the coach, and from them Messrs. Brown, Lashmar, & West, of the Brighton Union Bank, hired a box beneath the seat for the conveyance of remittances to and from London. On this day the Bank's London correspondents placed these notes in the box for transmission to Brighton, but on arrival the box was found to have been broken open and the notes all stolen. It would seem that a carefully planned conspiracy had been entered into by several persons, who must have had a thorough knowledge of the means by which the Union Bank sent and received money to and from the metropolis. On this morning six persons were booked for inside places. Of this number two only made an appearance—a gentleman and a lady. Two gentlemen were picked up as the coach proceeded. The lady was taken suddenly ill when Sutton was reached, and she and her husband were left at the inn there. When the coach arrived at Reigate the two remaining passengers went to inquire for a friend. Returning shortly, they told the coachman that the friend whom they had supposed to be at Brighton had returned to town, therefore it was of no use proceeding further.

Thus the coachman and guard had the remainder of the journey to themselves, while the cash-box, as was discovered at the journey's end, was minus its cash. A reward of £300 was immediately offered for information that would lead to recovery of the notes. This was subsequently altered to an offer of 100 guineas for information of the offender, in addition to £300 upon recovery of the total amount, or "ten per cent. upon the amount of so much thereof as shall be recovered." The reward-money was never paid, neither were the thieves ever discovered.

Mr. Whitchurch started in 1813 a coach which ran from London to Brighton, and returned the same day, time each way, six hours; calling up a rival, the "Eclipse," which performed the journey in the same time. Competition was now very severe, fares being reduced to, inside ten shillings, outside five shillings. Indeed, in 1816, a number of Jews started a coach which was to run from London to Brighton in six hours, or, failing to keep time, was to forfeit all fares. After it had run for three months, an information was laid against it for furious driving, when speed was reduced.

The mails, meanwhile, maintained a crawling pace of a little over six miles an hour, a sort of dignified, no-hurry, governmental progression.

Racing now became so common between stage-coaches, that proprietors were obliged to issue notices, to reassure the timid, that rival racing would not be allowed to continue. But accidents *would* happen. The "Coburg" was upset at Cuckfield in August 1819. Six of the passengers were so much injured that they could proceed no farther, and one of them died on the following day. The "Coburg" was one of the old-fashioned stage-coaches, heavy, clumsy, and slow, carrying six passengers inside and twelve outside. This type gave way to coaches of lighter build about 1823. "Viator Junior," writing in the *Sporting*

Magazine of 1828, says, "Great as the improvement made in modern travelling has everywhere been, it has on no road been more conspicuous than on that between Brighton and the metropolis. Twenty years ago, the quickest coaches never performed the journey in less than nine and a half or ten hours; and although still a young man, I can perfectly remember my father relating as an exploit, that he had posted, on a most particular and express occasion, to his own door, four miles short of London, in eight hours. It is needless to tell your readers that every coach now runs from yard to yard in seven, and some of them, the quickest, in less than six hours."

Two years before those words were written, in 1826, there ran, according to Cary, that coaching Cocker, seventeen coaches, starting for Brighton from London every morning, afternoon, or evening. They had all of them the most high-sounding of names, calculated to impress the mind either with a sense of swiftness, or to awe the understanding with visions of aristocratic and court-like grandeur. As for the times they individually made, and for the inns from which they started, you who are insatiable of dry bones of fact may go to the Library of the British Museum and find your Cary (without an "e") and do your gnawing of them. That they started at all manner of hours, even the most uncanny, you must rest assured; and that they took off from the (to ourselves) most impossible and romantic-sounding of inns, may be granted, when such examples as the strangely incongruous "George and Blue Boar," the Herrick-like "Blossoms" Inn, and the idyllic-seeming "Flower-pot" are mentioned.

They were, those seventeen coaches, the "Royal Mail," the "Coronet," "Magnet," "Comet," "Royal Sussex," "Sovereign," "Alert," "Dart," "Union," "Regent," "Times," "Duke of York," "Royal George," "True Blue," "Patriot," "Post," and the "Summer Coach," so called, and they started from the City and Holborn mostly, calling at West End booking-offices on their several ways. Most of the old inns from which they set out are pulled down, and the memory of them has faded.

The "Golden Cross" at Charing Cross, from whose doors started the "Comet" and the "Regent" in this year of grace 1826, and at which the "Times" called on its way from Holborn; the "White Horse," Fetter Lane, whence the "Duke of York" bowled away: these two old inns retain something, though little, of their old-time look; but the only one which still wears very much the same expression as when the "Alert," the "Union," and the "Times" drew up daily at its old-fashioned galleried courtyard is the Old Bell and Crown Inn, Holborn. Were Viator to return to-morrow, he would find little change in the inn's appearance. Around him would be, to his senses, an astonishing whirl and noise of traffic, for all the wood-paving that has superseded macadam, which itself displaced the road-paving he knew. Many strange and horrid portents he would note, and Holborn would be to him as an unknown street in a strange town, saving only the "Old Bell and

Crown" and a few other buildings close by, which have escaped the Scytheman thus far.

Than 1826 the informative Cary goes no further, and his "Itinerary," excellent though it be, and invaluable to he who would know aught of the coaches that plied in the years when it was published, gives no particulars of the many "butterfly" coaches and amateur drags that cut in upon the regular coaches during the rush and scour of the season.

In 1821 it was computed that over forty coaches ran to and from London daily; in September 1822 there were thirty-nine. In 1828 it was calculated that the sixteen permanent coaches then running, summer and winter, received between them a sum of £60,000 per annum, and the total sum expended in fares upon coaching on this road was taken as amounting to £100,000 per annum. That leaves the very respectable amount of £40,000 for the season's takings of the "butterflies."

An accident happened to the "Alert" on 9th October 1829, when the coach was taking up passengers at Brighton. The horses ran away, and dashed the coach and themselves into an area sixteen feet deep. The coach was battered almost to pieces, and one lady was seriously injured. The horses escaped unhurt. In 1832, August 25, the Brighton mail was upset near Reigate, the coachman being killed.

By 1839 the coaching business had in Brighton become concentrated in Castle Square, six of the seven principal offices being situated there. Five London coaches ran from the Blue Office (Strevens

& Co.), five from the Red Office (Mr. Goodman's), four from the "Spread Eagle" (Chaplin & Crunden's), three from the Age (T. W. Capps & Co.), two from Hine's, East Street; two from Snow's (Capps & Chaplin), and two from the "Globe" (Mr. Vaughan's).

To state the number of visitors to Brighton on a certain day will give an idea of how well this road was used during the decade that preceded the coming of steam. On Friday, 25th October 1833, upwards of 480 persons travelled to Brighton by stage-coach. A comparison of this number with the hordes of visitors cast forth from the Brighton Railway Station to-day would render insignificant indeed that little crowd of 1833; but in those times, when the itch of excursionising was not so acute as now, that day's return was remarkable; it was a day that fully justified the note made of it. Then, too, those few hundreds benefited the town more certainly than perhaps their number multiplied by ten does now. For, mark you, the Brighton visitor of sixty years ago, once set down in Castle Square, had to remain the night at least at Brighton; there was no returning to London the same day for him. And so the Brighton folks had their wicked will of him for a while, and made something out of him; while in these times the greater proportion of a day's excursionists find themselves either at home in London already when evening hours are striking from Westminster Ben, or else waiting with what patience they may the collecting of tickets at the bleak and dismal penitentiary platforms of Grosvenor Road

THE BRIGHTON DAY MAILS CROSSING HOOKWOOD COMMON, 1838.

(From an Engraving after J. Shayer.)

Station; and, after all, Brighton is little or nothing advantaged by their visit.

But though the tripper of the coaching era found it impracticable to have his morning in London, his day upon the King's Road, and his evening in town again, yet the pace at which the coaches went in the '30's was by no means despicable. Mail-coaches going at ten miles an hour, a better rate of progression than even "Viator Junior" could speak of, were now become slow and altogether behind the age.

In 1843 the Marquis of Worcester, together with a Mr. Alexander, put three coaches on the road, an up and down "Quicksilver" and a single coach, the "Wonder." The "Quicksilver," named probably in allusion to its swiftness (it was timed for four hours and three-quarters), ran to and from what was then a favourite stopping-place, the "Elephant and Castle." But on July 15th of the same year an accident, by which several persons were very seriously injured, happened to the up "Quicksilver" when starting from Brighton. Snow, who was driving, could not hold the team in, and they bolted away, and brought up violently against the railings by the New Steyne. Broken arms, fractured arms and ribs, and contusions were plenty. The "Quicksilver," chameleon-like, changed colour after this mishap; was repainted and renamed, and reappeared as the "Criterion:" the old name carried with it too great a spice of danger for the timorous.

On 4th February 1834 the "Criterion," driven by Charles Harbour, outstripping the old performances of the "Vivid," and beating the previous wonderfully quick journey of the "Red Rover," carried down King William's Speech on the opening of Parliament in 3 hours and 40 minutes, a coach record that has not yet been surpassed, nor quite equalled, on this road, not even by Selby on his great drive of 13th July 1888, his times being out and in respectively. 3 hours 56 minutes, and 3 hours 54 minutes. Then again, on another road, on May-Day 1830, the "Independent Tally-ho," running from London to Birmingham, covered those 109 miles in 7 hours 39 minutes, a better record than Selby's London to Brighton and back drive by 11 minutes, with an additional mile to the course. Another coach, the "Original Tally-ho," did the same distance in 7 hours 50 minutes. The "Criterion" fared ill under its new name; it gained an unenviable notoriety on 7th June 1834; being overturned in a collision with a drag in the Borough. Many of the passengers were injured; Sir William Cosway, who was climbing over the roof when the collision occurred, was killed.

In 1839, the coaching era, full-blown even to decay, began to pewk and wither before the coming of steam, long heralded and now but too sure. The tale of coaches now decreased to twenty-three; fares, which had fallen in the cut-throat competition of coach proprietors with their fellows in previous years to 10s. inside, 5s. outside for the single journey, now rose to 21s. and 12s. Every man that horsed a coach, seeing that now was the shearing time for the public, ere the now building railway was opened,

strove to make as much as possible ere he closed his yards, sold his stock and coach, and took himself off the road.

On 21st September 1841 the railway was opened from London to Brighton, and with that event the coaching era on this road virtually died. Professional coach proprietors, who wished to retain what gains they had, were well advised to shun all competition with steam; others had been wise to cut their losses, for the Road was a thing of the past: the Rail had superseded it.

In the prime era of coaching on this road a writer who adopted the pseudonym of "Viator Junior," wrote two papers upon its coaches and coachmen.

They are so admirable that merely to have made quotations from them would have been to spoil their peculiar flavour. Captain Malet has reprinted them in his "Annals of the Road;" but as they deal especially with the Brighton Road, no apology seems necessary for their reproduction here.

They appeared originally in the *Sporting Magazine*.

"THE BRIGHTON ROAD.

I.

"*October* 1828.

"Great as the improvement in modern travelling has everywhere been, it has on no road been more conspicuous than on that between Brighton and the metropolis. Twenty years ago the quickest coaches never performed the journey in less than nine hours and a half or ten hours; and although still a young man, I can perfectly remember my father's relating as an exploit that he had posted on a most particular and express occasion to his own door, four miles short of London, in eight hours! It is needless to tell your readers that *every* coach now runs *yard* to *yard* in *seven*, and some of them, the quickest, in less than *six* hours. It is not at all unusual to see Mr. Snow's *Dart* at the 'Elephant and Castle' at a quarter-past eleven, having left Brighton at six; and several others—Goodman's coaches and the *Item*, for instance—keep the same time.

"Within my recollection the Brighton Road was always a good one; but from the innumerable improvements made on it during the last ten or twelve years, it is now as close to perfection, and very nearly as much shortened, as it ever can be. On neither of the new lines of road is there occasion more than twice or thrice for the drag-chain, even with the most stiff-necked team; and the old road, with the exception of Reigate and Clayton Hills (which are certainly puzzles for a fresh-catched one to take a load either up or down), is equally free from difficulty or danger; and both are capitally hard and good for wheels at all seasons of the year!

"This excellence of the roads, however, has produced one defect—it has nearly annihilated the breed of coachmen between Brighton and London. Out of a list of forty-five that I have now before me, who are regularly at work, there are not more than seven or eight who are worth looking at as real artists—*workmen who can hit 'em and hold 'em*—and I could name more than one or two of the lot who are, even on such a road as this, unfit to be trusted with the lives of their passengers, and totally incompetent to take along a heavy load in safety at the pace at which their coaches are timed. This very day I saw one of 'the awkward squad' keep his coach on her legs by pure accident, in bringing her with a heavy load round the corner by the King's Stables; and as his attitude was rather good, I'll endeavour to describe it. His bench was very low, and he himself is rather a tall man; his legs, tucked under him as far as possible, were as wide apart as if he was across one of his wheelers; both hands had hold of his reins, which, though perfectly slack, were all but within his teeth: his whip was stuck beside him (in general, however, it is hanging down between his wheel-horses about the middle of the foot-board); and, to complete the picture, his mouth was gaping wide open, like Curran's Irishman endeavouring to catch the English accent. *South of York* I have not often seen this man's fellow; but surely Providence must keep a most especial guard over him, for I understand he has worked for some years on the same coach without an accident; and, judging from appearances, it is a daily miracle that he gets to his journey's end.

"Not long ago, too, I had the fortune of witnessing, as a passenger, one or two hair-breadth escapes on one of the professed flash afternoon-coaches. First or last, I never saw a fellow with more conceit and less knowledge of the art than our self-styled coachman; and I could not help thinking it a great pity to have deprived the shop-board of his services to expose him on the bench. We were very near having a *case* with our first team out of Brighton. Both his wheel-horses were bad holders, and the leaders (both of them thoroughbred) were impatient and fidgety at the rattling of the bars, and could not be kept, at least my friend could not keep them, out of a canter. He put his chain on down the hill by New Timber, and all was right enough; but being too busy with his cigar (the march of intellect!!!), he let his team get well on the crown of the hill, *just above his change*, before he attempted to pull up: the consequence was, they could not be stopped, and away we went. I have no hesitation in saying, with a top-heavy load, or with anything like a ditch at hand, nothing could have saved us from being floored; for, from his awkward pulling and hauling at them (he had his reins clubbed into the bargain), instead of keeping his coach steady in the middle of the road, we were alternately in the watercourse on each side, and we pulled up at last only in consequence of the horses getting to their own stable door. In his next team a little fanning was necessary; and *Dominie Sampson* himself could not have made a more diabolical attempt at hitting a near leader. I can scarcely, however, expect to be believed when I tell you that he actually hit his off-side passenger on the roof behind him every time he endeavoured to hit his off-side wheel-horse. Such, nevertheless, was the fact. But to cut a long story short, we got to London safe and sound in rather more than six hours, having been in jeopardy of our lives the whole time.

"Now I would not have you imagine, Mr. Editor, that I am more nervous on a coach-box than my neighbours: on the contrary, having been much attached to, and worked a great deal on, the road ever since I was the height of a whip, I have no reason to be so; but I must confess that with such 'impostors' it is rather nervous work, and I think no coachmaster is warranted in committing the lives of his customers, the public, to such incompetent hands. I shall keep my eye on one or two of these 'flying Brightons,' and if there is not an alteration, and an improvement too, before long, I will show up the delinquents, both master and servant, by name.

"There is a very old and good servant of the public still at work on this road, whose long and praiseworthy career deserves to be recorded; his name is Hine, and though never a first-rate performer, has been, as far back as I can remember, from his constant sobriety, civility, and steadiness, the chief favourite (especially with families) on the old Reigate and Clayton road. When I first knew him, fully twenty years ago, he had been for a great length of time on Orton and Bradford's coach, which gradually declined after he left it, out of the Bull Yard, Holborn; and it is only within the last fourteen years that he has turned 'rioter'[1] on the coach which he now drives, the *Alert*, and a capital coach

[1] Proprietor.

it is. I should be happy to take an even bet that he has carried more families for the last ten years than any other three coachmen out of Brighton; and I am delighted to see the old man still in good health, and feathering his nest so comfortably.

"Goodman's *Times* and *Regent* are among the best-horsed coaches going, and, from what I can see, have their full share of business. Sam, however, himself, though a tolerable coachman, is not to be named in the same day with Mr. Snow; but it must be allowed that few can equal, and none, not even Peer himself or Bill Williams, can excel this great artist. It is quite a treat to compare his perfect ease and elegant attitude on his box in turning out of the 'Spread Eagle' yard in Gracechurch Street, with the uncouth gestures and awkward catchings and clawings of some of his brethren—his own man, Ned Russell, for instance. Ned, however, once started over London Bridge, is not worse than some of his neighbours. Gray, on the *Regent*, is a very fair, steady coachman. I remember him fourteen or fifteen years ago on a very seedy concern called the *Princess of Wales*, through Horsham; and having had my eye a good deal on him since that period, I have no hesitation in pronouncing him a very efficient coachman, and a most excellent servant in every respect. Mosely, too, who used to be against him on the same road on the *Duke of Norfolk*, and is now at work on Goodman's mid-day *Times*, is nothing less than a very capital performer.

"Of Mr. Stevenson, as I have never seen enough of him at work to enable me to judge, I shall of course say nothing; but he has the reputation of being a good coachman, and I wish him success. He is warmly patronised by the public, which, I am sorry to say, has had the effect of creating a good deal of illiberality and jealousy against him with some of the other coachmen; and I took the liberty of giving one of them with whom I was travelling the other day a good jobation for his selfishness and impertinence.

"As I hold all *safety patents* about coaches exceedingly cheap, I have not given myself the trouble of examining 'Cook's Patent Life Preserver,' which is fitted to Mr. Gray's 'Bolt-in-Tun' coach, the *Patriot;* but I will relate a rather good anecdote of an incident of which I was a witness a few days ago. Just as Pickett was starting with his 'Union' coach out of Holborn, up comes a fussy old citizen, puffing and blowing like a grampus: 'Pray, coachman, is this here the Patriotic Life Preserver Safety-coach?' 'Yes, sir,' says Pickett, not hearing above one-half of his passenger's question; 'room behind, sir; jump up, if you please; very late this morning.' 'Why, where's the machinery?' cries the old one. 'There, sir,' replied a passenger (a young Cantab, I suspect), pointing to a heavy trunk of mine that was swung beneath; 'in that box, sir, that's where the machinery works.' 'Ah!' quoth the old man, climbing up quite satisfied, 'wonderful inventions now-a-days, sir; we shall all get safe to Brighton; no chance of an accident by this coach.'

"Doubtless it would have been no very difficult task to have persuaded this old fool that we were going by steam; for the day was wet, and the cigars were smoking most merrily in front all the road down.

"Few of your readers, I dare say, have an idea of the money that is annually dropped on this favourite road. There are at this moment (in the height of the season) twenty-four coaches (including the mail) out of Brighton, with a corresponding number out of London, every day. Now, at a moderate computation, *sixteen* of these at least are kept on through the winter; and they must each of them earn the whole year through ten pounds daily to pay anything like their expenses up and down. These sixteen permanent coaches alone, therefore, must receive nearly sixty thousand pounds a year, *merely to keep them going*; and the eight *butterflies*, as I have heard them called, or summer coaches for six months, must earn nearly fifteen thousand pounds more! Looking, however, at the lowness of my calculation as to expense, and at the excellent way-bills that most of them carry both summer and winter, I am quite satisfied that, including gratuities to coachmen, &c., not a farthing less than *one hundred thousand pounds per annum* is spent by the public between Brighton and London; and for the sake of the wheels, for which I have always been a staunch advocate, I wish it were twice as much.

"Taking up a newspaper a few days ago, I was very sorry to observe the death of Mr. Horne, the largest proprietor by far in England, and one of the best that ever put a horse to public conveyance.

The public has sustained a great loss by his decease, for he conducted the whole of his immense concern in a most creditable and spirited manner; and his coaches, taken altogether, were better horsed than those in any other yard in London—my old ally, Mrs. Nelson's, being always excepted. I have not heard what arrangements are likely to take place; but I should think it will be difficult to find any *one customer* with capital sufficient to take the whole of his various establishments, amounting as they do almost to a monopoly of the best roads out of London.

"It is now high time, I think, Mr. Editor, to bring these desultory remarks to a conclusion. A few weeks more, and what has with me been always first and first—FOX-HUNTING—will commence. I am told that the packs in this neighbourhood are well worth seeing, and that since NIMROD's visit there has been a great improvement in the Brighton harriers. I saw them in kennel about three years and a half ago, and must confess that I did not then think much of their appearance. However, *nous verrons;* and if I can pick up anything in the meantime worth sending, you shall hear again from

"VIATOR, JUN.

"*P.S.*—On looking over what I have written, I find that I have omitted noticing what I hear is a very steady, quiet, good coach—namely, George Sheward's *Magnet*. I have not seen much of it personally, except *into London;* but I must do Sheward the justice to say that, on that ground at least, he is most magnificently horsed, and I like the appearance of his coach altogether very much. Long, therefore, may the *Magnet* continue to *attract!*"

II.

"*November* 1828.

"In my last letter to you, I pulled up, I think, on George Sheward's *Magnet;* and the time allowed for washing out our mouths being now expired, I proceed once more to take hold of my whip and reins, and 'wag another yard or two' on the same coach, on the 'Brighton Road.' I am sorry, however, to say that my 'bill' is but a short one; and still more so to observe that for some time past it has been but too often the case; and that this very quick and capitally horsed coach has fallen off for the last two months most lamentably and unaccountably. Unaccountable it certainly appears, for no drag at the same hour is turned out better, if so well: the time is accurately kept; the fares are the same as all its neighbours; the coach itself affords the same accommodation for passengers. Yet, although all this, and more, is done for the satisfaction of the public, it carries decidedly the worst loads, by far, of anything out of Brighton or London, at ten o'clock. Were I, however, asked to find out the loose screw, I should say in the first place, that, coming out of private stables in London, instead of a regular public yard, such as the 'Cross,' 'Spread Eagle,' 'Bolt-in-Tun,' &c. &c., militates very greatly against every coach that adopts the plan, as there cannot be half the power either to form or to hold 'a connexion' well together; and chance custom, let the friends of the proprietor or coachman be ever so numerous, *genteel*, or zealous, will go but a short way towards paying the expenses for any great length of time. Secondly, the perpetual changing and turning back of the coachmen on the road must have annoyed the passengers not a little; and it has, moreover, been the means of Sheward's losing one of the very best waggoners out of Brighton—young Cook—who was at last so disgusted at being thus shifted and bandied about 'between Hell and Hackney,' that he cut the concern, and has taken, I have reason to believe, by no means a small number of the *Magnet's* old friends to the *Regulator*, on which he is now at work.

"Sheward has played his cards very ill in throwing this trump out of his hand, for he is not only a first-rate coachman, but one of the pleasantest fellows to travel with one can easily meet; and therefore a most dangerous customer on a cheap opposition, that starts half-an-hour earlier, and runs to the same end of 'the Village.' Neither am I by any means singular in the opinion that, had Sheward stuck to this one coach, without having anything to do with *The Age*, it would have been better both for him and it; for, in point of fact, the connexion is not large enough for the support of both; and as the one robs the other, they neither of them load as they should do, and the old proverb, 'between two stools' is most unhappily, but truly, exemplified. Splendidly, indeed, as his side of the last-mentioned flash concern is worked all through, and Corinthian as is the *tout ensemble* of the turnout, I cannot conceive that it does more than average its expenses, if so much; and on many journeys within the last month, I know that the up-coaches have been fed very plentifully from *The New Dart.* Sheward knows all this as well as I can tell him, and I hope he will take in good part what I have said, for he may be assured he has my best wishes, and that I would gladly see his coaches doing as well as he himself could desire. I will conclude by giving him 'one hint more.' If his down *Magnet* loads light, it is a bad job certainly; but let him give his stock the benefit of 'the chance,' and not wear them out in galloping and hunting them against a cocktail pair-horse concern, that there can be neither honour nor profit in beating.

"The mention of *The Age* induces me naturally to speak of Mr. Stevenson. Since I last addressed you, I have had the pleasure of seeing this gentleman at work, and have seldom, if ever, been more gratified. I am not aware, to quote a vulgar saying, if he was 'born with a silver spoon in his mouth,' but I certainly think he must have been brought into the world with a whip and reins in his hand, for in point of ease and elegance of execution as a light coachman, he beats nineteen out of twenty of the regular working dragsmen into fits, and, as an amateur, is only to be approached by two or three of the chosen few, whose names will live for ever in the annals of the B.D.C.—Sir Henry

THE "AGE," 1828, STARTING FROM CASTLE SQUARE, BRIGHTON

Peyton and Mr. Walker, for instance. What he may be with bad and heavy cattle, I will not pretend to say; but, judging from the manner in which his teams are put together (and he has some awkward customers amongst them), I think nothing could come much amiss to him. I sincerely hope his side of *The Age* is doing well; and that every one of the crowd assembled in Castle Square three times a week to see him start, may prove a passenger and a friend to him all through the winter.

"In giving you the anecdote about *The Patriot* to which I was a witness on Pickett's *Union*, in my last communication, I omitted to notice his partner, Egerton, who drives the other side of this (now) excellent coach. In point of manners, deportment, and conversation he ranks far above almost all dragsmen with whom I have at any time travelled; and, if he pursues the same obliging and unassuming mode of conducting himself (of which there is little doubt), there is no fear that he will be as popular on the road and as much patronised by the public as old Hine himself; and this, let me tell him, is not to be attained by every one. He was for some time at work out of the 'Spread Eagle Yard,' on Chaplin and Snow's Worthing *Sovereign*, and left, when he quitted that coach, a good name behind him. No man, indeed, is more highly spoken of amongst his associates; and it was only the other day that William Snow was regretting in my presence that he was not working for *their* party, instead of being where he now is, and where I hope and think he is doing as well as his best friends could wish.

"As I have mentioned William Snow's name, it may be as well to 'lug in' my opinion of him, as old John Lawrence would say, as a dragsman. Having heard a great deal of him as an artist, I took an opportunity of travelling with him a few days ago on the extra *Dart;* but, I am sorry to say, I was much disappointed in his performance, which, considering his reputation as a coachman, I thought extremely *mediocre;* and he certainly has no pretensions to the character of a first-rate workman. As to a comparison with his brother Bob (which I had understood he had no occasion to shrink from), there is more coachmanship and knowledge of the art in Robert's little finger than in all William's body put together; and, although a very civil and cheerful fellow to travel with, I cannot assign him even an 'Exeter class' in the 'honours' of dragsmanship, but must rank him only amongst the οἱ πολλοὶ, or 'vulgar herd,' as we used to say at Oxford. Before I dismiss the name of Snow, let me express my very great pleasure at the way in which the whole of Bob's coaches—the *Dart, Comet,* and *Sovereign*—have been loading this season; and if he takes my advice, he will not kick down any part of what he has earned with *them,* by continuing his horses on that suicidal night-opposition, *The Evening Star.* Both he and Sam Goodman may rely on it that old Crossweller does not care one button for the harm it can do the *Mail;* and, if they keep it on through the winter, their monthly accounts will speak pretty plainly for themselves as to the harm it will do their own summer earnings. It will be sure, moreover, to make the *Item* a fixture on the road (for, as they well know, this beautifully-horsed coach is in the hands of a terribly stiff-necked, obstinate party when once offended); and, in winter time, when *the City swells are behind their counters* and *minding the shop*, this will be by no means a pointless thorn in the side of *The Dart* and *New Times*. There is a coachman, by the way, at work on *The Star* who deserves a better place; and I hope before long that Bill Penny may be seen once more by daylight; for where you find one better, you will travel with twenty inferior performers.

"And here I may observe, that, in spite of all that Nimrod brings forward to justify his predilection for night-work, I cannot persuade myself to view it in the same favourable colours, or to consider the life of a night-coachman an enviable one for a constancy. It is all very pleasant for a gentleman on a fine night, either summer or winter, to work forty or fifty miles on a journey of business or amusement (and I have found as much delight in doing so as any man, and have often abandoned my claret for the coach-box, as poor Skinner on the Glasgow Mail, from Boroughbridge to Doncaster, if alive, and his partner, could testify). But when we take into account the perpetual privation of natural repose (for no man, as the Irishman says, can get a good night's rest by day), and the ravages on the constitution produced by it and incessant exposure to the worst vicissitudes of weather at the worst periods—the damps and fogs, and 'peltings of the storm,' which these poor fellows have constantly to endure in darkness, and sometimes almost in solitude, with no one but the guard and 'the mad-woman' about the coach; to say nothing of the teams—blind ones, bow-kickers, and cripples of every description unfit to show by day—that not a few of them have to drive; and the rotten reins and worn-out harness that some proprietors, to their eternal shame, persist in keeping at work in the dark; when we consider all this, I repeat, we shall not find much to envy in the situation of a night-coachman. There is 'balm in Gilead,' however, as 'Nicol Jarvie' observes; and where the guard and coachman have pulled well together, I have seen in my time an infinity of fun and lark upon the road between supper and breakfast. One night in particular on the Dover mail—but this, and another anecdote or two of night-work I must reserve for a future opportunity, and get back meantime to the neighbourhood of the Steyne.

"I have already spoken of *The Regulator*—not so, however, of the office from which it starts. By some of the dragsmen about Brighton it is called (and not inappropriately) 'The Beehive'—being the place that gives birth to the swarm of *cheap concerns*, the whole of which book at it; and an elegant lot, take them altogether, they certainly are. As I do not profess to be the historian of 'pair-horse coaches,' I shall waste but few words on *The Royal Exchange* and *Hero*, observing only that one of them (the first, I believe) was, and, for aught I know to the contary, still is, horsed out of Brighton by a dealer of the name of Hayler or Hamer—no bad judge, it would appear, of the value of the old saying, 'Short accounts make long friends;' for, every night after the coach comes in, he *draws the blunt*, or no 'flesh' is forthcoming the next morning. To the Adonis of *The Beehive*, Old Tommy (on Mr. Stevenson's late coach, *The Coronet*), in his white castor, it would take a far abler pen than mine to do justice. I shall make my bow to him, therefore, with the remark, that I believe him to be a very excellent judge of *stock* (would he not be therefore better placed on *The Exchange?*), and that if his passengers are at any time displeased with him, they must be guilty of the most gross ingratitude in the world; for he shows them, beyond a doubt, *the most extraordinary countenance of any man on the road.* Mr. Genn's old servant, Charles Newman, drives, and, I believe, horses part of, the other side of this concern; but were it not to notice his coach—I had almost written van—I should pass him over *sub silentio*, as it gives me no pleasure to find fault, and it is out of my power to compliment him on his performance as a dragsman; which, considering the number of years he has been at it, is but a slovenly piece of business, and, meet him whenever you will, his horses are never in hand as they should be. Let me, however, give him his due. I have ridden with him more than once (not on his present coach), and always found him exceedingly civil, obliging, and good-tempered; and I believe his career has been singularly fortunate so far as regards the chapter of accidents. The drag he is just now at work upon—his own fancy, I am given to understand—is certainly a most extraordinary one, considering the 'march of intellect' on the road, as elsewhere: being built—though on some fantastic, new-fangled construction, on the old principle of six *in* and twelve *out*—very *roomy*, high and lofty from the ground, and altogether as heavy in appearance and reality as the old waggons of fifty years back. If I mistake not, they advertise it to run in 'six hours;' but in my opinion the cattle have yet to be foaled that will keep this time with it three journeys together.

"If in anything that I have remarked I seem to under-rate the merits of *The Beehive* and its economists, I beg pardon very sincerely for so doing; but, having an unhappy prejudice against cheap articles in general, of all cheap things in this world (except cheap wine), I hold cheap coaches in the greatest and most particular abomination; and whenever I see the words, 'Cheap Travelling' posted up at the door of an office, I always feel disposed involuntarily to add, 'and nasty,' to the advertisement.

"I recognised the other day a well-known face on *The Royal Clarence* through Horsham and Kingston, and found on inquiry that it belonged to my old acquaintance Christopher, of Oxford, one of the largest country proprietors going, and the sharpest thorn that old Costar ever had or will have in his side. Will Mr. Goodman forgive me if I tell him that I looked twice before I would believe the evidence of my eyes, that it bore the name of the proprietor of *The Regent* and *New Times*.' Holmes and his son are both at work on this coach; but I certainly cannot compliment them on the appearance of their cattle—into Brighton at least; and if Mr. Goodman remembers some observations he once made at a coach-dinner at Huntingdon about one of the 'Stamfords,' on which he and I were travelling, he will find them apply pretty closely to this name-child of the late Lord High Admiral. I should observe that Holmes himself takes *The Clarence* from Horsham to Kingston; and having lately had an opportunity of comparing his stock with that of his partner into Brighton, I was not a little struck with the difference of condition; but twelve miles an hour over Mr. Goodman's ground, and *four and a half over his own*, will account for anything!

"I find I must once more retrace my steps to the office, No. 52 East Street, having hitherto omitted all notice of poor old Hine's partner, a very deserving young man of the name of Bristow, who, from being a porter in the establishment, has raised himself within the last few years to the situation of coach-man and proprietor of *The Alert.* He and the evergreen old veteran horse it between them up to Reigate, from which Mr. Grace, of Sutton, I believe, takes it to the village of that name, and thence Mr. Horne into the 'Old Bell' yard, Holborn. I cannot speak very intimately of Bristow's performance, but I believe him to be a fair coachman, and he appears uncommonly strong and powerful on his box.

"Of the artists of 'The Blue Office' it is not, of course, my intention to speak, having travelled with but one of them, who is now at work, *and of him I have already recorded my opinion.* I may say, however, that Mr. Crossweller's coaches in general are capitally horsed; he has, indeed, the reputation of doing his work as well as any man out of Brighton; and I think it must be a fastidious eye that could find much fault with the specimens of his stock that I have seen in the *Item, Rocket,*

&c., &c. He bears, moreover, amongst his servants a most excellent character, and, I have good reason to believe, is a very worthy man, as well as one of the best horsemasters in Christendom.

"I cannot conclude this article (and my paper reminds me speedily to do so) without once more adverting to the merits of a coach I have already named, *The New Dart*. Believe me, gentle reader, it is one of the very best on the road; and let me counsel you by no means to omit travelling this autumn with both George Deere and Ned Pattenden; for it would, I assure you, be a service of considerable difficulty to find two better dragsmen or more obliging fellows out of any yard, not in Brighton alone, but the whole of London. I hope the proprietors intend to keep both sides on during the winter, as it will be a thousand pities to throw such artists out of regular employment; and working alternate weeks, which, if one side is dropped, I suppose they will be obliged to do, is hardly sufficient (in winter) to make the pot boil, and not at all commensurate with the deserts of either one or the other.

"Your patience, Mr. Editor, I should think, must now be at an end. I beg your forgiveness for having trespassed on it so long, and conclude by giving you a list of coaches out of Brighton on the 1st October 1828, with the various hours at which they start for London, and the names of the dragsmen now at work. As a matter of reference, it may hereafter be interesting, and I think you will find it perfectly correct.

"VIATOR, JUN.

"*P.S.*—I must take an early opportunity of travelling with both Clary and Jordan on that first-rate coach *The Comet;* for, from everything I can learn of them, they are precisely the sort of artists that Bob Snow, for the sake of consistency, should have always about him.

Names.	Offices.	Hours.	Dragsmen.
Dart	18 Castle Square	6 A.M.	Bob Snow, up and down.
Item	Blue Coach Office		Mellish, up and down.
New Times . .	Goodman's, Castle Square . . .	7 A.M.	Sam Goodman, up and down.
Royal Exchange	Beehive, Castle Square . . .		
Royal Clarence	Goodman's . . .	9 A.M.	Tho. Holmes and Son.
Alert	52 East Street .		Hine and Bristow.
Regulator . .	Beehive, Castle Square	9.30 A.M.	Young Cook and Adams.
Comet . . .	18 Castle Square .	10 A.M.	Clary and Jordan
Patriot . . .	7 Castle Square .		Harding and Smart.
Magnet . . .	5 Castle Square .		Womack and Young Callow.
Regent . . .	Goodman's, Castle Square . . .		Gray and Goodman's brother.
True Blue . .	Blue Office . . .		Mellish and Scriven.
Union . . .	52 and 53 East St.	11 A.M.	Pickett and Egerton.
Age	5 Castle Square .	12 o'clock	Mr. Stevenson and Sheward.
Coronet . . .	Beehive, Castle Square . . .		Old Tommy and C. Newman.
New Dart . .	135 North St. and 18 Castle Square		George Deere and Ned Pattenden.
Royal George .	Blue Office . . .		Eugeroh and J. Newman.
Rocket . . .	Blue Office . . .	2 P.M.	Houldsworth and Young C. Newman.
Times . . .	Goodman's Office	3 P.M.	Mosely and Ellis.
Sovereign . .	18 Castle Square .		Ned Russell, up and down; sometimes W. Snow.
Hero . . .	Beehive, Castle Square . . .		...
Evening Star .	18 Castle Square and Goodman's .	10 P.M.	Penny and Bramble.
Royal Mail . .	Blue Office . . .	10.30 P.M.	Farley and Allen.

N.B.—An extra coach, from 18 Castle Square, at eight o'clock every Saturday morning, driven by William Snow.

"Your readers will observe a blank in the column

of dragsmen appointed to the *Hero* and *Royal Exchange*. To speak the truth, I have never thought it worth my while to inquire the names of these 'pair-horse' performers; but I believe that one carter has something to do with the driving of the *Hero* and Hayler's horse-keeper, perhaps, drives or drove the other."

The coaching age is an age so utterly passed away and forgotten that no young man of our time can have any conception of the hardships cheerfully, or at least passively, endured by our grandfathers when they travelled. It is but rarely one finds mention of these things by contemporary writers, because they were regarded as of such common experience as not to be worthy the mentioning. Most writers, too, in our time have been gentlemen coachmen, amateurs of the whip, who could have little or no experience of what old-time travelling really meant in all its discomforts of delay, danger, and expense. Of its romance, too, they cannot know much. It is, then, with gratitude that the searcher after these things lights upon such passages as the following from Shergold's "Recollections of Brighton in the Olden Time," written now many years ago, and published in a little paper-covered pamphlet that is now extremely scarce. It lies before me as I write, an account, with a certain literary flavour, of Brighton during Regency times, written by one who experienced or observed all those things of which he writes. Here is his account of coaching on the Brighton road in his time:—

"In my early days the setting out from Brighton and the arriving in London was a very formidable affair. It was really an event only to be well got through by men of a robust constitution and women who had been inured to fatigue by early rising and scrubbing and rubbing.

"There were three roads from Brighton to London. The first and chief passed through Cuckfield and Reigate. This was the Appian Way for the high nobility of England. The other two were vulgar. The one passed through Lewes, the other through Horsham. Genteel people never spoke of those roads but with a turn up of the nose and (!) a slight ejection of saliva from the lips. On both these roads there ran, from my earliest recollection, a four-horse coach, or genteel wagon, which had a rumble-tumble or basket behind, in which soldiers, sailors, workmen, and other rough materials travelled; and, as the rumble-tumble had no springs, the exercise in it must have been just as delightful as if a person were to employ a man to kick him all the way from Brighton to London. These coaches or wagons generally arrived in London before midnight; but sometimes, it is said, they fell short, and stopped the night on the road, for the benefit of some innkeeper, a relation of the coachman.

"The best method of conveyance on the Cuckfield road was by pair-horse coaches. These started at eight o'clock in the morning, and, if nothing intervened, proceeded steadily and boldly as far as Preston, where they stopped at the public-house—it being a prescriptive right of all coachmen in those days never to pass a public-house without calling. Coachmen were also persons of much consideration, a great deal of the business of the country being transacted by them. After quitting Preston, the coach 'snailed it on,' if I may be allowed to invent a term, to Withdean and Patcham, stopping, of course, a little time at each. The next stoppage was at the bottom of Clayton Hill—the formidable Clayton Hill—where the coachman descended from his box and civilly obliged all the passengers, outside and in, to walk up, on the plea 'that the roads were very heavy; it being absolutely killing to his horses.' This walk to the top of Clayton Hill took about half-an-hour, and was very fatiguing, especially if a man had the gallantry to offer his arm to a fat widow. From the top of Clayton Hill you had a most delightful view. You saw the Surrey Hills, and some people asserted you could see St. Paul's; but I believe the persons who saw St. Paul's were Londoners and men of very extensive imagination. From Clayton Hill the coach 'snailed it on' towards Cuckfield, the coachman not deeming it proper to ask the passengers to walk above three or four times until he arrived at that little town. At St. John's Common, on the hither side of Cuckfield, was a neat little public-house where the coachman usually took a snack, which consisted of a mouthful of bread and cheese and five or six glasses of gin and bitters, for that was the liquor *par excellence* of coachmen in that day. When the coach arrived at Cuckfield, it was usual for some of the passengers to say to one another, 'Well, as the coach will stop here for some time, we will walk on.' This walking on often consisted of a hard tug, up hill and down, over five or six miles of slimy, slippery road. But then you had your recompense. You cultivated the acquaintance of some agreeable fellow, who had begun to interest you by his manners. You heard every man's business; where he came from and where he was going; where his father and mother lived; how many brothers and sisters he had, and what was his occupation. One told you he was going to London to get employment; another, that he was going to France; a third, that he was going to India; and a fourth that he was going to the d—l,[1] and so forth. Now compare this to the taciturn, sulky method of travelling by railroad, and you will immediately see the difference. There was an advantage and an interest in travelling by coach which travelling by rail can never communicate. In the former you saw men and their faces, and acquired some information; in the latter you learn nothing except the number of persons killed or injured by the last accident. A young man who entered the coach at eight o'clock in the morning at Brighton took his seat perhaps opposite a young lady whom he thought pretty and interesting. When he arrived at Cuckfield he began to be in love; at Crawley he was desperately smitten; at Reigate his passion became irretrievable, and when he gave her an arm to ascend the steep ridges of Reigate Hill—a just emblem, by the way, of human life—he declared his passion,

[1] Why palter with the Devil, my good Shergold; has he not a right to his name?

was accepted, and they were married soon after. Nothing of this sort ever occurs on railroads. Sentiment never blooms on the iron soil of these sulky conveyances. A woman was a creature to be looked at, admired, courted, and beloved in a stage-coach; but on a railway a woman is nothing but a package, a bundle of goods committed to the care of the railway company's servants, who take care of the poor thing as they would take care of any other bale of goods. It is said that matches are made in heaven; it may likewise be said that matches more often begin in the old stage-coaches, and that railroads are the antipodes of love.

"Before the coach overtook the passengers who had purposed to walk forward, they arrived at Hand Cross, a complete rustic inn, of which the landlord bore the impress of Sussex rusticity. With that kind and benevolent attention to the happiness and comfort of walking travellers which innkeepers by the roadside usually possess, a number of stools and benches were always placed in front of the inn to receive the wearied muscles of the promenaders. What ought to be done? Something must be ordered to recruit the strength of the exhausted passengers and to repay the landlord for his kind attention. Hand Cross was out of the world. It was quite as far from London—at least, apparently so—as the deserts of Arabia. There were no dandies near. Brummel had left England and repaired to Caen, in Normandy. Nature had returned to what she originally was, and Englishmen had become what Englishmen always are when left to themselves—simple and unostentatious. Bannister, the publican of Hand Cross, walked forth from his inn, carrying a gallon bottle of gin in one hand and a small wicker basket of slices of gingerbread in the other. 'You must be tired, gentlemen,' said he; 'come, take a glass and a slice.' Hand Cross was not Bond Street, nor was it St. James's Street, nor White's, nor Boodle's, nor any other great place, but simply Hand Cross; and gin and gingerbread became it as well in those days as whitebait now becomes Blackwall. So we all partook of gin and gingerbread; and I can safely aver that I never heard a gentleman's character disputed or his reputation blackened because he took a glass of gin and ate a slice of gingerbread at the rustic hostelrie of Hand Cross.

But the coach was soon seen tending towards Hand Cross, and the outside and inside passengers, leaping up, took each person his place, and off we went at the quiet and everlasting rate of four miles and a half an hour. As we had a down-hill passage from Hand Cross, and not above four or five houses to stop at, we soon arrived at Crawley, a miserable place, the sight of which always gave me, and many other persons whom I could mention, were it necessary, the stomach-ache. At Crawley we delayed not more than was sufficient just to kick the dust from our feet, which Horace, or some other poet, mentions as a demonstration of contempt. We then bundled on to Reigate, and arrived at the 'King's Arms,' the horses absolutely trotting up to the door as if they took a real pleasure in presenting their passengers in grand style.

"At the door of this comfortable inn there was always standing (I mean in the days of coaching) a waiter, who, after handing out the passengers, informed them that dinner was ready and would be on the table in five minutes. Every man felt hungry; for, out of the thirty-two miles which lie between Brighton and Reigate, they had walked twenty. When they entered the room where dinner was to be served, they found some other passengers, who had come by a downward coach, waiting to dine. Here, then, we were, about fifteen ladies and gentlemen of the coach-going community—and who were not coach-goers in those simple and happy days?—about to sit down to a plain dinner, with two bottles of wine, at two o'clock in the day, at one of the best inns of the sort in the kingdom. The waiter put everything expeditiously on the table, wine and all—even *et cætera* and *et consequentia* (I don't know the Latin words for pies and tarts—I think the Romans, poor fellows! never knew what they were—or else I would quote the words), and said, very obligingly, 'Ladies and gentlemen, you have just two minutes for dinner! The coachman is putting-to his horses, and he will be round at the door immediately.' 'My friends,' said an Irishman, 'don't be after troubling yourselves about the botheration of the serving-man. It's all a got-up business between the innkeeper and the coachman; they wish to keep the good things for themselves. But they shan't have their own way; I'd sooner put the leg of mutton and the custards in my pocket. But let's call in the landlord and the coachman, and give them such a drubbing that they'll not quit their beds for a fortnight.' This might have been done, for bad advice is amazingly attractive—it is as catching as bird-lime—had not a Mr. Prudent, who often travelled the roads in those days, proposed to call in the coachman, that he might be argued with in two ways: firstly, to his stomach, by a tumbler of sherry; and, secondly, to his brains, by plain and solid argument. The coachman was summoned, and Mr. Prudent proved to his stomach, by a tumbler of sherry, and to his head, by a few words of good sense, that 'they who sit down to a dinner, and mean to pay for it, should be allowed time to eat it.' The coachman was convinced; he gave us time to eat our dinner; we paid for it, wine and all, conjointly—the ladies being considered as visitors: and then went on as fast as two horses (one of which was lame and the other broken-winded) could carry us. The coachman, after we had quitted Reigate, entered into an able soliloquy, addressed to me, to prove that eating dinners at two o'clock and drinking heavy port wine was imprudent. I was sitting on the box, and perfectly agreed with him. He did not say anything about drinking sherry, so I did not allude to it; but when he told me that he was quite sure he should lose his place for staying so long at Reigate, we on the outside all gave him a shilling apiece: so that, by delaying ten minutes, he gained about seven shillings and a tumbler of sherry. The coachmen of those days were such honest men—not at all cunning! But those were the days of the olden time, before the slippery railroads came into fashion!

"When the coach arrived at Reigate Hill"—our writer, you see, takes the old route—"all passengers were requested to descend. This hill was the most formidable tug on the road. Like the Alps or the Pyrenees, it presented obstacles which could only be surmounted by sound lungs and strong limbs. The best and easiest way of arriving at the summit of the hill was to follow humbly the movements of the coach; but some ladies and gentlemen ventured up a steep which led almost perpendicularly up the hill, and joined the road by a transverse path. Here was the trial of sound lungs and easy and comfortable lacing. Ladies who looked more to dapper shapes than easy respiration were sure to be brought to a *non-plus* about the middle of the path, and it was necessary sometimes to despatch a deputation of the gentlemen who were walking up the hill near the coach to aid in dragging the impeded ladies up the path. The fair passengers, however squeamish, were obliged to submit to the pulling and pushing movement: for there was only this method of surmounting these difficulties, unless they preferred to be rolled down the steep like a bundle of goods, and thus rejoin their fellow-passengers below. There was always a little merry nonsense of this sort which was attached to coach-travelling, and now, alas! forms part of the category of laughable incidents of the olden times.

"When we arrived at the top of Reigate Hill, we—the travellers of the ancient epoch—considered the journey to London almost as completed; for we were so accustomed to slow travelling, that an

hour in a coach was as patiently borne as five minutes now are on the railroad.

"At the 'Cock,' at Sutton,[1] we delayed a little half hour, as the French say, and then valiantly proceeded on to the noted 'Elephant and Castle,' where we waited for the completion of many businesses, such as change of coach, if you were going into the City, and other necessary duties. The destination of the Brighton coaches in those days was the 'Golden Cross,' Charing Cross—a nasty inn, remarkable for filth and apparent misery—whence it was usual to be conveyed to the place to which you were going in one of those large lumbering hackney-coaches, with two jaded, broken-winded, and broken-kneed hacks, which were common in those days, before the introduction of safety cabs and light flies. These vehicles were always damp and dreary, the very epitomes of misery. On arriving at the house you were going to in London, of some friends or relations, the following conversation often occurred:—'Happy to see you; but what brings you so soon?—didn't expect you before nine, and it's now only seven.' 'We have been eleven hours on the road—is not that enough?' 'Oh! quite enough; but formerly the Brighton coaches arrived at midnight. Travelling improves every day. I wonder what we shall arrive at next! Only eleven hours from Brighton to London! Wonderful! Almost incredible!'

[1] "Gentleman" Jackson, the pugilist, kept the "Cock Inn" at Sutton after he had retired from the "Ring" with a fortune. He enjoyed the patronage of George IV., died here, and is buried at Brompton.

"It may be remarked, in reference to roads and the travelling on them in bygone days, that our ancestors had a predilection for the tops of hills. Whether they loved the passage over hills because they presented them with extensive views, or because the air on the tops of hills inflated delightfully their lungs and cheered their minds. I know not, but so it was; and I have no doubt if Skiddaw had been placed where Clayton Hill is, and Snowdon where Reigate Hill is, they would have gone right over the tops of those two hills. But a road from one place to another, as from London to Brighton, became, after a time, no longer a way of agreeable passage, which you lingered along for recreation and pleasure, and from which you contemplated charming objects, but a road over which you desired to be conveyed with impatient speed lest you should have time for sober reflection. When our ancestors of the Sussex breed bethought them how they might hasten from one place to another with the greatest rapidity, they discovered, great geniuses as they were, that every hill has a valley near it, or a flat level at no great distance, and that by following this valley or level you went a few miles about, but avoided all the inconveniences of the hills, and accomplished the journey in half the time. Two new roads were, therefore, made; the one avoided Clayton Hill; the other, by leaving Reigate Hill to the left, passed through a village called, I think, Merstham, and enabled you to arrive in London without material inequality of surface.

"After the above alterations were made on the

Brighton Road, came on the time of expeditious travelling by four-horse coaches. Then lived and laboured in their vocation Bob Pointer, Black Sam, the Newnhams, and other celebrated coachmen who handled the 'ribbons' most skilfully, and drove four blood-horses, tackled to elegant coaches, with the same facility as they could have driven a donkey in a go-cart. Then was the time of the gentlemen coachmen, when some members of the Four-in-Hand Club thought they could exercise profitably the three avocations of gentlemen, coach proprietors, and coachmen. One saw in those days fair and agreeable countenances peering out of the coach-windows, and heard sweet and silvery voices saying in tuned accents, 'Mr. Coachman, please to put me down at Preston Gate,' &c. I remember a Captain Gwynne, about the time I am now dwelling on, who horsed a Brighton coach, and was always attended by two servants in livery: the one executed his master's orders about the steeds; the other took care of the passengers and luggage, and received the money which was due. I think, also, I recollect a Marquess of Worcester and other noblemen horsing coaches to Brighton. It became a kind of fashionable mania to imitate coachmen in all things—to talk like coachmen, look like coachmen, and act like coachmen. A man, whose name I think was Whitchurch, started a coach to go from Brighton to London and return the same day. This was a great event, and people assembled in numbers to see it arrive. After that a coach called the 'Eclipse' was immensely reputed. The horses galloped all the way from Brighton to

London! It was overturned two or three times a week, and some persons were killed. After the 'Eclipse' came the railroads; and after the railroads, nobody can tell what will follow—perhaps we may travel by 'electric telegraph.'"

Between 1841, when the railway was opened all the way from London, and 1866, during a period of twenty-five years, coaching, if not dead, at least showed but few and intermittent signs of life. "The Age," which then was owned by Mr. F. W. Capps, was the last coach to run regularly on the direct road to and from London. The "Victoria," however, was on the road until November 8, 1845.

"The Age" had been one of the best equipped and driven of all the smart drags in that period when aristocratic amateur dragsmen frequented this road; when the Marquis of Worcester drove the "Beaufort," and when the Hon. Fred Jerningham, a son of the Earl of Stafford, a whip of consummate skill, drove the day-mail; a time when "The Age" itself was driven by that sportsman of gambling memory, Sir St. Vincent Cotton, and by that Mr. Stevenson who was its founder, mentioned more particularly on page 182. When Mr. Capps became proprietor, he had as coachmen several distinguished men. For twelve years, for instance, Robert Brackenbury drove "The Age" for the nominal pay of twelve shillings per week, enough to keep him in whips.

In later years, about 1852, a revived "Age," owned and driven by the present Duke of Beaufort and

George Clark, the "Old" Clark of coaching acquaintance, was on the road to London, *viâ* Dorking and Kingston, in the summer months. It was discontinued in 1862. A picture of this coach crossing Ham Common *en route* for Brighton was painted in 1852 and engraved. A reproduction of it is shown here.

From 1862 to 1866, the rattle of the bars and the sound of the guard's yard of tin were silent on the Brighton Road; but in the latter year of horsey memory and the coaching revival, a number of aristocratic and wealthy amateurs of the whip, among whom were representatives of the best coaching talent of the day, subscribed a capital, in shares of £10; and a little yellow coach, the "Old Times," was put on the highway. Among the promoters of the venture were Captain Haworth, the Duke of Beaufort, Lord H. Thynne, Mr. Chandos Pole, Mr. "Cherry" Angell, Colonel Armytage, Captain Lawrie, and Mr. Fitzgerald. The experiment proved unsuccessful; but in the following season, commencing in April 1867, when the goodwill and a large portion of the stock had been purchased by the original subscribers, by the Duke of Beaufort, Mr. E. S. Chandos Pole, and Mr. Angell, the coach was doubled, and two new coaches built by Holland & Holland.

The Duke of Beaufort was chief among the sportsmen who horsed the coaches during this season, and Alfred Tedder was professional whip, in conjunction with Pratt. Mr. Chandos Pole, at the termination of the summer season, determined to carry on by himself, throughout the winter, a service of one coach. This he did, and, aided by Mr. Pole-Gell, doubled it in the following summer.

Mr. Chandos Pole, "the Squire," as he was known, was dined at Hatchett's at the season's close by enthusiastic lovers of the road, and was presented with an elaborate silver flagon of considerable value, by way of recognition of his qualities as whip and sportsman. Tedder, the coachman, who was also at that time landlord of the "Chequers" at Horley, was presented with a similar, though smaller flagon.

The following year, 1869, the coach had so prosperous a season, that it showed never a clean bill all the summer, either way. The partners this year were the Earl of Londesborough, Mr. Pole-Gell, Colonel Stracey Clitherow, Mr. Chandos Pole, and Mr. G. Meek, who each provided horses for one stage, with the exception of Mr. Chandos Pole, who horsed two stages.

From this season coaching became extremely popular on the Brighton Road, Mr. Chandos Pole running his coach until 1872, when, in December, Tedder died. In the following year, an American amateur, Mr. Tiffany, kept up the tradition with two coaches. Late in the season of 1874, Captain Haworth put in an appearance.

In 1875 "The Age" was put upon the road by Mr. Stewart Freeman, and ran in the season up to and including 1880, in which year it was doubled. John Thorogood was professional whip

in this series of years, joined in 1880 by Harry Ward. Captain Blyth had the "Defiance" on the road to Brighton this year, by the circuitous route of Tunbridge Wells. In 1881 Mr. Freeman's coach was absent from the road: but Edwin Fownes put "The Age" on late in the season. In the following year Mr. Freeman's coach ran, doubled again, and single in 1883. It was again absent in 1884, 1885, and 1886, in which last year it ran to Windsor; but it reappeared on this road in 1887 as "The Comet." In the winter of this year the service was continued by Captain Beckett, who had Selby and Fownes as whips. In 1888 Mr. Freeman ran in partnership with Colonel Stracey Clitherow, Lord Wiltshire, and Mr. Hugh M'Calmont, and in 1889 became partner in an undertaking to run the coach doubled. The two "Comets," therefore, served the road in this season, supported by two additional subscribers, the Honourable H. Sandys and Mr. Randolph Wemyss.

In 1888 the "Old Times," forsaking the Oatlands Park drive, had appeared on the Brighton Road as a rival of "The Comet," and continued throughout the winter months, until Selby met his death in that December.

"The Comet," as a single coach, ran in the winter season from October 1889 to April 1890, when it was again doubled for the summer, running single in 1891 and the present year.

By the courtesy of Mr. Freeman I am enabled to give the following particulars of the Brighton coaches in which he has been a leading partner:

1875.

Proprietor, .	Stewart Freeman.
No. of horses,	33. Coachman, Pope, succeeded by John Thorogood.
Ran, . . .	15 weeks and 3 days.
Route, . . .	Sutton, Woodhatch, Crawley, Hand Cross, Warminglid, Bolney, Dale, and Patcham. Paying tolls.

1876.

Proprietor, .	Stewart Freeman.
No. of horses,	43. Coachman, John Thorogood.
Ran, . . .	19 weeks and 5 days, carrying 1003 passengers.
Route, . . .	Vauxhall, Sutton, Reigate, Crawley, Warninglid, Dale, and Patcham. Paying tolls.

1877.

Proprietor, .	Stewart Freeman,
No. of horses,	39. Coachman, John Thorogood.
Ran, . . .	June 2 to October 5, carrying 835 passengers. Five changes.
Route, .	Croydon, Merstham, Horley, Hand Cross, Albourne. Paying tolls.

1878.

Proprietors,	Stewart Freeman and Colonel Stracey-Clitherow.
No. of horses,	40. Coachman, John Thorogood.
Ran, . .	19 weeks and 2 days, carrying 863 passengers. Five changes. Paying tolls.
Route, .	As before.

1879.

Proprietors,	Stewart Freeman, Colonel Stracey-Clitherow, Chandos Pole.
No. of horses,	51. Coachman, John Thorogood.
Ran, .	19 weeks and 2 days, carrying 882 passengers.
Route, .	As before. Paying tolls.

1880.

Proprietors, . Stewart Freeman, Colonel Stracey-Clitherow, Lord Algernon Lennox, Mr. Craven (doubled coach).
No. of horses, 100. Coachmen, John Thorogood, Harry Ward.
Ran, . . June 26 to November 9.
Route, . . As before.

1881.

Coach discontinued.

1882.

Proprietors, Stewart Freeman and Baron Oppenheim (doubled coach).
No. of horses, 100. Coachmen, John Thorogood, Edwin Fownes, senior.
Ran, . . June 17 to October 16.
Route, . . As before.

1883.

Proprietors, . Stewart Freeman and Colonel Stracey-Clitherow.
No. of horses, 50. Coachman, John Thorogood.
Ran, . . August 11 to October 29.
Route, . . . As before.

1884, 1885.

Coach discontinued.

1886.

Ran to Windsor.

1887.

Proprietors, Stewart Freeman, Capt. A. F. MacAdam, and Capt. H. L. Beckett.
No. of horses, 50. Coachman, John Thorogood.
Ran, . . June 11 to October 6.
Route, . . . As before.

1888.

Proprietors,	Stewart Freeman, Colonel Stracey-Clitherow, Lord Wiltshire, and Mr. Hugh M'Calmont.
No. of horses,	50. Coachman, John Thorogood.
Ran,	May 15 to October 22.
Route, .	As before.

1889.

Proprietors,	Stewart Freeman, Colonel Stracey-Clitherow, Mr. Hugh M'Calmont, Hon. H. Sandys, and Mr. Randolph Wemyss (doubled coach).
No. of horses,	100. Coachman, John Thorogood, Pennington.
Ran, .	May 11 to October 5.
Route, .	As before.

1889–90.

Winter Coach.

Proprietors,	Stewart Freeman, Colonel Stracey-Clitherow, Mr. Hugh M'Calmont, and Mr W. H. Mackenzie.
No. of horses,	50. Coachman, Pennington.
Ran, . .	October 1889 to April 1890.
Route, .	As before.

1890.

Proprietors, .	Stewart Freeman, Colonel Stracey-Clitherow, Mr. Hugh M'Calmont, and Sir John Poynder, Bart. (doubled coach).
No. of horses,	100. Coachmen, W. H. Wragg, Arthur Woodland.
Ran,	May 10 to October 4.
Route, .	As before.

1891.

Proprietors, .	Stewart Freeman, Colonel Stracey-Clitherow, and Sir John Poynder, Bart.
No. of horses,	45. Coachman, W. H. Wragg.
Ran, .	May 2 to October 10, carrying 1446 passengers.
Route, .	As before.

1892.

Proprietors, .	Stewart Freeman and Colonel Stracey-Clitherow.

THE "COMET," 1890.

(From a Painting by Alfred S. Bishop, by permission of Stewart Freeman, Esq.)

Many of those who took part in the coaching revival on this road—the road on which the revival began—are now gone over to the great majority.

Selby's death and Tedder's have already been mentioned. On 12th May 1873, Mr. B. J. Angell died, followed by Mr. Meek in December 1874; Mr. Willis, November 1876; Mr. W. H. Cooper, 25th March 1878; and Mr. E. S. Chandos-Pole.

But revive coaching as you may, 'tis but an amusement in this era of steam, or, let us say, this transitional era from steam to electricity. Nothing can give us the experiences of our grandfathers, which is perhaps as well for we of a degenerate generation.

In those times you took your seat on your particular fancy in coaches, and paid your sixteen shilling fare from London to Brighton, trusting (yet with heavy heart) in Providence to bring you to a happy issue from all the dangers and discomforts of travelling, and they were many. Contemporary newspapers give, for instance, particulars of what befell upon the road in the great snowstorm of 24th December 1836, a storm which paralysed communications throughout the kingdom.

"The Brighton up-mail of Sunday had travelled about eight miles from that town, when it fell into a drift of snow, from which it was impossible to extricate it without assistance. The guard immediately set off to obtain all necessary aid, but when he returned no trace whatever could be found either of the coach, coachman, or passengers, three in number. After much difficulty the coach was found, but could not be extricated from the hollow into which it had got. The guard did not reach town until seven o'clock on Tuesday night, having been obliged to travel with the bags on horseback, and in many instances to leave the main road and proceed across fields in order to avoid the deep drifts of snow.

"The passengers, coachman, and guard slept at Clayton, seven miles from Brighton. The road from Hand Cross was quite impassable. The non-arrival of the mail at Crawley induced the postmaster there to send a man in a gig to ascertain the cause on Monday afternoon. No tidings being heard of man, gig, or horse for several hours, another man was despatched on horseback, and after a long search he found horse and gig completely built up in the snow. The man was in an exhausted state. After considerable difficulty the horse and gig were extricated, and the party returned to Crawley. The man had learned no tidings of the mail, and refused to go out again on any such exploring mission."

The Brighton mail from London, too, reached Crawley, but was compelled to return.

Sentiment hung round the expiring age of coaching, and has cast a halo upon old-time ways of travelling, so that we often fail to note the disadvantages and discomforts endured in those days; but amid regrets which were often simply maudlin occur now and again witticisms true and tersely epigrammatic, as thus—

"For the neat wayside inn and a dish of cold meat
You've a gorgeous saloon, but there's nothing to eat;"

THE FASHION, 1828.

and a contributor to the *Sporting Magazine* observes, very happily, that "even in a 'case' in a coach, it's 'there you are;' whereas in a railway carriage it's 'where are you?'"

But sentiment is a fearsome thing, and few things are more certain than that if the sulphurous fumes of our Metropolitan Railway were replaced to-morrow by less objectionable vapours, there would be found those who would regret the change, for the sake of old association's charm.

Why, coaching itself in its very beginnings was as roughly assailed as were railways on their first introduction. Towards the close of the seventeenth century, when hired stages began to supersede in many country towns and districts the use of horses for riding, an indignant writer[1] unburdened his soul in this wise:—

"Will any man keep a horse for himself and another for his servant, all the year round, for to ride one or two journeys, that at pleasure when he hath occasion can slip to any place where his business lies for two or three shillings, if within twenty miles of London, and so proportionately to any part of England? No, there is no man, unless some noble soul that seems to abhor being confined to so ignoble, base, and sordid a way of travelling as these coaches oblige him to, and who prefers a public good before his own ease and advantage, that will breed or keep horses. . . . Travelling in these coaches can neither prove advantageous to men's health or business, for what advantage is it to men's

[1] "The Grand Concern of England Explained," 1673.

health to be called out of their beds into their coaches an hour before day in the morning, to be hurried in them from place to place till one, two, or three hours within night, insomuch that sitting all day in the summer time, stifled with heat and choked with dust, or in the winter time, starving or freezing with cold, or choked with filthy fogs! They are often brought into their inns by torchlight, when it is too late to sit up to get a supper, and next morning they are forced into the coach so early that they can get no breakfast. What addition is this to men's health or business, to ride all day with strangers oftentimes sick, or with diseased persons, or young children crying, to whose humours they are obliged to be subject, forced to bear with, and many times are poisoned with their nasty scents, and crippled by the crowd of their boxes and bundles?"

I seem to know that man; he was doubtless a choleric specimen of the fossilised country gentleman, stuck fast in his own ruts, and all uncaring how slowly the world wagged to the millennium. He says a great deal of "man" and "men's business," but never says a word of the ladies. Are we to infer that they travelled little, or does the writer write in the larger sense of mankind, and hold, with the philosopher, that "man embraces woman"?

However, protests to the contrary, coaching came in, and horse-riding practically went out. The spirit of conservatism, however, beaten back from one ditch, clung always tenaciously to the next. The fine old crusted spirit of exclusiveness shown above is admirably put by De Quincey when he describes the difference of caste supposed to exist between inside and outside passengers on the mail coaches when this dying century was born.

There was then a rigid rule which limited the number of passengers on a mail coach to four inside and three out, exclusive, of course, of driver and guard. The three outsides were seated, by an irrefragable regulation of the Post Office, in the following position, to afford some degree of security to the mail custodians. One sat on the box beside the driver; the other two immediately behind the box, and well out of reach of the guard and mails, perched securely behind the main structure of the coach, armed with cutlass and blunderbuss, and furnished in addition with a horn.

"It had been," says De Quincey, "the fixed assumption of the four inside people that they, the illustrious quaternion, constituted a porcelain variety of the human race, whose dignity would have been compromised by exchanging one word of civility with the three miserable delf-ware outsides. Even to have kicked an outsider might have been held to attaint the foot concerned in that operation, so that perhaps it would have required an Act of Parliament to restore its purity of blood. What words, then, could express the horror and the sense of treason, in that case, which *had* happened, where all three outsides (the trinity of Pariahs) made a vain attempt to sit down at the same breakfast-table or dinner-table with the consecrated four? I myself witnessed such an attempt; and on that occasion a benevolent old gentleman endeavoured to soothe his three holy associates by suggesting that if the outsides were indicted for this criminal attempt at the next assizes, the court would regard it as a case of lunacy or delirium tremens rather than that of treason. England owes much of her grandeur to the depth of the aristocratic element in her social composition when pulling against her strong democracy. I am not the man to laugh at it. But sometimes, undoubtedly, it expressed itself in comic shapes. The course taken with the infatuated outsiders, in the particular attempt which I have noticed, was that the waiter, beckoning them away from the privileged *salle-à-manger*, sang out, 'This way, my good men,' and then enticed these good men away to the kitchen. But that plan had not always answered. Sometimes, though rarely, cases occurred where the intruders, being stronger than usual, or more vicious than usual, resolutely refused to budge, and so far carried their point as to have a separate table arranged for themselves in a corner of the general room. Yet if an Indian screen could be found ample enough to plant them out from the very eyes of the high table or dais, it then became possible to assume as a fiction of law that the three delf fellows after all were not present. They could be ignored by the porcelain men under the maxim that objects not appearing and not existing are governed by the same logical construction."

And so an end of coaching gossip. Half a mile or so below Cuckfield is the picturesque hamlet of Ansty Cross, a cluster of a few cottages and an inn.

the "Green Cross," a sign which probably derives from the arms of some long-forgotten local family. A turnpike gate was used to stand here. The beginning of turnpike gates was in 1700, when Turnpike Acts began to pass the Houses of Parliament, and when good roads began to be made between large towns. Road-making had ended in Britain with the end of the Roman occupation, and was not revived until the beginning of the eighteenth century. Between 1700 and 1710 twelve Turnpike Acts received the royal assent, and by 1770, 530 such Acts were in existence, and were continually being added to. The period of authorisation for the collection of tolls was at first twenty-one years, but in 1830 these terms were extended to thirty-one years. Such Acts were, however, renewed from time to time as became necessary. Tolls were originally chargeable according to the number of wheels, without reference to weight carried; but in 1767 the first of a series of Acts was passed, by which tolls were lowered in proportion as the breadth of wheels was increased. By two Acts passed in the 42nd and 58th of George III., two out of a number dealing with Surrey and Sussex roads, the following scale of tolls was authorised:—

"For every horse, mare, gelding, mule, or ass, laden or unladen, and not drawing, the sum of one penny halfpenny:

"For every chaise, chair, or other such like carriage, drawn by one horse, mare, gelding, or other beast of draught, the sum of threepence:

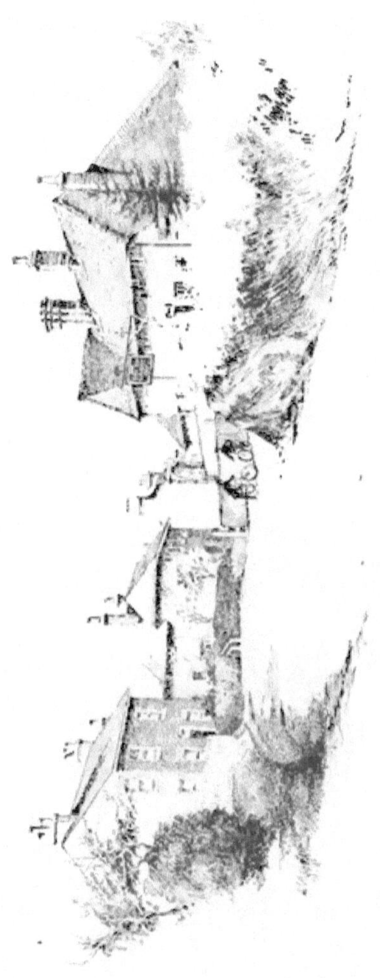

"For every curricle or chair, or other such like carriage, on two wheels only, drawn by two or more horses or other beasts of draught, the sum of sixpence:

"For every coach, chariot, landau, berlin, hearse, chaise, curricle, barouche, calash, or other such like carriage on more than two wheels, drawn by two or three horses or other beasts of draught only, the sum of ninepence:

"For every coach, chariot, landau, berlin, hearse, chaise, curricle, barouche, calash, or other such like carriage, drawn by four horses or other beasts of draught, the sum of one shilling:

"For every coach, chariot, landau, berlin, hearse, chaise, curricle, barouche, calash, or other such like carriage, drawn by more than four horses or other beasts of draught, the sum of one shilling and sixpence:

"For every cart, dray, or other such like carriage, drawn by one horse or other beast of draught only, the sum of threepence:

"For every cart, dray, or other such like carriage, with wheels of less breadth than six inches, drawn by two horses or other beasts of draught only, the sum of fourpence:

"For every cart, dray, or such like carriage, with wheels of less breadth than six inches, drawn by three horses or other beasts of draught only, the sum of sixpence:

"For every cart, dray, or such like carriage, with wheels of the breadth of six inches and upwards, drawn by four horses or other beasts of draught, the sum of fourpence:

"For every waggon laden with hay or straw, the sum of sixpence:

"For every cart laden with hay or straw, the sum of threepence:

"For every waggon laden with turnips, grains, cabbages, potatoes, or any other green fodder, the sum of sixpence:

"For every cart laden with turnips, grains, cabbages, potatoes, or any other green fodder, the sum of threepence:

"For every waggon not laden with hay or straw, with wheels of less breadth than six inches, drawn by more than two and not exceeding four horses or other beasts of draught, the sum of one shilling:

"For every such waggon with wheels of the breadth of six inches and upwards, not drawn by more than four horses or other beasts of draught, the sum of sixpence:

"For every such waggon with wheels of the breadth of six inches and upwards, not drawn by more than six horses or other beasts of draught, the sum of ninepence:

"And for every such waggon with wheels of the breadth of nine inches and upwards, drawn by more than six horses or other beasts of draught, the sum of sixpence:

"For every drove of oxen, cows, or neat cattle, the sum of tenpence per score, and so in proportion for any greater or less number: And for every drove of calves, pigs, sheep, or lambs, the sum of fivepence per score, and so in proportion for any greater or less number."

At Riddens Farm, a picturesque little homestead with tiled front and clustered chimneys, on the left hand below Austy, is one of those old Sussex cast-iron firebacks, whose manufacture is mentioned in an earlier page. It is dated 1622, and is in design and execution above the average.

Below Ansty, two miles or thereby down the road, the little river Adur is passed at Bridge Farm, and the twin towns of St. John's Common and Burgess Hill are reached.

SUSSEX IRON FIREBACK, RIDDENS FARM.

Before 1820 their sites were fields and common land, wild and gorse-covered, free and open. Few houses were then in sight; the "Anchor Inn," by Burgess Hill, the reputed haunt of smugglers, who stored their contraband in the woods and heaths close by; and the "King's Head," at St. John's Common, with two or three cottages—these were all.

St. John's Common, partly in Keymer and partly in Clayton parishes, was enclosed piecemeal, between 1828 and 1855, by an arrangement between the lords of the manors and the copyholders, who divided the plunder between them. This large tract of land presently became the site of these towns of St. John's Common and Burgess Hill, which sprang up, if not with quite the rapidity of a Californian mining town, at least with a celerity almost unknown in England. Their rapid rise is due to the making of the Brighton Railway, which has now a station for Burgess Hill. Four acres only of common land were left, set apart for the purpose of a recreation ground for these land-grabbing, mushroom townsfolk; but either they required no recreation, or else hungered for this poor fragment to build upon; for although powers existed for the expenditure of public money for its cultivation, yet it remained for over thirty years as a place of desolation, covered with ant-hills, and a receptacle for the potsherds of the community.

We shook the dust of this rising brick-making, tile, and drain-pipe manufacturing place from off our feet, and made haste to leave it behind, coming in two miles to Friar's Oak.

"Friar's Oak Inn" is very old—of unknown date. It stands by the roadside at a spot just before you come to the forty-third milestone from London.

Tradition, little else, hath it that here was once a monastery (of what order tradition saith not) in the meadow opposite the inn; but to-day that meadow is innocent of all but cows and grass, and the ancient oak that gives its name to this wayside tavern. That tree measures fifteen feet six inches in circumference, and is supposed to be at least five hundred years old. The pious monks or friars are supposed to have given doles to poor wayfarers beside its trunk. Upstairs, in a bedroom of the inn, hangs its original sign, an oil painting upon a wooden panel, mellowed and obscured by time, representing a monk of sinister

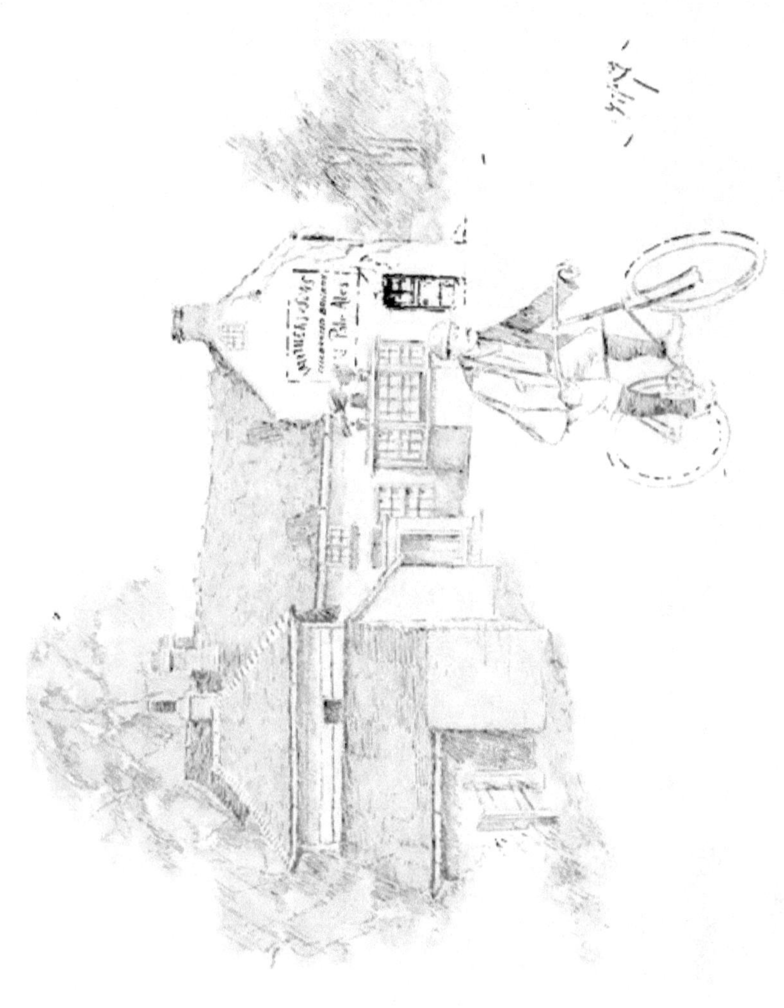

and austere aspect dancing beneath the oak, as the Scotchman joked, "wi' deeficulty." This sign was used to hang outside the inn. Stolen many years ago, it was subsequently discovered in London by the merest accident, was purchased for a trifling sum, and restored to its bereft signpost. The innkeeper, however, thinking that what befell once might happen again, hung the cherished panel within the house, where it remains to this day.

We left our knapsacks at the inn, intending to spend the afternoon on the Downs above Clayton, and to return here for the night.

From Friar's Oak it is but a step to that newest creation among Brighton's suburbs, Clayton Park, its clustering red-brick villas, building estates, and half-formed roads adjoining the station of Hassocks Gate, which, by the way, the railway authorities term "Hassocks," *tout court.* The name recalls certain dusty contrivances of straw and carpeting artfully contrived for the devout to stumble over in church. But not to incur the suspicion of tripping over the name as here applied, it may be mentioned that "hassock" is the Anglo-Saxon name for a coppice or small wood; and there are really many of these at and around Hassocks Gate to this day. At Stonepound, where a road, leading on the left hand to Clayton Park and on the right to Hurstpierpoint, crosses the Brighton road, there stood formerly Stonepound turnpike gate, one of the nine gates that barred the way from London in 1826. They began at Kennington Church, with one at Croydon; another at Foxley Hatch by the twelfth milestone.

half a mile past Purley House; and one at Frenches, nineteen miles four furlongs from London—that is to say, just before you come into Red Hill streets. Across Earlswood Common, at Salford, another gate spanned the road; with one each at Horley and Ansty Cross. After Stonepound, there was but one more, and that was at Preston.[1] The amount of toll was regulated not only by the number of wheels to a vehicle, but also by their width. The broad dished wheels of the old stage-waggons were not so constructed solely for strength and durability, but because the broader the wheels the smaller the toll, the idea being that a wheel of say twenty inches in breadth would do little in the way of rutting the doughy highways of an era which knew not a Telford nor a M'Adam.

Parishes in those days borrowed money for the improvement of their roads upon the security of their turnpike tolls, and it was a frequent practice for them to farm out sections of the highway to speculative folk for an annual sum, the speculator in each case to make what he could out of his particular pike, bound though by the recognised tariff. In those cases the bilking of a pikeman proved an engrossing matter: it was merely a question of whether you "had" the pikeman or he cheated you—there was no question of morals in the affair at all. A turnpike ticket was available for return the same day, and would, in addition, admit through the

[1] In 1829 there were three additional gates: one at Crawley, another at Hand Cross, before you came to the "Red Lion," and one more at Slough Green. Meanwhile the Horley gate on this route had disappeared. Salford gate was the last remaining on the Brighton road.

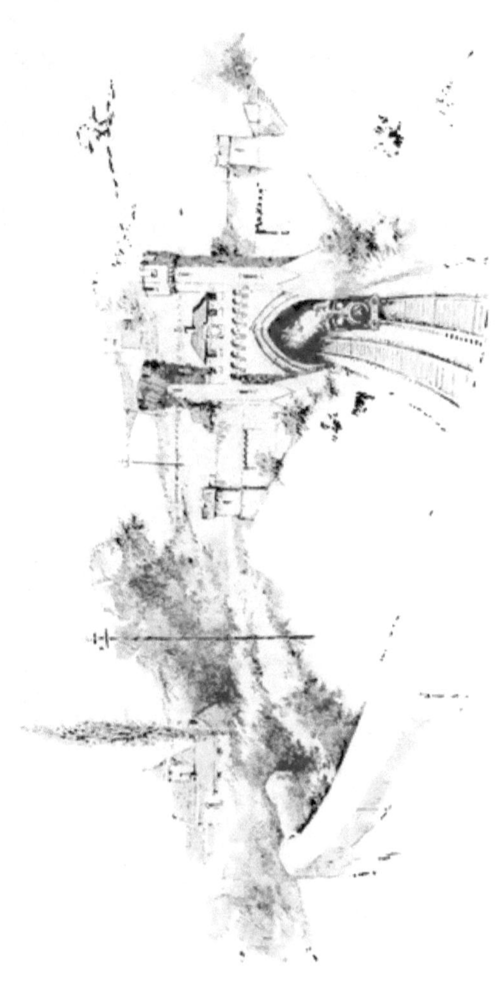

next gate. If the pikeman found it possible to chouse you out of your free return, or his colleague at the next gate could manage to charge you for its passage, he would do so. A few gates lingered on even until the velocipede made its appearance on the road. The toll for one was three-halfpence.

Twenty years ago, in this part of Sussex, the cost of maintaining the road was, at an average, £35 a mile. Under the new authority, the East Sussex County Council, the amount has been usually £81 a mile, and now the country folk declare that the roads were in better condition under the old regime.

Here the South Downs come full upon the view, crowned at Clayton Hill with windmills. Ditchling Beacon to the left, and the more commanding height of Wolstonbury to the extreme right, flank this great wall of earth, chalk, and grass—Wolstonbury semicircular in outline and bare, save only for some few clumps of yellow gorse and other small bushes. And now the road begins to climb Clayton Hill, a "name," to paraphrase Shakespeare, "of fear, unpleasing to a 'cyclist's' ear," and the Gothic battlemented entrance to Clayton Tunnel looms large on the right hand as you cross the railway bridge. Was ever Gothic architecture so misplaced as here, where that fine convention of bye-gone centuries in brick and masonry is lugged in to set off with an attempt at beauty the crowning achievement in usefulness of the nineteenth!

From the summit of Clayton Hill, above the blowholes and telegraph posts that plentifully garnish the tunnel's course, is a splendid and wide-embracing view. Clayton Hill has been thrice fatal to rash cyclists, who, ere the "safety" type of machine was introduced, adventured down its steep and winding roadway. To-day, though its descent can be, and often is, accomplished on the cycle, it is only your hare-brained wheelman who will attempt it. Better walk down and lose a few minutes than rush it on

THE HOBBY-HORSE AND THE SAFETY BICYCLE.

wheels and be knocked, perchance, into a jelly and eternity. But the cyclist was ever of a reckless, devil-daring nature, else how could he in the beginning have bestrode the hobby-horse, or later the velocipede-boneshaker?

THE VELOCIPEDE.

A breast secured with triple brass
(As Horace hath it) his had been
Who first, poor wretch, essayed to pass,
Good lack!
Along the road's uncertain track
On this machine.

His iron-shod wheel and creaking spokes,
Of solid timber, down the hills
Would rumble, and the country folks
Would stare,
With horrid jokes and stupid air
To see his "spills."

And ever, as from out the dust
The Thing, uninjured from the fray,

Would rise, the rider stood and cussed
Like mad,
And presently, all torn and sad,
Would ride away.

The hero of that early day
Is changed by Time's all-changing hand:
His raven locks are scant and grey,
Alas!
He learns, full-well, all flesh is grass:
'Twill pass away.

BONESHAKER OF 1868. BUILT OF IRON, WITH IRON-SHOD WHEELS AND WOODEN SPOKES.

But changeless, though time fly away,
Will be that cycle. Nothing can
Affect its massive frame. Decay
To seek
Its youth remains. 'Tis (so to speak)
The Better Man.

But a tragedy of the awfullest and most heart-shaking description belongs to Clayton Hill, for in the tunnel below, on Sunday, August 25, 1861, befell a railway accident of the most horrible nature, by which twenty-four persons in all lost their lives, and one hundred and seventy-five were injured.

Three trains were timed to leave Brighton Station shortly after eight o'clock on that fatal morning, two of them filled to crowding with excursionists, the other, an ordinary train, well filled and bound for London. Their times for starting were 8, 8.5, and 8.30 respectively, but owing to delays occasioned by press of traffic, they did not set out until considerably later, at 8.28, 8.31, and 8.35. At such terribly short intervals were they started in times when no block system existed to render such close following comparatively safe.

But by reason of Clayton Tunnel being considered then so dangerous a place, there was situated at either end (north and south entrances) a signal-cabin furnished with telegraphic instruments and signal apparatus, by which the signalman at one end of the tunnel could communicate with his fellow at the other, and could notify "train in" or "train out," as might happen. This practically formed a primitive sort of "block system," especially devised for use in this mile and a quarter's gloomy burrow.

But now, see what happened. The first train from Brighton passed in, and, on its way to the tunnel, failed to turn a "self-acting" signal placed in the cutting some distance from the southern entrance, a signal which upon the passage of every train would, in theory, set itself at "danger" for any following train, until placed at "line clear" from the nearest cabin.

On this occasion the theory failed of becoming practice, and the second train, following upon the heels of the first, passed all unsuspecting, and dashed from daylight into the tunnel's mouth; the signalman, who had not received a message from the other end of the tunnel being clear, frantically waving his red flag to stop it. This signal apparently unnoticed by the driver, the train passed in.

At this moment the third train came into view, and at the same time the signalman was advised of the tunnel being clear of the first. Meanwhile, the driver of the second train, who *had* noticed the red flag, was, unknown to the signalman, backing his train out again. A signal was sent to the north cabin for it, "train in;" but the signalman there, thinking this to be a mere repetition of the first message, replied, "train out," referring, of course, to the first train.

The tunnel being to the southern signalman apparently clear, the third train was allowed to proceed, and met, midway, away from daylight, the retreating second train. The collision was terrible; the two rearward carriages of the second train were smashed to pieces, and the engine of the third, reared upon their wreck, poured fire and steam and scalding water upon the poor wretches who, wounded but not killed by the impact, were struggling to free themselves from the splintered and twisted remains of the two carriages.

The heap of wreckage was piled up to the roof of the tunnel, whose interior presented a dreadful scene, the engine fire throwing a lurid glare around, but partly obscured by the blinding, scalding clouds of steam; while this suddenly created Inferno resounded with the prayers, shrieks, shouts, and curses of injured and scatheless alike, all fearful of the coming of another train to add to the already sufficiently hideous ruin.

Fortunately no further catastrophe occurred; but nothing of horror was wanting, neither in the magnitude nor in the circumstances of the disaster, which long remained in the memories of those who read, and was impossible of oblivion in those who witnessed it.

On the Downs we lay and lingered all the afternoon and watched the sheep and shepherds, and, high above the Weald, saw in the blue distance the wall of the North Downs stretching east and west, and in the level lands between these two ranges noted the white steam-trails of the crawling trains. Snail-like they seemed from the vantage of this happy eminence, and feeble their starting whistles as they moved out of Hassocks station down below, presently to burrow with many rumblings beneath these sunny hillsides.

Sheep graze here in thousands, and South Down mutton is still more in the land than a memory. Shepherds, with crooks of traditional pattern, though they be no longer of the famous Pyecombe make, still watch their flocks here. All along the hillsides is heard the dull and hollow sound of the sheep-bells, as the sheep, whose fleeces begin now to show promise of a good crop for the shears in June, move about all reckless of Smithfield. The shearing will be shorn as in uncounted seasons past, but I fear that neither the words nor the airs of

these old shearing-songs will ever again awaken the echoes of hillsides in the daytime, nor make the roomy interiors of barns ring again o' nights, as they were wont to do langsyne, when the convivial shearing supper was held, and the ale hummed in the cup, and, later in the evening, in the head also.

Here are the two old country songs referred to. Their scansion is not of the best, and their sentiments are calculated to give the patrons of the pump an effect as of shameless bacchanalian revels; but though they are so redolent of ale, and though the feet of their lines have what may be construed by the uncharitable into a beery stumble, yet they are greatly preferable to the songs the shepherd sings to-day—when he sings at all. Musical he is not; it is only your idyllic Watteau shepherd who, decked out with ribbons, pipes plaintively to his wondering flock.

OLD SHEEP-SHEARING SONG.

Come all my jolly boys, and we'll together go
Abroad with our masters, to shear the lamb and ewe;
All in the merry month of June, of all times in the year,
It always comes in season, the ewes and lambs to shear;
And then we must work hard, boys, until our backs do ache,
And our master he will bring us beer whenever we do lack.

Our master he comes round to see our work is doing well,
And he cries, "Shear them close, men, for there is little wool;"
"Oh, yes, good master," we reply, "we'll do the best we can;"
When our captain calls, "Shear close, boys," to each and ev'ry man;
And at some places still we have this story all day long;—
"Close them, boys! shear them well!" and this is all their song.

And then our noble captain doth unto our master say,
"Come, let us have one bucket of your good ale, I pray."
He turns unto our captain, and makes him this reply:—
"You shall have the best of beer, I promise, presently."
Then out with a bucket pretty Betsy she doth come,
And master says, "Maid, mind and see that ev'ry man has some."

THE DOWNS.

This is our merry pastime while we the sheep do shear,
And though we are such merry boys, we work hard, I declare;
And when 'tis night, and we have done, our master is more free,
And stores us well with good strong beer, and pipes and tobaccee.
So sit we all, and drink and smoke and sing and roar,
Till we become more merry far than e'er we were before.

When all our work is done, and all our sheep are shorn,
Then home with our captain to drink the ale that's strong:

'Tis a barrel, then, of hum-cap, which we call the Black Ram,
And each does sit and swagger, and swear that he's a man;
But yet, before 'tis night, I'll stand you half-a-crown,
That, if you ha'n't a special care, that ram will knock you down.

OLD SHEEP-SHEARING SONG.

Here the rosebuds in June and the violets are blowing,
The small birds they warble from every green bough;
Here's the pink and the lily,
And the daffydowndilly,
To adorn and perfume the sweet meadows in June.
'Tis all before the plough the fat oxen go slow;
But the lasses and lads to the sheep-shearing go.

Our shepherds rejoice in their fine heavy fleeces,
And frisky young lambs which their flocks do increase;
Each lad takes his lass,
All on the green grass,
Where the pink and the lily, &c.

Here stands our brown jug, and 'tis filled wi' good ale,
Our table, our table, increase and not fail:
We'll joke and we'll sing,
And we'll dance in a ring.
Where the pink and the lily, &c.

When the shearing is over, and harvest is nigh.
We prepare for the fields, our strength for to try:
We reap and we mow,
We plough and we sow:
Oh! the pink and the lily, &c.

Later in the day, after having scorched in the hot afternoon sun on the hills of Ditchling Beacon, we returned to Friar's Oak, to a late tea, welcome after the climbings and pantings up and along the Downs.

While we discussed the cheerful meal, there came from other regions of the house—from the sanded public parlour of the inn, as we afterwards discovered—sounds of revelry and song: the rustics were making merry after work was done. A confused hammering, interspersed with the hum of voices and the ear-grating scratching of hob-nailed boots on gritty floors, preceded an interminable song, whose words, saving only those of the chorus, were indistinguishable, and even those were only pieced together by the attentive ear after several repetitions.

The singer of the song could have urged no claims to regard by reason of his singing, neither was there any quality, other than that of volume, to be discerned in the choral voices, whose curiously staccato efforts at length resolved themselves into this refrain:—

> "For—we're—all—jol-ly—fel-lows—that—fol-low—the—plough."

Curious to see what manner of company this might be, we took the earliest opportunity of looking in upon the jovial gathering. They proved to be, as might be inferred from their inharmonic chorus, farm labourers, ploughmen, shepherds, and others, bent evidently upon contriving a mellow evening, altogether independent of atmospheric conditions. Descendants these of many generations of South Down shepherds, not though, alas! so parochial as their forbears, and so, less interesting. It was of a simpler generation that the following story was told; not, indeed, that even the modern rustic understands hydraulics, but familiarity has banished curiosity.

When beer-pumps were first introduced into the bars of country inns, they excited a great deal of curiosity amongst the bumpkins, and they would continually pry into and handle them, the more inquisitive in that they could understand little or nothing of the principle of hydraulics upon which these machines work. This meddling curiosity greatly annoyed the landlord of one of these old roadside inns, and he, having a kind of unlettered fancy for writing verses, chose to set up a metrical notice forbidding any interference with the machines:—

"CAUTION.

"Whoever presumes with these here cocks for to meddle,
Shall pay a *pint* of beer: that there is the riddle;
But whoever presumes these here cocks for to draw,
Shall pay a *pot* of beer; that there is the law.
But if he doesn't pay that, he shall be soused in the pond
with the ducks:
All this here comes of meddling with them there cocks."

But the Sussex peasant is not by any means altogether bereft of provincialism. Sussex, till lately a remote and difficulty county, plunged in its sloughs and isolated by reason of its forests, is still a stronghold of the stolid Saxon, and its peasantry, even in these times of racial displacements, are rooted, it seems, as firmly as ever to what Camden calls this "queachy soil." Words of Saxon origin are still current in the talk of the country-side; folk-tales, told in times when the South Saxon kingdom was yet a power of the Heptarchy, still exist in remote corners, currently with the latest ribald song from the London halls; superstitions linger, as may be proved by he who pursues his inquiries judiciously, and thought moves slowly still in the bucolic mind.

The Norman conquest has left few traces upon the population. They are the ruling families only who show Norman descent or admixture of blood. The peasant is still the fair-haired, blue-eyed Saxon he ever has been; his occupations, too, tend to slowness of speech and mind. The Sussex man is by the very rarest chance engaged in any manufacturing industries. He is by choice and by force of circumstances ploughman, woodman, shepherd, market-gardener, or carter, and is become heavy as his soil, and curiously old-world in habit. All which traits are delightful to the preternaturally sharp Londoner, whose nerves occupy the most important place in his being. These country folk are new and interesting creatures for study to him who is weary of that acute product of *fin-de-siècle* civilisation—the London arab.

Sussex ways are, many of them, still curiously patriarchal. But a few years ago, and ploughing was commonly performed in these fields by oxen: even to-day those teams are still met with. Shepherds watched their flocks on the South Downs as they have done here since history became a chronology of four figures. Their speech, like their dress, has varied somewhat in the flight of centuries, but their occupation has changed not a whit since the

THE SOUTH DOWNS, CLAYTON.

declining period of Saxon rule, when the tenth century merged into the eleventh.

Their cottages are the same as ever; thatched for the greater part, and within, the old household scene of living room, with yawning fireplace, and, commonly, red-bricked floor. The capacious settle is drawn up to the blaze; brass candlesticks of many mouldings shine upon the high mantelshelf, flanked, indeed, by specimens of a modern science, daguerreotypes, silhouettes, and photographs of the cotter's relatives; but these, with the occasional weekly paper and the familiar gaudy calendar from the village grocer's, are generally the only distinctive products of our times you shall readily find. To the contrary, the ancient home-made sampler and the time-honoured tankard are more frequently met with.

Outside, in the garden, grow homely flowers and useful vegetables, and perhaps by the gnarled apple-trees there stands in the sun a row of beehives, which may indeed be purchased, but, so lingering superstition hath it, with, perhaps, a subtle touch of worldly wisdom and modern commercialism, only with gold; for

> "If you wish your bees to thrive,
> Gold must be paid for ev'ry hive;
> For when they're bought with other money,
> There will be neither swarm nor honey."

Indeed, the year was used to be one long round of superstitious customs and observances for the Sussex peasant, and, under favourable circumstances and in favouring places, it is so even now. But superstition is shy, and not to be discovered of the casual wayfarer; it is here, though, and will remain while human nature remains what it is.

In January began the round, for from Christmas Eve to Twelfth Day was the proper time for "worsling," that is "wassailing" the orchards, but more particularly the apple-trees. The country-folk would gather round the trees and chant in chorus, rapping the trunks the while with sticks—

"Stand fast root, bear well top;
Pray, good God, send us a howling crop;
Ev'ry twig, apples big;
Ev'ry bough, apples enow';
Hats full, caps full,
Full quarters, sacks full."

These wassailing folk were generally known as "howlers;" "doubtless rightly," says a Sussex archaeologist, "for real old Sussex music is in a minor key, and can hardly be distinguished from howling." This knowledge enlightens our reading of the pages of the Rev. Giles Moore, of Horsted Keynes, when he records:—"1670, 26th Dec., I gave the howling boys 6d.;" a statement which, if not illumined by acquaintance with these old customs, would be altogether incomprehensible.

Then, if mud were brought into the house in the month of January, the cleanly housewife, at other times jealous of her spotless floors, would have nothing of reproof to say, for was this not "January butter," and the harbinger of luck to all beneath the roof-tree?

Saints' days, too, had their observances; the

habits of bird and beast were the almanacs and weather warnings of the villagers, all innocent of any other meteorological department, and they have been handed down in doggerel rhyme, like this of the Cuckoo, to the present day:—

> "In April he shows his bill,
> In May he sings o' night and day,
> In June he'll change his tune,
> By July prepares to fly,
> By August away he must.
> If he stay till September,
> 'Tis as much as the oldest man
> Can ever remember."

If he stayed till September, he might possibly see a sight which no mere human eye ever beheld: he might observe a practice to which old Sussex folk know the Evil One to be addicted. For on Old Michaelmas Day, September 10th, the Devil goes round the country, and—dirty fellow—spits on the blackberries. Should any persons eat one on the 11th of September, they, or some one of their kin, will surely die or fall into great trouble before the close of the year.

But to come down from these malignant doings to domestic matters, we shall find that the Sunday next before Advent is widely known as "Stir-up Sunday," from the Collect for that day, which commences "Stir up, we beseech Thee, O Lord." and reminds both the grocer to lay in his stock of Christmas fruits, and the housewife to think upon the "stirring up" of her plum-pudding.

Sussex has neither the imaginative Celtic race

of Cornwall nor that county's fantastic scenery to inspire legends; but is it at all wonderful that old beliefs die hard in a county so inaccessible as this has hitherto been? We have read travellers' tales of woful happenings on the road; hear now Defoe, who is writing in the year 1724, of another proof of heavy going on the highways:—"I saw," says he, "an ancient lady, and a lady of very good quality, I assure you, drawn to church in her coach by six oxen; nor was it done in frolic or humour, but from sheer necessity, the way being so stiff and deep that no horses could go in it." All which says much for the piety of this ancient lady. Only a few years later, in 1729, died Dame Judith, widow of Sir Henry Hatsell, who in her will, dated 10th January 1728, directed that her body should be buried at Preston, should she happen to die at such a time of year when the roads were passable; otherwise, at any place her executors might think suitable. It so happened that she died in the month of June, so compliance with her wishes was possible.

We took an evening walk in the neighbourhood of Ditchling and Wivelsfield, starting as the sun began to set.

The gloaming is, apart from the bleating sentimentalist of the drawing-room ballad, a charming time. Noon-day glare is gone; the sharp photograph-like distinctness of objects near and far is vanished with the sun, and in its place come the tender tones and suggestive haze of 'tween lights. Now does the prosaic villa of commerce loom largely upon the imagination in the misty valley, and the trees and wayside bushes begin to assume delightfully dreadful forms, with beckoning fingers of topmost branches, and trunks of strange and awesome shapes. Now does the cool breeze of evening rise

AT CLAYTON.

and play upon the electric wires in tunes now low, now in throbbing loudness, now in some witch-inspired æolian melody, and again in an access of demoniacal frenzy. It is only the circumstance of sunlight that makes the telegraph wire a prosaic object.

Ditchling and Wivelsfield villages were, as night fell, mere formless blots upon the whiteness of bye-roads, glimmering faintly from commons and waifs and strays and selvedges of common land; lights in cottage windows only accentuated the murk and gloom of their thatched roofs and heavy chimneys set against the sky. Jacob's Post, standing, as it has done since 1734, on Ditchling Common, an authentic fragment of a gibbet, seemed well suited to such a place and hour. It takes its name from Jacob Harris, a Jew pedlar, who committed a triple murder at the inn close by, and was hanged for it at Horsham Gaol, afterwards being swung in chains near the scene of his crime. Pieces of wood from this gallows-tree were long and highly esteemed by country-folk as charms, and were often carried about with them as preventatives of all manner of accidents and diseases; indeed, its present meagre proportions are due to this practice and belief.

From Ditchling we returned to Friar's Oak, there to sup and sleep and dream horribly of Jacob and the "Dancing Friar."

FIFTH DAY.

And now for Brighton, nine miles away, past the little Early English church of Clayton, and over Clayton Hill to Pyecombe Street, where the alternative route *viâ* Albourne rejoins the classic road, and where the equally meagre church of Pyecombe stands beside a blacksmith's forge, on a commanding spur of the rolling downs.

The churches of Pyecombe, Patcham, Preston, and Clayton are very similar in appearance exteriorly, all with a shingled spirelet of insignificant proportions. This little Norman church, consisting of nave (a tiny nave) and chancel only, is chiefly interesting as possessing a triple chancel arch and an ancient font.

Over the chancel arch hangs a painting of the Royal Arms, painted in the time of George III., faded and tawdry, with dandified unicorn and a gamboge lion, all teeth and mane, regarding the congregation on Sundays, and empty benches at other times, with the most amiable of grins. Other points of interest there are none at Pyecombe, except the "Plough" Inn, at the junction of the roads, a hostelry of some age and of pleasant appearance.

And so down the few remaining miles, past Pangdean, where, by an unkempt farm, several acrobatic ducks were performing astonishing feats of agility, standing on their heads and somersaulting in a roadside pond of dirty water, to Patcham, which rejoices, or may be supposed to rejoice, in the possession of a delusive Jubilee horse-trough, wearing, a way off, with its unvarnished oak and shingled peaked roof, and inscription of Gothic character, the appearance of some mediæval lychgate strayed upon the road.

OLD DOVECOT, PATCHAM.

But Patcham has, in a meadow beside its church, one of those ancient dovecots seen now and again in the land; buttressed structures of an astonishing solidity, bearing in mind their use. This is a picturesque, half-ruinated example, built, in a district where building stone is not found, of plenteous Sussex flints, deep-embedded in mortar and diversified by occasional bands of red brick. Close by is the church, swept and garnished and encaustic-tiled, and containing on the tympanum above the chancel arch the remains of a mediæval fresco, discovered at a restoration, deep beneath layers of Puritan-churchwarden whitewash.

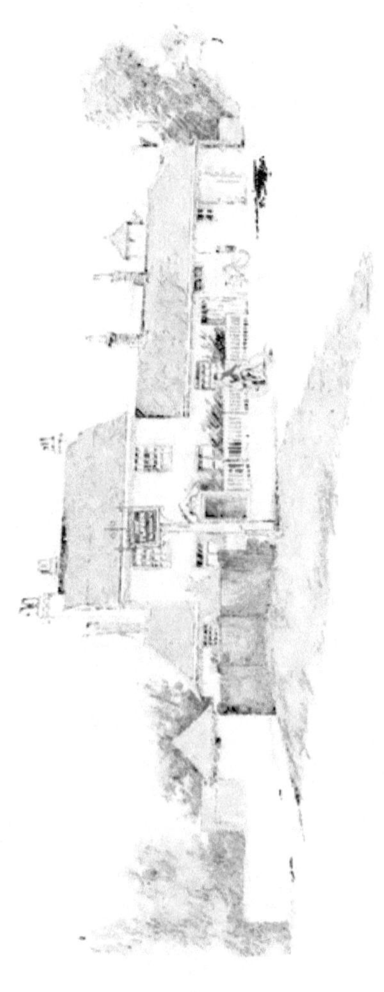

And now for a tale of smuggling times. In the churchyard at Patcham, to the north of the church, is a tombstone with almost illegible inscription, to this effect:—

> "Sacred to the memory of DANIEL SCALES,
> who was unfortunately shot on Thursday evening,
> November 7th, 1796.
>
> "Alas! swift flew the fatal lead,
> Which piercéd through the young man's head.
> He instant fell, resigned his breath,
> And closed his languid eyes in death.
> All you who do this stone draw near,
> Oh! pray let fall the pitying tear.
> From this sad instance may we all
> Prepare to meet Jehovah's call."

Poor fellow! Now this young man was a desperate smuggler, one of a daring gang which had long carried on its risky business practically unmolested on these downs. On the night when he was "unfortunately shot," he was, with many others, coming from Brighton, the gang of them laden heavily with smuggled goods, when they fell in with a number of soldiers and excise officers near this place. The smugglers fled, leaving their casks of liquor to take care of themselves, careful only to make good their own escape, saving only Daniel Scales, who, met by a "riding officer," as mounted excisemen were termed, was called upon by him to surrender himself and his booty, which he refused to do. The officer, who himself had been in early days engaged in many smuggling transactions, knew that Daniel was "too good a man for him, for they had tried it out before;" so he shot him through the head. Alas! poor Daniel.

I think that is the most romantic incident in the history of Patcham, a little village that lines the road for a space by the forty-eighth milestone, and thereafter clambers up the foot-hills of the Downs. Patcham is not unbeautiful, especially as you view it looking southward down the road, beside barren-looking fields, in which flints stand in the same proportion to soil as do quibbles to truths in the speeches of your vote-hunting politician. Opposite these ungenerous fields, on the other side of the highway, runs the railroad, deep in chalk cuttings, and between goes the high-road, enveloped in clouds of chalk-dust, and further along is the pinched-in, bleached-looking street of Patcham. Beyond this is the stretch of road and gritty pathways leading to the welcome shade of Withdean trees, and in another mile, diversified now with many villas, and dusty and gritty beyond mere words, is Preston.

To attempt to draw here a character sketch of Preston would be to attempt the impossible, for now-a-days Preston is so assimilated to Brighton as to have few independent features of its own beyond the Park, which, indeed, belongs also to the borough, and is the heritage of Brightonians and Preston folk alike—if, again, you *can* class your Brighton and Preston residents under two heads.

Preston Church, though patched and pieced and altered, remains practically the little Early English church it ever has been. It contains little of inte-

PATCHAM.

rest beyond the Shirley tomb and the frescoes upon the chancel arch, one representing the murder of Thomas à Beckett, while in the other the Virgin Mary is, together with an angel, contending with the Devil for the possession of a departed soul. The angel, like some celestial grocer, appears to be weighing the soul in a balance, while the fiend, sitting in one scale, makes the unfortunate soul in the other "kick the beam." That Devil is a weighty person in the matter of avoirdupois.

When it is said that Preston Church is also the burial-place of the fiery, disputatious, seventeenth-century Cheynell, the claims of the building to notice are done.

Preston turnpike gate, erected about 1807, was removed in May 1854 to a point a hundred yards north of Withdean, as the result of an agitation started in 1853, when the Highway Trustees were applying to Parliament for another term of years. It and its hateful legend, "NO TRUST," painted large for all the world to see, were a nuisance and a gratuitous satire upon human nature; no one regretted them when their time came.

Passing the modernised coaching inn, the "Crown and Anchor," the tall elms beside the park railings come in view, and, obtruding upon the roadway, break happily the ever-growing streets; but they will have, are having, their day, which cannot last long, and then the Park will be seen with its hem of houses complete.

Presently we are upon the pavements and the great span of the lofty railway viaduct confirms our entry of the town. A great wall of roofs and houses, lines upon lines of streets, rows and rows of never-ending terraces and squares and crescents, rise up before the eye, framed in by that soaring arch, and it seems as if London, a brighter, cleaner London, certainly, had appeared.

And so we came at length into the centre, the very heart of this Brighton, the Old Steyne, the rendezvous of fashion in the days of the Regency and George IV.'s reign, filled with reminiscences of Perdita Robinson and Mrs. Fitzgerald, and the many who flourished so bravely for awhile in the favour of Prince Florizel.

For all its history, the place wears a passé, decayed appearance, because those days of its brilliancy are past, and *are* historic now. The houses, stuccoed, with those intolerable bay windows so characteristic of the time and place, are not old enough to be interesting, nor sufficiently new for smartness' sake, and so fail of satisfying on any count. Mrs. Fitzgerald's house, No. 55 Old Steyne, is now the chosen home of the Brighton Young Men's Christian Association. Time brings, most certainly, many strange revenges!

The Pavilion is still here, with its grounds and trees—the few trees the town can boast. Treeless Brighton has been the derision alike of Doctor Johnson and Tom Hood, to name no others. Johnson, who visited Brighton in 1770 in the company of the Thrales and Fanny Burney, declared the neighbourhood to be so desolate that "if one had a mind to hang one's self for desperation at being

obliged to live there, it would be difficult to find a tree on which to fasten a rope."

Hood, on the other hand, is jocular in an airier and lighter-hearted fashion. His punning humour (a kind of witticism which Johnson hated with the hatred of a man who delved deep after Greek and Latin roots) is to Johnson's as the footfall of a cat to the earth-shaking tread of the elephant. His, too, is a manner of gibe that is susceptible of being construed into praise by the townsfolk. "Of all the trees," says he, "I ever saw, none could be mentioned in the same breath with the magnificent beach at Brighton."

But though these trees of the Pavilion give a grateful shelter from the glare of the sun and the roughness of the wind, they hide little of the tawdriness of that architectural enormity. The gilding has faded, the tinsel become tarnished, and the whole pile of cupolas and minarets is reduced to one even tint, that is not white nor grey, nor any distinctive shade of any colour. How the preposterous building could ever have been admired (as it undoubtedly was at one time) surpasses belief. Its cost, one shrewdly suspects—it is supposed to have cost over £1,000,000—was what appealed to the imagination.

That reptile Croker, the creature of that Lord Hertford whom one recognises as the "Marquis of Steyne" in "Vanity Fair," admired it, as assuredly did not rough-and-ready Cobbett, who opines, "A good idea of the building may be formed by placing the pointed half of a large turnip upon the middle of a board, with four smaller ones at the (*sic*) corner."

That is not a bad comparison of this monument of extravagance and bad taste. Commenced in 1784, and, after numerous alterations, pullings-down, and rebuildings, finally completed in 1818, it set the seal of a certain permanence upon the royal favours extended to the town, whose population rose from 3600 in the year of its completion to the remarkable total of 24,429, shown in the census of 1821,[1] the last of George the Fourth's reign.

One of the best stories connected with this sorry building is that told so well in the "Four Georges:"—

And now I have one more story of the bacchanalian sort, in which Clarence of York and the very highest personage in the realm, the great Prince Regent, all play parts.

"The feast took place at the Pavilion at Brighton, and was described to me by a gentleman who was present at the scene. In Gilray's caricatures, and amongst Fox's jolly associates, there figures a great nobleman, the Duke of Norfolk, called Jockey of Norfolk in his time, and celebrated for his table exploits. He had quarrelled with the Prince, like the rest of the Whigs; but a sort of reconciliation

[1] Population of Brighton, from the earliest authenticated lists, to the present time:—

1761	. 2,000	1821	. 24,429	1861	. 77,693-88,361[1]
1786	. 3,600	1831	. 40,634	1871	. 90,011-103,760[1]
1794	. 5,669	1841	. 46,661	1881	. 99,049-128,382[1]
1801	. 7,339	1851	. 65,583	1891	. 102,699-136,419[1]
1811	. 12,012				

[1] Parliamentary borough, including Hove and Preston.

had taken place, and now, being a very old man, the Prince invited him to dine and sleep at the Pavilion, and the old Duke drove over from his Castle of Arundel with his famous equipage of grey horses, still remembered in Sussex.

"The Prince of Wales had concocted with his royal brothers a notable scheme for making the old man drunk. Every person at table was enjoined to drink wine with the Duke—a challenge which the old toper did not refuse. He soon began to see that there was a conspiracy against him; he drank glass for glass: he overthrew many of the brave. At last the first gentleman of Europe proposed bumpers of brandy. One of the royal brothers filled a great glass for the Duke. He stood up and tossed off the drink. 'Now,' says he, 'I will have my carriage and go home.'

"The Prince urged upon him his previous promise to sleep under the roof where he had been so generously entertained. 'No,' he said; 'he had had enough of such hospitality. A trap had been set for him; he would leave the place at once, and never enter its doors more.'

"The carriage was called, and came; but, in the half-hour's interval, the liquor had proved too potent for the old man; his host's generous purpose was answered, and the Duke's old grey head lay stupefied on the table. Nevertheless, when his post-chaise was announced, he staggered to it as well as he could, and stumbling in, bade the postillions drive to Arundel.

"They drove him for half an hour round and

round the Pavilion lawn; the poor old man fancied he was going home.

"When he awoke that morning, he was in a bed at the Prince's hideous house at Brighton. You may see the place now for sixpence; they have fiddlers there every day, and sometimes buffoons and mountebanks hire the Riding-House and do their tricks and tumbling there. The trees are still there, and the gravel walks round which the poor old sinner was trotted."

But indeed practical joking was carried to the extreme—was elevated to the status of a fine art at Brighton by the Prince and his merry men. A characteristic story of him is that told of a drive to Brighton races, when he was accompanied in his great yellow barouche by Townsend, the Bow Street runner, who was present to protect the Prince from insult or robbery at the hands of the multitude. 'It was a position,' says my authority, 'which gave His Royal Highness an opportunity to practise upon his guardian a somewhat unpleasant joke. Turning suddenly to Townsend, just at the termination of a race, he exclaimed, 'By Jove, Townsend, I've been robbed; I had with me some damson tarts, but they are now gone.' 'Gone!' said Townsend, rising; 'impossible!' 'Yes,' rejoined the Prince, 'and you are the purloiner,' at the same time taking from the seat whereon the officer had been sitting the crushed crust of the asserted missing tarts, and adding, 'This is a sad blot upon your reputation as a vigilant officer.' 'Rather say, your Royal Highness, a sad stain upon my escutcheon,' added Townsend, raising the gilt-buttoned tails of his blue coat and exhibiting the fruit-stained seat of his nankeen inexpressibles."

But it was not this practical-joking Prince who first discovered Brighton. It would never have attained its great vogue without him, but it would have been the health resort of a certain circle of fashion—an inferior Bath, in fact. To Dr. Richard Russell, who visited the little village of Brighthelmstone in 1750, belongs the credit of discovering the place to an ailing fashionable world. He died in 1759, long ere the sun of royal splendour first rose upon the fishing-village; but even before the Prince of Wales first visited Brighthelmstone in 1782, it had attained a certain popularity, as the "Brighthelmstone Guide" of July 1777 attests in these halting verses:—

"This town or village of renown,
Like London Bridge, half broken down,
Few years ago was worse than Wapping,
Not fit for a human soul to stop in;
But now, like to a worn out shoe,
By patching well, the place will do.
You'd wonder much, I'm sure to see
How it's becramm'd with quality."

And so on.

Brighthelmstone, indeed, has had more Guides written upon it than even Bath has had, and very curious some of them are become in these days. They range from lively to severe, from grave to gay, from the serious screeds of Russell and Dr. Relhan, his successor, to the light and airy, and not too admirable puffs of to-day. But however these guides may vary, they all agree in harking back to that shadowy Brighthelm who is supposed to have given his peculiar name to the ancient fisher-village here established time out of mind. In the days when "County Histories" were first let loose, in folio volumes, upon an unoffending land, historians, archæologists, and other interested parties seemed at a loss for the derivation of the place-name, and, rather than confess themselves ignorant of its meaning, they conspired together to invent a Saxon archbishop, who, dying in the odour of sanctity and the ninth century, bequeathed his appellation to what is now known, in a contracted form, as Brighton.

But the man is not known who has unassailable proofs to show of this Brighthelm's having so honoured the fisher-folk's hovels with his name.

Thackeray, greatly daring, considering that the Fourth George is the real patron—saint, we can hardly say; let us make it—king, of the town, elected to deliver his lectures upon the "Four Georges" at Brighton, among other places, and to that end made, with monumental assurance, a personal application at the Town-Hall for the hire of the banqueting-room in the Royal Pavilion.

But one of the Aldermen, who chanced to be present, suggested, with extra-aldermanic wit, that the Town-Hall would be equally suitable, intimating at the same time that it was not considered as strictly etiquette to "abuse a man in his own house." The witty Alderman's suggestion, we are

THE AQUARIUM

told, was acted upon, and the Town Hall engaged forthwith.

It indeed argued considerable courage on the lecturer's part to declaim against George IV. anywhere in that town which His Majesty had, by his example, conjured up from almost nothingness. It does not seem that Thackeray was, after all, ill-received at Brighton; whence thoughts arise as to the ingratitude and fleeting memories of them that were, either in the first or second generation, advantaged by the royal preference for this bleak stretch of shore beneath the bare South Downs, open to every wind that blows. Surely gratitude is well described as a "lively sense of favours to come," and what more was there to expect from a dead hand?

Did not Her Majesty, unmindful of Brighton's charms, sell the Royal Pavilion to the (then) Commissioners of Brighton in 1850 for the goodly sum of £53,000, and thereafter deny the place her presence?

Has royalty in the present generation advantaged Brighton anything whatever? I trow not. Therefore, perhaps, the townsfolk resented nothing of all the lecturer's gall and wormwood, doubtless secure in the sense of favours acknowledged by the tardy setting up of a brazen image to the memory of him who is really the genius of the place, *vice* Brighthelm superannuated.[1]

[1] This statue was erected in October 1828. The idea of setting up a memorial to him who had so plenished their pockets originated with a number of Brighton tradesmen, "who," says Erredge, in his valuable "History of Brighthelmstone," "were accustomed to assemble nightly

For they have set up on the Old Steyne an image of the King, by Chantrey; and there he stands, on his granite pedestal, smooth-faced and smirking, as unlike one's conception of that easy-going, roystering blade as may well be. It seems as incongruous as though the Y.M.C.A. were to call him brother, to perpetuate this characterless travesty. The salt sea-breeze blows upon that brazen statue facing toward the King's Road, so that there has become deposited on that characterless countenance a partial green coating of oxide. They let it remain; what right, then, should they have to resent a stranger's depreciatory remarks upon the original of that neglected image?

This space, in whose midst rises the counterfeit presentment of His Majesty, is sacred to Corinthian days and memories of the Regency. Bay-windowed frontages, red-bricked paves, Pavilion pinnacles, what frolics have you not witnessed in the long-past days before Mrs. Grundy had become the infinitely more tyrannical British Matron; when men travelled, not by steam, but drawn by horses, and when the short-waisted frock, the curly wig, and knee-breeches were still the vogue.

Roysterers all are gone. The Prince and King, the Barrymores—Hellgate, Newgate, and Cripplegate—brothers three; Mrs. Fitzgerald, "the only woman whom George the Fourth ever really loved;" Sir John Lade, the reckless, the frolicsome, who is

at the 'King's Arms,' George Street; but a subscription which remained open for more than eight years and a half did not provide the sum—£3000—agreed to be paid Chantrey for his artistic skill."

in so far historic that he was the first man who (with the courage and "æs triplex" of the Horatian mariner who first put off to sea) publicly wore the trouser: these, with innumerable others, are long since silent, and their places know them no more. No more are they heard who, with unseemly revelry, disturbed the midnight moon, and upset the decrepit watchman in his box, the while his companion swung his creaking rattle for timely succour.

WATCHMAN.

Those days are done, and we live in a time which, if more to be desired from comfort's point of view, is certainly less picturesque and more gravely decorous than the closing years of the last and the opening decade of the present century.

And now we had reached the end of our journey, but there were two places in this town which we wished to see ere we departed hence. They are both of them connected with the one historical escapade of any antiquity that belongs to the town, and which, safely carried through, ensured the death of the Commonwealth, the ultimate restoration of the monarchy, and the return of Charles the Second.

The one is in West Street, at the sign of the

King's Head. In 1651, after the disastrous result of Worcester fight, Charles was driven to wander, a fugitive, through the land, seeking the coast from which he could embark and reach safety until such time as he could come in power and claim his own again.

Hunted by relentless Roundheads, and sheltered

DR. RICHARD RUSSELL (*from a picture by Zoffany*).

on his way by only a few faithful adherents, he at length reached the village of Brighthelmstone with his small party, and lodged at the inn, which was then the "George."

That evening, after much negotiation, Colonel Gunter, the King's companion, arranged with Nicholas Tettersell, the master of a small trading

vessel, to convey the King across the Channel to Fécamp, on the coast of France, to sail in the early hours of the following morning, October 14th. How they sailed, and the account of their journeyings, shall be found fully set forth in the "Narrative" of Colonel Gunter by he who lists to hear a romantic episode in English history.

The inn is still standing, a small building of brick, with low-ceiled parlour and upstairs rooms, upon which the loyal may look with reverence, but which, were their history unknown, would be accounted mean.

The sign was altered upon the King's triumphant return to that name it bears to-day, but the picture of the miscalled "Merry" Monarch has long since vanished. Fanny Burney, visiting Brighton in the company of the Thrales, who resided opposite, was familiar with this sign, for she says of the place, "I fail not to look at it with loyal satisfaction, and his black-wigged Majesty has from the time of his restoration been its sign."[1]

Then from West Street we found our way to the old parish church of Brighton, St. Nicholas, standing upon the topmost eyrie of the borough, and overlooking from its crowded graveyard the heaped and jostling roofs below.

This is probably the place referred to by a viva-

[1] Alas! some scientific historian has demolished the legend of the King's Head. This ruthless destroyer of a picturesque falsehood has proved that there was no "George" until a very much later date than that of Charles's escape, and also that in later times the inn of that name was in Middle Street, on the site of the present No. 44. *Sic transit gloria, &c.*

cious Frenchman, who, just over a hundred years ago, summed up "Brigtemstone" as "a miserable village, commanded by a cemetery and surrounded by barren mountains." That this populous burying-place should be a place of pilgrimage for all them that are historically inclined may well be granted, but I do not know that visitors to it are many of all the crowds that come here to court the sea.

But from here you can, with some trouble, catch just a glimpse of the watery horizon through the grey haze that rises from countless chimney-pots, and never a breeze but blows laden with the scent of soot and smoke. Yet, for all the changed fortune that changeful Time has brought this hoary and grimy place, he has not yet deprived it of interesting mementoes. You may, with patience, discover the tombstone of Phœbe Hassall, a centenarian of pith and valour, who, in her youthful days, in male attire, joined His Majesty King George the Second's army, and warred with her regiment in many lands; and all around are the resting-places of many celebrities, who, denied a wider fame, have yet their place in local annals; but prominent in place and in fame is the tomb of that Captain Tettersell who (it must be owned, for a consideration) sailed away that October morn, two hundred and forty years ago, across the Channel, carrying with him the hope of the clouded Royalists aboard his grimy craft.

His altar-tomb stands without the southern doorway of the church, and reads curiously to modern ears. That not one of all the many who have had

ST. NICHOLAS—THE OLD PARISH CHURCH OF BRIGHTHELMSTONE.

occasion to print it has transcribed the quaintness of that epitaph aright seems a strange thing, but so it is :—

"P.M.S.

"Captain NICHOLAS TETTERSELL, through whose Prudence ualour an Loyalty Charles the second King of England & after he had escaped the sword of his merciless rebells and his fforses received a fatall ouerthrowe at Worcester Septr 3^{d} 1651, was ffaithfully preserued & conueyed into ffrance. Departed this life the 26th day of July 1674.

→ → →

"Within this monument doth lye,
Approued Ffaith, hono^{r} and Loyalty.
In this Cold Clay he hath now tane up his statio^{n},
At once preserued ye Church, the Crowne and nation.
When Charles ye Greate was nothing but a breat^{h}
This ualiant soule stept betweene him & death.
Usurpers threats nor tyrant rebells frowne
Could not affright his duty to the Crowne :
Which glorious act of his for Church & state,
Eight princes in one day did Gratulate
Professing all to him in debt to bee
As all the world are to his memory
Since Earth Could not Reward his worth have give^{n},
Hee now receiues it from the King of heauen."

And so, Tettersell, farewell !

We left the churchyard and its memories and descended the steep street to Brighton of to-day ; to where, ye gods ! stands the Jubilee Clock Tower at the parting of the ways. And so down North Street to the Steyne once more. Hasting from the ruddy brick pavements of the Old Steyne, past the entrance to the Aquarium, we presently happened, rather than walked, upon that beach of which Wigstead speaks in his "Excursion," talking with amusing gusto of the "number of beautiful women who every morning court the embraces of the Watery God."

Alas! when we reached the beach there were no beautiful women courting embraces. Perhaps we were too late; perhaps their absence was to be accounted for in the fact of the Watery God being at low ebb. Perhaps the bye-laws of the corporation of Brighton . . . . ?!

This was Saturday; not yet, though, had the smart London "Saturday to Monday" horde arrived upon the scene, and the King's Road was comparatively clear. Neither was this the season when the cheap tripper disports himself in his thousands upon the beach, and the Cockney treats his *inamorata* to a fleeting five hours at the seaside. No; Brighton was, for the time, quiet.

There yet remained to us two hours ere the fashionable invasion began, so we sheltered on the painful pebbles under the welcome lee of a groyne, and gazed awhile across this sailless sea and upon the doomed Chain Pier. C—— fingered his stubby beard reflectively; the writer regarded with something akin to shame his travel-stained attire. A passing fair one looked curiously at us two pilgrims, and went her way smiling.

. . . . . .

Then our eyes met with a mute intelligence. We rose simultaneously and made to depart. Brighton is no place for the travel-worn. We would away to some rural resting-place, less public and with a wider

THE CHAIN PIER, 1839.
(From a contemporary Lithograph.)

latitude in the matter of dress than this, whose Bond Street air shamed our knapsacks and dusty boots.

"Where shall it be?" asked the other man. "Rottingdean." "Very well, quartermaster, make it so;" and we, disregarding Horace Greeley's advice to the "young man," went east.

DAY TRIPPERS.

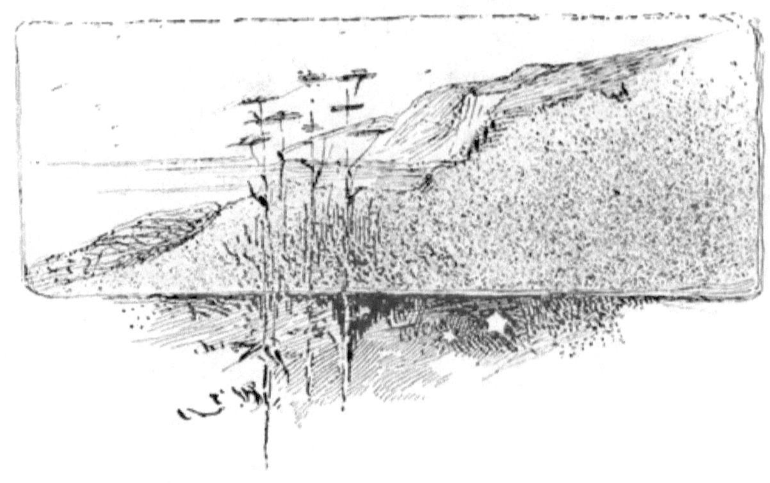

THE ROAD TO BRIGHTON.

	Miles.
Westminster Bridge (Surrey side) to—	
St. Mark's Church, Kennington	$1\frac{1}{2}$
Brixton Church .	3
Streatham . .	$5\frac{1}{2}$
Norbury . .	$6\frac{3}{4}$
Thornton Heath	8
Croydon (Whitgift's Hospital) .	$9\frac{1}{2}$
Purley House . . .	$11\frac{1}{2}$
Smitham Bottom	$13\frac{1}{2}$
Coulsdon Railway Station	$14\frac{1}{4}$
Merstham . .	$17\frac{3}{4}$
Redhill (Market Hall)	$20\frac{1}{2}$
Horley (Chequers) .	24
Povey Cross	$25\frac{3}{4}$
Kimberham Bridge (cross River Mole)	26
Lowfield Heath . .	27

	Miles.
Crawley . .	29
Pease-Pottage Gate . .	31¼
Hand Cross . . .	33½
Staplefield Common	34¾
Slough Green	36¼
Whiteman's Green .	37¼
Cuckfield	37½
Ansty Cross	38
Bridge Farm (cross River Adur)	40¼
St. John's Common	40¾
Friar's Oak Inn	42¾
Stonepound .	43½
Clayton .	44½
Pyecombe	45½
Patcham	48
Withdean	48¾
Preston . . .	49¾
Brighton (Aquarium)	51½

INDEX.

THE END.

PRINTED BY BALLANTYNE, HANSON AND CO.
EDINBURGH AND LONDON.

A List of Books

PUBLISHED BY

CHATTO & WINDUS,

214, Piccadilly, London, W.

Sold by all Booksellers, or sent post-free for the published price by the Publishers.

ABOUT.—THE FELLAH: An Egyptian Novel. By EDMOND ABOUT. Translated by Sir RANDAL ROBERTS. Post 8vo, illustrated boards, **2s.**

ADAMS (W. DAVENPORT), WORKS BY.

A DICTIONARY OF THE DRAMA. Being a comprehensive Guide to the Plays, Playwrights, Players, and Playhouses of the United Kingdom and America. Crown 8vo, half-bound, **12s. 6d.** [*Preparing.*

QUIPS AND QUIDDITIES. Selected by W. D. ADAMS. Post 8vo, cloth limp, **2s. 6d.**

ADAMS (W. H. D.).—WITCH, WARLOCK, AND MAGICIAN: Historical Sketches of Magic and Witchcraft in England and Scotland. By W. H. DAVENPORT ADAMS. Demy 8vo, cloth extra, **12s.**

AGONY COLUMN (THE) OF "THE TIMES," from 1800 to 1870. Edited, with an Introduction, by ALICE CLAY. Post 8vo, cloth limp, **2s. 6d.**

AIDE (HAMILTON), WORKS BY. Post 8vo, illustrated boards, **2s.** each.

CARR OF CARRLYON. | **CONFIDENCES.**

ALBERT.—BROOKE FINCHLEY'S DAUGHTER. By MARY ALBERT. Post 8vo, picture boards, **2s.**; cloth limp, **2s. 6d.**

ALEXANDER (MRS.), NOVELS BY. Post 8vo, illustrated boards, **2s.** each.

MAID, WIFE, OR WIDOW? | **VALERIE'S FATE.**

ALLEN (F. M.).—GREEN AS GRASS. By F. M. ALLEN, Author of "Through Green Glasses." With a Frontispiece by JOSEPH SMYTH. Crown 8vo, cloth extra, **3s. 6d.**

ALLEN (GRANT), WORKS BY. Crown 8vo, cloth extra, **6s.** each.

THE EVOLUTIONIST AT LARGE. | **COLIN CLOUT'S CALENDAR.**

Crown 8vo, cloth extra, **3s. 6d.** each; post 8vo, illustrated boards, **2s.** each.

PHILISTIA.
BABYLON.
STRANGE STORIES.
BECKONING HAND.
FOR MAIMIE'S SAKE.
IN ALL SHADES.
THE DEVIL'S DIE.
THIS MORTAL COIL.
THE TENTS OF SHEM.
THE GREAT TABOO.

DUMARESQ'S DAUGHTER. Crown 8vo, cloth extra, **3s. 6d.**

THE DUCHESS OF POWYSLAND. Three Vols., crown 8vo.

AMERICAN LITERATURE, A LIBRARY OF, from the Earliest Settlement to the Present Time. Compiled and Edited by EDMUND CLARENCE STEDMAN and ELLEN MACKAY HUTCHINSON. Eleven Vols., royal 8vo, cloth extra. A few copies are for sale by Messrs. CHATTO & WINDUS, price **£6 12s.** the set.

ARCHITECTURAL STYLES, A HANDBOOK OF. By A. ROSENGARTEN. Translated by W. COLLETT-SANDARS. With 639 Illusts. Cr. 8vo, cl. ex., **7s. 6d.**

ART (THE) OF AMUSING: A Collection of Graceful Arts, GAMES, Tricks, Puzzles, and Charades. By FRANK BELLEW. 300 Illusts. Cr. 8vo, cl. ex., **4s. 6d.**

ARNOLD (EDWIN LESTER), WORKS BY.
THE WONDERFUL ADVENTURES OF PHRA THE PHŒNICIAN. With Introduction by Sir EDWIN ARNOLD, and 12 Illusts. by H. M. PAGET. Cr. 8vo, cl., **3s. 6d.**
BIRD LIFE IN ENGLAND. Crown 8vo, cloth extra, **6s.**

ARTEMUS WARD'S WORKS: The Works of CHARLES FARRER BROWNE, better known as ARTEMUS WARD. With Portrait and Facsimile. Crown 8vo, cloth extra, **7s. 6d.**—Also a POPULAR EDITION, post 8vo, picture boards, **2s.**
THE GENIAL SHOWMAN: Life and Adventures of ARTEMUS WARD. By EDWARD P. HINGSTON. With a Frontispiece. Crown 8vo, cloth extra, **3s. 6d.**

ASHTON (JOHN), WORKS BY. Crown 8vo, cloth extra, **7s. 6d.** each.
HISTORY OF THE CHAP-BOOKS OF THE 18th CENTURY. With 334 Illusts.
SOCIAL LIFE IN THE REIGN OF QUEEN ANNE. With 85 Illustrations.
HUMOUR, WIT, AND SATIRE OF SEVENTEENTH CENTURY. With 82 Illusts.
ENGLISH CARICATURE AND SATIRE ON NAPOLEON THE FIRST. 115 Illusts.
MODERN STREET BALLADS. With 57 Illustrations.

BACTERIA.—A SYNOPSIS OF THE BACTERIA AND YEAST FUNGI AND ALLIED SPECIES. By W. B. GROVE, B.A. With 87 Illustrations. Crown 8vo, cloth extra, **3s. 6d.**

BARDSLEY (REV. C. W.), WORKS BY.
ENGLISH SURNAMES: Their Sources and Significations. Cr. 8vo, cloth, **7s. 6d.**
CURIOSITIES OF PURITAN NOMENCLATURE. Crown 8vo, cloth extra, **6s.**

BARING GOULD (S., Author of "John Herring," &c.**), NOVELS BY.**
Crown 8vo, cloth extra, **3s. 6d.** each; post 8vo, illustrated boards, **2s.** each.
RED SPIDER. | **EVE.**

BARRETT (FRANK, Author of "Lady Biddy Fane,"**) NOVELS BY.**
Post 8vo, illustrated boards, **2s.** each; cloth, **2s. 6d.** each.
FETTERED FOR LIFE. | **BETWEEN LIFE AND DEATH.**
THE SIN OF OLGA ZASSOULICH.

BEACONSFIELD, LORD: A Biography. By T. P. O'CONNOR, M.P. Sixth Edition, with an Introduction. Crown 8vo, cloth extra, **5s.**

BEAUCHAMP.—GRANTLEY GRANGE: A Novel. By SHELSLEY BEAUCHAMP. Post 8vo, illustrated boards, **2s.**

BEAUTIFUL PICTURES BY BRITISH ARTISTS: A Gathering of Favourites from our Picture Galleries, beautifully engraved on Steel. With Notices of the Artists by SYDNEY ARMYTAGE, M.A. Imperial 4to, cloth extra, gilt edges, **21s.**

BECHSTEIN.—AS PRETTY AS SEVEN, and other German Stories. Collected by LUDWIG BECHSTEIN. With Additional Tales by the Brothers GRIMM, and 98 Illustrations by RICHTER. Square 8vo, cloth extra, **6s. 6d.**; gilt edges, **7s. 6d.**

BEERBOHM.—WANDERINGS IN PATAGONIA; or, Life among the Ostrich Hunters. By JULIUS BEERBOHM. With Illusts. Cr. 8vo, cl. extra, **3s. 6d.**

BESANT (WALTER), NOVELS BY.
Cr. 8vo, cl. ex., **3s. 6d.** each; post 8vo, illust. bds., **2s.** each; cl. limp, **2s. 6d.** each.
ALL SORTS AND CONDITIONS OF MEN. With Illustrations by FRED. BARNARD.
THE CAPTAINS' ROOM, &c. With Frontispiece by E. J. WHEELER.
ALL IN A GARDEN FAIR. With 6 Illustrations by HARRY FURNISS.
DOROTHY FORSTER. With Frontispiece by CHARLES GREEN.
UNCLE JACK, and other Stories. | **CHILDREN OF GIBEON.**
THE WORLD WENT VERY WELL THEN. With 12 Illustrations by A. FORESTIER.
HERR PAULUS: His Rise, his Greatness, and his Fall.
FOR FAITH AND FREEDOM. With Illustrations by A. FORESTIER and F. WADDY.
TO CALL HER MINE, &c. With 9 Illustrations by A. FORESTIER.
THE BELL OF ST. PAUL'S.
THE HOLY ROSE, &c. With Frontispiece by F. BARNARD.

Crown 8vo, cloth extra, **3s. 6d.** each.
ARMOREL OF LYONESSE: A Romance of To-day. With 12 Illusts. by F. BARNARD.
ST. KATHERINE'S BY THE TOWER. With 12 page Illustrations by C. GREEN.
VERBENA CAMELLIA STEPHANOTIS, &c. With a Frontispiece by GORDON BROWNE.

FIFTY YEARS AGO. With 144 Plates and Woodcuts. Cheaper Edition, Revised, with a New Preface, &c. Crown 8vo, cloth extra, **5s.**
THE EULOGY OF RICHARD JEFFERIES. With Portrait. Cr. 8vo, cl. extra, **6s.**
THE ART OF FICTION. Demy 8vo, **1s.**
LONDON. With 124 Illustrations. Demy 8vo, cloth extra, **18s.** [*Preparing.*

BESANT (WALTER) AND JAMES RICE, NOVELS BY.
Cr. 8vo, cl. ex., 3s. 6d. each; post 8vo, illust. bds., 2s. each; cl. limp, 2s. 6d. each.

READY-MONEY MORTIBOY.
MY LITTLE GIRL.
WITH HARP AND CROWN.
THIS SON OF VULCAN.
THE GOLDEN BUTTERFLY.
THE MONKS OF THELEMA.
BY CELIA'S ARBOUR.
THE CHAPLAIN OF THE FLEET.
THE SEAMY SIDE.
THE CASE OF MR. LUCRAFT, &c.
'TWAS IN TRAFALGAR'S BAY, &c.
THE TEN YEARS' TENANT, &c.

*** There is also a LIBRARY EDITION of the above Twelve Volumes, handsomely set in new type, on a large crown 8vo page, and bound in cloth extra, 6s. each.

BENNETT (W. C., LL.D.), WORKS BY. Post 8vo, cloth limp, 2s. each.
A BALLAD HISTORY OF ENGLAND. | SONGS FOR SAILORS.

BEWICK (THOMAS) AND HIS PUPILS. By AUSTIN DOBSON. With 95 Illustrations. Square 8vo, cloth extra, 6s.

BIERCE.—IN THE MIDST OF LIFE: Tales of Soldiers and Civilians. By AMBROSE BIERCE. Crown 8vo, cloth extra, 6s.

BLACKBURN'S (HENRY) ART HANDBOOKS.
ACADEMY NOTES, separate years, from 1875-1887, 1889-1891, each 1s.
ACADEMY NOTES, 1892. With Illustrations. 1s.
ACADEMY NOTES, 1875-79. Complete in One Vol., with 600 Illusts. Cloth limp, 6s.
ACADEMY NOTES, 1880-84. Complete in One Vol., with 700 Illusts. Cloth limp, 6s.
GROSVENOR NOTES, 1877. 6d.
GROSVENOR NOTES, separate years, from 1878 to 1890, each 1s.
GROSVENOR NOTES, Vol. I., 1877-82. With 300 Illusts. Demy 8vo, cloth limp, 6s.
GROSVENOR NOTES, Vol. II., 1883-87. With 300 Illusts. Demy 8vo, cloth limp, 6s.
THE NEW GALLERY, 1888-1891. With numerous Illustrations, each 1s.
THE NEW GALLERY, 1892. With Illustrations. 1s.
ENGLISH PICTURES AT THE NATIONAL GALLERY. 114 Illustrations. 1s.
OLD MASTERS AT THE NATIONAL GALLERY. 128 Illustrations. 1s. 6d.
ILLUSTRATED CATALOGUE TO THE NATIONAL GALLERY. 242 Illusts. cl., 3s.
THE PARIS SALON, 1892. With Facsimile Sketches. 3s.
THE PARIS SOCIETY OF FINE ARTS, 1892. With Sketches. 3s. 6d.

BLAKE (WILLIAM): India-proof Etchings from his Works by WILLIAM BELL SCOTT. With descriptive Text. Folio, half-bound boards, 21s.

BLIND (MATHILDE), Poems by. Crown 8vo, cloth extra, 5s. each.
THE ASCENT OF MAN.
DRAMAS IN MINIATURE. With a Frontispiece by FORD MADOX BROWN.

BOURNE (H. R. FOX), WORKS BY.
ENGLISH MERCHANTS: Memoirs in Illustration of the Progress of British Commerce. With numerous Illustrations. Crown 8vo, cloth extra, 7s. 6d.
ENGLISH NEWSPAPERS: The History of Journalism. Two Vols., demy 8vo, cl., 25s.
THE OTHER SIDE OF THE EMIN PASHA RELIEF EXPEDITION. Crown 8vo, cloth extra, 6s.

BOWERS.—LEAVES FROM A HUNTING JOURNAL. By GEORGE BOWERS. Oblong folio, half-bound, 21s.

BOYLE (FREDERICK), WORKS BY. Post 8vo, illustrated boards, 2s. each.
CHRONICLES OF NO-MAN'S LAND. | CAMP NOTES.
SAVAGE LIFE. Crown 8vo, cloth extra, 3s. 6d.; post 8vo, picture boards, 2s.

BRAND'S OBSERVATIONS ON POPULAR ANTIQUITIES; chiefly illustrating the Origin of our Vulgar Customs, Ceremonies, and Superstitions. With the Additions of Sir HENRY ELLIS, and Illustrations. Cr. 8vo, cloth extra, 7s. 6d.

BREWER (REV. DR.), WORKS BY.
THE READER'S HANDBOOK OF ALLUSIONS, REFERENCES, PLOTS, AND STORIES. Fifteenth Thousand. Crown 8vo, cloth extra, 7s. 6d.
AUTHORS AND THEIR WORKS, WITH THE DATES: Being the Appendices to "The Reader's Handbook," separately printed. Crown 8vo, cloth limp, 2s.
A DICTIONARY OF MIRACLES. Crown 8vo, cloth extra, 7s. 6d.

BREWSTER (SIR DAVID), WORKS BY. Post 8vo cl. ex. 4s. 6d. each.
MORE WORLDS THAN ONE: Creed of Philosopher and Hope of Christian. Plates.
THE MARTYRS OF SCIENCE: GALILEO, TYCHO BRAHE, and KEPLER. With Portraits.
LETTERS ON NATURAL MAGIC. With numerous Illustrations.

BRET HARTE, WORKS BY.

LIBRARY EDITION. In Seven Volumes, crown 8vo, cloth extra, **6s.** each.

BRET HARTE'S COLLECTED WORKS. Arranged and Revised by the Author.
Vol. I. COMPLETE POETICAL AND DRAMATIC WORKS. With Steel Portrait.
Vol. II. LUCK OF ROARING CAMP—BOHEMIAN PAPERS—AMERICAN LEGENDS.
Vol. III. TALES OF THE ARGONAUTS—EASTERN SKETCHES.
Vol. IV. GABRIEL CONROY.
Vol. V. STORIES—CONDENSED NOVELS, &c.
Vol. VI. TALES OF THE PACIFIC SLOPE.
Vol. VII. TALES OF THE PACIFIC SLOPE—II. With Portrait by JOHN PETTIE, R.A.

THE SELECT WORKS OF BRET HARTE, in Prose and Poetry With Introductory Essay by J. M. BELLEW, Portrait of Author, and 50 Illusts. Cr. 8vo, cl. ex., **7s. 6d.**
BRET HARTE'S POETICAL WORKS. Hand-made paper & buckram. Cr. 8vo, **4s. 6d.**
THE QUEEN OF THE PIRATE ISLE. With 28 original Drawings by KATE GREENAWAY, reproduced in Colours by EDMUND EVANS. Small 4to, cloth, **5s.**

Crown 8vo, cloth extra, **3s. 6d.** each.

A WAIF OF THE PLAINS. With 60 Illustrations by STANLEY L. WOOD.
A WARD OF THE GOLDEN GATE. With 59 Illustrations by STANLEY L. WOOD.
A SAPPHO OF GREEN SPRINGS, &c. With Two Illustrations by HUME NISBET.
COLONEL STARBOTTLE'S CLIENT, AND SOME OTHER PEOPLE. With a Frontispiece by FRED. BARNARD.

Post 8vo, illustrated boards, **2s.** each.

GABRIEL CONROY. | **THE LUCK OF ROARING CAMP, &c.**
AN HEIRESS OF RED DOG, &c. | **CALIFORNIAN STORIES.**

Post 8vo, illustrated boards, **2s.** each; cloth limp, **2s. 6d.** each.

FLIP. | **MARUJA.** | **A PHYLLIS OF THE SIERRAS.**

Fcap. 8vo picture cover, **1s.** each.

THE TWINS OF TABLE MOUNTAIN. | **JEFF BRIGGS'S LOVE STORY.**
SNOW-BOUND AT EAGLE'S.

BRILLAT-SAVARIN.—GASTRONOMY AS A FINE ART.

By BRILLAT-SAVARIN. Translated by R. E. ANDERSON, M.A. Post 8vo, half-bound, **2s.**

BRYDGES.—UNCLE SAM AT HOME.

By HAROLD BRYDGES. Post 8vo, illustrated boards, **2s.**; cloth limp, **2s. 6d.**

BUCHANAN'S (ROBERT) WORKS.

Crown 8vo, cloth extra, **6s.** each.

SELECTED POEMS OF ROBERT BUCHANAN. With Frontispiece by T. DALZIEL.
THE EARTHQUAKE; or, Six Days and a Sabbath.
THE CITY OF DREAM: An Epic Poem. With Two Illustrations by P. MACNAB.
THE OUTCAST: A Rhyme for the Time. With 15 Illustrations by RUDOLF BLIND, PETER MACNAB, and HUME NISBET. Small demy 8vo, cloth extra, **8s.**

ROBERT BUCHANAN'S COMPLETE POETICAL WORKS. With Steel-plate Portrait. Crown 8vo, cloth extra, **7s. 6d.**

Crown 8vo, cloth extra, **3s. 6d.** each; post 8vo, illustrated boards, **2s.** each.

THE SHADOW OF THE SWORD.
A CHILD OF NATURE. Frontispiece.
GOD AND THE MAN. With 11 Illustrations by FRED. BARNARD.
THE MARTYRDOM OF MADELINE. With Frontispiece by A. W. COOPER.
LOVE ME FOR EVER. Frontispiece.
ANNAN WATER. **FOXGLOVE MANOR.**
THE NEW ABELARD.
MATT: A Story of a Caravan. Front.
THE MASTER OF THE MINE. Front.
THE HEIR OF LINNE.

BURTON (CAPTAIN).—THE BOOK OF THE SWORD:

Being a History of the Sword and its Use in all Countries, from the Earliest Times. By RICHARD F. BURTON. With over 400 Illustrations. Square 8vo, cloth extra **32s.**

BURTON (ROBERT).

THE ANATOMY OF MELANCHOLY: A New Edition, with translations of the Classical Extracts. Demy 8vo, cloth extra, **7s. 6d.**
MELANCHOLY ANATOMISED Being an Abridgment, for popular use, of BURTON'S ANATOMY OF MELANCHOLY. Post 8vo, cloth limp, **2s. 6d.**

CAINE (T. HALL), NOVELS BY.

Crown 8vo, cloth extra, **3s. 6d.** each; post 8vo, illustrated boards, **2s.** each; cloth limp, **2s. 6d.** each.

SHADOW OF A CRIME. | **A SON OF HAGAR.** | **THE DEEMSTER.**

CAMERON (COMMANDER).—THE CRUISE OF THE "BLACK PRINCE" PRIVATEER.

By V. LOVETT CAMERON, R.N., C.B. With Two Illustrations by P. MACNAB. Crown 8vo, cloth extra, **5s.**; post 8vo, illustrated boards, **2s.**

CAMERON (MRS. H. LOVETT), NOVELS BY.

Post 8vo, illust. bds., **2s.** each.

JULIET'S GUARDIAN. | **DECEIVERS EVER.**

CARLYLE (THOMAS) ON THE CHOICE OF BOOKS. With Life by R. H. SHEPHERD, and Three Illustrations. Post 8vo, cloth extra, **1s. 6d.**

THE CORRESPONDENCE OF THOMAS CARLYLE AND RALPH WALDO EMERSON, 1834 to 1872. Edited by CHARLES ELIOT NORTON. With Portraits. Two Vols., crown 8vo, cloth extra, **24s.**

CARLYLE (JANE WELSH), LIFE OF. By Mrs. ALEXANDER IRELAND. With Portrait and Facsimile Letter. Small demy 8vo, cloth extra, **7s. 6d.**

CHAPMAN'S (GEORGE) WORKS. Vol. I. contains the Plays complete, including the doubtful ones. Vol. II., the Poems and Minor Translations, with an Introductory Essay by ALGERNON CHARLES SWINBURNE. Vol. III., the Translations of the Iliad and Odyssey. Three Vols., crown 8vo, cloth extra, **6s.** each.

CHATTO AND JACKSON.—A TREATISE ON WOOD ENGRAVING, Historical and Practical. By WILLIAM ANDREW CHATTO and JOHN JACKSON. With an Additional Chapter by HENRY G. BOHN, and 450 fine Illusts. Large 4to, hf.-bd., **28s.**

CHAUCER FOR CHILDREN: A Golden Key. By Mrs. H. R. HAWEIS. With 8 Coloured Plates and 30 Woodcuts. Small 4to, cloth extra, **6s.**

CHAUCER FOR SCHOOLS. By Mrs. H. R. HAWEIS. Demy 8vo, cloth limp, **2s. 6d.**

CLARE.—FOR THE LOVE OF A LASS: A Tale of Tynedale. By AUSTIN CLARE. Post 8vo, picture boards, **2s.**; cloth limp, **2s. 6d.**

CLIVE (MRS. ARCHER), NOVELS BY. Post 8vo, illust. boards, **2s.** each.
PAUL FERROLL. | **WHY PAUL FERROLL KILLED HIS WIFE.**

CLODD.—MYTHS AND DREAMS. By EDWARD CLODD, F.R.A.S. Second Edition, Revised. Crown 8vo, cloth extra, **3s. 6d.**

COBBAN.—THE CURE OF SOULS: A Story. By J. MACLAREN COBBAN. Post 8vo, illustrated boards, **2s.**

COLEMAN (JOHN), WORKS BY.
PLAYERS AND PLAYWRIGHTS I HAVE KNOWN. Two Vols., 8vo, cloth, **24s.**
CURLY: An Actor's Story. With 21 Illusts. by J. C. DOLLMAN. Cr. 8vo, cl., **1s. 6d.**

COLLINS (C. ALLSTON).—THE BAR SINISTER. Post 8vo, **2s.**

COLLINS (MORTIMER AND FRANCES), NOVELS BY.
Crown 8vo, cloth extra, **3s. 6d.** each; post 8vo, illustrated boards, **2s.** each.
FROM MIDNIGHT TO MIDNIGHT. | **BLACKSMITH AND SCHOLAR.**
TRANSMIGRATION. | **YOU PLAY ME FALSE.** | **A VILLAGE COMEDY.**
Post 8vo, illustrated boards, **2s.** each.
SWEET ANNE PAGE. | **SWEET AND TWENTY.**
A FIGHT WITH FORTUNE. | **FRANCES.**

COLLINS (WILKIE), NOVELS BY.
Cr. 8vo, cl. ex., **3s. 6d.** each; post 8vo, illust. bds., **2s.** each; cl. limp, **2s. 6d.** each.
ANTONINA. With a Frontispiece by Sir JOHN GILBERT, R.A.
BASIL. Illustrated by Sir JOHN GILBERT, R.A., and J. MAHONEY.
HIDE AND SEEK. Illustrated by Sir JOHN GILBERT, R.A., and J. MAHONEY.
AFTER DARK. With Illustrations by A. B. HOUGHTON.
THE DEAD SECRET. With a Frontispiece by Sir JOHN GILBERT, R.A.
QUEEN OF HEARTS. With a Frontispiece by Sir JOHN GILBERT, R.A.
THE WOMAN IN WHITE. With Illusts. by Sir J. GILBERT, R.A., and F. A. FRASER.
NO NAME. With Illustrations by Sir J. E. MILLAIS, R.A., and A. W. COOPER.
MY MISCELLANIES. With a Steel-plate Portrait of WILKIE COLLINS.
ARMADALE. With Illustrations by G. H. THOMAS.
THE MOONSTONE. With Illustrations by G. DU MAURIER and F. A. FRASER.
MAN AND WIFE. With Illustrations by WILLIAM SMALL.
POOR MISS FINCH. Illustrated by G. DU MAURIER and EDWARD HUGHES.
MISS OR MRS.? With Illusts. by S. L. FILDES, R.A., and HENRY WOODS, A.R.A.
THE NEW MAGDALEN. Illustrated by G. DU MAURIER and C. S. REINHART.
THE FROZEN DEEP. Illustrated by G. DU MAURIER and J. MAHONEY.
THE LAW AND THE LADY. Illusts. by S. L. FILDES, R.A., and SYDNEY HALL.
THE TWO DESTINIES.
THE HAUNTED HOTEL. Illustrated by ARTHUR HOPKINS.
THE FALLEN LEAVES. | **HEART AND SCIENCE.** | **THE EVIL GENIUS.**
JEZEBEL'S DAUGHTER. | **"I SAY NO."** | **LITTLE NOVELS.**
THE BLACK ROBE. | **A ROGUE'S LIFE.** | **THE LEGACY OF CAIN.**
BLIND LOVE. With Preface by WALTER BESANT, and Illusts. by A. FORESTIER.

COLLINS (JOHN CHURTON, M.A.), BOOKS BY.
ILLUSTRATIONS OF TENNYSON. Crown 8vo, cloth extra, **6s.**
A MONOGRAPH ON DEAN SWIFT. Crown 8vo, cloth extra, **8s.**

COLMAN'S HUMOROUS WORKS: "Broad Grins," "My Nightgown and Slippers," and other Humorous Works of GEORGE COLMAN. With Life by C. B. BUCKSTONE, and Frontispiece by HOGARTH. Crown 8vo, cloth extra, **7s. 6d.**

COLMORE.—A VALLEY OF SHADOWS. By G. COLMORE, Author of "A Conspiracy of Silence." Two Vols., crown 8vo.

COLQUHOUN.—EVERY INCH A SOLDIER: A Novel. By M. J. COLQUHOUN. Post 8vo, illustrated boards, **2s.**

CONVALESCENT COOKERY: A Family Handbook. By CATHERINE RYAN. Crown 8vo, **1s.**; cloth limp, **1s. 6d.**

CONWAY (MONCURE D.), WORKS BY.
DEMONOLOGY AND DEVIL-LORE. With 65 Illustrations. Third Edition. Two Vols., demy 8vo, cloth extra, **28s.**
A NECKLACE OF STORIES. 25 Illusts. by W. J. HENNESSY. Sq. 8vo, cloth, **6s.**
PINE AND PALM: A Novel. Two Vols., crown 8vo, cloth extra, **21s.**
GEORGE WASHINGTON'S RULES OF CIVILITY Traced to their Sources and Restored. Fcap. 8vo, Japanese vellum, **2s. 6d.**

COOK (DUTTON), NOVELS BY.
PAUL FOSTER'S DAUGHTER. Cr. 8vo, cl. ex., **3s. 6d.**; post 8vo, illust. boards, **2s.**
LEO. Post 8vo, illustrated boards, **2s.**

CORNWALL.—POPULAR ROMANCES OF THE WEST OF ENGLAND; or, The Drolls, Traditions, and Superstitions of Old Cornwall. Collected by ROBERT HUNT, F.R.S. Two Steel-plates by GEO. CRUIKSHANK. Cr. 8vo, cl., **7s. 6d.**

COTES.—TWO GIRLS ON A BARGE. By V. CECIL COTES. With 44 Illustrations by F. H. TOWNSEND. Crown 8vo, cloth extra, **3s. 6d.**

CRADDOCK.—THE PROPHET OF THE GREAT SMOKY MOUNTAINS. By CHARLES EGBERT CRADDOCK. Post 8vo, illust. bds., **2s.**; cl. limp, **2s. 6d.**

CRIM.—ADVENTURES OF A FAIR REBEL. By MATT CRIM. With a Frontispiece by DAN. BEARD. Crown 8vo, cloth extra, **3s. 6d.**

CRUIKSHANK'S COMIC ALMANACK. Complete in Two SERIES: The FIRST from 1835 to 1843; the SECOND from 1844 to 1853. A Gathering of the BEST HUMOUR of THACKERAY, HOOD, MAYHEW, ALBERT SMITH, A'BECKETT, ROBERT BROUGH, &c. With numerous Steel Engravings and Woodcuts by CRUIKSHANK, HINE, LANDELLS, &c. Two Vols., crown 8vo, cloth gilt, **7s. 6d.** each.
THE LIFE OF GEORGE CRUIKSHANK. By BLANCHARD JERROLD. With 84 Illustrations and a Bibliography. Crown 8vo, cloth extra, **7s. 6d.**

CUMMING (C. F. GORDON), WORKS BY. Demy 8vo, cl. ex., **8s. 6d.** each.
IN THE HEBRIDES. With Autotype Facsimile and 23 Illustrations.
IN THE HIMALAYAS AND ON THE INDIAN PLAINS. With 42 Illustrations.
VIA CORNWALL TO EGYPT. With Photogravure Frontis. Demy 8vo, cl., **7s. 6d.**

CUSSANS.—A HANDBOOK OF HERALDRY; with Instructions for Tracing Pedigrees and Deciphering Ancient MSS., &c. By JOHN E. CUSSANS. With 408 Woodcuts, Two Coloured and Two Plain Plates. Crown 8vo, cloth extra, **7s. 6d.**

CYPLES (W.)—HEARTS of GOLD. Cr. 8vo, cl., 3s. 6d.; post 8vo, bds., 2s.

DANIEL.—MERRIE ENGLAND IN THE OLDEN TIME. By GEORGE DANIEL. With Illustrations by ROBERT CRUIKSHANK. Crown 8vo, cloth extra, **3s. 6d.**

DAUDET.—THE EVANGELIST; or, Port Salvation. By ALPHONSE DAUDET. Crown 8vo, cloth extra, **3s. 6d.**; post 8vo, illustrated boards, **2s.**

DAVENANT.—HINTS FOR PARENTS ON THE CHOICE OF A PROFESSION FOR THEIR SONS. By F. DAVENANT, M.A. Post 8vo, **1s.**; cl., **1s. 6d.**

DAVIES (DR. N. E. YORKE-), WORKS BY.
Crown 8vo, **1s.** each; cloth limp, **1s. 6d.** each.
ONE THOUSAND MEDICAL MAXIMS AND SURGICAL HINTS.
NURSERY HINTS: A Mother's Guide in Health and Disease.
FOODS FOR THE FAT: A Treatise on Corpulency, and a Dietary for its Cure.
AIDS TO LONG LIFE. Crown 8vo, **2s.**; cloth limp, **2s. 6d.**

DAVIES' (SIR JOHN) COMPLETE POETICAL WORKS, including Psalms I. to L. in Verse, and other hitherto Unpublished MSS., for the first time Collected and Edited, with Memorial-Introduction and Notes, by the Rev. A. B. GROSART, D.D. Two Vols., crown 8vo, cloth boards, **12s.**

DAWSON.—THE FOUNTAIN OF YOUTH: A Novel of Adventure. By ERASMUS DAWSON, M.B. Edited by PAUL DEVON. With Two Illustrations by HUME NISBET. Crown 8vo, cloth extra, 3s. 6d.

DE GUERIN.—THE JOURNAL OF MAURICE DE GUERIN. Edited by G. S. TREBUTIEN. With a Memoir by SAINTE-BEUVE. Translated from the 20th French Edition by JESSIE P. FROTHINGHAM. Fcap. 8vo, half-bound, 2s. 6d.

DE MAISTRE.—A JOURNEY ROUND MY ROOM. By XAVIER DE MAISTRE. Translated by HENRY ATTWELL. Post 8vo, cloth limp, 2s. 6d.

DE MILLE.—A CASTLE IN SPAIN. By JAMES DE MILLE. With a Frontispiece. Crown 8vo, cloth extra, 3s. 6d.; post 8vo, illustrated boards, 2s.

DERBY (THE).—THE BLUE RIBBON OF THE TURF: A Chronicle of the RACE FOR THE DERBY, from Diomed to Donovan. With Notes on the Winning Horses, the Men who trained them, Jockeys who rode them, and Gentlemen to whom they belonged; also Notices of the Betting and Betting Men of the period, and Brief Accounts of THE OAKS. By LOUIS HENRY CURZON. Cr. 8vo, cloth extra, 6s.

DERWENT (LEITH), NOVELS BY. Cr. 8vo, cl., 3s. 6d. ea.; post 8vo, bds., 2s. ea.

OUR LADY OF TEARS. | CIRCE'S LOVERS.

DICKENS (CHARLES), NOVELS BY. Post 8vo, illustrated boards, 2s. each.

SKETCHES BY BOZ. | NICHOLAS NICKLEBY.
THE PICKWICK PAPERS. | OLIVER TWIST.

THE SPEECHES OF CHARLES DICKENS, 1841-1870. With a New Bibliography. Edited by RICHARD HERNE SHEPHERD. Crown 8vo, cloth extra, 6s.—Also a SMALLER EDITION, in the *Mayfair Library*, post 8vo, cloth limp, 2s. 6d.

ABOUT ENGLAND WITH DICKENS. By ALFRED RIMMER. With 57 Illustrations by C. A. VANDERHOOF, ALFRED RIMMER, and others. Sq. 8vo, cloth extra, 7s. 6d.

DICTIONARIES.

A DICTIONARY OF MIRACLES: Imitative, Realistic, and Dogmatic. By the Rev. E. C. BREWER, LL.D. Crown 8vo, cloth extra, 7s. 6d.

THE READER'S HANDBOOK OF ALLUSIONS, REFERENCES, PLOTS, AND STORIES. By the Rev. E. C. BREWER, LL.D. With an ENGLISH BIBLIOGRAPHY. Fifteenth Thousand. Crown 8vo, cloth extra, 7s. 6d.

AUTHORS AND THEIR WORKS, WITH THE DATES. Cr. 8vo, cloth limp, 2s.

FAMILIAR SHORT SAYINGS OF GREAT MEN. With Historical and Explanatory Notes. By SAMUEL A. BENT, A.M. Crown 8vo, cloth extra, 7s. 6d.

SLANG DICTIONARY: Etymological, Historical, and Anecdotal. Cr. 8vo, cl., 6s. 6d.

WOMEN OF THE DAY: A Biographical Dictionary. By F. HAYS. Cr. 8vo, cl., 5s.

WORDS, FACTS, AND PHRASES: A Dictionary of Curious, Quaint, and Out-of-the-Way Matters. By ELIEZER EDWARDS. Crown 8vo, cloth extra, 7s. 6d.

DIDEROT.—THE PARADOX OF ACTING. Translated, with Annotations, from Diderot's "Le Paradoxe sur le Comédien," by WALTER HERRIES POLLOCK. With a Preface by HENRY IRVING. Crown 8vo, parchment, 4s. 6d.

DOBSON (AUSTIN), WORKS BY.

THOMAS BEWICK & HIS PUPILS. With 95 Illustrations. Square 8vo, cloth, 6s.

FOUR FRENCHWOMEN: MADEMOISELLE DE CORDAY; MADAME ROLAND; THE PRINCESS DE LAMBALLE; MADAME DE GENLIS. Fcap. 8vo, hf. roxburghe, 2s. 6d.

EIGHTEENTH CENTURY VIGNETTES. Crown 8vo, cloth extra, 6s. [*Preparing.*

DOBSON (W. T.), WORKS BY. Post 8vo, cloth limp, 2s. 6d. each.

LITERARY FRIVOLITIES, FANCIES, FOLLIES, AND FROLICS.
POETICAL INGENUITIES AND ECCENTRICITIES.

DONOVAN (DICK), DETECTIVE STORIES BY.

Post 8vo, illustrated boards, 2s. each; cloth limp, 2s. 6d. each.

THE MAN-HUNTER. | WHO POISONED HETTY DUNCAN?
CAUGHT AT LAST! | A DETECTIVE'S TRIUMPHS.
TRACKED AND TAKEN. | IN THE GRIP OF THE LAW.

THE MAN FROM MANCHESTER. With 23 Illustrations. Crown 8vo, cloth extra, 3s. 6d.; post 8vo, illustrated boards, 2s.

TRACKED TO DOOM. With 6 full-page Illustrations by GORDON BROWNE. Crown 8vo, cloth extra, 3s. 6d.

DRAMATISTS, THE OLD. With Vignette Portraits. Cr. 8vo, cl. ex., 6s. per Vol.

BEN JONSON'S WORKS. With Notes Critical and Explanatory, and a Biographical Memoir by WM. GIFFORD. Edited by Col. CUNNINGHAM. Three Vols.

CHAPMAN'S WORKS. Complete in Three Vols. Vol. I. contains the Plays complete; Vol. II., Poems and Minor Translations, with an Introductory Essay by A. C. SWINBURNE; Vol. III., Translations of the Iliad and Odyssey.

MARLOWE'S WORKS. Edited, with Notes, by Col. CUNNINGHAM. One Vol.

MASSINGER'S PLAYS. From GIFFORD'S Text. Edit. by Col. CUNNINGHAM. One Vol.

DOYLE (CONAN).—THE FIRM OF GIRDLESTONE. By A. CONAN DOYLE, Author of "Micah Clarke." Crown 8vo, cloth extra, 6s.

DUNCAN (SARA JEANNETTE), WORKS BY. Crown 8vo, cloth extra, 7s. 6d. each.
A SOCIAL DEPARTURE: How Orthodocia and I Went round the World by Ourselves. With 111 Illustrations by F. H. TOWNSEND.
AN AMERICAN GIRL IN LONDON. With 80 Illustrations by F. H. TOWNSEND.

DYER.—THE FOLK-LORE OF PLANTS. By Rev. T. F. THISELTON DYER, M.A. Crown 8vo, cloth extra, 6s.

EARLY ENGLISH POETS. Edited, with Introductions and Annotations, by Rev. A. B. GROSART, D.D. Crown 8vo, cloth boards, 6s. per Volume.
FLETCHER'S (GILES) COMPLETE POEMS. One Vol.
DAVIES' (SIR JOHN) COMPLETE POETICAL WORKS. Two Vols.
HERRICK'S (ROBERT) COMPLETE COLLECTED POEMS. Three Vols.
SIDNEY'S (SIR PHILIP) COMPLETE POETICAL WORKS. Three Vols.

EDGCUMBE.—ZEPHYRUS: A Holiday in Brazil and on the River Plate. By E. R. PEARCE EDGCUMBE. With 41 Illustrations. Crown 8vo, cloth extra, 5s.

EDWARDES (MRS. ANNIE), NOVELS BY:
A POINT OF HONOUR. Post 8vo, illustrated boards, 2s.
ARCHIE LOVELL. Crown 8vo, cloth extra, 3s. 6d.; post 8vo, illust. boards, 2s.

EDWARDS (ELIEZER).—WORDS, FACTS, AND PHRASES: A Dictionary of Curious, Quaint, and Out-of-the-Way Matters. By ELIEZER EDWARDS. Crown 8vo, cloth extra, 7s. 6d.

EDWARDS (M. BETHAM-), NOVELS BY.
KITTY. Post 8vo, illustrated boards, 2s.; cloth limp, 2s. 6d.
FELICIA. Post 8vo, illustrated boards, 2s.

EGGLESTON (EDWARD).—ROXY: A Novel. Post 8vo, illust. bds., 2s.

EMANUEL.—ON DIAMONDS AND PRECIOUS STONES: Their History, Value, and Properties; with Simple Tests for ascertaining their Reality. By HARRY EMANUEL, F.R.G.S. With Illustrations, tinted and plain. Cr. 8vo, cl. ex., 6s.

ENGLISHMAN'S HOUSE, THE: A Practical Guide to all interested in Selecting or Building a House; with Estimates of Cost, Quantities, &c. By C. J. RICHARDSON. With Coloured Frontispiece and 600 Illusts. Crown 8vo, cloth, 7s. 6d.

EWALD (ALEX. CHARLES, F.S.A.), WORKS BY.
THE LIFE AND TIMES OF PRINCE CHARLES STUART, Count of Albany (THE YOUNG PRETENDER). With a Portrait. Crown 8vo, cloth extra, 7s. 6d.
STORIES FROM THE STATE PAPERS. With an Autotype. Crown 8vo, cloth, 6s.

EYES, OUR: How to Preserve Them from Infancy to Old Age. By JOHN BROWNING, F.R.A.S. With 70 Illusts. Eighteenth Thousand. Crown 8vo, 1s.

FAMILIAR SHORT SAYINGS OF GREAT MEN. By SAMUEL ARTHUR BENT, A.M. Fifth Edition, Revised and Enlarged. Crown 8vo, cloth extra, 7s. 6d.

FARADAY (MICHAEL), WORKS BY. Post 8vo, cloth extra, 4s. 6d. each.
THE CHEMICAL HISTORY OF A CANDLE: Lectures delivered before a Juvenile Audience. Edited by WILLIAM CROOKES, F.C.S. With numerous Illustrations.
ON THE VARIOUS FORCES OF NATURE, AND THEIR RELATIONS TO EACH OTHER. Edited by WILLIAM CROOKES, F.C.S. With Illustrations.

FARRER (J. ANSON), WORKS BY.
MILITARY MANNERS AND CUSTOMS. Crown 8vo, cloth extra, 6s.
WAR: Three Essays, reprinted from "Military Manners." Cr. 8vo, 1s.; cl., 1s. 6d.

FENN (MANVILLE).—THE NEW MISTRESS: A Novel. By G. MANVILLE FENN, Author of "Double Cunning," &c. Crown 8vo, cloth extra, 3s. 6d.

FICTION.—A CATALOGUE OF NEARLY SIX HUNDRED WORKS OF FICTION published by CHATTO & WINDUS, with a Short Critical Notice of each (40 pages, demy 8vo), will be sent free upon application.

FIN-BEC.—THE CUPBOARD PAPERS: Observations on the Art of Living and Dining. By FIN-BEC. Post 8vo, cloth limp, 2s. 6d.

FIREWORKS, THE COMPLETE ART OF MAKING; or, The Pyrotechnist's Treasury. By THOMAS KENTISH. With 267 Illustrations. Cr. 8vo, cl., 5s.

FITZGERALD (PERCY, M.A., F.S.A.), WORKS BY.
THE WORLD BEHIND THE SCENES. Crown 8vo, cloth extra, 3s. 6d.
LITTLE ESSAYS: Passages from Letters of CHARLES LAMB. Post 8vo, cl., 2s. 6d.
A DAY'S TOUR: Journey through France and Belgium. With Sketches. Cr. 4to, 1s.
FATAL ZERO. Crown 8vo, cloth extra, 3s. 6d.; post 8vo, illustrated boards, 2s.

Post 8vo, illustrated boards, 2s. each.

BELLA DONNA. | **LADY OF BRANTOME.** | **THE SECOND MRS. TILLOTSON.**
POLLY. | **NEVER FORGOTTEN.** | **SEVENTY-FIVE BROOKE STREET.**

LIFE OF JAMES BOSWELL (of Auchinleck). With an Account of his Sayings, Doings, and Writings; and Four Portraits. Two Vols., demy 8vo, cloth, 24s.

FLAMMARION.—URANIA: A Romance. By CAMILLE FLAMMARION. Translated by AUGUSTA RICE STETSON. With 87 Illustrations by DE BIELER, MYRBACH, and GAMBARD. Crown 8vo, cloth extra, 5s.

FLETCHER'S (GILES, B.D.) COMPLETE POEMS: Christ's Victorie in Heaven, Christ's Victorie on Earth, Christ's Triumph over Death, and Minor Poems. With Notes by Rev. A. B. GROSART, D.D. Crown 8vo, cloth boards, 6s.

FLUDYER (HARRY) AT CAMBRIDGE: A Series of Family Letters. Post 8vo, picture cover, 1s.; cloth limp, 1s. 6d.

FONBLANQUE (ALBANY).—FILTHY LUCRE. Post 8vo, illust. bds., 2s.

FRANCILLON (R. E.), NOVELS BY.
Crown 8vo, cloth extra, 3s. 6d. each; post 8vo, illustrated boards, 2s. each.

ONE BY ONE. | **QUEEN COPHETUA.** | **A REAL QUEEN.** | **KING OR KNAVE?**

OLYMPIA. Post 8vo, illust. bds., 2s. | **ESTHER'S GLOVE.** Fcap. 8vo, pict. cover, 1s.
ROMANCES OF THE LAW. Crown 8vo, cloth, 6s.; post 8vo, illust. boards, 2s.

FREDERIC (HAROLD), NOVELS BY.
SETH'S BROTHER'S WIFE. Post 8vo, illustrated boards, 2s.
THE LAWTON GIRL. With Frontispiece by F. BARNARD. Cr. 8vo, cloth ex., 6s.; post 8vo, illustrated boards, 2s.

FRENCH LITERATURE, A HISTORY OF. By HENRY VAN LAUN. Three Vols., demy 8vo, cloth boards, 7s. 6d. each.

FRERE.—PANDURANG HARI; or, Memoirs of a Hindoo. With Preface by Sir BARTLE FRERE. Crown 8vo, cloth, 3s. 6d.; post 8vo, illust. bds., 2s.

FRISWELL (HAIN).—ONE OF TWO: A Novel. Post 8vo, illust. bds., 2s.

FROST (THOMAS), WORKS BY. Crown 8vo, cloth extra, 3s. 6d. each.
CIRCUS LIFE AND CIRCUS CELEBRITIES. | **LIVES OF THE CONJURERS.**
THE OLD SHOWMEN AND THE OLD LONDON FAIRS.

FRY'S (HERBERT) ROYAL GUIDE TO THE LONDON CHARITIES. Showing their Name, Date of Foundation, Objects, Income, Officials, &c. Edited by JOHN LANE. Published Annually. Crown 8vo, cloth, 1s. 6d.

GARDENING BOOKS. Post 8vo, 1s. each; cloth limp, 1s. 6d. each.
A YEAR'S WORK IN GARDEN AND GREENHOUSE: Practical Advice as to the Management of the Flower, Fruit, and Frame Garden. By GEORGE GLENNY.
HOUSEHOLD HORTICULTURE. By TOM and JANE JERROLD. Illustrated.
THE GARDEN THAT PAID THE RENT. By TOM JERROLD.

OUR KITCHEN GARDEN: The Plants we Grow, and How we Cook Them. By TOM JERROLD. Crown 8vo, cloth, 1s. 6d.
MY GARDEN WILD, AND WHAT I GREW THERE. By FRANCIS G. HEATH. Crown 8vo, cloth extra, gilt edges, 6s.

GARRETT.—THE CAPEL GIRLS: A Novel. By EDWARD GARRETT. Crown 8vo, cloth extra, 3s. 6d.; post 8vo, illustrated boards, 2s.

GENTLEMAN'S MAGAZINE, THE. 1s. Monthly. In addition to the Articles upon subjects in Literature, Science, and Art, for which this Magazine has so high a reputation, "**TABLE TALK**" by SYLVANUS URBAN appears monthly.
*** *Bound Volumes for recent years kept in stock,* 8s. 6d. *each. Cases for binding,* 2s.

GENTLEMAN'S ANNUAL, THE. Published Annually in November. 1s.

GERMAN POPULAR STORIES. Collected by the Brothers GRIMM and Translated by EDGAR TAYLOR. With Introduction by JOHN RUSKIN, and 22 Steel Plates after GEORGE CRUIKSHANK. Square 8vo, cloth, 6s. 6d.; gilt edges, 7s. 6d.

GIBBON (CHARLES), NOVELS BY.
Crown 8vo, cloth extra, 3s. 6d. each; post 8vo, illustrated boards, 2s. each.
ROBIN GRAY. | LOVING A DREAM. | THE GOLDEN SHAFT.
THE FLOWER OF THE FOREST. | OF HIGH DEGREE.

Post 8vo, illustrated boards, 2s. each.
THE DEAD HEART. | IN LOVE AND WAR.
FOR LACK OF GOLD. | A HEART'S PROBLEM.
WHAT WILL THE WORLD SAY? | BY MEAD AND STREAM.
FOR THE KING. | A HARD KNOT. | THE BRAES OF YARROW.
QUEEN OF THE MEADOW. | FANCY FREE. | IN HONOUR BOUND.
IN PASTURES GREEN. | HEART'S DELIGHT. | BLOOD-MONEY.

GIBNEY (SOMERVILLE).—SENTENCED! Cr. 8vo, 1s.; cl., 1s. 6d.

GILBERT (WILLIAM), NOVELS BY. Post 8vo, illustrated boards, 2s. each.
DR. AUSTIN'S GUESTS. | JAMES DUKE, COSTERMONGER.
THE WIZARD OF THE MOUNTAIN.

GILBERT (W. S.), ORIGINAL PLAYS BY. Two Series, 2s. 6d. each.
The FIRST SERIES contains: The Wicked World—Pygmalion and Galatea—Charity—The Princess—The Palace of Truth—Trial by Jury.
The SECOND SERIES: Broken Hearts—Engaged—Sweethearts—Gretchen—Dan'l Druce—Tom Cobb—H.M.S. "Pinafore"—The Sorcerer—Pirates of Penzance.

EIGHT ORIGINAL COMIC OPERAS written by W. S. GILBERT. Containing The Sorcerer—H.M.S. "Pinafore"—Pirates of Penzance—Iolanthe—Patience—Princess Ida—The Mikado—Trial by Jury. Demy 8vo, cloth limp, 2s. 6d.
THE "GILBERT AND SULLIVAN" BIRTHDAY BOOK: Quotations for Every Day in the Year, Selected from Plays by W. S. GILBERT set to Music by Sir A. SULLIVAN. Compiled by ALEX. WATSON. Royal 16mo, Jap. leather, 2s. 6d.

GLANVILLE (ERNEST), NOVELS BY.
THE LOST HEIRESS: A Tale of Love, Battle and Adventure. With 2 Illusts. by HUME NISBET. Cr. 8vo, cloth extra, 3s. 6d.; post 8vo, illustrated boards, 2s.
THE FOSSICKER: A Romance of Mashonaland. With Frontispiece and Vignette by HUME NISBET. Second Edition. Crown 8vo, cloth extra, 3s. 6d.

GLENNY.—A YEAR'S WORK IN GARDEN AND GREENHOUSE: Practical Advice to Amateur Gardeners as to the Management of the Flower, Fruit, and Frame Garden. By GEORGE GLENNY. Post 8vo, 1s.; cloth limp, 1s. 6d.

GODWIN.—LIVES OF THE NECROMANCERS. By WILLIAM GODWIN. Post 8vo, cloth limp, 2s.

GOLDEN TREASURY OF THOUGHT, THE: An Encyclopædia of QUOTATIONS. Edited by THEODORE TAYLOR. Crown 8vo, cloth gilt, 7s. 6d.

GOWING.—FIVE THOUSAND MILES IN A SLEDGE: A Midwinter Journey Across Siberia. By LIONEL F. GOWING. With 30 Illustrations by C. J. UREN, and a Map by E. WELLER. Large crown 8vo, cloth extra, 8s.

GRAHAM.—THE PROFESSOR'S WIFE: A Story. By LEONARD GRAHAM. Fcap. 8vo, picture cover, 1s.

GREEKS AND ROMANS, THE LIFE OF THE, described from Antique Monuments. By ERNST GUHL and W. KONER. Edited by Dr. F. HUEFFER. With 545 Illustrations. Large crown 8vo, cloth extra, 7s. 6d.

GREENWOOD (JAMES), WORKS BY. Cr. 8vo, cloth extra, 3s. 6d. each.
THE WILDS OF LONDON. | LOW-LIFE DEEPS.

GREVILLE (HENRY), NOVELS BY:
NIKANOR. Translated by ELIZA E. CHASE. With 8 Illustrations. Crown 8vo, cloth extra, 6s.; post 8vo, illustrated boards, 2s.
A NOBLE WOMAN. Crown 8vo, cloth extra, 5s.; post 8vo, illustrated boards, 2s.

GRIFFITH.—CORINTHIA MARAZION: A Novel. By CECIL GRIFFITH, Author of "Victory Deane," &c. Three Vols., crown 8vo.

HABBERTON (JOHN, Author of "Helen's Babies"), NOVELS BY.
Post 8vo, illustrated boards 2s. each; cloth limp, 2s. 6d. each.
BRUETON'S BAYOU. | COUNTRY LUCK.

HAIR, THE: Its Treatment in Health, Weakness, and Disease. Translated from the German of Dr. J. PINCUS. Crown 8vo, 1s.; cloth limp, 1s. 6d.

HAKE (DR. THOMAS GORDON), POEMS BY. Cr. 8vo, cl. ex., 6s. each.
NEW SYMBOLS. | LEGENDS OF THE MORROW. | THE SERPENT PLAY.
MAIDEN ECSTASY. Small 4to, cloth extra, 8s.

HALL.—SKETCHES OF IRISH CHARACTER. By Mrs. S. C. HALL. With numerous Illustrations on Steel and Wood by MACLISE, GILBERT, HARVEY, and GEORGE CRUIKSHANK. Medium 8vo, cloth extra, 7s. 6d.

HALLIDAY (ANDR.).—EVERY-DAY PAPERS. Post 8vo, bds., 2s.

HANDWRITING, THE PHILOSOPHY OF. With over 100 Facsimiles and Explanatory Text. By DON FELIX DE SALAMANCA. Post 8vo, cloth limp, 2s. 6d.

HANKY-PANKY: A Collection of Very Easy Tricks, Very Difficult Tricks, White Magic, Sleight of Hand, &c. Edited by W. H. CREMER. With 200 Illustrations. Crown 8vo, cloth extra, 4s. 6d.

HARDY (LADY DUFFUS).—PAUL WYNTER'S SACRIFICE. By Lady DUFFUS HARDY. Post 8vo, illustrated boards, 2s.

HARDY (THOMAS).—UNDER THE GREENWOOD TREE. By THOMAS HARDY, Author of "Far from the Madding Crowd." With Portrait and 15 Illustrations. Crown 8vo, cloth extra, 3s. 6d.; post 8vo, illustrated boards, 2s.

HARWOOD.—THE TENTH EARL. By J. BERWICK HARWOOD. Post 8vo, illustrated boards, 2s.

HAWEIS (MRS. H. R.), WORKS BY. Square 8vo, cloth extra, 6s. each.
THE ART OF BEAUTY. With Coloured Frontispiece and 91 Illustrations.
THE ART OF DECORATION. With Coloured Frontispiece and 74 Illustrations.
CHAUCER FOR CHILDREN. With 8 Coloured Plates and 30 Woodcuts.

THE ART OF DRESS. With 32 Illustrations. Post 8vo, 1s.; cloth, 1s. 6d.
CHAUCER FOR SCHOOLS. Demy 8vo, cloth limp, 2s. 6d.

HAWEIS (Rev. H. R., M.A.).—AMERICAN HUMORISTS: WASHINGTON IRVING, OLIVER WENDELL HOLMES, JAMES RUSSELL LOWELL, ARTEMUS WARD, MARK TWAIN, and BRET HARTE. Third Edition. Crown 8vo, cloth extra, 6s.

HAWLEY SMART.—WITHOUT LOVE OR LICENCE: A Novel. By HAWLEY SMART. Crown 8vo, cloth extra, 3s. 6d.; post 8vo, illustrated boards, 2s.

HAWTHORNE.—OUR OLD HOME. By NATHANIEL HAWTHORNE. Annotated with Passages from the Author's Note-book, and Illustrated with 31 Photogravures. Two Vols., crown 8vo, buckram, gilt top, 15s.

HAWTHORNE (JULIAN), NOVELS BY.
Crown 8vo, cloth extra, 3s. 6d. each; post 8vo, illustrated boards, 2s. each.
GARTH. | ELLICE QUENTIN. | BEATRIX RANDOLPH. | DUST.
SEBASTIAN STROME. | DAVID POINDEXTER.
FORTUNE'S FOOL. | THE SPECTRE OF THE CAMERA.

Post 8vo, illustrated boards, 2s. each.
MISS CADOGNA. | LOVE—OR A NAME.

MRS. GAINSBOROUGH'S DIAMONDS. Fcap. 8vo, illustrated cover, 1s.
A DREAM AND A FORGETTING. Post 8vo, cloth limp, 1s. 6d.

HEATH.—MY GARDEN WILD, AND WHAT I GREW THERE. By FRANCIS GEORGE HEATH. Crown 8vo, cloth extra, gilt edges, 6s.

HELPS (SIR ARTHUR), WORKS BY. Post 8vo, cloth limp, 2s. 6d. each.
ANIMALS AND THEIR MASTERS. SOCIAL PRESSURE.

IVAN DE BIRON: A Novel. Cr. 8vo, cl. extra, 3s. 6d.; post 8vo, illust. bds., 2s.

HENDERSON.—AGATHA PAGE: A Novel. By ISAAC HENDERSON. Crown 8vo, cloth extra, 3s. 6d.

HERMAN.—A LEADING LADY. By HENRY HERMAN, joint-Author of "The Bishops' Bible." Post 8vo, illustrated boards, 2s.; cloth extra, 2s. 6d.

HERRICK'S (ROBERT) HESPERIDES, NOBLE NUMBERS, AND COMPLETE COLLECTED POEMS. With Memorial-Introduction and Notes by the Rev. A. B. GROSART, D.D.; Steel Portrait, &c. Three Vols., crown 8vo, cl. bds., 18s.

HERTZKA.—FREELAND: A Social Anticipation. By Dr. THEODOR HERTZKA. Translated by ARTHUR RANSOM. Crown 8vo, cloth extra, 6s.

HESSE-WARTEGG.—TUNIS: The Land and the People. By Chevalier ERNST VON HESSE-WARTEGG. With 22 Illustrations. Cr. 8vo, cloth extra, 3s. 6d.

HINDLEY (CHARLES), WORKS BY.

TAVERN ANECDOTES AND SAYINGS: Including Reminiscences connected with Coffee Houses, Clubs, &c. With Illustrations. Crown 8vo, cloth, 3s. 6d.

THE LIFE AND ADVENTURES OF A CHEAP JACK. By ONE OF THE FRATERNITY. Edited by CHARLES HINDLEY. Crown 8vo, cloth extra, 3s. 6d.

HOEY.—THE LOVER'S CREED. By Mrs. CASHEL HOEY. Post 8vo, 2s.

HOLLINGSHEAD (JOHN).—NIAGARA SPRAY. Crown 8vo, 1s.

HOLMES.—THE SCIENCE OF VOICE PRODUCTION AND VOICE PRESERVATION. By GORDON HOLMES, M.D. Crown 8vo, 1s.; cloth, 1s. 6d.

HOLMES (OLIVER WENDELL), WORKS BY.

THE AUTOCRAT OF THE BREAKFAST-TABLE. Illustrated by J. GORDON THOMSON. Post 8vo, cloth limp, 2s. 6d.—Another Edition, in smaller type, with an Introduction by G. A. SALA. Post 8vo, cloth limp, 2s.

THE PROFESSOR AT THE BREAKFAST-TABLE. Post 8vo, cloth limp, 2s.

HOOD'S (THOMAS) CHOICE WORKS, in Prose and Verse. With Life of the Author, Portrait, and 200 Illustrations. Crown 8vo, cloth extra, 7s. 6d.

HOOD'S WHIMS AND ODDITIES. With 85 Illustrations. Post 8vo, printed on laid paper and half-bound, 2s.

HOOD (TOM).—FROM NOWHERE TO THE NORTH POLE: A Noah's Arkæological Narrative. By TOM HOOD. With 25 Illustrations by W. BRUNTON and E. C. BARNES. Square 8vo, cloth extra, gilt edges, 6s.

HOOK'S (THEODORE) CHOICE HUMOROUS WORKS; including his Ludicrous Adventures, Bons Mots, Puns, and Hoaxes. With Life of the Author, Portraits, Facsimiles, and Illustrations. Crown 8vo, cloth extra, 7s. 6d.

HOOPER.—THE HOUSE OF RABY: A Novel. By Mrs. GEORGE HOOPER. Post 8vo, illustrated boards, 2s.

HOPKINS.—"'TWIXT LOVE AND DUTY:" A Novel. By TIGHE HOPKINS. Post 8vo, illustrated boards, 2s.

HORNE.—ORION: An Epic Poem. By RICHARD HENGIST HORNE. With Photographic Portrait by SUMMERS. Tenth Edition. Cr. 8vo, cloth extra, 7s.

HORSE (THE) AND HIS RIDER: An Anecdotic Medley. By "THORMANBY." Crown 8vo, cloth extra, 6s.

HUNT.—ESSAYS BY LEIGH HUNT: A TALE FOR A CHIMNEY CORNER, &c. Edited by EDMUND OLLIER. Post 8vo, printed on laid paper and half-bd., 2s.

HUNT (MRS. ALFRED), NOVELS BY.

Crown 8vo, cloth extra, 3s. 6d. each; post 8vo, illustrated boards, 2s. each.

THE LEADEN CASKET. | SELF-CONDEMNED. | THAT OTHER PERSON.

THORNICROFT'S MODEL. Post 8vo, illustrated boards, 2s.

HUTCHISON.—HINTS ON COLT-BREAKING. By W. M. HUTCHISON. With 25 Illustrations. Crown 8vo, cloth extra, 3s. 6d.

HYDROPHOBIA: An Account of M. PASTEUR'S System. Containing a Translation of all his Communications on the Subject, the Technique of his Method, and Statistics. By RENAUD SUZOR, M.B. Crown 8vo, cloth extra, 6s.

IDLER (THE): A Monthly Magazine. Edited by JEROME K. JEROME and ROBERT E. BARR. Profusely Illustrated. Sixpence Monthly.

INGELOW (JEAN).—FATED TO BE FREE. With 24 Illustrations by G. J. PINWELL. Cr. 8vo, cloth extra, 3s. 6d.; post 8vo, illustrated boards, 2s.

INDOOR PAUPERS. By ONE OF THEM. Crown 8vo, 1s.; cloth, 1s. 6d.

IRISH WIT AND HUMOUR, SONGS OF. Collected and Edited by A. PERCEVAL GRAVES. Post 8vo, cloth limp, **2s. 6d.**

JAMES.—A ROMANCE OF THE QUEEN'S HOUNDS. By CHARLES JAMES. Post 8vo, picture cover, **1s.**; cloth limp, **1s. 6d.**

JANVIER.—PRACTICAL KERAMICS FOR STUDENTS. By CATHERINE A. JANVIER. Crown 8vo, cloth extra, **6s.**

JAY (HARRIETT), NOVELS BY. Post 8vo, illustrated boards, **2s.** each.
THE DARK COLLEEN. | THE QUEEN OF CONNAUGHT.

JEFFERIES (RICHARD), WORKS BY. Post 8vo, cloth limp, **2s. 6d.** each.
NATURE NEAR LONDON. | THE LIFE OF THE FIELDS. | THE OPEN AIR.
THE EULOGY OF RICHARD JEFFERIES. By WALTER BESANT. Second Edition. With a Photograph Portrait. Crown 8vo, cloth extra, **6s.**

JENNINGS (H. J.), WORKS BY.
CURIOSITIES OF CRITICISM. Post 8vo, cloth limp, **2s. 6d.**
LORD TENNYSON: A Biographical Sketch. With a Photograph. Cr. 8vo, cl., **6s.**

JEROME.—STAGELAND: Curious Habits and Customs of its Inhabitants. By JEROME K. JEROME. With 64 Illustrations by J. BERNARD PARTRIDGE. Square 8vo, picture cover, **1s.**; cloth limp, **2s.**

JERROLD.—THE BARBER'S CHAIR; & THE HEDGEHOG LETTERS. By DOUGLAS JERROLD. Post 8vo, printed on laid paper and half-bound, **2s.**

JERROLD (TOM), WORKS BY. Post 8vo, **1s.** each; cloth limp, **1s. 6d.** each.
THE GARDEN THAT PAID THE RENT.
HOUSEHOLD HORTICULTURE: A Gossip about Flowers. Illustrated.
OUR KITCHEN GARDEN: The Plants, and How we Cook Them. Cr. 8vo, cl., **1s. 6d.**

JESSE.—SCENES AND OCCUPATIONS OF A COUNTRY LIFE. By EDWARD JESSE. Post 8vo, cloth limp, **2s.**

JONES (WILLIAM, F.S.A.), WORKS BY. Cr. 8vo, cl. extra, **7s. 6d.** each.
FINGER-RING LORE: Historical, Legendary, and Anecdotal. With nearly 300 Illustrations. Second Edition, Revised and Enlarged.
CREDULITIES, PAST AND PRESENT. Including the Sea and Seamen, Miners, Talismans, Word and Letter Divination, Exorcising and Blessing of Animals, Birds, Eggs, Luck, &c. With an Etched Frontispiece.
CROWNS AND CORONATIONS: A History of Regalia. With 100 Illustrations.

JONSON'S (BEN) WORKS. With Notes Critical and Explanatory and a Biographical Memoir by WILLIAM GIFFORD. Edited by Colonel CUNNINGHAM. Three Vols., crown 8vo, cloth extra, **6s.** each.

JOSEPHUS, THE COMPLETE WORKS OF. Translated by WHISTON. Containing "The Antiquities of the Jews" and "The Wars of the Jews." With Illustrations and Maps. Two Vols., demy 8vo, half-bound, **12s. 6d.**

KEMPT.—PENCIL AND PALETTE: Chapters on Art and Artists. By ROBERT KEMPT. Post 8vo, cloth limp, **2s. 6d.**

KERSHAW.—COLONIAL FACTS AND FICTIONS: Humorous Sketches. By MARK KERSHAW. Post 8vo, illustrated boards, **2s.**; cloth, **2s. 6d.**

KEYSER.—CUT BY THE MESS: A Novel. By ARTHUR KEYSER. Crown 8vo, picture cover, **1s.**; cloth limp, **1s. 6d.**

KING (R. ASHE), NOVELS BY. Cr. 8vo, cl., **3s. 6d.** ea.; post 8vo, bds., **2s.** ea.
A DRAWN GAME. | "THE WEARING OF THE GREEN."
Post 8vo, illustrated boards, **2s.** each.
PASSION'S SLAVE. | BELL BARRY.

KINGSLEY (HENRY), NOVELS BY.
OAKSHOTT CASTLE. Post 8vo, illustrated boards, **2s.**
NUMBER SEVENTEEN. Crown 8vo, cloth extra, **3s. 6d.**

KNIGHTS (THE) OF THE LION; A Romance of the Thirteenth Century. Edited, with an Introduction, by the MARQUESS OF LORNE, K.T. Cr. 8vo, cl. ex., **6s.**

KNIGHT.—THE PATIENT'S VADE MECUM: How to Get Most Benefit from Medical Advice. By WILLIAM KNIGHT, M.R.C.S., and EDWARD KNIGHT, L.R.C.P. Crown 8vo, **1s.**; cloth limp, **1s. 6d.**

LAMB'S (CHARLES) COMPLETE WORKS, in Prose and Verse, including "Poetry for Children" and "Prince Dorus." Edited, with Notes and Introduction, by R. H. SHEPHERD. With Two Portraits and Facsimile of a page of the "Essay on Roast Pig." Crown 8vo, half-bound, **7s. 6d.**

THE ESSAYS OF ELIA. Post 8vo, printed on laid paper and half-bound, **2s.**

LITTLE ESSAYS: Sketches and Characters by CHARLES LAMB, selected from his Letters by PERCY FITZGERALD. Post 8vo, cloth limp, **2s. 6d.**

THE DRAMATIC ESSAYS OF CHARLES LAMB. With Introduction and Notes by BRANDER MATTHEWS, and Steel-plate Portrait. Fcap. 8vo, hf.-bd., **2s. 6d.**

LANDOR.—CITATION AND EXAMINATION OF WILLIAM SHAKSPEARE, &c., before Sir THOMAS LUCY, touching Deer-stealing, 19th September, 1582. To which is added, **A CONFERENCE OF MASTER EDMUND SPENSER** with the Earl of Essex, touching the State of Ireland, 1595. By WALTER SAVAGE LANDOR. Fcap. 8vo, half-Roxburghe, **2s. 6d.**

LANE.—THE THOUSAND AND ONE NIGHTS, commonly called in England **THE ARABIAN NIGHTS' ENTERTAINMENTS.** Translated from the Arabic, with Notes, by EDWARD WILLIAM LANE. Illustrated by many hundred Engravings from Designs by HARVEY. Edited by EDWARD STANLEY POOLE. With a Preface by STANLEY LANE-POOLE. Three Vols., demy 8vo, cloth extra, **7s. 6d.** each.

LARDER.—A SINNER'S SENTENCE: A Novel. By A. LARDER. 3 vols.

LARWOOD (JACOB), WORKS BY.

THE STORY OF THE LONDON PARKS. With Illusts. Cr. 8vo, cl. extra, **3s. 6d.**

ANECDOTES OF THE CLERGY: The Antiquities, Humours, and Eccentricities of the Cloth. Post 8vo, printed on laid paper and half-bound, **2s.**

Post 8vo, cloth limp, **2s. 6d.** each.

FORENSIC ANECDOTES. | **THEATRICAL ANECDOTES.**

LEIGH (HENRY S.), WORKS BY.

CAROLS OF COCKAYNE. Printed on hand-made paper, bound in buckram, **5s.**

JEUX D'ESPRIT. Edited by HENRY S. LEIGH. Post 8vo, cloth limp, **2s. 6d.**

LEYS (JOHN).—THE LINDSAYS: A Romance. Post 8vo, illust. bds., **2s.**

LIFE IN LONDON; or, The History of JERRY HAWTHORN and CORINTHIAN TOM. With CRUIKSHANK'S Coloured Illustrations. Crown 8vo, cloth extra, **7s. 6d.** [*New Edition preparing.*

LINTON (E. LYNN), WORKS BY. Post 8vo, cloth limp, **2s. 6d.** each.

WITCH STORIES. | **OURSELVES:** ESSAYS ON WOMEN.

Crown 8vo, cloth extra, **3s. 6d.** each; post 8vo, illustrated boards, **2s.** each.

SOWING THE WIND. | **UNDER WHICH LORD?**
PATRICIA KEMBALL. | **"MY LOVE!"** | **IONE.**
ATONEMENT OF LEAM DUNDAS. | **PASTON CAREW, Millionaire & Miser.**
THE WORLD WELL LOST.

Post 8vo, illustrated boards, **2s.** each.

THE REBEL OF THE FAMILY. | **WITH A SILKEN THREAD.**

FREESHOOTING: Extracts from the Works of Mrs. LYNN LINTON. Post 8vo, cloth, **2s. 6d.**

LONGFELLOW'S POETICAL WORKS. With numerous Illustrations on Steel and Wood. Crown 8vo, cloth extra, **7s. 6d.**

LUCY.—GIDEON FLEYCE: A Novel. By HENRY W. LUCY. Crown 8vo, cloth extra, **3s. 6d.**; post 8vo, illustrated boards, **2s.**

LUSIAD (THE) OF CAMOENS. Translated into English Spenserian Verse by ROBERT FFRENCH DUFF. With 14 Plates. Demy 8vo, cloth boards, **18s.**

MACALPINE (AVERY), NOVELS BY.

TERESA ITASCA, and other Stories. Crown 8vo, bound in canvas, **2s. 6d.**

BROKEN WINGS. With 6 Illusts. by W. J. HENNESSY. Crown 8vo, cloth extra, **6s.**

MACCOLL (HUGH), NOVELS BY.

MR. STRANGER'S SEALED PACKET. Second Edition. Crown 8vo, cl. extra, **5s.**

EDNOR WHITLOCK. Crown 8vo, cloth extra, **6s.**

McCARTHY (JUSTIN, M.P.), WORKS BY.

A HISTORY OF OUR OWN TIMES, from the Accession of Queen Victoria to the General Election of 1880. Four Vols. demy 8vo, cloth extra, **12s.** each.—Also a POPULAR EDITION, in Four Vols., crown 8vo, cloth extra, **6s.** each.—And a JUBILEE EDITION, with an Appendix of Events to the end of 1886, in Two Vols., large crown 8vo, cloth extra, **7s. 6d.** each.

A SHORT HISTORY OF OUR OWN TIMES. One Vol., crown 8vo, cloth extra, **6s.** —Also a CHEAP POPULAR EDITION, post 8vo, cloth limp, **2s. 6d.**

A HISTORY OF THE FOUR GEORGES. Four Vols. demy 8vo, cloth extra, **12s.** each. [Vols. I. & II. *ready*.

Crown 8vo, cloth extra, **3s. 6d.** each; post 8vo, illustrated boards, **2s.** each.

THE WATERDALE NEIGHBOURS.
MY ENEMY'S DAUGHTER.
A FAIR SAXON.
LINLEY ROCHFORD.
DEAR LADY DISDAIN.
MISS MISANTHROPE.
DONNA QUIXOTE.
THE COMET OF A SEASON.
MAID OF ATHENS.
CAMIOLA: A Girl with a Fortune.

"THE RIGHT HONOURABLE." By JUSTIN McCARTHY, M.P., and Mrs. CAMPBELL-PRAED. Fourth Edition. Crown 8vo, cloth extra, **6s.**

McCARTHY (JUSTIN H., M.P.), WORKS BY.

THE FRENCH REVOLUTION. Four Vols., 8vo, **12s.** each. [Vols. I. & II. *ready*.

AN OUTLINE OF THE HISTORY OF IRELAND. Crown 8vo, **1s.**; cloth, **1s. 6d.**

IRELAND SINCE THE UNION: Irish History, 1798-1886. Crown 8vo, cloth, **6s.**

HAFIZ IN LONDON: Poems. Small 8vo, gold cloth, **3s. 6d.**

HARLEQUINADE: Poems. Small 4to, Japanese vellum, **8s.**

OUR SENSATION NOVEL. Crown 8vo, picture cover, **1s.**; cloth limp, **1s. 6d.**

DOOM! An Atlantic Episode. Crown 8vo, picture cover, **1s.**

DOLLY: A Sketch. Crown 8vo, picture cover, **1s.**; cloth limp, **1s. 6d.**

LILY LASS: A Romance. Crown 8vo, picture cover, **1s.**; cloth limp, **1s. 6d.**

THE THOUSAND AND ONE DAYS: Persian Tales. Edited by JUSTIN H. McCARTHY. Two Vols., crown 8vo, cloth extra, **12s.**

MACDONALD (GEORGE, LL.D.), WORKS BY.

WORKS OF FANCY AND IMAGINATION. Ten Vols., cl. extra, gilt edges, in cloth case, **21s.** Or the Vols. may be had separately, in grolier cl., at **2s. 6d.** each.

Vol. I. WITHIN AND WITHOUT.—THE HIDDEN LIFE.
,, II. THE DISCIPLE.—THE GOSPEL WOMEN.—BOOK OF SONNETS.—ORGAN SONGS.
,, III. VIOLIN SONGS.—SONGS OF THE DAYS AND NIGHTS.—A BOOK OF DREAMS.—ROADSIDE POEMS.—POEMS FOR CHILDREN.
,, IV. PARABLES.—BALLADS.—SCOTCH SONGS.
,, V. & VI. PHANTASTES: A Faerie Romance. | Vol. VII. THE PORTENT.
,, VIII. THE LIGHT PRINCESS.—THE GIANT'S HEART.—SHADOWS.
,, IX. CROSS PURPOSES.—THE GOLDEN KEY.—THE CARASOYN.—LITTLE DAYLIGHT.
,, X. THE CRUEL PAINTER.—THE WOW O' RIVVEN.—THE CASTLE.—THE BROKEN SWORDS.—THE GRAY WOLF.—UNCLE CORNELIUS.

THE COMPLETE POETICAL WORKS OF DR. GEORGE MACDONALD. Collected and arranged by the Author. Crown 8vo, buckram, **6s.** [*Shortly*.

A THREEFOLD CORD. Poems by Three Friends. Edited by Dr. GEORGE MACDONALD. Post 8vo, cloth, **5s.**

MACDONELL.—QUAKER COUSINS: A Novel. By AGNES MACDONELL.

Crown 8vo, cloth extra, **3s. 6d.**; post 8vo, illustrated boards, **2s.**

MACGREGOR. — PASTIMES AND PLAYERS: Notes on Popular Games.

By ROBERT MACGREGOR. Post 8vo, cloth limp, **2s. 6d.**

MACKAY.—INTERLUDES AND UNDERTONES; or, Music at Twilight.

By CHARLES MACKAY, LL.D. Crown 8vo, cloth extra, **6s.**

MACLISE PORTRAIT GALLERY (THE) OF ILLUSTRIOUS LITERARY CHARACTERS: 85 PORTRAITS;

with Memoirs — Biographical, Critical, Bibliographical, and Anecdotal—illustrative of the Literature of the former half of the Present Century, by WILLIAM BATES, B.A. Crown 8vo, cloth extra, **7s. 6d.**

MACQUOID (MRS.), WORKS BY. Square 8vo, cloth extra, 7s. 6d. each.

IN THE ARDENNES. With 50 Illustrations by THOMAS R. MACQUOID.

PICTURES AND LEGENDS FROM NORMANDY AND BRITTANY. With 34 Illustrations by THOMAS R. MACQUOID.

THROUGH NORMANDY. With 92 Illustrations by T. R. MACQUOID, and a Map.

THROUGH BRITTANY. With 35 Illustrations by T. R. MACQUOID, and a Map.

ABOUT YORKSHIRE. With 67 Illustrations by T. R. MACQUOID.

Post 8vo, illustrated boards, **2s.** each.

THE EVIL EYE, and other Stories. | **LOST ROSE.**

MAGIC LANTERN, THE, and its Management: including full Practical Directions for producing the Limelight, making Oxygen Gas, and preparing Lantern Slides. By T. C. HEPWORTH. With 10 Illustrations. Cr. 8vo, **1s.**; cloth, **1s. 6d.**

MAGICIAN'S OWN BOOK, THE: Performances with Cups and Balls, Eggs, Hats, Handkerchiefs, &c. All from actual Experience. Edited by W. H. CREMER. With 200 Illustrations. Crown 8vo, cloth extra, **4s. 6d.**

MAGNA CHARTA: An Exact Facsimile of the Original in the British Museum, 3 feet by 2 feet, with Arms and Seals emblazoned in Gold and Colours, **5s.**

MALLOCK (W. H.), WORKS BY.

THE NEW REPUBLIC. Post 8vo, picture cover, **2s.**; cloth limp, **2s. 6d.**
THE NEW PAUL & VIRGINIA: Positivism on an Island. Post 8vo, cloth, **2s. 6d.**
POEMS. Small 4to, parchment, **8s.**
IS LIFE WORTH LIVING? Crown 8vo, cloth extra, **6s.**

MALLORY'S (SIR THOMAS) MORT D'ARTHUR: The Stories of King Arthur and of the Knights of the Round Table. (A Selection.) Edited by B. MONTGOMERIE RANKING. Post 8vo, cloth limp, **2s.**

MARK TWAIN, WORKS BY. Crown 8vo, cloth extra, **7s. 6d.** each.

THE CHOICE WORKS OF MARK TWAIN. Revised and Corrected throughout by the Author. With Life, Portrait, and numerous Illustrations.
ROUGHING IT, and INNOCENTS AT HOME. With 200 Illusts. by F. A. FRASER.
MARK TWAIN'S LIBRARY OF HUMOUR. With 197 Illustrations.
A YANKEE AT THE COURT OF KING ARTHUR. With 220 Illusts. by BEARD.

Crown 8vo, cloth extra (illustrated), **7s. 6d.** each; post 8vo, illust. boards, **2s.** each.

THE INNOCENTS ABROAD; or New Pilgrim's Progress. With 234 Illustrations. (The Two-Shilling Edition is entitled **MARK TWAIN'S PLEASURE TRIP.**)
THE GILDED AGE. By MARK TWAIN and C. D. WARNER. With 212 Illustrations.
THE ADVENTURES OF TOM SAWYER. With 111 Illustrations.
A TRAMP ABROAD. With 314 Illustrations.
THE PRINCE AND THE PAUPER. With 190 Illustrations.
LIFE ON THE MISSISSIPPI. With 300 Illustrations.
ADVENTURES OF HUCKLEBERRY FINN. With 174 Illusts. by E. W. KEMBLE.

MARK TWAIN'S SKETCHES. Post 8vo, illustrated boards, **2s.**
THE STOLEN WHITE ELEPHANT, &c. Cr. 8vo, cl., **6s.**; post 8vo, illust. bds., **2s.**
THE AMERICAN CLAIMANT: The Adventures of Mulberry Sellers. With numerous Illustrations. Crown 8vo, cloth extra, **3s. 6d.** [*Preparing.*

MARLOWE'S WORKS. Including his Translations. Edited, with Notes and Introductions, by Col. CUNNINGHAM. Crown 8vo, cloth extra, **6s.**

MARRYAT (FLORENCE), NOVELS BY. Post 8vo, illust. boards, **2s.** each.

A HARVEST OF WILD OATS.	**FIGHTING THE AIR.**
OPEN! SESAME!	**WRITTEN IN FIRE.**

MASSINGER'S PLAYS. From the Text of WILLIAM GIFFORD. Edited by Col. CUNNINGHAM. Crown 8vo, cloth extra, **6s.**

MASTERMAN.—HALF-A-DOZEN DAUGHTERS: A Novel. By J. MASTERMAN. Post 8vo, illustrated boards, **2s.**

MATTHEWS.—A SECRET OF THE SEA, &c. By BRANDER MATTHEWS. Post 8vo, illustrated boards, **2s.**; cloth limp, **2s. 6d.**

MAYHEW.—LONDON CHARACTERS AND THE HUMOROUS SIDE OF LONDON LIFE. By HENRY MAYHEW. With Illusts. Crown 8vo, cloth, **3s. 6d.**

MENKEN.—INFELICIA: Poems by ADAH ISAACS MENKEN. With Biographical Preface, Illustrations by F. E. LUMMIS and F. O. C. DARLEY, and Facsimile of a Letter from CHARLES DICKENS. Small 4to, cloth extra, **7s. 6d.**

MERRICK.—THE MAN WHO WAS GOOD. By LEONARD MERRICK, Author of "Violet Moses," &c. Two Vols., crown 8vo.

MEXICAN MUSTANG (ON A), through Texas to the Rio Grande. By A. E. SWEET and J. ARMOY KNOX. With 265 Illusts. Cr. 8vo, cloth extra, **7s. 6d.**

MIDDLEMASS (JEAN), NOVELS BY. Post 8vo, illust. boards, **2s.** each.

TOUCH AND GO.	**MR. DORILLION.**

MILLER.—PHYSIOLOGY FOR THE YOUNG; or, The House of Life: Human Physiology, with its application to the Preservation of Health. By Mrs. F. FENWICK MILLER. With numerous Illustrations. Post 8vo, cloth limp, **2s. 6d.**

MILTON (J. L.), WORKS BY. Post 8vo, 1s. each; cloth, 1s. 6d. each.
THE HYGIENE OF THE SKIN. With Directions for Diet, Soaps, Baths, &c.
THE BATH IN DISEASES OF THE SKIN.
THE LAWS OF LIFE, AND THEIR RELATION TO DISEASES OF THE SKIN.
THE SUCCESSFUL TREATMENT OF LEPROSY. Demy 8vo, 1s.

MINTO (WM.)—WAS SHE GOOD OR BAD? Cr. 8vo, 1s.; cloth, 1s. 6d.

MOLESWORTH (MRS.), NOVELS BY.
HATHERCOURT RECTORY. Post 8vo, illustrated boards, 2s.
THAT GIRL IN BLACK. Crown 8vo, cloth, 1s. 6d.

MOORE (THOMAS), WORKS BY.
THE EPICUREAN; and ALCIPHRON. Post 8vo, half-bound, 2s.
PROSE AND VERSE, Humorous, Satirical, and Sentimental, by THOMAS MOORE; with Suppressed Passages from the MEMOIRS OF LORD BYRON. Edited by R. HERNE SHEPHERD. With Portrait. Crown 8vo, cloth extra, 7s. 6d.

MUDDOCK (J. E.), STORIES BY.
STORIES WEIRD AND WONDERFUL. Post 8vo, illust. boards, 2s.; cloth, 2s. 6d.
THE DEAD MAN'S SECRET; or, The Valley of Gold. With Frontispiece by F. BARNARD. Crown 8vo, cloth extra, 5s.; post 8vo, illustrated boards, 2s.
MAID MARIAN AND ROBIN HOOD: A Romance of Old Sherwood Forest. With 12 Illustrations by STANLEY L. WOOD. Crown 8vo, cloth extra, 5s. [Shortly.

MURRAY (D. CHRISTIE), NOVELS BY.
Crown 8vo, cloth extra, 3s. 6d. each; post 8vo, illustrated boards, 2s. each.

A LIFE'S ATONEMENT.	**HEARTS.**	**BY THE GATE OF THE SEA.**
JOSEPH'S COAT.	**WAY OF THE WORLD**	**A BIT OF HUMAN NATURE.**
COALS OF FIRE.	**A MODEL FATHER.**	**FIRST PERSON SINGULAR.**
VAL STRANGE.	**OLD BLAZER'S HERO.**	**CYNIC FORTUNE.**

MURRAY (D. CHRISTIE) & HENRY HERMAN, WORKS BY.
ONE TRAVELLER RETURNS. Crown 8vo, cloth extra, 6s.; post 8vo, illustrated boards, 2s.
Crown 8vo, cloth extra, 3s. 6d. each; post 8vo, illustrated boards, 2s. each.
PAUL JONES'S ALIAS. With 13 Illustrations by A. FORESTIER and G. NICOLET.
THE BISHOPS' BIBLE.

MURRAY (HENRY), NOVELS BY.
A GAME OF BLUFF. Post 8vo, illustrated boards, 2s.; cloth, 2s. 6d.
A SONG OF SIXPENCE. Post 8vo, cloth extra, 2s. 6d.

NISBET (HUME), BOOKS BY.
"BAIL UP!" A Romance of BUSHRANGERS AND BLACKS. Cr. 8vo, cl. ex., 3s. 6d.
LESSONS IN ART. With 21 Illustrations. Crown 8vo, cloth extra, 2s. 6d.
WHERE ART BEGINS. With 27 Illusts. Square 8vo, cloth extra, 7s. 6d. [Shortly.

NOVELISTS.—HALF-HOURS WITH THE BEST NOVELISTS OF THE CENTURY. Edit. by H. T. MACKENZIE BELL. Cr. 8vo, cl., 3s. 6d. [Preparing.

O'CONNOR.—LORD BEACONSFIELD: A Biography. By T. P. O'CONNOR, M.P. Sixth Edition, with an Introduction. Crown 8vo, cloth extra, 5s.

O'HANLON (ALICE), NOVELS BY. Post 8vo, illustrated boards, 2s. each.
THE UNFORESEEN. | **CHANCE? OR FATE?**

OHNET (GEORGES), NOVELS BY.
DOCTOR RAMEAU. Translated by MRS. CASHEL HOEY. With 9 Illustrations by E. BAYARD. Crown 8vo, cloth extra, 6s.; post 8vo, illustrated boards, 2s.
A LAST LOVE. Translated by ALBERT D. VANDAM. Crown 8vo, cloth extra, 5s.; post 8vo, illustrated boards, 2s.
A WEIRD GIFT. Translated by ALBERT D. VANDAM. Crown 8vo, cloth, 3s. 6d.; post 8vo, illustrated boards, 2s.

OLIPHANT (MRS.), NOVELS BY. Post 8vo, illustrated boards, 2s. each.
THE PRIMROSE PATH. | **THE GREATEST HEIRESS IN ENGLAND.**
WHITELADIES. With Illustrations by ARTHUR HOPKINS and HENRY WOODS, A.R.A. Crown 8vo, cloth extra, 3s. 6d.; post 8vo, illustrated boards, 2s.

O'REILLY (HARRINGTON).—FIFTY YEARS ON THE TRAIL: Adventures of JOHN Y. NELSON. By HARRINGTON O'REILLY. With 100 Illustrations by PAUL FRENZENY. Crown 8vo, cloth extra, 3s. 6d.

O'REILLY (MRS.).—PHŒBE'S FORTUNES. Post 8vo, illust. bds., 2s.

O'SHAUGHNESSY (ARTHUR), POEMS BY.
LAYS OF FRANCE. Crown 8vo, cloth extra, 10s. 6d.
MUSIC AND MOONLIGHT. Fcap. 8vo, cloth extra, 7s. 6d.
SONGS OF A WORKER. Fcap. 8vo, cloth extra, 7s. 6d.

OUIDA, NOVELS BY. Cr. 8vo, cl., **3s. 6d.** each; post 8vo, illust. bds., **2s.** each.

HELD IN BONDAGE. TRICOTRIN. STRATHMORE. CHANDOS. CECIL CASTLEMAINE'S GAGE. IDALIA. UNDER TWO FLAGS. PUCK. FOLLE-FARINE. A DOG OF FLANDERS. PASCAREL. TWO LITTLE WOODEN SHOES. SIGNA. IN A WINTER CITY. ARIADNE. FRIENDSHIP. MOTHS. PIPISTRELLO. A VILLAGE COMMUNE. IN MAREMMA. BIMBI. WANDA. FRESCOES. OTHMAR. PRINCESS NAPRAXINE. GUILDEROY. RUFFINO.

SYRLIN. Crown 8vo, cloth extra, **3s. 6d.**; post 8vo, illustrated boards, **2s.**
SANTA BARBARA, &c. Second Edition. Square 8vo, cloth extra, **6s.**

WISDOM, WIT, AND PATHOS, selected from the Works of OUIDA by F. SYDNEY MORRIS. Post 8vo, cloth extra, **5s.** CHEAP EDITION, illustrated boards, **2s.**

PAGE (H. A.), WORKS BY.
THOREAU: His Life and Aims. With Portrait. Post 8vo, cloth limp, **2s. 6d.**
ANIMAL ANECDOTES. Arranged on a New Principle. Crown 8vo, cloth extra, **5s.**

PARLIAMENTARY ELECTIONS AND ELECTIONEERING, A HISTORY OF, from the Stuarts to Queen Victoria. By JOSEPH GREGO. A New Edition, with 93 Illustrations. Demy 8vo, cloth extra, **7s. 6d.**

PASCAL'S PROVINCIAL LETTERS. A New Translation, with Historical Introduction and Notes by T. M'CRIE, D.D. Post 8vo, cloth limp, **2s.**

PAUL.—GENTLE AND SIMPLE. By MARGARET A. PAUL. With Frontispiece by HELEN PATERSON. Crown 8vo, cloth, **3s. 6d.**; post 8vo, illust. boards, **2s.**

PAYN (JAMES), NOVELS BY.

Crown 8vo, cloth extra, **3s. 6d.** each; post 8vo, illustrated boards, **2s.** each.

LOST SIR MASSINGBERD. WALTER'S WORD. LESS BLACK THAN WE'RE PAINTED. BY PROXY. HIGH SPIRITS. UNDER ONE ROOF. A CONFIDENTIAL AGENT. A GRAPE FROM A THORN. FROM EXILE. THE CANON'S WARD. THE TALK OF THE TOWN. HOLIDAY TASKS. GLOW-WORM TALES. THE MYSTERY OF MIRBRIDGE. THE WORD AND THE WILL.

Post 8vo, illustrated boards, **2s.** each.

HUMOROUS STORIES. THE FOSTER BROTHERS. THE FAMILY SCAPEGRACE. MARRIED BENEATH HIM. BENTINCK'S TUTOR. A PERFECT TREASURE. A COUNTY FAMILY. LIKE FATHER, LIKE SON. A WOMAN'S VENGEANCE. CARLYON'S YEAR. CECIL'S TRYST. MURPHY'S MASTER. AT HER MERCY. THE CLYFFARDS OF CLYFFE. FOUND DEAD. GWENDOLINE'S HARVEST. A MARINE RESIDENCE. MIRK ABBEY. SOME PRIVATE VIEWS. NOT WOOED, BUT WON. TWO HUNDRED POUNDS REWARD. THE BEST OF HUSBANDS. HALVES. THE BURNT MILLION. FALLEN FORTUNES. WHAT HE COST HER. KIT: A MEMORY. FOR CASH ONLY.

Crown 8vo, cloth extra, **3s. 6d.** each.

IN PERIL AND PRIVATION: Stories of MARINE ADVENTURE Re-told. With 17 Illustrations.
SUNNY STORIES, and some SHADY ONES. With a Frontispiece by FRED. BARNARD.
NOTES FROM THE "NEWS." Crown 8vo, portrait cover, **1s.**; cloth, **1s. 6d.**

PENNELL (H. CHOLMONDELEY), WORKS BY. Post 8vo, cl., **2s. 6d.** each.
PUCK ON PEGASUS. With Illustrations.
PEGASUS RE-SADDLED. With Ten full-page Illustrations by G. DU MAURIER.
THE MUSES OF MAYFAIR. Vers de Société, Selected by H. C. PENNELL.

PHELPS (E. STUART), WORKS BY. Post 8vo, **1s.** each; cloth, **1s. 6d.** each.
BEYOND THE GATES. By the Author of "The Gates Ajar." **AN OLD MAID'S PARADISE.** **BURGLARS IN PARADISE.**
JACK THE FISHERMAN. Illustrated by C. W. REED. Cr. 8vo, **1s.**; cloth, **1s. 6d.**

PIRKIS (C. L.), NOVELS BY.
TROOPING WITH CROWS. Fcap. 8vo, picture cover, **1s.**
LADY LOVELACE. Post 8vo, illustrated boards, **2s.**

PLANCHE (J. R.), WORKS BY.
THE PURSUIVANT OF ARMS; or, Heraldry Founded upon Facts. With Coloured Frontispiece, Five Plates, and 209 Illusts. Crown 8vo, cloth, **7s. 6d.**
SONGS AND POEMS, 1819-1879. Introduction by MRS. MACKARNESS. Cr. 8vo, cl., **6s.**

PLUTARCH'S LIVES OF ILLUSTRIOUS MEN. Translated from the Greek, with Notes Critical and Historical, and a Life of Plutarch, by JOHN and WILLIAM LANGHORNE. With Portraits. Two Vols., demy 8vo, half-bound, **10s. 6d.**

POE'S (EDGAR ALLAN) CHOICE WORKS, in Prose and Poetry. Introduction by CHAS. BAUDELAIRE, Portrait, and Facsimiles. Cr. 8vo, cloth, **7s. 6d.**
THE MYSTERY OF MARIE ROGET, &c. Post 8vo, illustrated boards, **2s.**

POPE'S POETICAL WORKS. Post 8vo, cloth limp, **2s.**

PRICE (E. C.), NOVELS BY.
Crown 8vo, cloth extra, **3s. 6d.** each; post 8vo, illustrated boards, **2s.** each.
VALENTINA. | **THE FOREIGNERS.** | **MRS. LANCASTER'S RIVAL.**
GERALD. Post 8vo, illustrated boards, **2s.**

PRINCESS OLGA.—RADNA; or, The Great Conspiracy of 1881. By the Princess OLGA. Crown 8vo, cloth extra, **6s.**

PROCTOR (RICHARD A., B.A.), WORKS BY.
FLOWERS OF THE SKY. With 55 Illusts. Small crown 8vo, cloth extra, **3s. 6d.**
EASY STAR LESSONS. With Star Maps for Every Night in the Year, Drawings of the Constellations, &c. Crown 8vo, cloth extra, **6s.**
FAMILIAR SCIENCE STUDIES. Crown 8vo, cloth extra, **6s.**
SATURN AND ITS SYSTEM. With 13 Steel Plates. Demy 8vo, cloth ex., **10s. 6d.**
MYSTERIES OF TIME AND SPACE. With Illustrations. Cr. 8vo, cloth extra, **6s.**
THE UNIVERSE OF SUNS. With numerous Illustrations. Cr. 8vo, cloth ex., **6s.**
WAGES AND WANTS OF SCIENCE WORKERS. Crown 8vo, **1s. 6d.**

PRYCE.—MISS MAXWELL'S AFFECTIONS. By RICHARD PRYCE, Author of "No Impediment." With a Frontispiece by HAL LUDLOW. Crown 8vo, cloth extra, **3s. 6d.**

RAMBOSSON.—POPULAR ASTRONOMY. By J. RAMBOSSON, Laureate of the Institute of France. With numerous Illusts. Crown 8vo, cloth extra, **7s. 6d.**

RANDOLPH.—AUNT ABIGAIL DYKES: A Novel. By Lt.-Colonel GEORGE RANDOLPH, U.S.A. Crown 8vo, cloth extra, **7s. 6d.**

READE (CHARLES), NOVELS BY.
Crown 8vo, cloth extra, illustrated, **3s. 6d.** each; post 8vo, illust. bds., **2s.** each.
PEG WOFFINGTON. Illustrated by S. L. FILDES, R.A.—Also a POCKET EDITION, set in New Type, in Elzevir style, fcap. 8vo, half-leather, **2s. 6d.**
CHRISTIE JOHNSTONE. Illustrated by WILLIAM SMALL.—Also a POCKET EDITION, set in New Type, in Elzevir style, fcap. 8vo, half-leather, **2s. 6d.**
IT IS NEVER TOO LATE TO MEND. Illustrated by G. J. PINWELL.
THE COURSE OF TRUE LOVE NEVER DID RUN SMOOTH. Illustrated by HELEN PATERSON.
THE AUTOBIOGRAPHY OF A THIEF, &c. Illustrated by MATT STRETCH.
LOVE ME LITTLE, LOVE ME LONG. Illustrated by M. ELLEN EDWARDS.
THE DOUBLE MARRIAGE. Illusts. by Sir JOHN GILBERT, R.A., and C. KEENE.
THE CLOISTER AND THE HEARTH. Illustrated by CHARLES KEENE.
HARD CASH. Illustrated by F. W. LAWSON.
GRIFFITH GAUNT. Illustrated by S. L. FILDES, R.A., and WILLIAM SMALL.
FOUL PLAY. Illustrated by GEORGE DU MAURIER.
PUT YOURSELF IN HIS PLACE. Illustrated by ROBERT BARNES.
A TERRIBLE TEMPTATION. Illustrated by EDWARD HUGHES and A. W. COOPER.
A SIMPLETON. Illustrated by KATE CRAUFURD.
THE WANDERING HEIR. Illustrated by HELEN PATERSON, S. L. FILDES, R.A., C. GREEN, and HENRY WOODS, A.R.A.
A WOMAN-HATER. Illustrated by THOMAS COULDERY.
SINGLEHEART AND DOUBLEFACE. Illustrated by P. MACNAB.
GOOD STORIES OF MEN AND OTHER ANIMALS. Illustrated by E. A. ABBEY, PERCY MACQUOID, R.W.S., and JOSEPH NASH.
THE JILT, and other Stories. Illustrated by JOSEPH NASH.
A PERILOUS SECRET. Illustrated by FRED. BARNARD.
READIANA. With a Steel-plate Portrait of CHARLES READE.
BIBLE CHARACTERS: Studies of David, Paul, &c. Fcap. 8vo, leatherette, **1s.**
SELECTIONS FROM THE WORKS OF CHARLES READE. With an Introduction by Mrs. ALEX. IRELAND, and a Steel-Plate Portrait. Crown 8vo, buckram, **6s.**

RIDDELL (MRS. J. H.), NOVELS BY.
Crown 8vo, cloth extra, 3s. 6d. each; post 8vo, illustrated boards, 2s. each.
THE PRINCE OF WALES'S GARDEN PARTY. | WEIRD STORIES.

Post 8vo, illustrated boards, 2s. each.
THE UNINHABITED HOUSE. | FAIRY WATER.
MYSTERY IN PALACE GARDENS. | HER MOTHER'S DARLING.

RIMMER (ALFRED), WORKS BY. Square 8vo, cloth gilt, 7s. 6d. each.
OUR OLD COUNTRY TOWNS. With 55 Illustrations.
RAMBLES ROUND ETON AND HARROW. With 50 Illustrations.
ABOUT ENGLAND WITH DICKENS. With 58 Illusts. by C. A. VANDERHOOF, &c.

ROBINSON CRUSOE. By DANIEL DEFOE. (MAJOR'S EDITION.) With 37 Illustrations by GEORGE CRUIKSHANK. Post 8vo, half-bound, 2s.

ROBINSON (F. W.), NOVELS BY.
WOMEN ARE STRANGE. Post 8vo, illustrated boards, 2s.
THE HANDS OF JUSTICE. Crown 8vo, cloth extra, 3s. 6d.; post 8vo, illustrated boards, 2s.

ROBINSON (PHIL), WORKS BY. Crown 8vo, cloth extra, 7s. 6d. each.
THE POETS' BIRDS. | THE POETS' BEASTS.
THE POETS AND NATURE: REPTILES, FISHES, INSECTS. [Preparing.

ROCHEFOUCAULD'S MAXIMS AND MORAL REFLECTIONS. With Notes, and an Introductory Essay by SAINTE-BEUVE. Post 8vo, cloth limp, 2s.

ROLL OF BATTLE ABBEY, THE: A List of the Principal Warriors who came from Normandy with William the Conqueror, and Settled in this Country, A.D. 1066–7. With Arms emblazoned in Gold and Colours. Handsomely printed, 5s.

ROWLEY (HON. HUGH), WORKS BY. Post 8vo, cloth, 2s. 6d. each.
PUNIANA: RIDDLES AND JOKES. With numerous Illustrations.
MORE PUNIANA. Profusely Illustrated.

RUNCIMAN (JAMES), STORIES BY.
Post 8vo, illustrated boards, 2s. each; cloth limp, 2s. 6d. each.
SKIPPERS AND SHELLBACKS. | GRACE BALMAIGN'S SWEETHEART.
SCHOOLS AND SCHOLARS.

RUSSELL (W. CLARK), BOOKS AND NOVELS BY:
Crown 8vo, cloth extra, 6s. each; post 8vo, illustrated boards, 2s. each.
ROUND THE GALLEY-FIRE. | A BOOK FOR THE HAMMOCK.
IN THE MIDDLE WATCH. | MYSTERY OF THE "OCEAN STAR."
A VOYAGE TO THE CAPE. | THE ROMANCE OF JENNY HARLOWE

ON THE FO'K'SLE HEAD. Post 8vo, illustrated boards, 2s.
AN OCEAN TRAGEDY. Cr. 8vo, cloth extra, 3s. 6d.; post 8vo, illust. bds., 2s.
MY SHIPMATE LOUISE. Crown 8vo, cl. extra, 3s. 6d.; post 8vo, illust., bds., 2s.
ALONE ON A WIDE WIDE SEA. Three Vols., crown 8vo.

SAINT AUBYN (ALAN), NOVELS BY.
A FELLOW OF TRINITY. With a Note by OLIVER WENDELL HOLMES and a Frontispiece. Crown 8vo, cloth extra, 3s. 6d.; post 8vo, illust. boards, 2s.
THE JUNIOR DEAN. Crown 8vo, cloth extra, 3s. 6d.

SALA.—GASLIGHT AND DAYLIGHT. By GEORGE AUGUSTUS SALA. Post 8vo, illustrated boards, 2s.

SANSON.—SEVEN GENERATIONS OF EXECUTIONERS: Memoirs of the Sanson Family (1688 to 1847). Crown 8vo, cloth extra, 3s. 6d.

SAUNDERS (JOHN), NOVELS BY.
Crown 8vo, cloth extra, 3s. 6d. each; post 8vo, illustrated boards, 2s. each.
GUY WATERMAN. | THE LION IN THE PATH. | THE TWO DREAMERS.
BOUND TO THE WHEEL. Crown 8vo, cloth extra, 3s. 6d.

SAUNDERS (KATHARINE), NOVELS BY.
Crown 8vo, cloth extra, 3s. 6d. each; post 8vo, illustrated boards, 2s. each.
MARGARET AND ELIZABETH. | HEART SALVAGE.
THE HIGH MILLS. | SEBASTIAN.

JOAN MERRYWEATHER. Post 8vo, illustrated boards, 2s.
GIDEON'S ROCK. Crown 8vo, cloth extra, 3s. 6d.

SCIENCE-GOSSIP: An Illustrated Medium of Interchange for Students and Lovers of Nature. Edited by Dr. J. E. TAYLOR, F.L.S., &c. Devoted to Geology, Botany, Physiology, Chemistry, Zoology, Microscopy, Telescopy, Physiography Photography, &c. Price 4d. Monthly; or 5s. per year, post-free. Vols. I. to XIX. may be had, 7s. 6d. each; Vols. XX. to date, 5s. each. Cases for Binding, 1s. 6d.

SECRET OUT, THE: One Thousand Tricks with Cards; with Entertaining Experiments in Drawing-room or "White Magic." By W. H. CREMER. With 300 Illustrations. Crown 8vo, cloth extra, **4s. 6d.**

SEGUIN (L. G.), WORKS BY.

THE COUNTRY OF THE PASSION PLAY (OBERAMMERGAU) and the Highlands of Bavaria. With Map and 37 Illustrations. Crown 8vo, cloth extra, **3s. 6d.**

WALKS IN ALGIERS. With 2 Maps and 16 Illusts. Crown 8vo, cloth extra, **6s.**

SENIOR (WM.).—BY STREAM AND SEA. Post 8vo, cloth, **2s. 6d.**

SHAKESPEARE FOR CHILDREN: LAMB'S TALES FROM SHAKESPEARE. With Illustrations, coloured and plain, by J. MOYR SMITH. Crown 4to, cloth, **6s.**

SHARP.—CHILDREN OF TO-MORROW: A Novel. By WILLIAM SHARP. Crown 8vo, cloth extra, **6s.**

SHARP (LUKE).—IN A STEAMER CHAIR. By LUKE SHARP (R. E. BARR). With Two Illusts. by DEMAIN HAMMOND. Crown 8vo, cloth extra, **3s. 6d.**

SHELLEY.—THE COMPLETE WORKS IN VERSE AND PROSE OF PERCY BYSSHE SHELLEY. Edited, Prefaced, and Annotated by R. HERNE SHEPHERD. Five Vols., crown 8vo, cloth boards, **3s. 6d.** each.

POETICAL WORKS, in Three Vols.:

Vol. I. Introduction by the Editor; Posthumous Fragments of Margaret Nicholson; Shelley's Correspondence with Stockdale; The Wandering Jew; Queen Mab, with the Notes; Alastor, and other Poems; Rosalind and Helen; Prometheus Unbound; Adonais, &c.

Vol. II. Laon and Cythna; The Cenci; Julian and Maddalo; Swellfoot the Tyrant; The Witch of Atlas; Epipsychidion; Hellas.

Vol. III. Posthumous Poems; The Masque of Anarchy; and other Pieces.

PROSE WORKS, in Two Vols.:

Vol. I. The Two Romances of Zastrozzi and St. Irvyne; the Dublin and Marlow Pamphlets; A Refutation of Deism; Letters to Leigh Hunt, and some Minor Writings and Fragments.

Vol. II. The Essays; Letters from Abroad; Translations and Fragments, Edited by Mrs. SHELLEY. With a Bibliography of Shelley, and an Index of the Prose Works.

SHERARD.—ROGUES: A Novel. By R. H. SHERARD. Crown 8vo, picture cover, **1s.**; cloth, **1s. 6d.**

SHERIDAN (GENERAL).—PERSONAL MEMOIRS OF GENERAL P. H. SHERIDAN. With Portraits and Facsimiles. Two Vols., demy 8vo, cloth, **24s.**

SHERIDAN'S (RICHARD BRINSLEY) COMPLETE WORKS. With Life and Anecdotes. Including his Dramatic Writings, his Works in Prose and Poetry, Translations, Speeches and Jokes. 10 Illusts. Cr. 8vo, hf.-bound, **7s. 6d.**

THE RIVALS, THE SCHOOL FOR SCANDAL, and other Plays. Post 8vo, printed on laid paper and half-bound, **2s.**

SHERIDAN'S COMEDIES: THE RIVALS and **THE SCHOOL FOR SCANDAL.** Edited, with an Introduction and Notes to each Play, and a Biographical Sketch, by BRANDER MATTHEWS. With Illustrations. Demy 8vo, half-parchment, **12s. 6d.**

SIDNEY'S (SIR PHILIP) COMPLETE POETICAL WORKS, including all those in "Arcadia." With Portrait, Memorial-Introduction, Notes, &c. by the Rev. A. B. GROSART, D.D. Three Vols., crown 8vo, cloth boards, **18s.**

SIGNBOARDS: Their History. With Anecdotes of Famous Taverns and Remarkable Characters. By JACOB LARWOOD and JOHN CAMDEN HOTTEN. With Coloured Frontispiece and 94 Illustrations. Crown 8vo, cloth extra, **7s. 6d.**

SIMS (GEORGE R.), WORKS BY.

Post 8vo, illustrated boards, **2s.** each; cloth limp, **2s. 6d.** each.

ROGUES AND VAGABONDS.
THE RING O' BELLS.
MARY JANE'S MEMOIRS.
MARY JANE MARRIED.
TALES OF TO DAY.
DRAMAS OF LIFE. With 60 Illustrations.
TINKLETOP'S CRIME. With a Frontispiece by MAURICE GREIFFENHAGEN.
ZEPH: A Circus Story, &c.

Crown 8vo, picture cover, **1s.** each; cloth, **1s. 6d.** each.

HOW THE POOR LIVE; and **HORRIBLE LONDON.**
THE DAGONET RECITER AND READER: being Readings and Recitations in Prose and Verse, selected from his own Works by GEORGE R. SIMS.
DAGONET DITTIES. From the *Referee*.
THE CASE OF GEORGE CANDLEMAS.

SISTER DORA: A Biography. By MARGARET LONSDALE. With Four Illustrations. Demy 8vo, picture cover, **4d.**; cloth, **6d.**

SKETCHLEY.—A MATCH IN THE DARK. By ARTHUR SKETCHLEY Post 8vo, illustrated boards, **2s.**

SLANG DICTIONARY (THE): Etymological, Historical, and Anecdotal. Crown 8vo, cloth extra, **6s. 6d.**

SMITH (J. MOYR), WORKS BY.
THE PRINCE OF ARGOLIS. With 130 Illusts. Post 8vo, cloth extra, **3s. 6d.**
TALES OF OLD THULE. With numerous Illustrations. Crown 8vo, cloth gilt, **6s.**
THE WOOING OF THE WATER WITCH. Illustrated. Post 8vo, cloth, **6s.**

SOCIETY IN LONDON. By A FOREIGN RESIDENT. Crown 8vo, **1s.**; cloth, **1s. 6d.**

SOCIETY IN PARIS: The Upper Ten Thousand. A Series of Letters from Count PAUL VASILI to a Young French Diplomat. Crown 8vo, cloth, **6s.**

SOMERSET.—SONGS OF ADIEU. By Lord HENRY SOMERSET. Small 4to, Japanese vellum, **6s.**

SPALDING.—ELIZABETHAN DEMONOLOGY: An Essay on the Belief in the Existence of Devils. By T. A. SPALDING, LL.B. Crown 8vo, cloth extra, **5s.**

SPEIGHT (T. W.), NOVELS BY.
Post 8vo, illustrated boards, **2s.** each.
THE MYSTERIES OF HERON DYKE.
BY DEVIOUS WAYS, &c.
THE GOLDEN HOOP.
HOODWINKED; and **THE SANDYCROFT MYSTERY.**
BACK TO LIFE.
Post 8vo, cloth limp, **1s. 6d.** each.
A BARREN TITLE.
WIFE OR NO WIFE?
THE SANDYCROFT MYSTERY. Crown 8vo, picture cover, **1s.**

SPENSER FOR CHILDREN. By M. H. TOWRY. With Illustrations by WALTER J. MORGAN. Crown 4to, cloth gilt, **6s.**

STARRY HEAVENS (THE): A POETICAL BIRTHDAY BOOK. Royal 16mo, cloth extra, **2s. 6d.**

STAUNTON.—THE LAWS AND PRACTICE OF CHESS. With an Analysis of the Openings. By HOWARD STAUNTON. Edited by ROBERT B. WORMALD. Crown 8vo, cloth extra, **5s.**

STEDMAN (E. C.), WORKS BY.
VICTORIAN POETS. Thirteenth Edition. Crown 8vo, cloth extra, **9s.**
THE POETS OF AMERICA. Crown 8vo, cloth extra, **9s.**

STERNDALE.—THE AFGHAN KNIFE: A Novel. By ROBERT ARMITAGE STERNDALE. Cr. 8vo, cloth extra, **3s. 6d.**; post 8vo, illust. boards, **2s.**

STEVENSON (R. LOUIS), WORKS BY. Post 8vo, cl. limp, **2s. 6d.** each.
TRAVELS WITH A DONKEY. Seventh Edit. With a Frontis. by WALTER CRANE.
AN INLAND VOYAGE. Fourth Edition. With a Frontispiece by WALTER CRANE.

Crown 8vo, buckram, gilt top, **6s.** each.
FAMILIAR STUDIES OF MEN AND BOOKS. Sixth Edition.
THE SILVERADO SQUATTERS. With a Frontispiece. Third Edition.
THE MERRY MEN. Third Edition. | **UNDERWOODS:** Poems. Fifth Edition.
MEMORIES AND PORTRAITS. Third Edition.
VIRGINIBUS PUERISQUE, and other Papers. Seventh Edition. | **BALLADS.**
ACROSS THE PLAINS, with other Memories and Essays.

NEW ARABIAN NIGHTS. Eleventh Edition. Crown 8vo, buckram, gilt top, **6s.**; post 8vo, illustrated boards, **2s.**
PRINCE OTTO. Sixth Edition. Post 8vo, illustrated boards, **2s.**
FATHER DAMIEN: An Open Letter to the Rev. Dr. Hyde. Second Edition. Crown 8vo, hand-made and brown paper, **1s.**

STODDARD.—SUMMER CRUISING IN THE SOUTH SEAS. By C. WARREN STODDARD. Illustrated by WALLIS MACKAY. Cr. 8vo, cl. extra, **3s. 6d.**

STORIES FROM FOREIGN NOVELISTS. With Notices by HELEN and ALICE ZIMMERN. Crown 8vo, cloth extra, **3s. 6d.**; post 8vo, illustrated boards, **2s.**

STRANGE MANUSCRIPT (A) FOUND IN A COPPER CYLINDER. With 19 Illustrations by GILBERT GAUL. Third Edition. Crown 8vo, cloth extra, 5s.

STRANGE SECRETS. Told by CONAN DOYLE, PERCY FITZGERALD, FLORENCE MARRYAT, &c. Cr. 8vo, cl. ex., Eight Illusts., 6s.; post 8vo, illust. bds., 2s.

STRUTT'S SPORTS AND PASTIMES OF THE PEOPLE OF ENGLAND; including the Rural and Domestic Recreations, May Games, Mummeries, Shows, &c., from the Earliest Period to the Present Time. Edited by WILLIAM HONE. With 140 Illustrations. Crown 8vo, cloth extra, 7s. 6d.

SUBURBAN HOMES (THE) OF LONDON: A Residential Guide. With a Map, and Notes on Rental, Rates, and Accommodation. Crown 8vo, cloth, 7s. 6d.

SWIFT'S (DEAN) CHOICE WORKS, in Prose and Verse. With Memoir, Portrait, and Facsimiles of the Maps in "Gulliver's Travels." Cr. 8vo, cl., 7s. 6d.

GULLIVER'S TRAVELS, and A TALE OF A TUB. Post 8vo, printed on laid paper and half-bound, 2s.

A MONOGRAPH ON SWIFT. By J. CHURTON COLLINS. Cr. 8vo, cloth, 8s. [*Shortly.*

SWINBURNE (ALGERNON C.), WORKS BY.

SELECTIONS FROM POETICAL WORKS OF A. C. SWINBURNE. Fcap. 8vo, 6s.
ATALANTA IN CALYDON. Crown 8vo, 6s.
CHASTELARD: A Tragedy. Cr. 8vo, 7s.
NOTES ON POEMS AND REVIEWS. Demy 8vo, 1s.
POEMS AND BALLADS. FIRST SERIES. Crown 8vo or fcap. 8vo, 9s.
POEMS AND BALLADS. SECOND SERIES. Crown 8vo or fcap. 8vo, 9s.
POEMS AND BALLADS. THIRD SERIES. Crown 8vo, 7s.
SONGS BEFORE SUNRISE. Crown 8vo, 10s. 6d.
BOTHWELL: A Tragedy. Crown 8vo, 12s. 6d.
SONGS OF TWO NATIONS. Cr. 8vo, 6s.
GEORGE CHAPMAN. (*See* Vol. II. of G. CHAPMAN'S Works.) Crown 8vo, 6s.
ESSAYS AND STUDIES. Cr. 8vo, 12s.
ERECHTHEUS: A Tragedy. Cr. 8vo, 6s.
SONGS OF THE SPRINGTIDES. Crown 8vo, 6s.
STUDIES IN SONG. Crown 8vo, 7s.
MARY STUART: A Tragedy. Cr. 8vo, 8s.
TRISTRAM OF LYONESSE. Cr. 8vo, 9s.
A CENTURY OF ROUNDELS. Sm. 4to, 8s.
A MIDSUMMER HOLIDAY. Cr. 8vo, 7s.
MARINO FALIERO: A Tragedy. Crown 8vo, 6s.
A STUDY OF VICTOR HUGO. Cr. 8vo, 6s.
MISCELLANIES. Crown 8vo, 12s.
LOCRINE: A Tragedy. Cr. 8vo, 6s.
A STUDY OF BEN JONSON. Cr. 8vo, 7s.
THE SISTERS: A Tragedy. Cr. 8vo, 6s.

SYMONDS.—WINE, WOMEN, AND SONG: Mediæval Latin Students' Songs. With Essay and Trans. by J. ADDINGTON SYMONDS. Fcap. 8vo, parchment, 6s.

SYNTAX'S (DR.) THREE TOURS: In Search of the Picturesque, in Search of Consolation, and in Search of a Wife. With ROWLANDSON'S Coloured Illustrations, and Life of the Author by J. C. HOTTEN. Crown 8vo, cloth extra, 7s. 6d.

TAINE'S HISTORY OF ENGLISH LITERATURE. Translated by HENRY VAN LAUN. Four Vols., small demy 8vo, cl. bds., 30s.—POPULAR EDITION, Two Vols., large crown 8vo, cloth extra, 15s.

TAYLOR'S (BAYARD) DIVERSIONS OF THE ECHO CLUB: Burlesques of Modern Writers. Post 8vo, cloth limp, 2s.

TAYLOR (DR. J. E., F.L.S.), WORKS BY. Cr. 8vo, cl. ex., 7s. 6d. each.

THE SAGACITY AND MORALITY OF PLANTS: A Sketch of the Life and Conduct of the Vegetable Kingdom. With a Coloured Frontispiece and 100 Illustrations.

OUR COMMON BRITISH FOSSILS, and Where to Find Them. 331 Illustrations.

THE PLAYTIME NATURALIST. With 366 Illustrations. Crown 8vo, cloth, 5s.

TAYLOR'S (TOM) HISTORICAL DRAMAS. Containing "Clancarty," "Jeanne Darc," "'Twixt Axe and Crown," "The Fool's Revenge," "Arkwright's Wife," "Anne Boleyn," "Plot and Passion." Crown 8vo, cloth extra, 7s. 6d.
*** The Plays may also be had separately, at 1s. each.

TENNYSON (LORD): A Biographical Sketch. By H. J. JENNINGS. With a Photograph-Portrait. Crown 8vo, cloth extra, 6s.

THACKERAYANA; Notes and Anecdotes. Illustrated by Hundreds of Sketches by WILLIAM MAKEPEACE THACKERAY, depicting Humorous Incidents in his School-life, and Favourite Characters in the Books of his Every-day Reading. With a Coloured Frontispiece. Crown 8vo, cloth extra, 7s. 6d.

THAMES.—A NEW PICTORIAL HISTORY OF THE THAMES. By A. S. KRAUSSE. With 340 Illustrations Post 8vo, **1s.**; cloth, **1s. 6d.**

THOMAS (BERTHA), NOVELS BY. Cr. 8vo, cl., **3s. 6d.** ea.; post 8vo, **2s.** ea.
THE VIOLIN-PLAYER. | **PROUD MAISIE.**

CRESSIDA. Post 8vo, illustrated boards, **2s.**

THOMSON'S SEASONS, and CASTLE OF INDOLENCE. With Introduction by ALLAN CUNNINGHAM, and 48 Illustrations. Post 8vo, half-bound, **2s.**

THORNBURY (WALTER), WORKS BY. Cr. 8vo, cl. extra, **7s. 6d.** each.
THE LIFE AND CORRESPONDENCE OF J. M. W. TURNER. Founded upon Letters and Papers furnished by his Friends. With Illustrations in Colours.
HAUNTED LONDON. Edit. by E. WALFORD, M.A. Illusts. by F. W. FAIRHOLT, F.S.A.

Post 8vo, illustrated boards, **2s.** each.
OLD STORIES RE-TOLD. | **TALES FOR THE MARINES.**

TIMBS (JOHN), WORKS BY. Crown 8vo, cloth extra, **7s. 6d.** each.
THE HISTORY OF CLUBS AND CLUB LIFE IN LONDON: Anecdotes of its Famous Coffee-houses, Hostelries, and Taverns. With 42 Illustrations.
ENGLISH ECCENTRICS AND ECCENTRICITIES: Stories of Wealth and Fashion, Delusions, Impostures, and Fanatic Missions, Sporting Scenes, Eccentric Artists, Theatrical Folk, Men of Letters, &c. With 48 Illustrations.

TROLLOPE (ANTHONY), NOVELS BY.
Crown 8vo, cloth extra, **3s. 6d.** each; post 8vo, illustrated boards, **2s.** each.
THE WAY WE LIVE NOW. | **MARION FAY.**
KEPT IN THE DARK. | **MR. SCARBOROUGH'S FAMILY.**
FRAU FROHMANN. | **THE LAND-LEAGUERS.**

Post 8vo, illustrated boards, **2s.** each.
GOLDEN LION OF GRANPERE. | **JOHN CALDIGATE.** | **AMERICAN SENATOR.**

TROLLOPE (FRANCES E.), NOVELS BY.
Crown 8vo, cloth extra, **3s. 6d.** each; post 8vo, illustrated boards, **2s.** each.
LIKE SHIPS UPON THE SEA. | **MABEL'S PROGRESS.** | **ANNE FURNESS.**

TROLLOPE (T. A.).—DIAMOND CUT DIAMOND. Post 8vo, illust. bds., **2s.**

TROWBRIDGE.—FARNELL'S FOLLY: A Novel. By J. T. TROWBRIDGE. Post 8vo, illustrated boards, **2s.**

TYTLER (C. C. FRASER-).—MISTRESS JUDITH: A Novel. By C. C. FRASER-TYTLER. Crown 8vo, cloth extra, **3s. 6d.**; post 8vo, illust. boards, **2s.**

TYTLER (SARAH), NOVELS BY.
Crown 8vo, cloth extra, **3s. 6d.** each; post 8vo, illustrated boards, **2s.** each.
THE BRIDE'S PASS. | **BURIED DIAMONDS.**
NOBLESSE OBLIGE. | **LADY BELL.** | **THE BLACKHALL GHOSTS.**

Post 8vo, illustrated boards, **2s.** each.
WHAT SHE CAME THROUGH. | **BEAUTY AND THE BEAST.**
CITOYENNE JACQUELINE. | **DISAPPEARED.**
SAINT MUNGO'S CITY. | **THE HUGUENOT FAMILY.**

VILLARI.—A DOUBLE BOND. By LINDA VILLARI. Fcap. 8vo, picture cover, **1s.**

WALT WHITMAN, POEMS BY. Edited, with Introduction, by WILLIAM M. ROSSETTI. With Portrait. Cr. 8vo, hand-made paper and buckram, **6s.**

WALTON AND COTTON'S COMPLETE ANGLER; or, The Contemplative Man's Recreation, by IZAAK WALTON; and Instructions how to Angle for a Trout or Grayling in a clear Stream, by CHARLES COTTON. With Memoirs and Notes by Sir HARRIS NICOLAS, and 61 Illustrations. Crown 8vo, cloth antique, **7s. 6d.**

WARD (HERBERT), WORKS BY.
FIVE YEARS WITH THE CONGO CANNIBALS. With 92 Illustrations by the Author, VICTOR PERARD, and W. B. DAVIS. Third ed. Roy. 8vo, cloth ex., **14s.**
MY LIFE WITH STANLEY'S REAR GUARD. With a Map by F. S. WELLER, F.R.G.S. Post 8vo, **1s.**; cloth, **1s. 6d.**

WARNER.—A ROUNDABOUT JOURNEY. By CHARLES DUDLEY WARNER. Crown 8vo, cloth extra, **6s.**

WALFORD (EDWARD, M.A.), WORKS BY.

WALFORD'S COUNTY FAMILIES OF THE UNITED KINGDOM (1892). Containing the Descent, Birth, Marriage, Education, &c., of 12,000 Heads of Families, their Heirs, Offices, Addresses, Clubs, &c. Royal 8vo, cloth gilt, **50s.**

WALFORD'S WINDSOR PEERAGE, BARONETAGE, AND KNIGHTAGE (1892). Crown 8vo, cloth extra, **12s. 6d.**

WALFORD'S SHILLING PEERAGE (1892). Containing a List of the House of Lords, Scotch and Irish Peers, &c. 32mo, cloth, **1s.**

WALFORD'S SHILLING BARONETAGE (1892). Containing a List of the Baronets of the United Kingdom, Biographical Notices, Addresses, &c. 32mo, cloth, **1s.**

WALFORD'S SHILLING KNIGHTAGE (1892). Containing a List of the Knights of the United Kingdom, Biographical Notices, Addresses, &c. 32mo, cloth, **1s.**

WALFORD'S SHILLING HOUSE OF COMMONS (1892). Containing a List of all Members of Parliament, their Addresses, Clubs, &c. 32mo, cloth, **1s.**

WALFORD'S COMPLETE PEERAGE, BARONETAGE, KNIGHTAGE, AND HOUSE OF COMMONS (1892). Royal 32mo, cloth extra, gilt edges, **5s.**

TALES OF OUR GREAT FAMILIES. Crown 8vo, cloth extra, **3s. 6d.**

WARRANT TO EXECUTE CHARLES I. A Facsimile, with the 59 Signatures and Seals. Printed on paper 22 in. by 14 in. **2s.**

WARRANT TO EXECUTE MARY QUEEN OF SCOTS. A Facsimile, including Queen Elizabeth's Signature and the Great Seal. **2s.**

WASSERMANN.—THE DAFFODILS: A Novel. By LILLIAS WASSERMANN. Crown 8vo, **1s.**; cloth, **1s. 6d.**

WEATHER, HOW TO FORETELL THE, WITH POCKET SPECTROSCOPE. By F. W. CORY. With 10 Illustrations. Cr. 8vo, **1s.**; cloth, **1s. 6d.**

WESTROPP.—HANDBOOK OF POTTERY AND PORCELAIN. By HODDER M. WESTROPP. With Illusts. and List of Marks. Cr. 8vo, cloth, **4s. 6d.**

WHIST.—HOW TO PLAY SOLO WHIST. By ABRAHAM S. WILKS and CHARLES F. PARDON. Crown 8vo, cloth extra, **3s. 6d.**

WHISTLER'S (MR.) TEN O'CLOCK. Cr. 8vo, hand-made paper, **1s.**

WHITE.—THE NATURAL HISTORY OF SELBORNE. By GILBERT WHITE, M.A. Post 8vo, printed on laid paper and half-bound, **2s.**

WILLIAMS (W. MATTIEU, F.R.A.S.), WORKS BY.

SCIENCE IN SHORT CHAPTERS. Crown 8vo, cloth extra, **7s. 6d.**

A SIMPLE TREATISE ON HEAT. With Illusts. Cr. 8vo, cloth limp, **2s. 6d.**

THE CHEMISTRY OF COOKERY. Crown 8vo, cloth extra, **6s.**

THE CHEMISTRY OF IRON AND STEEL MAKING. Crown 8vo, cloth extra, **9s.**

WILLIAMSON (MRS. F. H.).—A CHILD WIDOW. Post 8vo, bds., **2s.**

WILSON (DR. ANDREW, F.R.S.E.), WORKS BY.

CHAPTERS ON EVOLUTION. With 259 Illustrations. Cr. 8vo, cloth extra, **7s. 6d.**

LEAVES FROM A NATURALIST'S NOTE-BOOK. Post 8vo, cloth limp, **2s. 6d.**

LEISURE-TIME STUDIES. With Illustrations. Crown 8vo, cloth extra, **6s.**

STUDIES IN LIFE AND SENSE. With numerous Illusts. Cr. 8vo, cl. ex., **6s.**

COMMON ACCIDENTS: HOW TO TREAT THEM. Illusts. Cr. 8vo, **1s.**; cl., **1s. 6d.**

GLIMPSES OF NATURE. With 35 Illustrations. Crown 8vo, cloth extra, **3s. 6d.**

WINTER (J. S.), STORIES BY. Post 8vo, illustrated boards, **2s.** each.

CAVALRY LIFE. | **REGIMENTAL LEGENDS.**

A SOLDIER'S CHILDREN. With 32 Illustrations by E. G. THOMSON and E. STUART HARDY. Crown 8vo, cloth extra, **3s. 6d.** [Sept.

WISSMANN.—MY SECOND JOURNEY THROUGH EQUATORIAL AFRICA, from the Congo to the Zambesi, in 1886, 1887. By Major HERMANN VON WISSMANN. With Map and 92 Illustrations. Demy 8vo, cloth extra, **16s.**

WOOD.—SABINA: A Novel. By Lady WOOD. Post 8vo, boards, **2s.**

WOOD (H. F.), DETECTIVE STORIES BY.

Crown 8vo, cloth extra, **6s.** each; post 8vo, illustrated boards, **2s.** each.

PASSENGER FROM SCOTLAND YARD. | **ENGLISHMAN OF THE RUE CAIN.**

WOOLLEY.—RACHEL ARMSTRONG; or, Love and Theology. By CELIA PARKER WOOLLEY. Post 8vo, illustrated boards, **2s.**; cloth, **2s. 6d.**

WRIGHT (THOMAS), WORKS BY. Crown 8vo, cloth extra, **7s. 6d.** each.

CARICATURE HISTORY OF THE GEORGES. With 400 Caricatures, Squibs, &c.

HISTORY OF CARICATURE AND OF THE GROTESQUE IN ART, LITERATURE, SCULPTURE, AND PAINTING. Illustrated by F. W. FAIRHOLT, F.S.A.

YATES (EDMUND), NOVELS BY. Post 8vo, illustrated boards, **2s.** each.

LAND AT LAST. | **THE FORLORN HOPE.** | **CASTAWAY.**

LISTS OF BOOKS CLASSIFIED IN SERIES.

**** For fuller cataloguing, see alphabetical arrangement, pp. 1-25.*

THE MAYFAIR LIBRARY. Post 8vo, cloth limp, 2s. 6d. per Volume.

A Journey Round My Room. By Xavier de Maistre.
Quips and Quiddities. By W. D. Adams.
The Agony Column of "The Times."
Melancholy Anatomised: Abridgment of "Burton's Anatomy of Melancholy."
The Speeches of Charles Dickens.
Literary Frivolities, Fancies, Follies, and Frolics. By W. T. Dobson.
Poetical Ingenuities. By W. T. Dobson.
The Cupboard Papers. By Fin-Bec.
W. S. Gilbert's Plays. First Series.
W. S. Gilbert's Plays. Second Series.
Songs of Irish Wit and Humour.
Animals and Masters. By Sir A. Helps.
Social Pressure. By Sir A. Helps.
Curiosities of Criticism. H. J. Jennings.
Holmes's Autocrat of Breakfast-Table.
Pencil and Palette. By R. Kempt.
Little Essays: from Lamb's Letters.
Forensic Anecdotes. By Jacob Larwood
Theatrical Anecdotes. Jacob Larwood
Jeux d'Esprit. Edited by Henry S. Leigh.
Witch Stories. By E. Lynn Linton.
Ourselves. By E. Lynn Linton.
Pastimes & Players. By R. Macgregor.
New Paul and Virginia. W. H. Mallock.
New Republic. By W. H. Mallock.
Puck on Pegasus. By H. C. Pennell.
Pegasus Re-Saddled. By H. C. Pennell.
Muses of Mayfair. Ed. H. C. Pennell.
Thoreau: His Life & Aims. By H. A. Page.
Puniana. By Hon. Hugh Rowley.
More Puniana. By Hon. Hugh Rowley.
The Philosophy of Handwriting.
By Stream and Sea. By Wm. Senior.
Leaves from a Naturalist's Note-Book. By Dr. Andrew Wilson.

THE GOLDEN LIBRARY. Post 8vo, cloth limp, 2s. per Volume.

Bayard Taylor's Diversions of the Echo Club.
Bennett's Ballad History of England.
Bennett's Songs for Sailors.
Godwin's Lives of the Necromancers.
Pope's Poetical Works.
Holmes's Autocrat of Breakfast Table.
Holmes's Professor at Breakfast Table.
Jesse's Scenes of Country Life.
Leigh Hunt's Tale for a Chimney Corner.
Mallory's Mort d'Arthur: Selections.
Pascal's Provincial Letters.
Rochefoucauld's Maxims & Reflections.

THE WANDERER'S LIBRARY. Crown 8vo, cloth extra, 3s. 6d. each.

Wanderings in Patagonia. By Julius Beerbohm. Illustrated.
Camp Notes. By Frederick Boyle.
Savage Life. By Frederick Boyle.
Merrie England in the Olden Time. By G. Daniel. Illustrated by Cruikshank.
Circus Life. By Thomas Frost.
Lives of the Conjurers. Thomas Frost.
The Old Showmen and the Old London Fairs. By Thomas Frost.
Low-Life Deeps. By James Greenwood.
Wilds of London. James Greenwood.
Tunis. Chev. Hesse-Wartegg. 22 Illusts.
Life and Adventures of a Cheap Jack.
World Behind the Scenes. P. Fitzgerald.
Tavern Anecdotes and Sayings.
The Genial Showman. By E. P. Hingston
Story of London Parks. Jacob Larwood.
London Characters. By Henry Mayhew.
Seven Generations of Executioners.
Summer Cruising in the South Seas. By C. Warren Stoddard. Illustrated.

POPULAR SHILLING BOOKS.

Harry Fludyer at Cambridge.
Jeff Briggs's Love Story. Bret Harte.
Twins of Table Mountain. Bret Harte.
Snow-bound at Eagle's. By Bret Harte.
A Day's Tour. By Percy Fitzgerald.
Esther's Glove. By R. E. Francillon.
Sentenced! By Somerville Gibney.
The Professor's Wife. By L. Graham.
Mrs. Gainsborough's Diamonds. By Julian Hawthorne.
Niagara Spray. By J. Hollingshead.
A Romance of the Queen's Hounds. By Charles James.
The Garden that Paid the Rent. By Tom Jerrold.
Cut by the Mess. By Arthur Keyser.
Our Sensation Novel. J. H. McCarthy.
Doom! By Justin H. McCarthy, M.P.
Dolly. By Justin H. McCarthy, M.P.
Lily Lass. Justin H. McCarthy, M.P.
Was She Good or Bad? By W. Minto.
Notes from the "News." By Jas. Payn.
Beyond the Gates. By E. S. Phelps.
Old Maid's Paradise. By E. S. Phelps.
Burglars in Paradise. By E. S. Phelps.
Jack the Fisherman. By E. S. Phelps.
Trooping with Crows. By C. L. Pirkis.
Bible Characters. By Charles Reade.
Rogues. By R. H. Sherard.
The Dagonet Reciter. By G. R. Sims.
How the Poor Live. By G. R. Sims.
Case of George Candlemas. G. R. Sims.
Sandycroft Mystery. T. W. Speight.
Hoodwinked. By T. W. Speight.
Father Damien. By R. L. Stevenson.
A Double Bond. By Linda Villari.
My Life with Stanley's Rear Guard. By Herbert Ward.

MY LIBRARY.

Choice Works, printed on laid paper, bound half-Roxburghe, 2s. 6d. each.

Four Frenchwomen. By AUSTIN DOBSON.
Citation and Examination of William Shakspeare. By W. S. LANDOR.
The Journal of Maurice de Guerin.
Christie Johnstone. By CHARLES READE. With a Photogravure Frontispiece.
Peg Woffington. By CHARLES READE.
The Dramatic Essays of Charles Lamb.

THE POCKET LIBRARY.

Post 8vo, printed on laid paper and hf.-bd., 2s. each.

The Essays of Elia. By CHARLES LAMB.
Robinson Crusoe. Edited by JOHN MAJOR. With 37 Illusts. by GEORGE CRUIKSHANK.
Whims and Oddities. By THOMAS HOOD. With 85 Illustrations.
The Barber's Chair, and The Hedgehog Letters. By DOUGLAS JERROLD.
Gastronomy as a Fine Art. By BRILLAT-SAVARIN. Trans. R. E. ANDERSON, M.A.
The Epicurean, &c. By THOMAS MOORE.
Leigh Hunt's Essays. Ed. E. OLLIER.
White's Natural History of Selborne.
Gulliver's Travels, and The Tale of a Tub. By Dean SWIFT.
The Rivals, School for Scandal, and other Plays by RICHARD BRINSLEY SHERIDAN.
Anecdotes of the Clergy. J. LARWOOD.
Thomson's Seasons. Illustrated.

THE PICCADILLY NOVELS.

LIBRARY EDITIONS OF NOVELS BY THE BEST AUTHORS, many Illustrated, crown 8vo, cloth extra, 3s. 6d. each.

By F. M. ALLEN.

The Green Bird.

By GRANT ALLEN.

Philistia.
Babylon
Strange Stories.
Beckoning Hand.
In all Shades.
The Tents of Shem.
For Maimie's Sake.
The Devil's Die.
This Mortal Coil.
The Great Taboo.
Dumaresq's Daughter.

By EDWIN L. ARNOLD.

Phra the Phœnician.

By ALAN ST. AUBYN.

A Fellow of Trinity.

By Rev. S. BARING GOULD.

Red Spider. | Eve.

By W. BESANT & J. RICE.

My Little Girl.
Case of Mr. Lucraft.
This Son of Vulcan.
Golden Butterfly.
By Celia's Arbour.
Monks of Thelema.
The Seamy Side.
Ten Years' Tenant.
Ready-Money Mortiboy.
With Harp and Crown.
'Twas in Trafalgar's Bay.
The Chaplain of the Fleet.

By WALTER BESANT.

All Sorts and Conditions of Men.
The Captains' Room.
All in a Garden Fair
The World Went Very Well Then.
For Faith and Freedom.
Dorothy Forster.
Uncle Jack.
Children of Gibeon.
Herr Paulus.
Bell of St. Paul's.
To Call Her Mine.
The Holy Rose.
Armorel of Lyonesse.
St. Katherine's by the Tower.

By ROBERT BUCHANAN.

The Shadow of the Sword.
A Child of Nature.
The Martyrdom of Madeline.
God and the Man.
Love Me for Ever.
Annan Water.
Matt.
The New Abelard.
Foxglove Manor.
Master of the Mine.
Heir of Linne.

By HALL CAINE.

The Shadow of a Crime.
A Son of Hagar. | The Deemster.

MORT. & FRANCES COLLINS.

Transmigration.
From Midnight to Midnight.
Blacksmith and Scholar.
Village Comedy. | You Play Me False.

By WILKIE COLLINS.

Armadale.
After Dark.
No Name.
Antonina. | Basil
Hide and Seek.
The Dead Secret.
Queen of Hearts.
My Miscellanies.
Woman in White.
The Moonstone.
Man and Wife.
Poor Miss Finch.
Miss or Mrs?
New Magdalen.
The Frozen Deep.
The Two Destinies.
Law and the Lady
Haunted Hotel.
The Fallen Leaves.
Jezebel's Daughter.
The Black Robe.
Heart and Science.
"I Say No."
Little Novels.
The Evil Genius.
The Legacy of Cain
A Rogue's Life.
Blind Love.

By DUTTON COOK.

Paul Foster's Daughter.

By MATT CRIM.

Adventures of a Fair Rebel.

By WILLIAM CYPLES.

Hearts of Gold.

By ALPHONSE DAUDET.

The Evangelist; or, Port Salvation.

By ERASMUS DAWSON.

The Fountain of Youth.

By JAMES DE MILLE.

A Castle in Spain.

By J. LEITH DERWENT.

Our Lady of Tears. | Circe's Lovers.

By DICK DONOVAN.

Tracked to Doom.

By Mrs. ANNIE EDWARDES.

Archie Lovell.

By G. MANVILLE FENN.

The New Mistress.

By PERCY FITZGERALD.

Fatal Zero.

By R. E. FRANCILLON.

Queen Cophetua. | A Real Queen.
One by One. | King or Knave?

Pref. by Sir BARTLE FRERE.

Pandurang Hari.

By EDWARD GARRETT.

The Capel Girls.

THE PICCADILLY (3/6) NOVELS—*continued.*

By CHARLES GIBBON.

Robin Gray.
Loving a Dream.
The Golden Shaft.
Of High Degree.
The Flower of the Forest.

By E. GLANVILLE.

The Lost Heiress.
The Fossicker.

By THOMAS HARDY.

Under the Greenwood Tree.

By BRET HARTE.

A Waif of the Plains.
A Ward of the Golden Gate.
A Sappho of Green Springs.
Colonel Starbottle's Client.

By JULIAN HAWTHORNE.

Garth.
Ellice Quentin.
Sebastian Strome.
Dust.
Fortune's Fool.
Beatrix Randolph.
David Poindexter's Disappearance.
The Spectre of the Camera.

By Sir A. HELPS.

Ivan de Biron.

By ISAAC HENDERSON.

Agatha Page.

By Mrs. ALFRED HUNT.

The Leaden Casket. | Self-Condemned.
That other Person.

By JEAN INGELOW.

Fated to be Free.

By R. ASHE KING.

A Drawn Game.
"The Wearing of the Green."

By HENRY KINGSLEY.

Number Seventeen.

By E. LYNN LINTON.

Patricia Kemball.
Under which Lord?
"My Love!"
Ione.
Paston Carew.
Sowing the Wind.
The Atonement of Leam Dundas.
The World Well Lost.

By HENRY W. LUCY.

Gideon Fleyce.

By JUSTIN McCARTHY.

A Fair Saxon.
Linley Rochford.
Miss Misanthrope.
Donna Quixote.
Maid of Athens.
Camiola.
The Waterdale Neighbours.
My Enemy's Daughter.
Dear Lady Disdain.
The Comet of a Season.

By AGNES MACDONELL.

Quaker Cousins.

By D. CHRISTIE MURRAY.

Life's Atonement.
Joseph's Coat.
Coals of Fire.
Val Strange.
Hearts.
A Model Father.
Old Blazer's Hero.
By the Gate of the Sea.
A Bit of Human Nature.
First Person Singular.
Cynic Fortune.
The Way of the World.

By MURRAY & HERMAN.

The Bishops' Bible.
Paul Jones's Alias.

By HUME NISBET.

"Bail Up!"

THE PICCADILLY (3/6) NOVELS—*continued.*

By GEORGES OHNET.

A Weird Gift.

By Mrs. OLIPHANT.

Whiteladies.

By OUIDA.

Held in Bondage.
Strathmore.
Chandos.
Under Two Flags.
Idalia.
CecilCastlemaine's Gage.
Tricotrin. | Puck.
Folle Farine.
A Dog of Flanders.
Pascarel. | Signa.
Princess Napraxine.
Two Little Wooden Shoes.
In a Winter City.
Ariadne.
Friendship.
Moths. | Ruffino.
Pipistrello.
A Village Commune
Bimbi. | Wanda.
Frescoes.
In Maremma.
Othmar. | Syrlin.
Guilderoy.

By MARGARET A. PAUL.

Gentle and Simple.

By JAMES PAYN.

Lost Sir Massingberd.
Less Black than We're Painted.
A Confidential Agent.
A Grape from a Thorn.
In Peril and Privation.
The Mystery of Mirbridge.
The Canon's Ward.
Walter's Word.
By Proxy.
High Spirits.
Under One Roof.
From Exile.
Glow-worm Tales.
Talk of the Town.
Holiday Tasks.
The Burnt Million.
The Word and the Will.
Sunny Stories.

By E. C. PRICE.

Valentina.
The Foreigners.
Mrs. Lancaster's Rival.

By RICHARD PRYCE.

Miss Maxwell's Affections.

By CHARLES READE.

It is Never Too Late to Mend.
The Double Marriage.
Love Me Little, Love Me Long.
The Cloister and the Hearth.
The Course of True Love.
The Autobiography of a Thief.
Put Yourself in his Place.
A Terrible Temptation.
Singleheart and Doubleface.
Good Stories of Men and other Animals.
Hard Cash.
Peg Woffington.
ChristieJohnstone.
Griffith Gaunt.
Foul Play.
Wandering Heir.
A Woman-Hater
A Simpleton.
Readiana.
The Jilt.
A Perilous Secret.

By Mrs. J. H. RIDDELL.

The Prince of Wales's Garden Party.
Weird Stories.

By F. W. ROBINSON.

Women are Strange.
The Hands of Justice.

By W. CLARK RUSSELL.

An Ocean Tragedy.
My Shipmate Louise.

By JOHN SAUNDERS.

Guy Waterman. | Two Dreamers.
Bound to the Wheel.
The Lion in the Path.

THE PICCADILLY (3/6) NOVELS—*continued.*

By KATHARINE SAUNDERS.
Margaret and Elizabeth.
Gideon's Rock. | Heart Salvage.
The High Mills. | Sebastian.

By LUKE SHARP.
In a Steamer Chair.

By HAWLEY SMART.
Without Love or Licence.

By R. A. STERNDALE.
The Afghan Knife.

By BERTHA THOMAS.
Proud Maisie. | The Violin-player.

By FRANCES E. TROLLOPE.
Like Ships upon the Sea.
Anne Furness. | Mabel's Progress.

THE PICCADILLY (3/6) NOVELS—*continued.*

By ANTHONY TROLLOPE.
Frau Frohmann. | Kept in the Dark.
Marion Fay. | Land-Leaguers.
The Way We Live Now.
Mr. Scarborough's Family.

By IVAN TURGENIEFF, &c.
Stories from Foreign Novelists.

By C. C. FRASER-TYTLER.
Mistress Judith.

By SARAH TYTLER.
The Bride's Pass. | Lady Bell.
Noblesse Oblige. | Buried Diamonds.
The Blackhall Ghosts.

By MARK TWAIN.
The American Claimant.

By J. S. WINTER.
A Soldier's Children.

CHEAP EDITIONS OF POPULAR NOVELS.

Post 8vo, illustrated boards, 2s. each.

By ARTEMUS WARD.
Artemus Ward Complete.

By EDMOND ABOUT.
The Fellah.

By HAMILTON AIDE.
Carr of Carrlyon. | Confidences.

By MARY ALBERT.
Brooke Finchley's Daughter.

By Mrs. ALEXANDER.
Maid, Wife, or Widow? | Valerie's Fate.

By GRANT ALLEN.
Strange Stories. | The Devil's Die.
Philistia. | This Mortal Coil.
Babylon. | In all Shades.
The Beckoning Hand.
For Maimie's Sake. | Tents of Shem.
The Great Taboo.

By ALAN ST. AUBYN.
A Fellow of Trinity.

By Rev. S. BARING GOULD.
Red Spider. | Eve.

By FRANK BARRETT.
Fettered for Life.
Between Life and Death.
The Sin of Olga Zassoulich.

By SHELSLEY BEAUCHAMP.
Grantley Grange.

By W. BESANT & J. RICE.
This Son of Vulcan. | By Celia's Arbour.
My Little Girl. | Monks of Thelema.
Case of Mr. Lucraft. | The Seamy Side.
Golden Butterfly. | Ten Years' Tenant.
Ready-Money Mortiboy.
With Harp and Crown.
'Twas in Trafalgar's Bay.
The Chaplain of the Fleet.

By WALTER BESANT.
Dorothy Forster. | Uncle Jack.
Children of Gibeon. | Herr Paulus.
All Sorts and Conditions of Men.
The Captains' Room.
All in a Garden Fair.
The World Went Very Well Then.
For Faith and Freedom.
To Call Her Mine.
The Bell of St. Paul's.
The Holy Rose.

By FREDERICK BOYLE.
Camp Notes. | Savage Life.
Chronicles of No-man's Land.

By BRET HARTE.
Flip. | Californian Stories.
Maruja. | Gabriel Conroy.
An Heiress of Red Dog.
The Luck of Roaring Camp.
A Phyllis of the Sierras.

By HAROLD BRYDGES.
Uncle Sam at Home.

By ROBERT BUCHANAN.
The Shadow of the Sword. | The Martyrdom of Madeline.
A Child of Nature. | Annan Water.
God and the Man. | The New Abelard.
Love Me for Ever. | Matt.
Foxglove Manor. | The Heir of Linne.
The Master of the Mine.

By HALL CAINE.
The Shadow of a Crime.
A Son of Hagar. | The Deemster.

By Commander CAMERON.
The Cruise of the "Black Prince."

By Mrs. LOVETT CAMERON.
Deceivers Ever. | Juliet's Guardian.

By AUSTIN CLARE.
For the Love of a Lass.

By Mrs. ARCHER CLIVE.
Paul Ferroll.
Why Paul Ferroll Killed his Wife.

By MACLAREN COBBAN.
The Cure of Souls.

By C. ALLSTON COLLINS.
The Bar Sinister.

MORT. & FRANCES COLLINS.
Sweet Anne Page. | Transmigration.
From Midnight to Midnight.
A Fight with Fortune.
Sweet and Twenty. | Village Comedy.
Frances. | You Play me False.
Blacksmith and Scholar.

Two-Shilling Novels—*continued.*

By WILKIE COLLINS.

Armadale. | My Miscellanies.
After Dark. | Woman in White.
No Name. | The Moonstone.
Antonina. | Basil. | Man and Wife.
Hide and Seek. | Poor Miss Finch.
The Dead Secret. | The Fallen Leaves.
Queen of Hearts. | Jezebel's Daughter
Miss or Mrs? | The Black Robe.
New Magdalen. | Heart and Science.
The Frozen Deep. | "I Say No."
Law and the Lady. | The Evil Genius.
The Two Destinies. | Little Novels.
Haunted Hotel. | Legacy of Cain.
A Rogue's Life. | Blind Love.

By M. J. COLQUHOUN.

Every Inch a Soldier.

By DUTTON COOK.

Leo. | Paul Foster's Daughter.

By C. EGBERT CRADDOCK.

Prophet of the Great Smoky Mountains.

By WILLIAM CYPLES.

Hearts of Gold.

By ALPHONSE DAUDET.

The Evangelist; or, Port Salvation.

By JAMES DE MILLE.

A Castle in Spain.

By J. LEITH DERWENT.

Our Lady of Tears. | Circe's Lovers.

By CHARLES DICKENS.

Sketches by Boz. | Oliver Twist.
Pickwick Papers. | Nicholas Nickleby.

By DICK DONOVAN.

The Man-Hunter. | Caught at Last!
Tracked and Taken.
Who Poisoned Hetty Duncan?
The Man from Manchester.
A Detective's Triumphs.
In the Grip of the Law.

CONAN DOYLE, and others.

Strange Secrets.

By Mrs. ANNIE EDWARDES.

A Point of Honour. | Archie Lovell.

By M. BETHAM-EDWARDS.

Felicia. | Kitty.

By EDWARD EGGLESTON.

Roxy.

By PERCY FITZGERALD.

Bella Donna. | Polly.
Never Forgotten. | Fatal Zero.
The Second Mrs. Tillotson.
Seventy-five Brooke Street.
The Lady of Brantome.

ALBANY DE FONBLANQUE.

Filthy Lucre.

By R. E. FRANCILLON.

Olympia. | Queen Cophetua.
One by One. | King or Knave?
A Real Queen. | Romances of Law.

By HAROLD FREDERICK.

Seth's Brother's Wife.
The Lawton Girl.

Pref. by Sir BARTLE FRERE.

Pandurang Hari.

Two-Shilling Novels—*continued.*

By HAIN FRISWELL.

One of Two.

By EDWARD GARRETT.

The Capel Girls.

By CHARLES GIBBON.

Robin Gray. | In Honour Bound.
Fancy Free. | Flower of Forest.
For Lack of Gold. | Braes of Yarrow.
What will the World Say? | The Golden Shaft.
Of High Degree.
In Love and War. | Mead and Stream.
For the King. | Loving a Dream.
In Pastures Green. | A Hard Knot.
Queen of Meadow. | Heart's Delight.
A Heart's Problem. | Blood-Money.
The Dead Heart.

By WILLIAM GILBERT.

Dr. Austin's Guests. | James Duke.
The Wizard of the Mountain.

By ERNEST GLANVILLE.

The Lost Heiress.

By HENRY GREVILLE.

A Noble Woman. | Nikanor.

By JOHN HABBERTON.

Brueton's Bayou. | Country Luck.

By ANDREW HALLIDAY.

Every-Day Papers.

By Lady DUFFUS HARDY.

Paul Wynter's Sacrifice.

By THOMAS HARDY.

Under the Greenwood Tree.

By J. BERWICK HARWOOD.

The Tenth Earl.

By JULIAN HAWTHORNE.

Garth. | Sebastian Strome.
Ellice Quentin. | Dust.
Fortune's Fool. | Beatrix Randolph.
Miss Cadogna. | Love—or a Name.
David Poindexter's Disappearance.
The Spectre of the Camera.

By Sir ARTHUR HELPS.

Ivan de Biron.

By HENRY HERMAN.

A Leading Lady.

By Mrs. CASHEL HOEY.

The Lover's Creed.

By Mrs. GEORGE HOOPER.

The House of Raby.

By TIGHE HOPKINS.

'Twixt Love and Duty.

By Mrs. ALFRED HUNT.

Thornicroft's Model. | Self-Condemned.
That Other Person. | Leaden Casket.

By JEAN INGELOW.

Fated to be Free.

By HARRIETT JAY

The Dark Colleen.
The Queen of Connaught.

By MARK KERSHAW.

Colonial Facts and Fictions.

By R. ASHE KING.

A Drawn Game. | Passion's Slave.
"The Wearing of the Green."
Bell Barry.

Two-Shilling Novels—*continued.*

By HENRY KINGSLEY.

Oakshott Castle.

By JOHN LEYS.

The Lindsays.

By E. LYNN LINTON.

Patricia Kemball. | Paston Carew.
World Well Lost. | "My Love!"
Under which Lord? | Ione.
The Atonement of Leam Dundas.
With a Silken Thread.
The Rebel of the Family.
Sowing the Wind.

By HENRY W. LUCY.

Gideon Fleyce.

By JUSTIN McCARTHY.

A Fair Saxon. | Donna Quixote.
Linley Rochford. | Maid of Athens.
Miss Misanthrope. | Camiola.
Dear Lady Disdain.
The Waterdale Neighbours.
My Enemy's Daughter.
The Comet of a Season.

By AGNES MACDONELL.

Quaker Cousins.

KATHARINE S. MACQUOID.

The Evil Eye. Lost Rose.

By W. H. MALLOCK.

The New Republic.

By FLORENCE MARRYAT.

Open! Sesame! | Fighting the Air.
A Harvest of Wild Oats.
Written in Fire.

By J. MASTERMAN

Half-a-dozen Daughters.

By BRANDER MATTHEWS.

A Secret of the Sea.

By JEAN MIDDLEMASS.

Touch and Go. | Mr. Dorillion.

By Mrs. MOLESWORTH.

Hathercourt Rectory.

By J. E. MUDDOCK.

Stories Weird and Wonderful.
The Dead Man's Secret.

By D. CHRISTIE MURRAY.

A Model Father. | Old Blazer's Hero.
Joseph's Coat. | Hearts.
Coals of Fire. | Way of the World.
Val Strange. | Cynic Fortune.
A Life's Atonement.
By the Gate of the Sea.
A Bit of Human Nature.
First Person Singular.

By MURRAY and HERMAN.

One Traveller Returns.
Paul Jones's Alias.
The Bishops' Bible.

By HENRY MURRAY.

A Game of Bluff.

By ALICE O'HANLON.

The Unforeseen. | Chance? or Fate?

Two-Shilling Novels—*continued.*

By GEORGES OHNET.

Doctor Rameau. | A Last Love.
A Weird Gift.

By Mrs. OLIPHANT.

Whiteladies. | The Primrose Path.
The Greatest Heiress in England.

By Mrs. ROBERT O'REILLY.

Phœbe's Fortunes.

By OUIDA.

Held in Bondage. | Two Little Wooden Shoes.
Strathmore. | Friendship.
Chandos. | Moths.
Under Two Flags. | Pipistrello.
Idalia. | A Village Commune.
CecilCastlemaine's Gage. | Bimbi.
Tricotrin. | Wanda.
Puck. | Frescoes.
Folle Farine. | In Maremma.
A Dog of Flanders. | Othmar.
Pascarel. | Guilderoy.
Signa. | Ruffino.
Princess Napraxine. | Syrlin.
In a Winter City. | Ouida's Wisdom, Wit, and Pathos.
Ariadne.

MARGARET AGNES PAUL.

Gentle and Simple.

By JAMES PAYN.

Bentinck's Tutor. | £200 Reward.
Murphy's Master. | Marine Residence.
A County Family. | Mirk Abbey.
At Her Mercy. | By Proxy.
Cecil's Tryst. | Under One Roof.
Clyffards of Clyffe. | High Spirits.
Foster Brothers. | Carlyon's Year.
Found Dead. | From Exile.
Best of Husbands. | For Cash Only.
Walter's Word. | Kit.
Halves. | The Canon's Ward
Fallen Fortunes. | Talk of the Town.
Humorous Stories. | Holiday Tasks.
Lost Sir Massingberd.
A Perfect Treasure.
A Woman's Vengeance.
The Family Scapegrace.
What He Cost Her.
Gwendoline's Harvest.
Like Father, Like Son.
Married Beneath Him.
Not Wooed, but Won.
Less Black than We're Painted.
A Confidential Agent.
Some Private Views.
A Grape from a Thorn.
Glow-worm Tales.
The Mystery of Mirbridge.
The Burnt Million.
The Word and the Will.

By C. L. PIRKIS.

Lady Lovelace.

By EDGAR A. POE.

The Mystery of Marie Roget.

By E. C. PRICE.

Valentina. | The Foreigners.
Mrs. Lancaster's Rival.
Gerald.

TWO-SHILLING NOVELS—*continued.*

By CHARLES READE.

It is Never Too Late to Mend.
Christie Johnstone.
Put Yourself in His Place.
The Double Marriage.
Love Me Little, Love Me Long.
The Cloister and the Hearth.
The Course of True Love.
Autobiography of a Thief.
A Terrible Temptation.
The Wandering Heir.
Singleheart and Doubleface.
Good Stories of Men and other Animals.
Hard Cash. | A Simpleton.
Peg Woffington. | Readiana.
Griffith Gaunt. | A Woman-Hater.
Foul Play. | The Jilt.
A Perilous Secret.

By Mrs. J. H. RIDDELL.

Weird Stories. | Fairy Water.
Her Mother's Darling.
Prince of Wales's Garden Party.
The Uninhabited House.
The Mystery in Palace Gardens.

By F. W. ROBINSON.

Women are Strange.
The Hands of Justice.

By JAMES RUNCIMAN.

Skippers and Shellbacks.
Grace Balmaign's Sweetheart.
Schools and Scholars.

By W. CLARK RUSSELL.

Round the Galley Fire.
On the Fo'k'sle Head.
In the Middle Watch.
A Voyage to the Cape.
A Book for the Hammock.
The Mystery of the "Ocean Star."
The Romance of Jenny Harlowe.
An Ocean Tragedy.
My Shipmate Louise.

GEORGE AUGUSTUS SALA.

Gaslight and Daylight.

By JOHN SAUNDERS.

Guy Waterman. | Two Dreamers.
The Lion in the Path.

By KATHARINE SAUNDERS.

Joan Merryweather. | Heart Salvage.
The High Mills. | Sebastian.
Margaret and Elizabeth.

By GEORGE R. SIMS.

Rogues and Vagabonds.
The Ring o' Bells.
Mary Jane's Memoirs.
Mary Jane Married.
Tales of To-day. | Dramas of Life.
Tinkletop's Crime.
Zeph: A Circus Story.

By ARTHUR SKETCHLEY.

A Match in the Dark.

By HAWLEY SMART.

Without Love or Licence.

By T. W. SPEIGHT.

The Mysteries of Heron Dyke.
The Golden Hoop. | By Devious Ways.
Hoodwinked, &c. | Back to Life.

TWO-SHILLING NOVELS—*continued.*

By R. A. STERNDALE.

The Afghan Knife.

By R. LOUIS STEVENSON.

New Arabian Nights. | Prince Otto.

BY BERTHA THOMAS.

Cressida. | Proud Maisie.
The Violin-player.

By WALTER THORNBURY.

Tales for the Marines.
Old Stories Re-told.

T. ADOLPHUS TROLLOPE.

Diamond Cut Diamond.

By F. ELEANOR TROLLOPE.

Like Ships upon the Sea.
Anne Furness. | Mabel's Progress.

By ANTHONY TROLLOPE.

Frau Frohmann. | Kept in the Dark.
Marion Fay. | John Caldigate.
The Way We Live Now.
The American Senator.
Mr. Scarborough's Family.
The Land-Leaguers.
The Golden Lion of Granpere.

By J. T. TROWBRIDGE.

Farnell's Folly.

By IVAN TURGENIEFF, &c.

Stories from Foreign Novelists.

By MARK TWAIN.

A Pleasure Trip on the Continent.
The Gilded Age.
Mark Twain's Sketches.
Tom Sawyer. | A Tramp Abroad.
The Stolen White Elephant.
Huckleberry Finn.
Life on the Mississippi.
The Prince and the Pauper.

By C. C. FRASER-TYTLER.

Mistress Judith.

By SARAH TYTLER.

The Bride's Pass. | Noblesse Oblige.
Buried Diamonds. | Disappeared.
Saint Mungo's City. | Huguenot Family
Lady Bell. | Blackhall Ghosts.
What She Came Through.
Beauty and the Beast.
Citoyenne Jaqueline.

By Mrs. F. H. WILLIAMSON.

A Child Widow.

By J. S. WINTER.

Cavalry Life. | Regimental Legends.

By H. F. WOOD.

The Passenger from Scotland Yard.
The Englishman of the Rue Cain.

By Lady WOOD.

Sabina.

CELIA PARKER WOOLLEY.

Rachel Armstrong; or, Love & Theology

By EDMUND YATES.

The Forlorn Hope. | Land at Last.
Castaway.

OGDEN, SMALE AND CO. LIMITED, PRINTERS, GREAT SAFFRON HILL, E.C.

www.ingramcontent.com/pod-product-compliance
Lightning Source LLC
Chambersburg PA
CBHW021343110726
47900CB00005B/1584

* 9 7 8 3 7 4 4 7 2 9 9 3 2 *